WITHIN A SHADOWED FOREST

ALSO BY
JEFFREY D. BRIGGS

Out of the Cold Dark Sea

WITHIN A SHADOWED FOREST

A Waterfront Mystery
With Martha Whitaker

Jeffrey D. Briggs

Shoreline, Washington

Published 2020 by Water's End Press

First Edition

Cover design by Kari March. www.karimarch.com

Inquiries should be addressed to:
Water's End Press
P.O. Box 60282
Shoreline, Washington 98177
206.619.9139
www.watersendpress.com

ISBN: 978-1-7337316-2-1 (trade paperback)
ISBN: 978-1-7337316-3-8 (eBook)

Printed in the United States of America

For the Rochester Literary Guild

P.S. Duffy, Daniel Dietrich,
Shelley Mahannah & Debbie Lampi

For inspiring me to write about
the Minnesota waterfront.

"When I had journeyed half of our life's way,
I found myself within a shadowed forest,
for I had lost the path that does not stray."

Dante Alighieri, *Inferno*

ONE

Martha Whitaker leaned against the corner of the house in the night shadows of an overgrown rhododendron bush and the neighbor's dilapidated garage. If any bad neighborhoods remained in rapidly changing Ballard, this tiny house, once a garage, was at the epicenter. Gentrification had swept through old Ballard like Gran on a cleaning frenzy. Built on the alley just up the hill from the Sloop Tavern, the shack was a remnant of the Scandinavian fishing community that had existed here for over a century. Two bedrooms—if a person were being generous about that pantry-sized addition—a kitchen that rivaled her boat galley for lack of space, an occasionally working shower that spit out enough hot water for a spit bath. Emily was trying to raise two kids here. Barely out of her teens, she was losing the battle in a world indifferent to those on the economic fringes who had too little education and not enough family support.

Someone ghosted behind the curtained windows of the kitchen, paused, and then passed back toward the living room. The flickering television gave off bursts of light in the sliver where the curtains didn't quite meet. Noise from the Sloop carried up the hill. Shouts peppered the air; a motorcycle roared to life, followed by a second. The sound of shattering glass caused Martha to flinch in her hiding spot. The tavern was closing.

It wouldn't be long now.

She began stretching muscles that had tightened in the damp Seattle air. September was her favorite month in the Pacific Northwest. The clear, warm days of summer were beginning to see the first crisp, cool nights. She appreciated the irony that the stretch of beautiful weather broke on the day she finally got Emily to agree to serve Jerome with a restraining order. Whether it was the precursor to the autumn rains or an isolated storm, she didn't know. It was a drizzle, really, just a light, steady mist, not enough to end the summer drought or soak the parched earth. A typical Seattle rain. Still, after four hours of waiting in the back alley, she was cold and damp. Muscles in her shoulders, back, arms, legs groaned as she began to move. She persisted until warmth and flexibility began to seep back into her limbs.

Martha went motionless. Two large men half-carried a barefoot woman between them down the gravel alley. Jerome had company. One shoe dangled from the woman's clenched fist. When she squirmed, they tightened their grips. They were close to the house now. She recognized the one with the flattop and too-small jeans jacket as Jerome Olsen, Emily's boyfriend, father of her two kids, and frequent abuser.

The men were evenly sized, tall, maybe six one or two, broad across the shoulders, bellies beginning to protrude over their belts. Not even Jerome's seasonal job on his grandfather's crab boat could make up for too many nights at the Sloop. Family money paid under the table turned into liquid courage at the bar. When he stumbled home to his nagging girlfriend who harangued him about food and rent money and diapers, he lashed out with hands callused from hauling lines and setting pots.

The drinking had also left him soft where it counted. Overconfidence. She'd have no problem with him.

His companion had longer hair and a crooked nose. He wouldn't be afraid of a little alleyway dust-up, but the nose said he was a bad fighter. Still, he had no dog in this fight. Martha wasn't concerned, even if he decided to join his friend. If they had guns or knives, they were hidden. She could disable both of them before the weapons became a factor.

She wasn't here to fight, she reminded herself, but to serve papers. It had taken Emily months since their first meeting to reach this decision. Still, Martha felt the adrenaline rush that craved for the release of a good fight. That deep well of violence was never far from the surface with her, simmering, threatening to boil over. And Jerome certainly deserved a slap down. Despite his promises, despite begging for forgiveness, he hadn't changed since Emily first came into her office months ago. Most likely he never would.

Suddenly, they dropped the woman and jumped back, but not before she vomited all over their shoes.

"Oh, bitch, that is fuckin' rude," Broken Nose said. He shoved her away with a foot on her shoulder, and she lay on her side, continuing to retch. It dribbled down her face and into her hair. Broken Nose rubbed his boot clean on the woman's jeans.

"Ain't sticking Big Jerry in that now," Olsen said.

Martha had seen enough and stepped out into the alley. "You won't be sticking it anywhere tonight, Jerome." She strolled toward him, a ghost appearing into the dim light.

"The fuck you doin' at my house?" Olsen snapped. "Who the fuck are you anyway?"

"Waiting for you. I'm Emily's attorney."

"Didn't tell me you had another hot bitch," Broken Nose said. "Little skinny for my taste, but we can still have fun, bro."

Martha spun to face him. "Leave now before I break your nose again."

"Whoo, no call to get mean, woman." His hand lashed out to grab her jacket. Martha intercepted it inches from the target, twirled him around, and bent his arm behind his back to a point just short of an ugly break. She shoved him away hard. He landed on his knees. Hands skidded across gravel. "I've asked nicely for you to leave before I hurt you. I won't ask again. And I really, really want to hurt you—both of you—right now."

From inside her rain jacket, she pulled out an envelope and handed it to Olsen. "This is a restraining order, Jerome. I'm Emily's attorney. You are not to go near her or the children."

Broken Nose rose off his knees and edged toward her. Again, Martha spun toward him and snarled, "Dude, play like a rat and go hide in a dumpster. Now!" One step in his direction had him backing up the alley. "And don't forget your girlfriend here."

"Never met the bitch before. She's on her own."

"Nice guy," Martha said, turning back to Olsen. Again, she extended the envelope. "Jerome, you are required by law to stay at least two hundred feet away from Emily and the kids. If you want time with the children, have your attorney file a petition with the court."

"No one's keeping me out of my own fucking house." He slapped her hand away, but she caught his wrist and forced the envelope into his hand.

"Actually, yes, she can."

He brushed past her, took the two steps up to the front door in one bound, and fumbled with his keys. Martha just watched. Again and again, he stabbed the key into the lock to no avail.

"We've changed the locks, Jerome," Martha said. "By law,

you cannot enter the house without a police escort. If you choose to violate these laws, you'll spend time at the Seattle jail to contemplate your many sins."

Olsen began bashing his fist on the door. "Emily, honey, open this door right now. Sweetie, you know I love you. Emily. Goddamn it, Emily, open the fuckin' door."

The door swung open and bright light burst into the night. Olsen had taken a half-step forward, when he realized it wasn't Emily at the door. Officer Ray Palmer of the Seattle Police Department barred his way. In his blues, with his linebacker body adorned with a bullet-proof vest and with a gun strapped to his utility belt, Palmer filled the doorway. Glancing down at the envelope Olsen still clutched, he said, "Mr. Olsen, I see that you've been served with the restraining order. Good. You are not allowed to enter the house. If you'd like to schedule a time tomorrow to return to pick up your personal effects, I'll be glad to escort you here."

"Emily, honey," Olsen shouted over the officer's shoulder, "let's talk. Emily?" When he got no answer, he shouted, "Goddamn it, Emily, at least look me in the eye and tell me you're kicking me out. Honey, where'm I suppose to go? I've got rights, Emily. I've got fuckin' rights too, bitch. Those are my kids, too, you know. You ain't heard the last of this."

Again, no answer came from the house.

"Mr. Olsen," Palmer said, "I'm afraid you have to leave now. You are not allowed within two hundred feet of the house without permission and a police escort." He grasped Olsen's arm and forced him to pivot on the front stoop. "I must insist."

Olsen shook free. "Get your fuckin' hands off me, you—" A modicum of sense prevailed, and he cut off the insult. Over his shoulder he shouted, "You'll be fuckin' sorry for this, Emily. Fuckin' sorry."

Palmer remained rigid in the doorway despite, Martha knew, a desire to tear the stupid, foul-mouthed bastard apart inch by very slow inch. As Olsen brushed past her, she said, "Oh, by the way, Jerome, threatening, stalking—whether in person or by email, text, or letter—will also get you thrown into jail. And personally, I think that's where you ought to be, but I couldn't get Emily to press charges, even after you rearranged her nose and eye socket. And since I'm delivering the news, the Sloop is within two hundred feet of the house. Find a new place to pick up one-night stands. If I even hear a rumor of you nosing around Emily and the kids, you'll discover exactly what I can do when I'm angry."

Palmer stood beside Martha outside the front door of the house. They watched Olsen stormed over to the F-150 parked on a dirt patch beside the house. He wrenched the door open, and the truck rumbled to life. Gravel flew at them as he hurtled up the alley.

"Any problems?" Palmer asked.

"None I couldn't handle. Thanks for backing me up."

"You should've let me deliver the restraining order. That's what you paid me for."

"I know you think that, Ray." She touched his arm. "But the only way I could get Emily to agree to this was to promise that I'd personally deliver it. She almost backed out even then. I don't understand, but she really does love him."

"Yeah, welcome to my world. Reason's got nothing to do with it. I hope she doesn't go running back to him. Most do, you know."

"I know. But one of the kids got hurt. It raised the stakes."

The truck turned out of the alley and with a squeal of its tires, disappeared.

Palmer said, "Okay, think I'll grab a nap on the couch in case he comes back."

"Sure?"

"No problem. See you at the gym tomorrow?"

"Probably not," Martha replied. "But soon."

"Okay, take care of yourself."

"Always do. Backatcha. And thanks again, Ray."

"Just doing my job."

Martha knew it was more than that, but she said nothing. She'd flirted shamelessly with him while she routinely dropped him to the mat at the gym. He always got up for more. She'd shared an after-class beer with him at one of the trendy sushi bars on Ballard Avenue after she'd been particularly rough with him in their sparring session. The cold beer accompanied by spicy edamame and gyoza soon led to rolling waves of shared dishes. Too bad he was a cop. He was attractive, smart, good at his job, and appreciated good beer, good food, and good coffee. He took being reminded of his inadequacies well. He wasn't much of a sparring partner, but he was an enthusiastic acolyte.

It was also good to have a friend in the SPD, the primary reason she'd accepted Ray's invitation to Shiku Sushi. She hadn't known when or with which client she might need to ask for assistance, but she knew that day would come. She also knew she was a persona non grata with the Seattle police. A prompt response from the SPD to any request from her was unlikely. But the feelings were mutual. Harry Callison had been a corrupt cop, but he had been their corrupt cop. They had taken offense at her knocking out several of his teeth and leaving him nailed to the floor.

She knelt beside the prostrate woman, shaking her by the shoulder, gently at first, then with some insistence. She lay in her own vomit. Nothing in the past five minutes had affected her, if she was even aware that anything had happened. Her eyes blinked open, closed again. A burble and a moan escaped her lips. Martha shook her again. "Come on, sweetheart, let's get you home."

How much she'd changed in the past year came to her as she helped the woman struggle to her feet. Before, Martha would've left her lying in the alley in her own vomit, disgusted at the woman's poor decisions and lack of self-control. She'd made this mess of her life; let her lie in it. Maybe the change had come from working with Emily and too many of her troubled sisters. But she knew that working with these women was only one manifestation of a change started by Lance Trammell.

"Yep, gotta go home," the woman slurred. "Think they slipped me a mickey. Did I do anything too bad?"

"Nothing too bad," Martha said, slipping a hand under her arm and steering her in the right direction.

"I get off on women too if you're interested," she said.

"Not tonight, I'm afraid. Now, let's get you moving, Ms.—"

"Rhi—Rhiannon, goddamn Fleetwood Mac song."

By the time Martha had gotten her back up the alley, stopping once for Rhi to vomit again, another time to hunt for her missing shoe, the Lyft driver sat parked in front of the deserted Sloop. His red Toyota Prius, the ubiquitous Seattle car, was as quiet as the empty street. Martha paid for the driver to chauffer the drunk woman two blocks up the hill, as it turned out, and gave him a generous tip to make sure she got in her apartment okay. "Got you logged, dude," she warned.

"I resent the implication," he spat.

Still, she hadn't changed so much that she was going to apologize. "Nothing personal. I just log all drivers taking single women home at two thirty in the morning."

From the hedge lining her neighbor's front yard, Martha scanned the empty street and surrounding yards. No cars moved, and she didn't see anyone slinking from bush to tree, from shadow to shadow. Still, she decided to wait, in case Jerome wasn't as surprised about events as he'd seemed. The vantage point allowed her to see her house across the street and up the driveway to the apartment above the garage, where she had moved Emily and the two kids for safekeeping. A dim light shone from the upper window of the Carriage House. Martha recognized it as the nightlight from the bathroom. She gently rocked on her toes to keep blood flowing and tightened the rain hood around her face.

She knew she had to keep an eye on Emily, as well as Jerome. Restraining orders only worked when all involved were willing to abide by them.

TWO

Gulls swept over the gray waters of Lake Superior. Through the open hatch of his father's sailboat, James MacAuliffe watched them soar toward the shore in the cool autumn morning, like swirling patches of fog. The bread lady must be making her morning offering in the parking lot. With a bag of two-day-old loaves courtesy of Amazing Grace Bakery, she'd soon be engulfed by the screeching seagulls and crows, throwing handfuls of bread skyward as if she had never seen the Hitchcock movie.

He gave a bitter laugh. Why did he begrudge an old lady her small pleasures? Each morning, six days a week, the retired schoolteacher dressed as if she still had scores of knuckleheads awaiting her pronouncements on algebra and trig. She leashed up Newton, her old golden retriever, and they set out on a brisk three-mile walk, over the Duluth lift bridge, and around Canal Park before the morning throngs of tourists overran the place. Many days, MacAuliffe would already be seated in the cockpit, sipping his first cup of coffee, and he'd wave and yell, "Good morning."

One day, he'd approached her on the boardwalk and asked if he might buy her a cup of coffee. His reporter's knack for asking questions elicited stories from Ester P—"Forgive me for not telling you my last name, but I don't know if I can trust you, and we single women can't be too careful with strangers. But you seem like a nice young man." Being widowed too early had forced her to work longer than planned. She would love to travel—"I've always wanted to visit the Australian Outback. Such beauty in simplicity. Similar to a good math equation." But she refused to board Newton, and her sister had taken ill and could no longer watch him. "So we walk our three miles every day and enjoy the morning," she'd said, adding a hearty smile. "I just love the birds, the freedom to soar with the wind. It may be the most magical gift of all."

That same knack led him to discover online Ester Petrowski, two years retired as a math teacher at Denfeld, the public high school that served a disproportionate number of Duluth's lower income families. Her retirement announcement showed the same smiling white-haired lady, even then thin as yesterday's newspaper, dressed in slacks and a blouse and a simple tweed jacket. A carefully knotted scarf added a splash of color. Newton, his muzzle a little less white, had also made the party.

Every morning except Sundays—"I sing in the choir at Saint Andrew's by the Lake"—Ester P tied the golden retriever to the railing along the Duluth harbor and she fed the birds. Newton would lay his white muzzle across his paws, his eyes closed despite the avian cacophony going on around him. Old bones and aching hips most likely welcomed the reprieve.

So why, like the languid old dog, couldn't MacAuliffe welcome this reprieve between disasters? Why couldn't he shut out the dissonance of his life? Or like Ester P, be more understanding and accepting of what had happened? He couldn't make the brain noise disappear, and once started, it cycled louder and louder until he was reliving each moment again. In less than a year he'd lost everything: His best friend was dead. The newspaper they had started together had been shuttered. Then his employees and friends disappeared one by one as he either laid them off or they quit when the promised paychecks weren't delivered. When he was no longer able to make moorage payments, he'd sold his boat, his home. And then the woman who had seen him through all of this had stopped calling. Martha was mourning her own losses, he knew, but still, he missed her, missed her a lot.

Burying a friend and running the newspaper into insolvency had kept him busy. The more recent idleness had caused him to slip closer to the edge of the dark chasm of his own despair. The abyss suddenly opened up in front of him. He'd been over that edge before.

The water boiled, and MacAuliffe prepared the French press. He noticed again the folded sleeping bag and the stack of extra blankets and a pillow, his dry clothes on the settee. While his coffee steeped, he stowed them. The girl would be okay. Or so he hoped.

Last night, returning to the boat after another torturous party at his parents' house, he'd found the girl water-soaked and shivering along the railing where Ester P always tied Newton, as if some of the warmth from the dog lingered in the concrete pier. The storm had passed, but she'd obviously endured its fury with little if any shelter. She hugged herself in a wet, grimy jacket that would never keep her warm in the autumn chill.

As he approached, a young voice challenged him. "Touch me, perv, and I'll stab you in the dick."

A head half shorn and half with long purple hair that lay plastered to her skull popped up. A glint of metal flashed from the rings in her nose and from the blade in her hand. A table knife.

"The neck might be a better location," MacAuliffe offered, standing well back. "Just checking to make sure you're okay, if you need anything."

No answer. He extended a grocery bag. "It's my mom's homemade lasagna. It's not very good—don't *ever* tell my mom I said that—but it's edible. Probably even has some nutritional value. Certainly filling. You're welcome to it."

He set the bag on the ground and began to walk away. He half turned and pointed. "I'm staying down here on a boat. You'll see the light come on in a sec. If you get cold or require a fork to go with your knife, just knock."

MacAuliffe propped the gate open so it wouldn't lock. The knock came before he even had time to change into his sweats. The lasagna was gone—no fork required. "Here's your mom's dish. Thank you. And it was, you know, good. You should be nicer about your mom's cooking."

Gratitude with manners—and attitude. MacAuliffe was taking a liking to the young woman. "Yeah, I know, I'm a bit of a prig about food. It's supposed to frost tonight. You got a place to sleep?" It might have been a nervous tic, or it might have been the slightest shaking of her head. "Please, come aboard. I've got an extra sleeping bag if you want to crash here. I can give you a real knife if it'd help you sleep easier."

That elicited a smile, a faint one to be sure, but a smile, nonetheless. She ducked below and eased a pink backpack off her shoulder. The pink seemed out of character when the cabin light revealed a teenager dressed in torn black jeans and, under her dirty jacket, a black tee-shirt with Kurt Cobain emblazoned on the front. Black fingernails, half a head of greasy purple hair, piercings in all the orifices. A constellation of acne crossed her brow which she did nothing to hide. Frightened brown eyes darted from hatch to port to him and back.

MacAuliffe found some clean sweatpants and a sweatshirt for her. She swam in them, but they were clean and warm. He hung up her wet clothes and fired up the diesel boat heater. Soon the boat was warm and toasty, and MacAuliffe opened a porthole for some fresh air.

"Still hungry?" he asked.

She nodded.

They stayed up late talking, sharing cheese and day-old bread, carrots, the last of some mixed olives, and a bag of barbeque potato chips—all he had to offer. She even licked her fingers and ran them around the inside of the chip bag and then licked them clean. She hadn't eaten in two days, he learned. She slouched in the corner of the settee, as if hiding—which, it turned out, she was. She displayed the perfect combination of ennui and disdain; but with time and patience, with a willingness to let silences linger, he slowly elicited her story. Amy. From up north. Seventeen, well, in a few weeks. Amy was short for Amelia. Amelia Bumgarten—"that's a name all the dumbass boys will tease you about. Bunch of assholes anyway." She fidgeted, nervous as a cat at a dog park. She spooked with every lurch the boat made when the wind brought it tight on its mooring lines.

"You in trouble?" MacAuliffe asked.

"Something's happened to Mom."

"What happened?"

"Didn't come home. We live in Grand Marais. She always comes home. It's just, you know, her and me. She never stays away without telling me. Never. Calls if she's gonna be ten minutes late. I mean, I'm not six anymore. But Mom's cool."

"Maybe she had an accident, maybe she can't call. Did you tell the police?"

"No."

"That might be a good place to start."

"Mom didn't trust the cops."

"They're usually the good guys," MacAuliffe said. He didn't mention they weren't always the good guys. His best friend, Lance Trammell, was dead because of a rogue cop. An ache settled deep in MacAuliffe at the memory of his friend. The camaraderie they shared had been such an important part of his life, late nights putting the paper together and brainstorming story angles over cheap bourbon. Life seemed so much darker now for having once shared the light with such a friend.

"I know someone was in our house," Amelia said.

"Did you see them?" MacAuliffe asked. "Did someone ransack the place? How'd you know?"

"Kitchen light was off."

"The light was off?"

"It's like a rule me and Mom have. Always leave the kitchen light on. We never turn it off, even during the day. Mom calls it her beacon, so she can always find her way home. But I know she's doing it for me. Sometimes she still thinks I'm a little kid afraid of the monsters under my bed."

"Maybe she's afraid of the monsters."

"Mom's not afraid of anything. But she worries a lot. She worries when I have to work the evening classes. At the Folk School. We teach people to build things—canoes, kayaks, shit like that. I don't teach, but I'm like the cashier, janitor, and helper. Amy Do-All. I walked home after closing, maybe nine thirty, ten. The kitchen light was off. I didn't go in. I just ran."

"What if the bulb had just burned out or your mom forgot and turned it off?"

"She didn't forget. She never forgets. Never. Car's not home. She's not answering her phone. I guess I just freaked out.

No way I was going in that house. And I know she was worried about, you know, someone coming after her."

"What was she doing? Who'd come after her?"

"I don't know. Like she was working it out. Land and environmental shit and stuff like that. It's something to do with a development around Grand Marais. That's where we live. She was always hiking in the woods or paddling the shore. Kept all her work at home, like she couldn't let other people know. She didn't trust anyone but me. Said I shouldn't trust anyone but her. Warned me that if anything happened to her, I had to get out of town fast. Go to my dad's. He's down in the Cities. He's kinda like, you know, a hippie wannabe lawyer."

"Hey, I'm a hippie wannabe. What's wrong with that?" He pulled his blonde hair back into a man bun.

"Oh man, don't even. Not with those ears. Being a hippie is dope if you don't wanna grow up. Dad's all right—if you don't have to count on him for anything."

The coffee had steeped long enough, and MacAuliffe eased the plunger down on the French press. Amelia had been gone this morning when he rose after a few hours of fitful sleep punctuated by nightmares. The cabin was empty, the sleeping bag folded on the settee, the pillow on top.

A hint of blue sky through the cockpit revealed that last night's storm was passing. To longtime Duluthians, a late summer storm made little difference. His mother had planned a party for MacAuliffe's return home. Used to the vagaries of this inland sea, his folks and their guests considered rain and wind mere impositions, offering them a chance to watch waves thunder onto the beach and to remark upon the weather, a favorite local pastime. "Right blustery this evening, but ain't nothing to the night the *Edmund Fitzgerald* sank."

"Now, that storm would've blown the knickers off a nun," MacAuliffe said, finishing Uncle Chuck's familiar story.

The party had been held at his folks' small bungalow out on a spit of land called Park Point, a pinkie finger of sand that extended into Lake Superior. The MacAuliffes were native Duluthians and even the most violent storms could not persuade them to move, though waiting at the lift bridge for an ore freighter bound for the Inner Harbor was another matter. But that pique of frustration would pass—it always did—and they'd conclude it was just the price of living in paradise.

MacAuliffe hadn't wanted the party.

"Oh, sure you do, Jimmy," his mother, Virginia MacAuliffe, insisted in the sweet, raspy voice that had changed little through the years. "Chuck and Marie, Bill and Clair, the Thompsons and the Razinskis, they're all excited to see you. We'll have fun."

That settled the matter, and she hugged him.

The party was for MacAuliffe only in the sense he was the excuse to throw wide the doors of the waterfront house. All the guests would be his parents' friends—which was also the way it had always been. MacAuliffe and his sister Katie helped with serving and kept up a running commentary as if auditioning for *Mystery Science Theatre 3000.*

"Pattie's bringing back bad '80s fashion with the padded shoulders and wide lapels on that suit," Katie said.

"Suit?" Mac replied. "I thought she was a Storm Trooper. She's been waving that champagne glass like a lightsaber."

"Marie just poured Uncle Chuck into the couch."

"Think he asked for a divorce or a blow job?"

And they laughed at the shared memories of other parties when their inebriated uncle had been lowered onto the couch by his long-suffering wife—which had been all of the parties.

Their mother whisked by so fast with another pan of lasagna

that it made the hoops of her self-made earrings jangle. "You two should mingle with the company," she called out on her way by, only to immediately add, "Katie, would you put some coffee on? Uncle Chuck's in his cups again."

"Already brewing, Mom," Katie replied.

MacAuliffe sipped his coffee and prepared to climb the companionway ladder. From the cockpit, he'd watch the morning brighten across the harbor and the lake, wave at Ester P as she threw the last of the breadcrumbs out for the birds.

He hoped the girl made it to her father's okay. She planned to catch the morning bus, but he hadn't expected her to be already gone when he rose. Drifting awake from another dream of Lance being alive, their partnership at *The Ballard Gazette* intact, MacAuliffe had decided to offer her a ride to meet her father. He had nothing else to do with his day except stare over the edge of the abyss. Maybe he'd drive over to the bus—

An explosion slammed the boat hard against the dock.

MacAuliffe crashed against the companionway, his forehead taking much of the impact. He dropped to his knees, breaking his fall with the hand that had moments ago held the coffee cup. Jeans soaked up the coffee as he knelt, shocked and shaken, his mind dulled from the impact and from the blast. The boat rocked wildly against its mooring lines. He grabbed the ladder to steady himself against the roller coaster of motion. He shook his head. Nothing but a violent ringing in his ears. Then he heard the faint banging of a halyard against the mast. Next came a crescendo of lines slapping and boats groaning and metal clanging. Finally came the terrible screeching of hundreds of birds.

Beneath the dissonance of noise, he heard the wild barking of a dog.

Newton. Ester P.

He scrambled to his feet, only to stumble back to his knees as the boat lurched. Again he rose, practically crawling up the boat steps. Topside, he saw the row of boat masts pitching wildly like out-of-synch pendulums. A halyard swung free and slapped him in the face on the way by. Turning, he gaped at the sight of a ball of fire that exploded out and up, a surge of orange flames tipped with black, an inferno of heat and destruction. Just across the boardwalk, his truck was now engulfed in flames.

His truck had been the explosion.

Oh, fuck. This was going to be a really bad day.

Newton's mad barking snapped him out of it. With each bark, the old golden retriever, still leashed to the rail near the foot bridge, lunged to the end of his tether toward the water. MacAuliffe crab-walked out of the cockpit and onto the wooden dock. The unmoving dock surprised him, and it took a second for him to regain his equilibrium. He stumbled through the wrecked wire fence of a gate, throwing up a bare arm against the flames. Heat seared his lungs.

He ran toward the dog, escaping the blaze. Newton clawed at the railing, trying to get over the four-foot-high bars. Each failure only made him more frantic. MacAuliffe scanned the gray water where the dog focused his attention. Debris from the blast and feathers and dead birds littered a circle widening out from the bulkhead. That's when he saw the body, face down, drifting away from shore beyond the pedestrian walkway.

Taking a couple of quick strides down the pedestrian walkway, he plunged headfirst into the chilly waters of the harbor. Two, three strokes brought him alongside the body just starting to sink with the weight of waterlogged clothes and jacket. Pulling it back to the surface and flipping the body over, he recognized the familiar features of Ester Petrowski. An ear dangled only by the lobe. Grasping her under the arms and around the chest brought her head above the surface. Her unresponsive face oozed blood, a red sheen spreading across brow and cheeks. He darted a glance toward the pedestrian bridge, then the cement-wall pier. Each had to be three, four feet from the deck to the water. He'd never be able to hoist Ester over either of them. Frantic, he scanned the shore. He swam for the concrete wall over which the explosion had flung Ester. Finally he saw it—a narrow, rusty ladder right in the corner where the bulkhead met walkway. He began to sidestroke toward it.

A frantic Newton, his leash now chewed in two, appeared for a brief moment on the walkway, then flung himself into the water. The dog nipped at MacAuliffe and then tried to crawl on top of him, pushing both swimmer and body back underwater. MacAuliffe lashed out at the dog with his one free hand and was starting to yell when he swallowed a mouthful of water. Coughing and gagging, he kicked out hard, catching the dog solid in the ribs. The move separated them, and MacAuliffe stroked hard for shore.

At the ladder, he dipped underwater and resurfaced with the unresponsive body of the schoolteacher draped over his shoulder. He pinned her in place with his shoulder while he grabbed the nipping Newton by the collar and hauled him up as well. He pushed the dog over the railing.

Time did not tick by, but pulsed by with each beat of his heart, expanding and contracting with each gasp of air. He took a deep breath and started up the ladder. She may have been thin and waifish in person, but unresponsive and soaking wet, her body felt as if the weight of the world rested on his shoulder. His feet slipped on the algae-covered rung. He jolted to a stop with his arm fully extended, wrenching his shoulder. He started to pull himself up the ladder again, careful to place his feet securely on the rungs. Each step up was done in lurches. On the third one he heard her groan into his back. Nothing had ever sounded so good to him. Faint, weak, miserable, it was the sound of life. He got one foot on the pier, and she moaned, louder this time. Yes, yes! It was followed by a second, then a quick gagging, and then she vomited down his back.

A man in a suit and tie came running up from the parking lot. His outstretched arms took the body, and he eased her over the railing and to the ground, rolling her onto her side. She vomited again. Newton charged in and began licking the blood from her face. Her eyes opened. A trembling hand reached out to touch the old dog's muzzle.

Sirens filled the parking lot. First a police car, then a fire truck. Two ambulances followed, all arriving as if they were on parade. With few if any commands, people jumped to their jobs, pulling hoses, driving spectators back. Firemen began spraying water on MacAuliffe's truck. Other firemen doused the row of boats, separated from the burning truck by only the walkway.

MacAuliffe watched it all, hoping he might wake up from this nightmare. Dreams had troubled him for so long now he'd found that at the right moment his subconscious would tell him he was dreaming, and he could force himself awake. Not this time. Not today. Either he was awake, or he was so deep into the nightmare that nothing would pull him out.

The paramedics lifted Ester P and settled her on the stretcher. Like picking up a broken twig, MacAuliffe thought, so careful, so delicate. The paramedic working on her cradled her head as gently as if handling a newborn.

Suddenly, MacAuliffe was alone. An uncontrollable shivering wracked his body, and he realized he was soaking wet in jeans and a tee-shirt. Bare feet extended before him as he leaned against the railing. The crisp autumn air carried a breeze that chilled him even more. The adrenaline rush had worn off and fatigue came with uncontrollable shivering.

He caught something fluttering out of corner of his eye. The roller furling jib on his dad's boat was shredded into rags, and the pieces rustled in the wind. The main halyard, severed by flying shrapnel or melted by fire, swung in the breeze. The fire was almost out, leaving a charred hulk that had once been his truck. The tires had melted in the blaze. The cap over the truck bed resembled wales on a pair of corduroys.

The man who had helped him lift Ester over the rail reappeared, leading Newton as if at heel.

"Thanks for the help," MacAuliffe said. "Don't know if I could have managed by myself."

"No problem. You gonna be okay?"

"That's a question people have been asking for years. Seems to be differing opinions on the answer."

"I guess you're gonna be okay. Any ideas what I'm supposed to do with the dog?"

MacAuliffe reached out for the leash. "I'll take him. Come here, Newton."

With the wet dog lying beside him, he watched the firemen finish putting out the fire. MacAuliffe's head began to throb, and he remembered how his face had smashed into the companionway ladder with the explosion. How was he going to explain to his dad what happened to the boat? His mother always claimed that she was only his second true love.

And your point is? his father would respond. No apologies, no protests. There was the boat, then Virginia, and then everyone else. MacAuliffe never quite knew where he ranked on the list of his father's priorities.

A sudden burst of activity brought MacAuliffe's attention back to the burnt-out truck. Two firemen huddled near the cab and one began to wave. A paramedic came sprinting over. He peered in the shattered window and shook his head. He stepped back.

For an instant, MacAuliffe could see between the firemen and inside the truck. His really bad day suddenly got worse, a whole lot worse.

A charred body was clearly visible leaning over the steering wheel.

THREE

The body was pulled from his truck, placed in a body bag, and wheeled to an ambulance. It departed with no lights flashing, no sirens. The body had to be that of Amy. From Grand Marais. Seventeen in a couple of weeks. Amelia Bumgarten. Who knew her mom was in trouble and feared she was being followed. His heart was sick at the thought, but nothing else made sense. MacAuliffe suspected Amelia had decided that stealing his truck was an easier way to get to the Cities than catching the Greyhound bus.

None of this explained why his truck had exploded.

He waited, paced the parking lot, and eventually settled onto a bench along the boardwalk. Newton settled to the ground beside him with a deep sigh. He'd been asked not to leave by the police once he confirmed that, yes, it was his truck. As if he had someplace else to go.

He leaned back on the bench, absorbing as much sun as he could. In the distance he saw an old stone building with the windows boarded up. The city of Duluth had seen a slow fall into disrepair since he'd grown up here. The port had lost shipping business to towns up the shore on Lake Superior all the way to Thunder Bay and to its neighbors on the Wisconsin coast, particularly the neighboring harbor city of Superior.

Duluth-Superior. The Twin Ports. Sometimes called the Armpit of the Arrowhead—a well-deserved moniker. Roads with potholes big enough for a person to take a bath in jarred drivers as if they were navigating a warzone.

Still, MacAuliffe saw signs of hope in his hometown. Signs of revival were everywhere in the city's core. Century-old buildings of brick and stone had the work of graffiti artists scrubbed away, reopening as businesses or boutique hotels. Old Victorians received fresh paint to accommodate the busy tourist season as Airbnbs. In Canal Park, boutiques and craft breweries were intermixed with outdoor stores and art galleries. Coffee shops and bakeries catered to the morning crowd; restaurants and pubs satisfied those who came out in the evenings. New hotels promised them a familiar, if antiseptic, place to stay. A boardwalk lined the shore of Lake Superior, giving rollerbladers, bikers, and walkers like Ester P a place to enjoy the shore. A new hockey arena was sold out when the men's team from UMD played.

At the end of Canal Park, a lighthouse provided a beacon for freighters bound for Duluth's inner harbor. The iron-framed lift bridge, the symbol of the city, would rise to accommodate their passage.

He scanned the scene unfolding in front of him. There was no sign that his wait would end any time soon. Police officers and people in white jumpsuits—who MacAuliffe could only guess were forensic experts—had replaced the firemen on the frontline of the scene of the explosion, but the fire trucks remained onsite, their lights flashing. The crowd of gawkers had ebbed and flowed but was finally starting to disperse. The police cordon now kept him from really seeing anything.

His head throbbed with the pounding of a pile driver. His wet tee-shirt, wrung out, hung over the back of the bench. A police officer had given him a jacket, and a fireman had found a pair of oversized boots. He patted the top of Newton's head to distract himself and scratched the dog's white muzzle. The dog seemed content to remain at his side.

From across the parking lot, he saw Mark Monahan, the police officer who had dug him up a spare jacket. Monahan was large, both in frame and size. Thick shoulders were packed into a blue squall jacket. The first hint of a paunch that his belt couldn't hold in forced khaki pants lower on the waist so that he walked on the hems. The detective was a black man in typically white-bread northern Minnesota. He nodded toward MacAuliffe and walked over.

"Mr. MacAuliffe," Monahan said. "I need to ask you some questions."

"I'm all yours," MacAuliffe said. The dog rose and curled its lip; it was accompanied by a low growl. "And this is Newton. It was his owner who was taken away in the first ambulance." MacAuliffe stroked the dog's head and said, "It's okay, Newton."

Monahan stepped up and held his hand out for the dog to smell. "It was your truck that exploded?"

"Yeah."

"Do you know what might have caused it?"

"I have no idea." Years of being the one asking the questions had taught MacAuliffe that simple answers often hid the important information. He had nothing to hide, so he elaborated. "It had just been serviced before leaving Seattle. That's where I live now. I'm in Duluth visiting my folks for a few weeks, Ted and Virginia MacAuliffe. I'm staying down here on my dad's boat, the *Virginia V*. It's that Tartan 31 right in front of my truck. I came back after a party at my parents' house. Got back between eleven thirty and midnight, I guess. They live on Park Point, out past the Lafayette Community Center, near 32nd."

Monahan joined him on the bench and was scribbling notes. MacAuliffe remained silent to let him catch up. "You any relation to Matty Monahan?"

The police officer nodded. "Yeah, he's my older brother."

"Thought that might be the case. I played hoops with Matty at Central. Back when there still was a Central."

"Oh, sure, I recognize you now. Jimmy Mac. Played point. Couldn't shoot the rock into the lake."

"That's me."

"Guess we've all put on some weight and lost some hair since then. You traveling alone, Jimmy?"

"Yeah. But I have an idea whose body you found in my truck."

"How'd you know we found a body?" An edge crept into Monahan's voice.

"I'm not blind, Detective. You've had me sitting here for a couple of hours. I saw them pull a body out of the truck and load it into an ambulance. You don't close up a body bag unless the person is dead."

"Who do you think it is?"

"Name's Amelia Bumgarten, from Grand Marais. She'd have been seventeen in a couple of weeks." He proceeded to tell the story of how he'd discovered her alone, on the run, and tucked along the railing last night.

"So you were just the Good Samaritan? Nothing more? And she repaid you by stealing your truck?"

"Appears so. And, yes, nothing more happened between us—except she complimented my mother's lasagna, which is probably the first compliment Mom's cooking has received in thirty years. Made me think she was a decent kid."

"Nothing else?"

"Nothing. It's not what you think."

"I'm not thinking anything. Just gathering facts."

"I never touched her. I slept in the vee-berth. She was on the settee. This morning when I got up, she was gone."

"Seventeen, you say?"

"Detective, I didn't touch her. She didn't threaten to yell rape or anything. Besides, why would I blow up my own truck? It's the only wheels I've got. My insurance won't cover this. It would've been a lot easier, a lot quieter, and a lot harder to trace if I'd just taken her up the North Shore on the boat and dumped her in the big lake with an anchor tied to her feet."

"Sounds like you know a lot about that, which is maybe why you'd do the exact opposite."

MacAuliffe imagined lighting a smoke. He inhaled deeply, then exhaled slowly, all the while counseling himself not to react. He resumed. "I understand everyone's a suspect at the beginning of an investigation, but I wouldn't even know how to blow up a car."

"Are you a vet, Mr. MacAuliffe?" Monahan asked.

"No, I'm not," he said. Now was not the time to elaborate on his opinion about US imperialism in the twenty-first century. Monahan might be a vet or might well share an affinity with those who served in the military. Still, it was an odd question, unless—"You found something that makes that important."

"Can't say right now." He glanced at his notes. "The girl told you she was on the run. Maybe she was just a homeless kid playing on the kindness of strangers?"

"She was a frightened kid. She said her mom was missing. Amelia was no Blanche DuBois."

Monahan nodded. "Most homeless kids are scared and frightened, but they get good at preying on strangers. She might have been a throwaway kid. We've seen more of them since the recession. Parents who just walk away. Can't afford them anymore or don't want to afford them. Often kids of meth heads out in the woods, but it's not exclusive to addicts."

"Amelia didn't come across as a throwaway kid," MacAuliffe said. "She sounded close to her mom. Said she worked for a law firm in Grand Marais."

"Okay, I can run down the Bumgartens in Grand Marais. That shouldn't be too hard."

"Amelia mentioned working at a place called the Folk School," MacAuliffe said.

"The North House Folk School," Monahan nodded. "I took a class there on canoe building. I go camping in the Boundary Waters every year. Only way in."

MacAuliffe's summers had been spent sailing Lake Superior on some iteration of the *Virginia*, and he was probably the only kid born and raised in the Arrowhead region of Minnesota who had never dipped a paddle in the Boundary Waters Canoe Area Wilderness, a vast tract of mosquito-infested wilderness straddling the border with Canada. Thousands of lakes of all sizes dotted hundreds of square miles of sparsely populated forest.

"Amelia said her mother was trying to prevent a resort that was being built outside of Grand Marais," MacAuliffe said. "She was using water quality issues in the national forest as her leverage point. Seems she was pretty secretive about her work."

"That narrows it down to about the size of Connecticut."

Morning sunlight and the crisp autumn day couldn't conceal the ugliness of the burnt-out scene before MacAuliffe. It was a reminder that he couldn't go on wasting his days amidst the clutter strewn around his dad's boat, chin in hand, binge watching Netflix and pornography, rereading *The Lord of the Rings* and *Moby Dick*, and moping about his bad fortune. Life had taken a shitty turn this past year, but at least he had a future.

"If it was even her," Monahan said. "We'll get the pathology report back soon."

"Maybe it wasn't her," MacAuliffe said, though he didn't believe it. "There's always the possibility that she was right. That someone didn't appreciate what her mother was doing and thought she might have told her daughter about it."

"How'd they find her here?" Monahan asked. "We're a hundred miles from Grand Marais. Did she say how she traveled? A bus, hitchhiking, a friend?"

MacAuliffe shook his head. "Anyone following her would expect her to pass through Duluth if they knew or suspected she was on the run. Canal Park would be a natural landing place if she was hoping to bum a ride to the Cities."

"There's also the possibility that she wasn't the target," Monahan said. His notebook sat perched on his knee, but he gazed intently at MacAuliffe.

"Who—"

"Do you have anyone in your past who might wish you ill?"

Really? It never occurred to him that he might have been the target. Of course, from Monahan's point of view, it made sense. Who would've known that Amelia would spend the night with him on the boat and then steal his truck? Sometimes we're blind to the obvious.

"I'm a reporter, Detective," MacAuliffe said. "There's a pretty long list of folks who might 'wish me ill,' but not who'd wish to kill me. Literally, not figuratively, of course. I had to file bankruptcy in Seattle, which made some creditors unhappy. I laid off some good friends. I wrote some unflattering stories about some influential people. But nothing that anyone would put out a hit on me over."

"You haven't stiffed a drug dealer since you've been in town?"

"I don't do drugs, unless a good stout or merlot qualifies. I haven't even smoked a joint since I was in college. I struggle all the time with nicotine, but that's legal."

God, someone was trying to kill him? It didn't make any sense. But murder often didn't make sense. He racked his brain, searching for someone with means and motive. McGwire the Seattle parking lot king hadn't appreciated his investigative report on influence peddling, but the old man had gotten off on a technicality. The Seattle cops probably wouldn't respond to his call if someone was pointing a loaded gun at him after his exposé on corruption in the police force. But Lance was dead, and Martha had been shot because of it, so they weren't about to put out a hit on him. Kline & Associates had demanded a retraction, but when it wasn't forthcoming, the real estate developer had taken its millions from its shoddy Ballard condo projects and moved on to other projects. "Do you have some ibuprofen?"

Monahan shook his head. "Sorry, but I'll check with the paramedics."

Before he could rise, a woman's voice came floating across the parking lot. "Jimmy, Jimmy, thank goodness you're all right."

MacAuliffe looked up and saw his mother hurrying toward them. Her hair, now more silver than blonde, tickled his nose as she hugged him tightly. "We were so worried, so worried when we heard the news."

His father arrived right behind her. "You okay, son?"

"I'm fine, Dad." It was best to get it over with when there was an audience. "But the *Ginny* took a pretty hard hit."

It may have been the biggest surprise of his life to hear his father say, "All fixable, I'm sure. I've got good insurance and all winter to work on her."

"Mom, Dad, this is Detective Monahan from the Duluth Police Department. He's right in the middle of asking me some questions."

"We can continue later downtown," Monahan said.

"You one of the Monahan brothers?" his dad asked. "Reggie and Gwen your folks?"

"Yes, sir, I am. Hard to miss us in Duluth."

"Watched your brothers Luke and Matty play a lot of football at UMD. Luke could've been a great one but blew out that knee. It was an illegal pick block but that didn't make his knee any better. Is he doing okay?"

"Yes, sir, he is. Thank you for asking. He's got a beer distributorship. Lives up in Hermantown."

While his father talked football with the detective, MacAuliffe studied the burnt-out hulk of his truck. Someone had targeted him or a scared, frightened teenager who was now dead. Ester P was in the hospital.

What was happening in his hometown?

FOUR

Walking to the edge of the *tatami*, Martha slowed her breathing, bowed, turned to her *sensei*, and bowed again, deeper this time. She felt each rivulet of sweat that ran down her face, each reed of the *tatami* mat under her bare toes. Her body sang where the *gi* brushed her skin, light as the flutter of a moth's wings. Illuminated pinpricks of light sparkled in her vision, as if she could see through the worn fabric of time into another world that contained a far brighter light. Soon she'd feel the familiar ache of muscles that had been worked to their limit, but not now, not yet. Now she reveled in the sensation that each fiber of her body was alive.

The studio was empty except for the two of them. Yamamoto came in early three times a week for their private lessons. Other days, she taught and worked out at the local gym where Ray Palmer was one of her students. Maybe twice a month Martha and her *sensei* would spar, but most days, like today, she'd be given a series of drills to perfect footwork, remove a blemish from her technique, improve her anticipation, focus her concentration. Today, she finished with the *Bassai Dai kata*, which had become for her a ritual dance of grace and power that she moved through like a leopard before it attacks.

Yamamoto motioned for her to join him on the bench. She sat on his right side, near his good ear. Together they sat still and silent, as her breathing returned to normal.

"You smell of diesel this morning," Ichiro Yamamota said, his hands flat on his knees.

"I slept on the boat."

"Is all okay?"

"Yes, *sensei*, thank you. It will be okay."

They both remained quiet for a time. Martha could hear his shallow breaths, the ticking of the clock on the wall.

"You are ready for *shichidan*," Yamamoto said. "You know this; yet you resist."

"I'm not interested in the next level, *sensei*," she replied. She knew she was ready when she'd bested Yamamoto for the first time ever in a recent sparring match. He'd taken the defeat with graciousness and great pride. She hadn't been able to repeat the victory since, but that once had been enough to tell her she was ready to stand for her seventh-level black belt. Once driven by a yearning for success and validation, now she found no appeal in the pursuit.

"I do believe you are not interested, Martha, but I wonder if you deceive yourself with false humility. It is a dishonor to our tradition to not stand for the test when a student is ready."

"I certainly mean no dishonor to you or tradition, *sensei*."

"I believe you believe that, my dear. Still, I am worried. I once asked you, 'Why do you fight?' At that time I promised I would help you. Terrible things sometimes happen to good people. The journey back from them is long and difficult. You had a setback on that journey, Martha. A terrible setback, I know. But we must continue to look forward if we're not to be consumed by guilt and vengeance and despair. Now I'm afraid your focus is again backwards, not forwards. You live in the anger of your failure. I cannot help you on that journey. Please think about this. We can talk more on Monday."

Yamamoto sprang up with a grace that belied his age and short, stocky frame. The sash on his *gi* indicated his degree, *kudon*, ninth-level black belt. Martha saw the missing ear, a reminder to himself of his own vanity when he thought he could beat anyone and everyone. A street fight in LA had proved otherwise. "You have made tremendous progress, Martha. I could not be more proud if I had been the one to start your journey. But I worry that you have become driven for the wrong reasons."

His face carried a deep warmth and openness. "Now, my dear, I have to change and meet with Father Stan. I promised the rector I would review his sermon for Sunday, and I am derelict in my promises. I think he values my opinion because it gives him someone to have coffee with. A shepherd cannot have too many friends and still lead his flock."

Showered, towels wrapping her hair and lean body, Martha sat beside her locker. Yamamoto had shown himself out, trusting her to lock up behind her. The quiet of the locker room, still warm and moist from her steam bath and long shower, gave her time to reflect. Why did she train with such fury? Certainly not to reach the seventh-level *dan*. How could she explain to Yamamoto that with each kick of the *kata* she didn't see the faces of her enemies, but the faces of those she'd been unable to save—her sister Rachel and Lance Trammell. Now they were lost forever.

As she healed physically from the gunshot wound, she'd promised herself she'd never allow such a loss to happen again. Each time she trained, she imagined holding Trammell's face as he died. She was looking backwards, not forwards.

Yamamoto was right, of course. Damn him! She slipped an imaginary dollar into the profanity jar.

Was protecting Emily and the kids her attempt to move forward, or just another reason not to forgive herself for failing to save Trammell? Was opening her own shop—Whitaker, Attorney—in Ballard, where she had quietly put out the word that her preferred clientele was disenfranchised and abused women, mothers, and troubled teens looking to the future or still focusing on the past?

And what was she going to do with Emily? Her plans for the safe house were still a month or more from fruition. The offer had been accepted, but closing was still several weeks out, and the house required a lot of basic work to be habitable again. Old Mrs. Haagen hadn't touched the place, it appeared, since her husband had disappeared many years ago with his boat and three crew members one fishing season on the Bering Sea. Martha had found his name, Kollin Haagen, 1977, on the Fishermen's Memorial at Fishermen's Terminal. Before she'd even been born. The reclusive widow and her cats had slowly shuttered out the world until nobody remembered she still lived in the tiny house across from the old Nordic Heritage Museum.

Not for the first time, Martha noted the irony that it was Hewitt's money that was buying the safe house, which she planned to use as a shelter for women like Emily. She was surprised to discover he had not changed his will. Already weak and frail, Hewitt hadn't lasted long in prison, and she'd declined all opportunities to visit him on his death bed. He'd betrayed her in life but stood steadfast in death. She inherited his sizeable real estate holdings. At first, she was disgusted at the thought of accepting his money. It had been his quest for revenge that had resulted in Trammell dying on a Utah mountainside. His betrayal had felt like a stab to the heart.

In the following months, her feelings about the money evolved. She knew Hewitt would've approved of her idea to liquidate his estate and use his money to help other abuse victims. He'd once been one himself. Being gay in 1940s Utah had exacted its pound of flesh from him.

His estate was financing the safe house and would eventually fund the Rachel Whitaker Foundation. Soon, Martha would be able to provide help to women by offering education, job training, and daycare services, and by addressing the myriad needs a woman had when striking out on her own.

Dressed in faded jeans and a white blouse, her bare toes curling in the carpet, Martha ran the hair dryer over thick, ebony curls. A small makeup case and earrings were laid out on the counter. She set the heat on high and blew it through her hair. With another rainy, cool Seattle morning, it would never dry without a little help. Nine months had passed since she shaved her head, and the thick curls now extended to cover most of her ears. Seeing her reflection in the mirror, she ran her fingers through her hair and cocked her head from side to side. She tried to decide if she liked this look or if she should let her hair grow a little longer.

When she became a corporate attorney over a dozen years ago with regular seven o'clock meetings, she'd lived by the mantra: You could have long, beautiful hair or you could be on time. Those days were past. Still, the need to do something with her hair stared back at her from the mirror. But what style?

At thirty-six, she wasn't exactly a kid anymore. She waved the dryer to throw her hair into disarray. The tousled hair hinted at a woman who knew how to have a little fun. She laughed. Now that would be a new character for her to try out. Maybe she could call Crystal, her former admin assistant at Carey, Harwell and Niehaus and invite her out to coffee. Crystal understood fashion, knowing the right colors, producing the right accessory, highlighting without being flashy. More than once Crystal had produced a scarf from her desk drawer, knotted it expertly, and changed Martha's appearance. Besides, it'd be good to—

She felt the vibration of her phone against a butt cheek. She knew her calendar by heart and her first appointment wasn't for another two hours. Maybe Alexis was cancelling and had sent a text. Then, it occurred to her: What if Jerome had violated the restraining order? She dug the phone out of her jeans pocket and breathed a sigh of relief when the text wasn't from Emily. She didn't recognize the number and thumbed open the text.

"Call me at this number. Someone tried to kill me this morning. Mac."

Mac? James MacAuliffe texted about as often as he bought the beer. The Mariners made the playoffs with more frequency. She read the text again. What happened?

Together, they had spread Lance's ashes off the bluff over Neah Bay and supported Lance's father and each other when the grief became too much. He'd joined her when she made the difficult trip to the men's homeless mission in Pioneer Square where she found Hewitt, her one-time friend and mentor, passing out cookies. They sat together through most of the ensuing trials, both Hewitt's and Harry Callison's. At times holding each other's hand, at times letting the tears flow freely, they had watched as justice was done. It did little to comfort them.

The bankruptcy of the paper had brought them together again, working side by side for a couple of months. No longer able to pay the bills, Mac became, in effect, her pro bono client, and she watched the stress and frustration slowly turn into bitterness as he watched his dreams die with each creditor he couldn't pay, with each document he signed. Martha always bought the beer afterwards.

He answered on the second ring.

"Mac, it's Martha. I just got your text. Are you okay? What's going on?"

"A veritable beehive of misery is what's going on," he said. "And that's just having to listen to my parents bicker like an old married couple. Oh, they are an old married couple." After a pause, he added, "And someone blew up my truck this morning."

"Oh, my God! Were you hurt? What's happened?"

"First, I've got to ask—did you put a hit out on me?"

"Mac, this is serious."

"I'm being serious. All that free legal work, not to mention all the beer you had to buy, might have tipped you over the edge. You know, channeled your Darth Vader or something. Remember, I limped for days after our first meeting."

Martha recalled it well, and it made her smile. Which she knew he was trying to do. Mac and Lance had broken into Hewitt's Lake Union houseboat seeking clues to Hewitt's disappearance while she was also there searching for clues. She'd greeted the intruders in her style. "Yeah, I remember you whining about it for days. But blowing up your truck isn't my MO. I'd have tied your earlobes together behind your head and shattered your kneecap into enough pieces it'd take a jigsaw master to put them all back together again." After a slight hesitation, she added, "But I could be lying to you. I am a lawyer after all. It's in our DNA."

This time, she knew, it was his turn to smile.

"Tell me what happened," she said and heard him take a deep breath.

"My truck exploded this morning. Only I wasn't in it, but someone else was." With prompting here and there from

Martha, he proceeded to tell her the whole story of Amelia Bumgarten, the explosion, and how a casual bystander had been caught in the blast.

"Mac, why do the police suspect they were after you and not this young woman, if she was running scared?"

"No one knew she was with me or that she'd steal my truck in the morning. If the perps didn't know about Amelia, then they had to be after me."

"What reason would she have to lie to you? And she ended up dead. That seems to be a pretty powerful reason to at least consider her story. Besides, who wants you dead? Think."

"That and jogging are two things I tend to avoid."

"Oh, spare me. Mac, why'd you call?"

"Technically, you called me."

"Really, Mac? Maybe I'll kill you myself."

"You've already answered my question. If you thought any of the creditors from the newspaper might have reason to follow me to Duluth and to 'wish me ill'—as the local detective so euphemistically put it—you'd have mentioned it right away."

"Creditors in a bankruptcy don't do that, Mac. You just provided them with a little—and I emphasize *little*—tax write-off."

He gave a bitter laugh. "That *little* tax write-off cost Molly and Benji their jobs."

"And you. And the dream you and Lance shared. I know all that, Mac. They all knew what was happening. They saw how hard you were working to save the paper. It's why they stayed with you right until the end. They're still your friends. Just give them the chance."

"Thanks for the pep talk, solicitor."

Martha ignored him. "And me. You haven't called for a beer since we finalized the bankruptcy. But you call me in a crisis. How do you think that makes me feel? I'm not just some attorney you have on retainer. I'm your friend. At least I thought we were friends."

"Just one more person I disappointed. Seems the only thing I'm any good at."

"Oh, get over yourself, Mac. What a whiner. Poor, poor me. *Wah, wah.* You can help a runaway kid, but you can't call a friend."

"Jesus, Martha, how do you think it makes me feel to be thirty-five and have to ask my parents for money? I had to borrow gas money from mom just to get here. And I can't even tell you the ammunition that gives my dad. Thinking I'll write an advice book. I'll call it *You Should: The Two Dirtiest Words in the English Language.*

"Mac, you're not the only one who lost nearly everything. And maybe you've forgotten—we were the good guys."

A heavy silence hung between them. Martha didn't need to remind him of all that she'd lost since they first met a little less than a year ago. She felt like she still bore a gaping, open wound from the temporary insanity of loving Trammell so briefly and so intensely, then having him ripped violently from her. Every time she thought she might be healing, some image or memory would tear the scab off, beginning the bleeding anew. The woman known as the ice queen by her former work colleagues at CH&N had begun weeping the other day in the bookstore at the sight of a Raymond Chandler novel. She bought it, *The Big Sleep*, because Lance had once listed Chandler as one of the good things to remember when the world seemed to contain nothing but despair and loss. "Fresh strawberries, the Musée d'Orsay, and Raymond Chandler novels," he'd said. From there, one loss piled on top of another until she felt she would smother under its weight—

"I'm sorry," MacAuliffe said, interrupting her thoughts. "I didn't mean to take my frustrations out on you." He hesitated. "What do you know about land-use law? That's the other reason I called. Amelia said her mom was working on a land-use issue on the North Shore—that's the shore of Lake Superior from Duluth to the border. Actually, it goes all around the lake to Sault Ste. Marie, but that part's in Canada. And we're Americans so we don't care about that."

"Oh goodness, there're so many different ones. Environmental, public trust, commercial, preventing the commercial, mineral rights, water rights. I wouldn't know where to begin."

"You could begin by coming to Duluth to help me." When she didn't respond, he added, "I was just thinking—"

"Hang on," she said. She flipped open a new screen on her phone. Her calendar popped up. Today she had a meeting with Alexis Graham, followed by a meeting with a new client this afternoon. Appointments were scattered across the next week, but she checked each one off as cancel, do by phone, reschedule. And her personal life required no mental gymnastics to figure out. A benefit of having no personal life, really. Next weekend she was scheduled to walk in a fundraiser for Alzheimer's—a sop to a client. They'd take her money whether she walked or not. It also solved her problem of what to do with Emily and the kids. They could stay in the Carriage House. A text to Ray Palmer would get him to check in on her from time to time.

Why should she change even one appointment to fly to Duluth to help Mac? The person who couldn't pay her for her professional expertise before and who certainly couldn't now; the person who hadn't called when she began to flounder in her own recovery. But she was already mentally canceling appointments and buying a plane ticket. Mac had been Lance's best friend. He was her friend and had shown up every time she needed someone and had nowhere else to turn, no matter the turmoil that was happening in his life. And she knew the phone worked both ways. She hadn't called him to tell him she was drowning in her own despair. Or to throw him a lifeline as he floundered in his own.

"I'll text you when I get in," she said. "It'll probably be tomorrow."

On the way out, she left Yamamoto a note telling him she would reflect on their conversation and talk about it when she returned. She threw a ten into the profanity jar—paying it forward—and secured the door behind her. She stood in the foyer at the bottom of the steps and considered the damp, gray morning. Well, at least she hadn't tried to do anything with her hair.

She stepped into the mist. Why did moving forward feel so much like looking back?

FIVE

By afternoon, Detective Mark Monahan was finishing his sweep of the *Virginia V.* MacAuliffe had paced the boardwalk for the better part of the day outside the yellow tape cordoning off the crime scene. His folks had walked home with Newton, leaving him his mom's truck and mobile phone. She'd slipped him some cash. "Just in case you need something, honey."

Monahan's head appeared in the companionway. With surprising nimbleness for a guy who had to be six five, six six, he bounded off the boat.

"Okay," Monahan started, "I'm buying part of your story." He held an evidence bag. White latex gloves contrasted with his dark skin. He pulled out a note written on the back of a napkin. "Found this with your wallet, in the nav station."

Hey, Mac,

I'm sorry I had to borrow your truck without asking—which I suppose makes it stealing but I hope you'll understand and not call the cops on me. They'll be checking the buses I'm sure. I would if I were them. I also borrowed some money and a credit card—pay it all back, girl scouts honor. I'll text you Dads address where you can pick up your truck when I get to Mpls. Muchas arigato for the food and place to crash. You've got a nice yacht. And take it easy on your Moms cooking. At least you have a Mom to cook for you. Maybe you should cook for her for a change. ☺

Sincerely,

Amy

In addition to the smiley face, her signature included a tail with a heart symbol. It felt eerie getting a lecture from a dead girl, but it confirmed his suspicions about why she was in his truck.

"Money's gone too," Monahan added. "Of course, might not have had any to steal. Still, it doesn't mean you didn't do it yourself. But not for the insurance since it seems your policy's expired. It's illegal to drive without insurance, you know."

"Doesn't look like I'll be driving again anytime soon."

"Probably not. I'll have to get a writing sample from you."

"Of course."

To answer MacAuliffe's unspoken question, the detective said, "Okay, it's not that I didn't believe you. We still have to verify it was her. I hope they can pull some dental records. Still doesn't mean she was the intended victim."

He dropped the napkin back into an evidence bag.

Monahan strode over to the burnt-out chassis of the truck. He bent over and talked to someone whose legs stuck out from underneath, reminiscent of the cruel end to the Wicked Witch of the West. His butt crack forced MacAuliffe to study the graffiti on the distant wall.

The detective stood up and hitched up his pants. Turning back to MacAuliffe, he said, "The note explains why she was in the truck, but it doesn't explain what happened or who they were after. I talked with the Grand Marais police and they have no record of any missing Bumgartens."

"They wouldn't if Amelia never called the police."

"Why wouldn't she call the police?"

"Her mom told her not to trust anyone—including the police."

"And you trust her? The girl who was in the process of stealing your truck, who emptied your wallet?"

"And who left me a note telling me she was doing it. And who took time to lecture me on being nice to my mom."

"You never would've got your truck back. At least in one piece."

"I think you're wrong, Mark. I talk to people all the time. It's my job. Ask them enough questions and listen for the lies in their answers, and you start to get a good sense of who they are in a short period of time. I got the feeling that she was exactly who she said she was."

"But how often do you talk to teenagers? I work with them all the time. I ask them lots of questions, too. Kids are good at lying." The officer peered at MacAuliffe. "Any thoughts on who might've come after you? This didn't happen on its own. We're gonna have to tow the truck back to our lab, but my man here thinks someone planted an explosive on the fuel tank."

"I just talked with my attorney. She assures me I'm too small a number on some corporate ledger to be worth the trouble."

If it had been a bad day for him, MacAuliffe only had to think about Amelia Bumgarten or look at Ester Petrowski to realize how much worse it could have been. The retired schoolteacher dozed in a hospital bed at St. Mary's. An IV ran into her left arm; a wire attached to a monitor disappeared under her hospital gown. Her head was wrapped in gauze, which forced her white hair to stick out at various angles like an untrimmed hedge. Her thin, frail body appeared as little more than a wrinkle in the blanket. Her mouth hung open and each breath was a heavy intake of air followed by a heavy exhale, as if she were sighing.

Remnants of a half-eaten dinner had been pushed aside on a cart. Someone had already delivered flowers. A plant of burgundy red mums with some green spiky thistle-like things sat on the windowsill in the evening twilight. He'd thought about bringing flowers but settled on a book. And he'd brought something better than either—news about her dog.

Ester P snorted loud enough that he was sure she was waking up, but it was just the preamble to more snoring. Out the window, red taillights showed traffic fleeing downtown. Beyond the city streets, the lake swallowed all light to the horizon.

"I hear I have you to thank for being here." The voice was loud and harsh, as if she were lecturing a group of students who had forgotten to turn in their homework.

"That is true," MacAuliffe replied, turning away from the window and the giant black maw of the lake. Ester P's eyes were open. A smile graced her beaten-up face. Bruises and tiny dots and streaks—probably from flying debris—gave her the appearance of an aging fighter on the losing end of a bout. A Band-Aid stretched across her upturned nose.

"Sure beats the hell out of the alternative." Again, her voice was loud but clear, as if she was remembering how to use it. "Thank you for pulling me out of the drink. Don't remember any of it. But the police officer, the big fella, one of the Monahan gospel brothers—had 'em all in class, Matthew, Mark, Luke, and John, good students for the most part. Sorry, I digress. The Gospel According to Mark says you saved my life. Not something most people would've done, but I'm extremely grateful. I'm not ready for the alternative. Makes you a hero in my opinion. And my opinion is the only one that counts, I'll have you know."

"You're welcome," MacAuliffe said, with a nod. "I'm just glad I was there." He pulled his chair up to her bedside and took her hand. "And I've got some good news. Newton is fine. The police think most of the blast probably went right over top of him." He'd made that up, but it seemed like it could be true. She squeezed his hand and closed her eyes. Tears ran down her cheeks. "Now you may have to arm wrestle my mom to get him back. He's already sitting on the couch with Dad watching the evening news. They're out on Park Point. He'll get his regular walks every day until you're feeling better."

"I was afraid to ask. Oh thank you, young man, thank you."

The conversation stopped while she cried a little more. MacAuliffe handed her a tissue. She wiped her eyes and blew her nose.

"How you feeling?" he asked.

"The drugs must be working because I actually don't feel so bad. I've gotta see if I can take some of these home."

"Better living through chemistry. I brought you something." He handed her Neal Stephenson's book, *Quicksilver*. "It's a fictional account of the Newton-Leibniz rivalry. I thought you might enjoy it. When you're feeling up to reading, of course."

"My cat!" Ester attempted to sit up, but quickly sank back into the bed. "Oh, my."

"Easy, easy." MacAuliffe placed a hand on her arm. "What is it?"

"Leibniz, that's my cat." Her voice was loud. "He has to have his heart pill."

"No need to shout, Ester. I'm right here."

"Oh, sorry. Doctor said I blew out my eardrum on one side, maybe both. I don't hear myself shouting."

"Do you have someone who can give your cat his meds?" MacAuliffe spoke louder. "Family, friend, neighbor? Can I call someone for you?"

"Agnes can't. She's my sister. Lost her foot to diabetes. Horrible disease. Helen is off on a fall color bus tour to New England. She's my neighbor. Frank'd rummage my underwear drawer. Damn creep. And Spike'd have to haul his oxygen tank up to the third floor. I hate living around all these old people."

"I'll feed your cat and give him a pill," MacAuliffe said. "I have to drive right that way to get to my folks' place."

"Taking care of Leibniz is, well, complicated. But it'd be so nice of you. So nice. Maybe knock on Agnes's door and let her know I'm okay. She lives just down the hall."

A nurse in burgundy scrubs, her shoulder-length hair pulled back in a ponytail, interrupted them to take Ester's vitals. Blood pressure, temperature, pulse. She set two pills in a paper cup on the food cart and drew a glass of water. She handed the pills and the water to Ester, who dutifully took them. The nurse sat down and took Ester's hand. "All your vitals are normal. You're doing great, Mrs. Petrowski. The back fracture requires rest. Lots of time in bed. The doctor will be in shortly to look at that head wound and your ear."

"Where my ear used to be, sweetie. How do you wear a hearing aid if you don't have an ear?"

"They can do implants now," the nurse replied. "Just wear your hair a little longer. No one will ever know." She stood up and fussed with the blankets. "You may not remember, but I had you for eleventh-grade trig and then calculus. Tanya Miller. I was so upset when I heard you were the one caught in that horrible explosion down at Canal Park. They're saying it might have been a terrorist. Can you believe it? In Duluth? A terrorist?"

"Of course I remember you, honey. How many times did I have to separate you and the Bishop girl?"

The nurse laughed. "Too many times, I'm afraid. Oh, good, I was worried you didn't remember me. I loved your classes, Mrs. Petrowski. It's why I became a nurse." To MacAuliffe, she added. "Visiting hours are over. Oughta start wrapping it up."

"I will, thanks. She just has to finish giving me instructions on feeding her cat." The detailed instructions had already spread to a second napkin.

"You still have Leibniz?" the nurse said.

"Eighteen and ornery as ever," Ester said.

"Well, you'll be home to him soon enough." The nurse fluffed the bedding again and pulled the top blanket up over Ester's shoulders. She made a couple of notes on the wall board and departed.

Ester wiggled a finger for MacAuliffe to come closer.

"You have to get me out of here, James," she said, in what passed for a whisper. "Tanya Miller's a dunderhead. I'm surprised she knows how to put her privates on straight, let alone start an IV or something important. I'm sure she passed calc only because she cheated. I just couldn't catch her. A sly one. She and the Bishop girl, both. If she's my nurse, I might as well pack my suitcase now for the last big trip."

"I didn't pull you out of the harbor for you to give up now," MacAuliffe said. "I'm sure she's fine. You didn't tell me you also broke your back."

"Ain't giving up on life or love, young man. I just know when the odds are long. Appears I did break my back, as well. The Gospel According to Mark thinks the blasts probably threw me against the railing before my swan dive into the drink. Wish someone would've caught it on camera. It'd probably go viral on YouTube. 'Old Lady Sticks the Landing.'"

"I suspect you didn't stick the landing. Now, just rest. I'll take care of the cat, and Newton's fine with my folks." He patted her hand. "I did have a question for you, as well."

"Wondering when you were going to get around to the purpose of your visit."

"Making sure you're okay isn't enough reason to visit?"

"Young man, I may have been born at night, but I wasn't born last night."

"Fair enough." MacAuliffe nodded. "I was wondering if you saw anything before my truck blew up. A young girl was in it when it happened. Did you see her get in or did you see anyone else sneaking around?"

"Same questions Mark asked me. Do you think I should call him Detective Monahan now that he's professional and all?"

"No, I think Mark is okay. I might stay away from The Gospel According to, though."

"Good point. That's what we called the Monahan boys in the teachers' lounge. Anyway, to answer your question. No, I didn't see anyone else. Newton and I have our morning routine and the only thing different this time was I saw a young woman come off the docks. The reason I remember her is she said, 'Good morning' first when I approached. Not many kids do these days, you know. I was walking the boardwalk in front of the docks."

"Can you describe her?"

"It was just getting light. Didn't pay much attention to her really. But I remember she was dressed in black. Such a harsh color for a pretty girl. Carried a pink backpack. She'd shaved part of her hair, and the rest was purple." She closed her eyes, as if thinking, and then added, "Oh, she had her nose pierced, as well. Always wonder when I see that in kids how they blow their nose. Maybe when you get older you think about more practical matters like that."

"That was Amelia," MacAuliffe said. "She was the one who died in the explosion. Where did she go?"

"She headed off across the parking lot."

"Did she stop at the truck?"

"Might've, I suppose. I didn't pay that much attention. I just saw her a few minutes later walking toward Lake Avenue."

"Did you see her come back?"

"No."

"Was this before or after you went to Amazing Grace for your bird food?"

"Before."

"You're getting tired."

"Yeah, a little. Tanya must've given me a sleeping pill."

"Or a narcotic for the pain."

"I'm not in any pain."

His head throbbed and he wondered if he could get some of the same medication.

With Leibniz fed, medicated, and petted, MacAuliffe retreated to the third-floor balcony to nurse his wounds. He unwrapped the paper towel from around his hand. The bleeding from the cat scratches had slackened to a slow oozing.

On the way from the hospital, he'd succumbed to the craving and bought a pack of cigarettes. This would be his first one in weeks. Thank God he'd never gotten hooked on anything more powerful than nicotine. He'd be dead or in jail by now. He shook a smoke from the pack and stared at it for a long time. The road to perdition starts here. A legal, addictive narcotic. And I am an addict.

He torched the end and inhaled deeply, holding the smoke in his lungs before exhaling. He felt the calming effect course through his body, like he was sinking into a warm bath.

Ester P's apartment had a view of Duluth's inner harbor. Specks of light outlined the shore, circling the dark water of the harbor. He could see a couple of docks where freighters were moored, lights blazing as crews worked through the evening. The bridge leading to Wisconsin soared high over the south end of the harbor and showed light traffic this evening.

Had he or Amelia been the intended victim? He wished Martha were here so they could kick this can around the bush a time or two. Her text said she'd be arriving in the morning and driving up from the Cities. Really what he wished was for Lance to be here. They had fed on each other's creativity, questioning logic, playing the foil, asking more questions, shooting holes into assumptions. He missed that right now.

Nothing about the day made any sense. If Amelia's story were true—question that assumption, dude, he heard Lance argue—but *if* it were true, he argued back, she was the likely victim. But how did they know where she'd be, that she'd steal his truck? But did they have to know those things? If he were hunting for a runaway girl, where would he search? Certainly the bus stop. In Duluth, Canal Park was the place where tourists gathered and dispersed. If he were seeking a quiet ride out of town, he'd chat someone up at a coffee shop and hope to find a generous soul heading home to Minneapolis or St. Paul who might offer a ride. He heard himself preparing the lie—my car died, it's in the shop, it's taken all my cash. Any chance you have room to give me a lift to the Cities? Cry on cue. It'd be so much more believable coming from a young girl.

He stubbed out his cigarette in one of Ester P's potted plants and lit another one. He leaned against the railing.

He realized now that he must have woken up to the sound of her leaving or the rocking of the boat when she stepped off. He'd risen and immediately turned the stove on to begin boiling water for his coffee. When Amelia had passed Ester P on the dock, she headed off across the parking lot. To where? Nothing on Lake Street would've been open. A block over, all of the shops on Canal Park Drive would have been closed—except Caribou Coffee. A coffee for the road? With cash stolen from him, the little shit. And that's where he'd wait if he were searching for a young girl on the run. It's where he'd be if he had someone at the bus stop, checking passengers for the seven o'clock bus to the Cities. That meant there had to be at least two people involved.

Did the bomb in the truck have to be planted prior to the explosion? That'd be important to know to determine who they were targeting.

MacAuliffe pecked out the message, 'do u have time to talk?' and sent it to Mark Monahan.

Before he could sit down on a patio chair, his mom's cell phone was ringing.

"You wanted to talk?" Monahan said by way of greeting.

"Yeah, I did. Thanks for calling back." When the detective didn't respond, MacAuliffe continued, "I was wondering about the bomb that blew up my truck. I know you can't talk about it as it's part of an open investigation, but maybe you can help me understand it in broad terms. See, I'm not remembering anyone in my past who'd care enough to blow me to kingdom come. I'm still thinking that Amelia had to be the target, not me. Can you at least tell me, was the bomb hardwired to the truck in some manner? You know, hotwired to the ignition switch for example, something a person would have to do ahead of time? Or was it something that a person could have placed on or under or near the truck at any time, including the last minute?"

"I see where you're going." Now it was MacAuliffe's turn to wait. "It wasn't hardwired to the truck. The explosion wasn't predicated on starting the truck. It was line-of-sight remote."

"So the person with their finger on the trigger had to be nearby?"

"Exactly."

"Any surveillance cameras in the area?"

"This is Duluth. You've been watching too much British television."

"Could someone have put it there at the last minute?"

"My understanding is that it's possible. But the bomb was affixed to the undercarriage of the truck, right next to the fuel tank. Get more explosion that way. That couldn't have been done on a run by. It's not like throwing a Molotov cocktail through an open window."

"How long would it take a person to secure it to the undercarriage?"

"I don't know, Mac. It probably depends on the level of expertise. It'd probably take me half an hour—if I could even fit under there."

"So the person had to be small—or at least smaller than you—plus know about how and where to place the bomb."

"Or they could have placed it there anytime during the night and waited."

"But don't you see, Mark, if the trigger was line-of-sight, then someone had to see it was Amelia, not me, getting into the truck."

"Shit, you're right," Monahan said. "Forensics is pretty sure it was a line-of-sight switch. Maybe the person couldn't see clearly in the dawn light, just saw someone get in the truck and thought it was you. I don't know how close the person on the trigger had to be."

"Ester Petrowski saw Amelia come off the docks before the explosion. There was enough light for Ester to know she had purple hair and a nose ring. I'm a balding dirty blonde with a beard and about twice the size of Amelia. It'd be hard to confuse us, even at a distance."

"Mrs. P never mentioned that to me."

"I probably asked her different questions." A thought occurred to MacAuliffe. "Do you know if Amelia was alive when the bomb exploded?"

"The ME hasn't done an autopsy yet."

"But you have an idea."

There was another long hesitation. "The body showed no visible signs of blunt trauma or anything that would lead us to believe she wasn't alive at the time of the blast."

"Other than being burnt to a crisp, of course. Would that hide a blunt trauma, say?"

"Some kinds, but not a fractured skull or a broken neck. Not a stab wound as the body's soft tissue isn't all consumed unless it burns longer, hotter than this. Firetrucks got there pretty fast."

"I have a friend—you'll probably meet her tomorrow, in fact—who can knock you out cold and not leave a bruise. I know this for a fact because she did it to my best friend. She wasn't as gentle with me."

"You hang out with all the fun people."

"But couldn't someone have done that to Amelia?"

"Maybe, but we keep coming back to the problem of how they found her."

"Ester saw her walk across the parking lot. My truck was parked right in front of the boats. She wouldn't have had to cross the parking lot to get to it." MacAuliffe explained his idea that Amelia might have headed to the coffee shop this morning and run into someone. God, was it really just this morning? "If you're a runaway teen and you think the bus depot is being watched, where would you go in Duluth?"

"Canal Park. People from out of town, people with money."

"Would the fire have burned up all the evidence?"

"It never burns up all the evidence."

"What about her backpack?"

Monahan didn't respond at first. "What backpack?"

"Amelia was carrying a pink backpack. She had it when she arrived last night, and Ester saw her with it this morning. If her mom told her to run if anything happened to her, she might have given Amelia something to take to her father. He's an attorney in the Cities. Amelia said he'd know what to do, so it makes sense that she had to take something to him."

"It wasn't in the truck when we searched it."

"You're sure?"

"Not positive, but everything leaves some residue. A pile of ashes, a puddle of goo, something. There was nothing like that in the truck. We found her phone and the body."

"Still, I'm thinking they were after Amelia, not me."

"You've given me plenty to think about." Mark's voice grew firm. "As far as I'm concerned, we haven't talked tonight."

MacAuliffe walked back into the apartment and joined Leibniz on the couch. The cat hissed at him before settling on his lap. One thing he was now sure of was that he hadn't been the intended target. Someone had been after Amelia and had succeeded. What was Amelia's mother up to that could get her daughter killed? Amelia had been a good kid running scared, but running scared from what and whom remained unknown.

He had nothing else to do in Duluth. He'd see if he could help figure it out.

SIX

Martha crested a hill and immediately knew why Mac had settled in Seattle after a childhood in Duluth. Lake Superior spread before her like a vast ocean, glittering blue under a clear sky to the distant horizon. Green hills with just a hint of the autumn colors still to come descended to the shore that wrapped around toward a harbor where two freighters lay at anchor. A sailboat, a mere whiff of a white cloud on the surface of the blue water, ghosted between the two freighters.

A river delta created a labyrinth of channels, gradually widening into an expansive inner harbor. A lift bridge of beams and trusses posed as gatekeeper between the lake and the inner harbor. The white speck of a powerboat glided east, following a narrow spit of land that jutted out between the large lake and the inner harbor. The vista left her with a sensation akin to topping Queen Anne hill to see Elliott Bay spreading out in front of her. For Mac, seeing Elliott Bay for the first time must have been like seeing a piece of home.

She descended into Duluth, and the scene vanished. She drove past businesses and warehouses and storage silos, some active, some shuttered, all signs of a struggling port town on the far edge of a big lake. Downtown came into view, but before she could take it in the GPS talked her off the interstate and toward something called Amazing Grace in Canal Park.

She parked and exited the rented Forester, yawning, stretching, shaking life into her body, her brain. She ran fingers through her hair. She doubted Mac would have an opinion about her hairstyle. He had all the creativity of a fast-food hamburger when it came to appearance. Jeans, wrinkled button-down Oxford in either blue or white, and boat shoes. With socks in the winter, without socks in the summer. Little else ever changed. If he didn't have food stains down the front of his shirt, he was dressed up.

Martha scanned the messages on her phone. She'd received two texts from Palmer who assured her that all was quiet at the Carriage House.

She descended the steps and entered the basement bakery. The aromas of yeast and baking bread, cinnamon, and coffee mingled in the air, flooding her senses with all that was good about mornings. The smell also made her realize she was ravenous. She saw MacAuliffe, his computer open in front of him, seated against the far wall, his head down, staring intently at the screen. His blonde hair and beard had grown shaggy since she last saw him, and just a hint of his elephantine ears poked through the hair. He was handsome in a way, with a strong patrician nose and cornflower blue eyes. Either he'd lost more weight, or he wore a borrowed wrinkled Oxford shirt—blue—that was too big in the shoulders and chest.

"Hey, Mac," she said, causing his head to pop up.

"Martha." He jumped up and enveloped her in a deep, long hug. At six feet, she had him by an inch or two. She smelled that he'd started smoking again. The smell of stale tobacco reminded her of home and family. Gran had been a smoker; her father was a smoker. The smell of smoke was part of the last memory she had of her mother, who had walked away from the family when Martha went for her first day of kindergarten. She knew Mac had struggled on and off since she met him to quit, occasionally succeeding, often not.

She hated the smell of cigarette smoke in everyone except the people she loved. She held him at arms' length and took in his red, swollen nose. "You're looking a little beat up, my friend."

"Yeah, you should see the other guy. Can I get you a cup of coffee, some lunch? I recommend the Chip's Eggs Mess, if you're hungry. Goes great with a cinnamon roll. God, I can't tell you how much I appreciate your coming out."

Over lattés, cinnamon rolls, hash browns, and eggs scrambled with everything in them—she *was* famished—and another latté, he updated her on all that had happened in the past thirty hours. Fully sated and a little buzzed, she sat back. "Wow. That's a lot. And you're sure you're not the target of this psycho bomber?"

"I'm sure, even if the cops are not," MacAuliffe said. "If it was a line-of-sight remote switch, they had to be after Amelia. A blind person wouldn't confuse us at a hundred yards, even if it was early morning."

"Do you think the kid had information about the work her mother was doing? Maybe files or a thumb drive in that backpack?"

"I have no idea, but it's possible someone thought so."

"So what's the next step?"

MacAuliffe rotated his computer so she could see the screen. The open file showed the minutes from the Cook County Council meeting from two months ago. He said, "The only person from Grand Marais named Bumgarten that I can locate is a woman named Rose Bumgarten. She testified against every proposed development in the area, but especially this one for a complex of condos and private residences situated around an eighteen-hole golf course south of town. The North Shore has seen a lot of development in the past couple of decades. It used to be a place where a few people had summer cottages. Now everyone has a cabin up north or rents one. Lutsen has a small ski resort—bunny hills mostly, but it's still downhill skiing in the Sawtooth Mountains. That's what they call the bigger hills around here. Don't confuse them for real mountains. This development would be the biggest yet. Nearly two hundred housing units and a top-ranked golf course. Conference centers, two restaurants, and year-round jobs. There's talk of adding downhill skiing sometime in the future. Rose Bumgarten wasn't drinking the Kool-Aid."

"On what grounds?"

"NIMBYism, I'd imagine, but the records show she did her homework. Cited environmental degradation, need to protect the watershed, overdevelopment in or near a national forest. Much of it's located along the edge of Superior National Forest. This has big money written all over it. It's taken years and probably hundreds of thousands of dollars—if not millions—to design the development, jump through the hoops of regulations, secure permits, and conduct EISs. Rose Bumgarten demanded it be stopped. Claimed the environmental impact statements were incomplete and misleading—basically they cherry-picked their data to show minimal impact. Questioned whether the water table could support that many housing units, and golf courses take huge amounts of water in the summer. They use lots of fertilizer, which ends up in the watershed, which ends up in the lake, which ends up in the drinking water. Wondered why public land was being considered for a private development."

"Was she being effective or just making lots of noise?"

"Again, hard to tell. But they haven't started digging yet."

"What are you thinking?"

"The representative for NorthShore Resorts who spoke at the public meetings is a guy named Craig Nettles. He lives here in Duluth, out in the Congdon neighborhood where the rich folks live. I've known the name since I was kid. Family has a long history in the area. A hundred years ago they made a lot of money in logging and mining in the Arrowhead. When that dried up, the family went into real estate development. They were part of the group that built the Miller Hill Mall, and they've been investing in the redevelopment of downtown. Now it appears they want to add Grand Marais to their list of projects. I thought we should pay Nettles a visit."

"Just going to walk in and ask him if he blew up your truck with Amelia in it?"

"I'm a freelance journalist working on a story about the economic development on the North Shore. It's a chance for him to set the record straight, to tell his side of the story. In fact, I've already got a meeting scheduled with him. Four o'clock. Care to join me?"

"And you'd bring your attorney, why?"

"We're partnering on the story. There are bound to be legal concerns about the development and you'll be much better at identifying them than me. Just ask good questions, like you were in court questioning a witness. You'll be fine."

"Can we swear him in to tell the whole truth and nothing but the truth?"

"And if you believe they do that in the courtroom, sure."

Outside, the sun had started to warm the day, but this far north and after the equinox, the promise of warmth was misleading. Still, the autumn rains had started in Seattle in recent days, and Martha enjoyed basking in its glow as she walked down the sidewalk with MacAuliffe at her side. He pointed out Caribou Coffee, said someone should take a picture of Amelia and show it to the early morning baristas. They cut across a parking lot. They passed an old brick warehouse with The Suites embossed on the door.

"Want to see if your room's available?" he asked.

"Later," she said.

Across the parking lot, a single row of boats appeared—mostly small powerboats with a few small sailboats mixed in. Martha recognized the powerboats instantly as fishing boats by the trolling gear mounted on the stern, much like the Grady White 23 she kept moored at Shilshole. When she'd quit her job as a corporate attorney—and with it, the paycheck—she had had to downsize to stay afloat. Raising the rent on the main house had helped—and the Heidens didn't care since the University of Washington sent the check every month. She sold her Lexus and her brother's vintage '57 T-Bird. Her Grady White had been for sale when she got word that Hewitt had died in prison.

It seemed so much of her life of late had been about dealing with loss. Her job, her friend, her lover. She took the boat off the market and spent the afternoon fishing the underwater bank near Richmond Bay. The memory of a night spent making love with Trammell on the boat while anchored there was more powerful, more important than selling the boat because Hewitt had once walked its decks. She refused to let a monster dictate her actions. Not Walt Boudreau. Not Hewitt.

Now, could she build a new life from the ashes of the old?

She wanted to believe she could trust MacAuliffe to help her do that.

Like she had trusted Hewitt? The thought stopped her cold on the boardwalk.

MacAuliffe turned when he sensed she was no longer at his side and saw her studying the transom of a navy blue vessel with *Mac's Place* in silver lettering across the stern. "That's my Uncle Chuck's fish killer," he said. "From what I can tell the only thing he catches is the bottle of Fireball he chills in the lake when he's trolling."

Martha chuckled and rejoined Mac on the boardwalk. He often made her laugh, and Lance had always trusted him. She remembered that once, during the work to complete the bankruptcy of the *Gazette*, she'd entered a room, and he was sitting there weeping. It was as if she had seen him for the first time—grieving for a friend, for the loss of their shared dream. She touched his shoulder but said nothing. The whole time he hadn't moved. Tears spilled out of unblinking blue eyes; his lips quivered, quick and brief like the flutter of a bee's wing. He wasn't embarrassed and didn't turn away. Moments passed in silence. And then he wiped his nose on his shirtsleeve, and they continued on as if it never happened.

Now, Martha hooked her hand in his arm and tried to look ahead and not back as they strode down the boardwalk.

She could smell the fire, that combination of soot and ash and charcoal. What was left of a small building, more like a hut really, was a twisted pile of scorched plywood and a collapsed roof. The paint on the fencing separating the boardwalk and the marina had blistered and peeled.

"This is where my truck exploded," MacAuliffe said, pointing to a black spot on the pavement. "They towed it away yesterday afternoon to their forensics lab. They won't say what they've found so far, but it's something to do with the bomb. Asked me if I'd ever been in the military." He nodded across the boardwalk, toward a boat beyond the fence. "And that is my dad's boat. The *Virginia V*, but we just call her *Ginny*, after my mom."

Mattresses from the vee-berth and settee were spread out on the deck. A halyard with a large knot in it was tied to the lifeline. It'd never haul a sail again. The roller furling jib had taken the brunt of the damage and was a combination of ragged edges and melted Kevlar.

"A rag bagger; I should have known," she said, studying the vessel. This got the smile she'd hoped for.

"What'd you expect? The acorn doesn't fall far from the tree. I grew up sailing this lake. I'd circumnavigated it before I was a teenager."

Martha knew he felt the loss of his own boat keenly. It had been his home as well as a passion for him. Couldn't afford the monthly moorage, he'd told her, but she knew he'd put the money into the newspaper in a last-ditch effort to publish for another week to pay his friends. It had been for naught in the end, just one more casualty in a life lived too much on the edge. "How bad's the damage?"

"Not as bad as it seems, actually. The jib's ruined, of course, but otherwise the *Ginny* came through in pretty good shape. I sleep with the hatches open, and water from the fire hoses drenched all the bedding and mattresses and most of my clothes. But they'll dry out. Mom's doing the laundry now. Helps her feel useful. Dad's already talked to his insurance agent about a new jib, I'm sure. The mechanics of the roller furling are fine. I can replace the halyard when I have some time and someone to haul me up the mast. I thought I'd put on the storm jib to get to the end of the season. He'll haul the boat pretty soon anyway. Not much sailing happens around here once you need an icebreaker to get to open water."

"When's that?"

"About a month. They haul the docks in November."

"No bubblers?"

He scoffed. "Not for boats this size. Easier and cheaper to haul them and store them on the hard for the winter. Wimpy stink potters will go inside a barn, of course."

"Of course," Martha replied and smiled.

"I've got to flip the mattresses, grab a couple of things. Then we can run out and you can meet the folks. I've got to get a phone charger from Mom and some clean clothes. I didn't make it home last night."

Martha looked at him askance. "You didn't stay here, that's obvious."

"Slept with an ornery cat. Figured he'd be good protection—just in case I'm wrong about all this."

They set out from the marina toward Martha's car. The air was cool with pockets of cold in places where the buildings blocked the sun. She nodded and made appropriate comments as MacAuliffe told the story of the retired math teacher—an innocent victim of yesterday's tragedy—and her appropriately named animals, how he was feeding her cat and had convinced his mother to care for the old dog, despite the objections of his father.

"But dad's grumpy about everything since he retired. Mom and I agree—he needs a hobby or a girlfriend."

"I thought sailing was his hobby."

"Doesn't feel sure enough of his balance to single-hand the *Ginny* anymore. Mom's too busy most of the time to go out with him. Katie has her own life and her kids aren't old enough to be yelled at nonstop for two, three hours."

"Have you gone out with him?"

"Oh, that's a recipe for a bad reality TV show. Murder on

Lake Gitche Gumee. Nah, we've both been captain of our own ships too long for that to work."

"You let Lance take the helm of the paper. You know how to be first mate, let others make the decisions."

"Lance knew what he was doing and how to do it in a way that didn't just piss everyone off. That's a skill my dad never learned walking his postal route. He didn't have to deal with people much."

"He got you safely around the largest lake in the world before you were a teenager."

MacAuliffe didn't respond. He steered them toward a brick building where he stepped into line at the Northern Waters Smokehaus. Martha made a quick phone call to Ray Palmer while she waited. All was quiet at home, he assured her. He'd checked in at the Carriage House this morning. Emily and kids were staying put, doing fine—if a little bored. How *did* she survive with no television?

Next, she browsed through a kitchen store and bought a gift pack of smoked olive oil and balsamic vinegar. She imagined the old building with its brick walls, glass windows, and hardwood floors had once been a busy office building, probably something related to the port and shipping. Now it was a central part of the tourist mecca called Canal Park. Change. Change or wither away.

They pulled into the driveway of a little bungalow set back off the one road that ran out onto the spit Mac had called Park Point. The house was painted green with gold trim and had a burgundy-red front door. A dog barked as they advanced up a walk made of flat sandstone rocks. The front yard resembled an overgrown English cottage garden filled with beds of late blooming flowers, tall wispy grasses, a deep purple clematis climbing a trellis. Overflowing pots of mums, two each of gold and burgundy, led up the steps.

"Mom's a Gopher," MacAuliffe said. "That's University of Minnesota in the Cities. She lives in Bulldog country, that's UMD, University of Minnesota Duluth. They hate each other. Especially during hockey season. But they have the same colors, maroon and gold. The garden's Mom's way of declaring a detente, I suppose." He opened the door. "Mom, Dad, it's me. I have company."

They were instantly greeted by a white-muzzled golden retriever with a wiggly butt and an active tail. He slobbered on MacAuliffe and then sniffed Martha's offered hand. She passed whatever test dogs give for approval and Newton licked her fingers. MacAuliffe was massaging the dog's ears when a woman's voice called out from somewhere inside the house.

"We're in the kitchen, Jimmy."

Martha arched a brow. "Jimmy? I never pictured you as a Jimmy."

"Kids can never outgrow their childhood with their parents."

In the kitchen, a warm, well-lit place of chaos and aromas, they found a petite woman with an unruly mass of silver and blonde curls gesturing with a wooden spoon in one hand and a potholder in the other. She wore a MOMA apron of Klimt's *The Kiss* over jeans and a yellow sweatshirt. She pointed the spoon at a second woman who could have been MacAuliffe's fraternal twin. A scarf of autumn leaves was pinned around her shoulders.

The younger woman said, "Mom was just giving me the blow-by-blow of how you saved the schoolteacher by doing a Johnny Weissmuller into the water." She rose and extended a hand to Martha. "I'm Katie, Jimmy's older, more mature, and better-looking sister."

"I agree on all accounts. Martha Whitaker."

MacAuliffe's mother set down the spoon and potholder. She took Martha's hand between hers. "They've been doing this for thirty-five years. Made for, shall we say, a lively household growing up. I'm Virginia. I'm sorry Teddy's not here to meet you. He's talking with his insurance agent about the boat. It's nice to meet you. Jimmy's talked about you on the phone."

"Lawyer jokes, I'm sure."

"Just a few. Which means he likes you, you know."

"I'll have to remember that." Turning to MacAuliffe, Martha said, "You never mentioned *you* were the one who saved the schoolteacher."

He shrugged. "It wasn't a big deal."

"I bet Mrs. Petrowski doesn't feel like that," his mother said.

Virginia offered food, which was respectfully declined, and then coffee, which Martha accepted and MacAuliffe declined. After a sip, Martha understood why. It may have been the worst coffee she'd ever tasted. Burnt and weak as truck stop coffee with some kind of flavoring, maybe hazelnut. She sipped it reluctantly while listening to Virginia recap the story of her son's heroic dive into the harbor to save the unconscious and drowning Ester Petrowski from certain death, a tale now embellished, Martha was sure, in the retelling.

MacAuliffe disappeared, leaving the three women in the kitchen. When Virginia moved to refill her coffee, Martha held up her hand and shook her head. "Oh, I couldn't but thank you."

Katie said to Martha, "Love your hair. How do you think I'd look if I cut my hair short?" Blonde hair fell to her shoulders; she pulled it back behind her head.

No one had asked her advice on style before, and at first she wasn't sure if Mac's sister was serious or was teasing her about her hairstyle. Her older sisters—as older sisters were wont to do—had given advice freely, but never asked for any in return; they had pooh-poohed her suggestions when offered. Rachel hadn't lived long enough for them, the two youngest girls in the Whitaker clan, to have that kind of relationship.

Katie still held her hair back. She wasn't teasing. Katie was a pretty woman, fine featured, nice high cheekbones, the same strong nose as Mac. And the same ears.

"You have beautiful hair the way it is," Martha equivocated.

"The ears?"

MacAuliffe saved her from having to either lie or possibly offend his sister when he reappeared in the doorway.

"Of course it's the ears," he said.

"Oh, shut up, Dumbo," Katie replied.

He'd changed into another blue Oxford, this one ironed with sharp creases extending down the arms. He'd washed his face and run a comb through his hair. A tweed sport jacket hung over one arm. He was carrying a notebook with a pen clipped to the cover, a professional journalist going to work.

Martha handed Virginia the bag with the smoked olive oil and balsamic vinegar. "I brought this for you."

"Oh, thank you, hon," she said. "That wasn't necessary. Please come visit any time. The door's always open."

"You don't even have to bring Jimmy," Katie added. "Probably be more fun without him.

"You've been talking about me again," MacAuliffe said.

"Not even," Katie said. "Guys are so vain. They think any time women get together we have to be talking about them, when nothing could be further from the truth."

They strolled through the English cottage garden. At the edge of the yard, they hesitated. The sweet light of afternoon slanted across the flowers and grasses, casting long shadows amid the colors.

"Your family's nice," Martha said.

"Minnesota nice," he replied.

"What's that mean?"

"They'll give you directions to anyplace but their own home."

"Mac, they're good, decent folks."

"Amelia Bumgarten said the same about me. See what that got her."

SEVEN

The woman who answered the door stood straight-backed but relaxed. Her eyes darted once between them and then remained still. "Yes?"

"We have a four o'clock appointment with Craig Nettles," MacAuliffe said. He noticed the wavy brown hair was laced with gray streaks. It framed an elegant face with a strong, square chin. Crow's feet touched the corners of her eyes and the corners of her mouth. She wore a sensible navy skirt and a fitted lighter blue blouse. A simple gold chain hung around her neck.

"May I tell him who's calling, please?"

"James MacAuliffe and Martha Whitaker."

She nodded. "Just a moment please." She left them outside with the door ajar.

"If we were burglars, we could just barge on in," MacAuliffe whispered.

"If we were burglars, we wouldn't knock on the front door," Martha replied, her voice soft in his ear. "She expected us. It's just a way to—"

The door swung open. "This way, please," the woman said with a tight smile.

They stepped into the foyer of the lakeside mansion. The entryway, MacAuliffe noted, was larger than the entire living space on the *Ginny*. He saw that Sophia wore slippers, and he slipped out of his boat shoes. Martha stooped to remove her boots. The woman waited patiently, hands clasped in front of her.

She led them toward the rear of the house where the space opened up to a living room of cream chairs and matching sofas. Hardwood floors of golden maple and a large abstract area rug added contrast to the stark décor.

As they stepped into an open kitchen, a man in an apron raised a finger, and attacked a large pot with an immersion blender. MacAuliffe's attention went to the floor-to-ceiling windows where a panoramic view of Lake Superior unfolded beyond an expanse of perfectly trimmed grass. Halfway to the horizon, a freighter steamed north on its way across the lake, the waters coruscating blue and gold in the afternoon sun. Off to one side of the putting green, the edge of a cottage was visible. A large powerboat, about fifty feet, he guessed, rocked in its moorage from the wake of a passing fishing boat. He wondered how many millions the yacht cost. A smaller boat, maybe a ski boat or a fishing boat, sat on rollers beside a hoist. The lifestyle of a one-percenter on full display.

The blender ceased whirling, and the man glanced up.

"Thank you, Sophia," he said. The woman slipped away without a word.

He wiped his hands on an apron he wore over a navy polo shirt and khaki trousers. His face was as pitted as an Iron Range mine. Nettles was tall, broad-shouldered and thick with the barrel- chested sturdiness of an old man.

"You must be James MacAuliffe," he said, extending a hand. "Craig Nettles."

MacAuliffe took the hand but studied his face. A bulbous nose stuck out from a clean-shaven face that was red enough MacAuliffe feared he might be having a stroke. White eyelashes and eyebrows and pale blue eyes created a raccoon look. A crew cut of white hair topped it all.

"This is my colleague, Martha Whitaker," MacAuliffe said. "Thank you for seeing us this afternoon."

"I'm afraid we'll have to conduct our interview in the kitchen," Nettles said. "I'm making butternut squash soup. First course for a dinner party tonight. You caught me right in the middle of it."

Nettles moved about the kitchen with an odd gait to his step, not quite a limp and not quite a shuffle. MacAuliffe wondered if he might be rehabbing from a hip or knee replacement.

The kitchen was a contrast of stainless steel appliances offset by a contemporary black and white decor. A refrigerator, a six-burner Bertazzoni range and oven, and two dishwashers, each with an over-sized stainless-steel sink, all gleamed under LED lights. White cupboards covered two walls and contrasted with countertops of black onyx streaked with white bands. The same onyx countertop covered an island the size of New Jersey.

MacAuliffe watched Nettles move behind the range. His original offer had been to meet at a coffee shop or bar downtown, where they could discuss the proposed development in Grand Marais. Instead, Nettles had insisted he come out to the house. He wants to show he has money, MacAuliffe realized now. And power. That he's not someone to be messed with. MacAuliffe had long ago stopped being impressed by money and power. People with both tended to trample over others who stood in their way to gaining even more.

Nettles motioned for them to take seats on the bar stools opposite. With the immersion blender in hand, he worked over the range in a large stainless-steel pot, the blender whirling as he pumped it up and down, adding cream to the orange puree. Dinner appeared to be about two gallons of butternut squash soup.

While the blender worked, he sipped an amber liquid from a cocktail glass. "Join me for a little bourbon to ease us into work?" he asked. "It's a Pappy's 23."

MacAuliffe smiled at the deliberate showing off. Or maybe this was really how the affluent spent their days: running around in stocking feet, making homemade soup—organic, he was sure—and sipping Pappy Van Winkle bourbon that ran a thousand dollars a bottle. If you could even get it.

"Sure," MacAuliffe said. "Neat. Best not to pollute perfection."

"Wise choice," Nettles said.

"Designated driver," Martha added, shaking her head.

Nettles poured liberal amounts for both men. They clinked glasses and exchanged nods. MacAuliffe sipped the bourbon. A hint of caramel, a touch of nuts, all creamy smooth with an oaky finish. Damn, that is perfection.

"I'm sorry to read about *The Ballard Gazette* folding," Nettles said.

And so began the thrust and parry. "You've done your homework."

"As you have as well, I'm sure. Who are you writing for these days?"

"I'm freelancing."

"Not a real lucrative position from what I understand."

"Craig, may I call you Craig?" Martha interjected. "That soup smells divine. Maybe some rosemary?"

"Ah, a woman after my culinary heart. You're absolutely right. Also apples. I use Honeycrisp for their sweetness. A home-grown Minnesota apple, you know. Don't have to add any sweetener that way. What you're probably not smelling is the cayenne pepper. It adds a bite to the mix, but that's balanced by the apples. The trick is creating the right combination of zesty and sweet."

"May I taste it?"

"Of course." He handed a spoonful across the counter.

"That is delicious. The cayenne does give it a bite, but it's not overwhelming. You didn't mention the nutmeg."

A smile crossed Nettles' face. He just nodded.

"Your guests will love it," Martha added. "I'd love to have the recipe—if it's not a family secret."

"Of course—" he paused, his gaze intent on her face.

MacAuliffe knew he was seeing the one blue eye and the one hazel eye for the first time. It always had this effect on people. Nettles recovered quickly. "I'm sorry. I'm not very good with names."

"Martha, Martha Whitaker."

"Of course, Martha. Always happy to share the family secrets." He placed the immersion blender in the sink, took another sip of bourbon and said, "Now, what can I do for you today?"

Martha knew very well that he'd caught her name. The diversion had been both a genuine interest in his soup and an opportunity to let Mac allow the fuse to burn out on the escalating tension between the two men. She also wanted to show that she, too, could piss in the boys' sandbox.

"I'm interested in a feature story highlighting the economic development and prosperity of what's happening on the North Shore," MacAuliffe said. "Do you mind if I tape this? I don't want to misquote you and get any of the details wrong."

He laid his phone on the counter and pressed the Record button.

For nearly half an hour, with a break only long enough to fill the glasses a second time, Nettles explained the NorthShore Resorts proposal to build a golf course, residential and vacation housing, and a business center just south of Grand Marais. Plans included a bar and grill for casual dining and a five-star restaurant featuring organic, local products for upscale clientele. And he was currently in negotiations with the Ojibwe about building a casino onsite. The conference center could accommodate up to 450 people with state-of-the-art technology. The area was already world-famous for its hiking trails and paddling and fishing. All outdoor activities to be highlighted, of course.

Martha refrained from asking why, if it was world-famous, she'd never heard of it.

But what was missing from the outdoor activities, Nettles continued, was a world-class golf course. The NorthShore Resort would add this to the mix. The golf course would be limited to eighteen holes in the first stage—as you probably know, land is difficult to obtain along the North Shore. Most of it's National Forest and the feds aren't feeling inclined to sell—but it'll be a championship-level par 70 and would feature four holes that played along the bluff overlooking Lake Superior. It was going to be brutal if your game included a serious slice off the tee.

He paused to laugh at his own joke.

The course would rival Pebble Beach as one of the most scenic golf courses in North America, he continued. It'll make the golf course at Lutsen play like a round for duffers. He had already begun informal conversations with a couple of friends at the PGA about bringing a tournament to the region.

In all, the proposed facility would sit on about three hundred acres and provide the community with about a hundred and fifty full-time jobs, a number he emphasized by slowing down and repeating it again, with plenty more in the peak season.

Nettles had given this spiel before, his facts and figures readily available as if he were reading off a marketing brochure. His delivery was part salesman, part revival preacher, and part father confessor. When MacAuliffe asked him for clarification, he listened intently, nodded his head, answered the question, and proceeded as if he had a cue card for the spot where he'd left off. MacAuliffe was astute, pressing him on the number and quality of jobs—aren't most of them going to be low-income service jobs?—how much business might the conference center attract?—it's a long way to Grand Marais from anywhere—and how might it help the local economy if the resort was a self-contained facility with little need for guests to venture off the premises? He even had Martha half-believing that he planned to write a pro-business, pro-economic development feature.

"I'm from the North Shore, my family's from the North Shore," Nettles said. "We've been here for going on a hundred and forty years. A development of this kind isn't going to be successful overnight. It will take time to create a brand, time to grow that brand, time to develop market share. We're committed to the long-term future of the North Shore, and we fully believe in the future of NorthShore Resorts."

"But there has to be some opposition to the development," MacAuliffe said. "Grand Marais is a sleepy little town that gets busy for a few months every summer. Then it goes into hibernation for the long northern winter. Not everyone can be happy with this proposed land use."

"You change the status quo and you're always going to upset some folks," Nettles said. "That's expected and planned for. And you're right. The long winters are a problem. That's why we've planned a ski resort for the second stage of the development.

The golf course becomes a first-class cross-country ski area, we develop snowmobiling trails, and we add downhill skiing. We're slowly acquiring the property now. Come to my office, and I'll show you."

He removed his apron and laid it on the counter. He fiddled with the knobs on the stove until just a thin blue flame was visible under the large pot. Carrying his bourbon, he led them back toward the front of the house.

Passing by an open set of French doors, Martha saw Sophia laying out silverware around a large wooden table.

Nettles opened a door and gestured them into a room with bookcases and a computer that seemed to float in midair. Nothing else sat on the glass desktop.

What she couldn't see from the doorway was a 3-D topographical model of the proposed development. It reminded Martha of those topographical displays at the Visitor Centers in national parks. Lake Superior in blue framed one edge of the model. The golf course, complete with fairways and greens, was displayed in varying shades of green, each hole numbered, 1 through 18. A gray ribbon with yellow divider stripes marked Highway 61. It bisected the course, four holes on the lake side, the rest inland. A cluster of buildings was built along one side of the inland holes, and a central compound was built on the shores of a small lake. From the lake, ski lifts ran up the hillsides with an intricate pattern of ski runs carved through the trees.

Nettles pointed out where they planned to develop hiking trails that would meet up with the Superior Hiking Trail and double as snowmobile runs in the winter. The ski resort would cover three hills with about forty runs and have a vertical drop of about a thousand feet.

"That's not championship skiing, I'll grant you," Nettles said. "But folks who can't get to Colorado or the Alps can come up from the Cities for a weekend and get some quality skiing in. These aren't just bunny runs. We'll attract people from the Cities and Minnesota, of course, but also from Thunder Bay, Wisconsin, and most of the northern Midwest."

"I was reading the minutes to the Cook County Council meeting," MacAuliffe said. "There seemed to be some objections to the development. A woman named Rose Bumgarten seemed the most vocal."

"Oh, Rosie, God bless her, is just making a lot of noise. She's a Johnny-come-lately to Grand Marais and doesn't want it to change. She's got this romantic notion of raising her daughter in a sleepy little burg, away from the temptations of the big city. But she may be losing that battle anyway. Seems the temptations are coming to her regardless of where she's living."

Nettles paused to sip his bourbon before adding, "Rosie's got good intentions, but they're good intentions for her, someone with a decent income, not for the people of Grand Marais who're scrambling for work in a place where mining has dwindled and the white pines for logging are long gone. The future of jobs on the North Shore is tourism, and I'm proposing bringing more tourists to the region, a lot more. Rosie doesn't like that. That's okay. I respect her position and understand it. But it's not going to stop our project."

"She claims you cherry-picked the information from your environmental impact statements," Martha said.

"We haven't cherry-picked anything. It's all available for anyone to read."

"Golf courses require a lot of fertilizer to keep those fairways and greens at championship-level quality. How do you plan to address the runoff that will end up in Lake Superior? This isn't a short-term problem, but a long-term issue. The build-up of chemicals leeching into the water table and into the lake."

"It won't be a problem. Environmental engineers with the state have all been satisfied with the way we've designed our containment system. The runoff will be captured and filtered before being released. It poses no environmental threat or degradation. It's all in the EIS, if you bother to read it—which clearly Rosie didn't. She was just throwing shit against the wall to see if anything would stick."

"But runoff is different than water leeching into the soil."

A sudden sharpness entered Nettles' voice. "I'd encourage you to read the EIS, Martha."

"Do you also have the mineral rights to the land?" she asked.

"Oh, lord," Nettles said. A gnarled hand rubbed his white crewcut, and he took a sip of his drink. He shook his head. "This is not, as Rosie claims, just a conspiracy to get mineral rights and to start a mining operation. The days of mining in the Arrowhead are essentially over. Anyone who thinks they're coming back is smoking the really good stuff."

"But isn't the Department of Natural Resources Lands and Minerals Division actively promoting copper and nickel exploration in this region?" MacAuliffe asked.

Nettles stepped over to a framed map on the wall of Lake Superior and all of the Arrowhead. His hand swept an arc from Duluth on one end to the Canadian border. The arc started and ended on the Lake Superior shore but in the middle extended deep into the interior of the Arrowhead region. "This is the Duluth Complex of the Midcontinent Rift System. The section along the shore has been determined to have no mineral value. All mining is further inland, toward Hibbing and that area. The DNR wouldn't have agreed to sell the land if it had timber or mineral deposits of economic value. Our proposal is actually what it appears to be—a resort, business center, casino, and golf course. It's not camouflage for a new mining operation."

"You haven't started building yet," MacAuliffe said. "Why's that?"

"Takes time to acquire all the property, file the permits, do the public hearings, complete the EIS. I've been working on this for literally decades. In fact, my father started it. He bought the first piece of land before he started the Miller Hill Mall in '72. It's been a pet project of mine since I joined the family business after college in the mid-'70s."

"Is everything in place now?" MacAuliffe asked.

Nettles hesitated.

Martha heard the sound of the front door opening and a shout, "It's me, Dad." Softer, "Hey, Soph, you're looking great."

"In the office, Buzz," Nettles replied, his voice loud.

A tall, thick man appeared in the doorway, strong, tanned forearms crossed over his chest. Martha placed him in his mid to late thirties. He wore jeans and a gray tee-shirt with the National Forest Service embossed over the pocket. Short hair the color of a new-born chick topped a brown, leathery face that carried the Nettles family heritage.

Nettles introduced Craig Junior. The man dutifully shook hands but spoke only to his father. "I've got everything loaded. Thinking I'll head back home before it gets dark."

"Getting late if you're taking the boat," Nettles said.

"Maybe next week. Weather forecasts say this storm system will settle down."

"Excuse us," the older Nettles said. He placed his hand on his son's shoulder. If Martha hadn't been watching closely, she'd have missed how Craig Junior had flinched at the touch and quickly created separation. They departed the office toward the kitchen, Nettles moving with that awkward, stiff-legged gait.

His voice fading, Martha heard him insist, "Come on, stay for dinner, son. I have some folks . . ."

Craig Junior's response was unintelligible, but the tone and volume clearly indicated he had no intentions of honoring his father's request. An argument ensued.

For the first time, Martha had a chance to study the rest of the room. The large map of the lake and the Arrowhead hung on one wall. Bookshelves lined two others; the fourth wall was mostly windows facing the front of the house. The bookshelves contained few books. Half of one shelf offered books on real estate—management, acquisition, development, deeds and liens—and *The Art of the Deal.* The other half displayed a photo of Nettles holding some kind of award and shaking hands with another white-haired man. Behind them was a banner for the University of Minnesota Duluth.

"Martha," MacAuliffe said, and indicated that she should join him. He stood in front of the other wall of bookshelves.

Through the doorway, faint voices drifted into the office. The words were indistinct, but it was obvious to Martha that father and son were continuing their disagreement. He glanced at Martha.

"Probably can't agree on the dinner menu," MacAuliffe said.

He pointed to a photo. A young man lay in a hospital bed, shaking hands with President Richard Nixon. Men in military attire framed the photo. The prone man had the same square jaw and high forehead of the two Nettles men. It must be a younger Nettles Senior.

"Had to be Vietnam," Martha said.

From the next shelf, Martha removed what must be a family photo. It was a formal studio shot. Nettles was now dressed in a suit and tie, still sporting a crew cut, his face severe, as if smiling would violate orders. An attractive woman sat in front of him, wearing a dress and a string of pearls. Her brunette hair was layered and highlighted, a long bang hanging over the right side of her face. Chic, sassy. Dated. The Rachel. Her radiant smile became the focal point of the photo. A young towheaded boy, also in suit and tie, stood military stiff beside the woman. The woman held a child on her lap. From the dress and the ribbon in her hair, Martha knew it to be a girl.

A second photo showed Nettles in a public café in Florence, Martha knew. The crenellated tower of the Palazzo Vecchio was visible over his shoulder. Two empty wine carafes were on the table in front of him. On one side of him sat a younger Craig Junior, showing lots of perfect teeth, a bit of an overbite. His blonde hair hung to his shoulders. His blue eyes exuded boredom—or maybe he was stoned.

On the other side was a young woman, her dark hair in a classic low-maintenance crew cut. The front flip showed a tinge of blonde. She wore a white tee under an open white sun shirt. The delicate, fine-featured face neither smiled nor frowned, but appeared more annoyed than anything. An attractive woman, if a bit severe. She resembled the woman in the first photo but with shorter hair. Nettles sat with an arm casually slung across her shoulder. It must have been the daughter. A bright smile shone from his face.

"We were in Europe," Nettles said. His face was flushed, even redder than when he'd met them in the kitchen. The white eyebrows and eyelashes stood out in stark contrast. He moved into the room and took the photo from Martha. "That's Buzz, of course. And that's my daughter Bess. Elizabeth. Looks so much like her mom."

Sorrow touched his voice; the words came out fractured, a window that had shattered into jagged pieces. "She was twenty-one, just graduated with top honors from UMD with her engineering degree. She'd been commissioned a second lieutenant. We were on a Grand Tour before she left for boot camp. She was always a daddy's girl. When she was little, I had a small desk for her in my office where she did her homework after school. The plan was for her to serve her country, get some leadership experience, then join the business."

He put the photo back on the shelf. "Things didn't work out the way we planned. She was assigned to a demolitions unit, same as her old man. First in to blow up bridges, rebuild them afterwards for the boys coming behind. She never came home from Afghanistan. She's officially listed as MIA. Never even found her dog tags. Her unit got caught in a firestorm up near the Khyber Pass. They were chasing a group of Taliban soldiers who were hightailing it toward Pakistan. Bess's unit drove right into an ambush. Half of them never made it back." His voice grew harsh when he continued. "It's fucking Vietnam all over again. No point, no strategy, just send our young men and women out to slaughter. Bess was just another goddamn number to some politician in Washington."

"I'm sorry," Martha said.

"So am I, so am I. We had planned that she'd take over the Grand Marais project after her tour of duty. It'd be her introduction into the business. She loved the north woods."

"Buzz?"

He shook his head. "Two different kids completely. He thinks of himself as the rebel. If the old man says yes, he says no, if the old man says maybe, he says fuck you." He moved back toward the scale model. "I'm sorry for the interruption. I'm still trying to entice Buzz to join the business. I had invited some folks over this evening who he might like, might listen to. Younger folks his age, a couple of old friends. He declined my invitation, as you probably heard."

"Yeah, we caught parts of it."

"I'm sorry. Thinks he can be a seasonal ranger for the Forest Service forever. Having someone else's money of course helps every rebel's cause." Nettles shrugged, a profound sadness contained in that simple gesture. "I allow all of it, of course. What's the word they use today? Enable. I enable it. He's family. He's my kid, for good or bad. He's all that's left with Bessie and her mom gone. It's just me and Buzz."

Nettles grew quiet, distant, as if he was conjuring up memories and images that Martha could only guess at, a father contemplating daughter and son, and a future he had once dreamed about that now would never be. No daughter to pass the business on to, no son to share his success. Surrounded by money and unhappiness, success and regrets. She suspected he'd trade it all to have his children at his side.

"You also served?" MacAuliffe said, his voice quiet. "The photo with Nixon."

"Yeah," Nettles said. "No one knew at the time he was a crook. It was a photo op, of course, the president handing out Purple Hearts. In 'Nam, they were as easy to get as candy at Halloween. Got a paper cut? Here's a Purple Heart. Still, you don't see me giving it back."

He bent over and rapped his lower leg. It gave off a dull, metallic ring. He offered a faint chuckle. "Gave a goddamn leg for my country. Always seemed a steep price until Bessie didn't come home. Now doesn't seem such a big deal. I'd gladly swap the other one if it'd bring her back."

"That's good family background material for the feature," MacAuliffe said. "Is there any problem if I use it?"

He shook his head. "It's all public record. No secrets. Just be aware, Buzz'll probably sue you for slander—or is it libel?—if you print anything about him."

"Comes with the territory," MacAuliffe said. He pushed the

Record button again on his phone. "So why aren't you breaking ground on the resort?"

"There's one last parcel that we need to buy before we can start," Nettles said. Confession was over. He stood straighter, enunciated clearly, spoke in complete sentences. "Next month, DNR is auctioning off sixty-five acres of lakefront that sits smack dab in the middle of our plans, right where the clubhouse sits and portions of the first four holes. Without it, I can't start. Next month I'll own it, and in the spring, we'll dig the first hole. We'll use the winter to put the finishing touches on the design, clean up any lingering problems."

"I didn't know DNR could sell public land to private developers," Martha said. "Is that legal?"

"Of course it is. They can sell if they determine it has no economic value to the state. The timber was logged off a long time ago, and it has no value in mineral rights. It's held in trust, and that trust supports the state's public education system. DNR can decide that it's better to sell and feed the state's coffers for education rather than let it sit idle and unproductive. And nonrevenue generating. Opening bid is set at eight hundred grand. It'll go for more than that, I'm sure. Might be a lot more, depending on the bidding. All of it goes into the education fund."

"You're not worried about being outbid?" MacAuliffe said.

"I won't be outbid. I've come too far and worked too hard for that to happen."

"Rose Bumgarten was seeking investors to oppose you, wasn't she?" MacAuliffe asked.

"Of course. But we expected that. Rosie can barely keep up with her mortgage, so she had to seek out investors. Nature Conservancy, Wolf Ridge, some others, mostly nonprofits who will leave it as is. As if we don't have enough woods already in northern Minnesota. But they won't commit the resources necessary to stop us."

"Has she filed an injunction to halt the sale?" Martha said.

"She filed. But the state legislature took itself out of the permission process a few years ago and gave DNR the right to sell lakeshore property if it was deemed of limited economic value. They deemed it such and decided to sell. They have the right and the authority. That doesn't change just because someone like Rosie doesn't like it. The judge dismissed her case out of hand—as I knew he would."

"Knew how?" MacAuliffe asked.

"The law's clear."

Martha saw MacAuliffe scribble "QPQ?" Aloud he said, "I wish I had that much confidence in the law.

"There's more than economic value," Martha said. "Preservation of important resources. Environmental degradation. Holding in trust the rights of future generations to have access to the wilderness."

"You sound like a lawyer for the goddamn tree huggers."

"I am a lawyer, though not for any environmental groups. James asked me to help with his story because of the complex legal issues involved."

He nodded. "Rosie played all those cards, and I trumped them. I too can lawyer up, and I've been at this a lot longer than Rosie Bumgarten. We've played by the rules. We've applied for no variances, no special considerations. This is a long game that my father started nearly fifty years ago when he bought the first twenty acres. Rosie's played a short game, and I've been three steps ahead of her the whole way. My three hundred acres, or a thousand acres—if you add the ski slope option—is so tiny within the scope of the north woods as to be negligible. DNR agreed with me. Rosie was out of options."

Nettles picked up a model car that ran down Highway 61 and fiddled with it before setting it back on the road. "I could use more good people on my team if you two are interested in staying in northern Minnesota for a while. You ask good questions. You understand the complexity of the issues. We're not trying to rape the land but trying to create a way for the community of Grand Marais to grow into the twenty-first century and stay viable with jobs and growth."

"Thank you," MacAuliffe said. He kept his face and voice friendly and amiable, even while he gagged inside. "But I'm pretty happy in Seattle. Got webs growing between my toes."

"That's too kind," Martha added. "But I've worked corporate before and am much happier on my own. And as Mac says, Seattle's home. I'm sure you understand."

"Of course. Now, unless you have any more questions, I have dinner guests coming and a salmon to prepare."

"Don't forget you promised me that soup recipe," Martha said.

"Of course."

"If I have any follow up questions, may I call?" MacAuliffe asked.

"Of course. I'm going to the Cities tomorrow for a meeting with tribal leaders about the casino. I'll be back sometime Monday evening."

"Actually, there is one more thing." MacAuliffe flipped a couple of pages back in his notebook. "You mentioned that Rose Bumgarten was losing the battle to keep drugs away from her daughter. What did you mean by that?"

Nettles glared at him. "What's this got to do with the resort?"

"I don't know. I'm not sure if it does. But you heard Rose Bumgarten's daughter was killed yesterday? In that explosion down at Canal Park."

Nettles' words became precise, taut, like wire stretched to breaking. "I did not know that. I only listen to the news in passing these days—it's campaign season and you can't believe anything you hear. I will have to send the poor woman a condolence card. She has to be terribly upset. I know the profound pain she must be experiencing."

He looked hard at MacAuliffe, the lines around his eyes and mouth deepening. "I hope you're not suggesting anything else."

"Not at all," MacAuliffe said. For the first time, he actually believed that. "But if you thought the mother was losing control of her daughter, it might be relevant to the police investigation."

Briefly, Nettles seemed to swell in size, staring hard at MacAuliffe who didn't break eye contact.

"Grand Marais," Nettles started, "is similar to so many small towns across America. It has a thriving drug community—meth, pot, now opiates. I had Rose Bumgarten investigated—as I do all my opponents. I want to know who I'm up against beforehand, not after. Seems Rose has her JD but is working as a paralegal and a waitress in Grand Marais. A few years back she did time in rehab for an addiction problem. My source told me she'd come to enjoy heroin a little too much. And they also discovered her daughter was a pothead and had been arrested at least once. Someone's growing weed in the backwoods and selling it to kids who're selling it to other kids. Rose's daughter was arrested for using and may have been one of the kids selling."

"So have you guys bought into Dad's shtick about bringing jobs to Grand Marais?" Craig Junior stood in the doorway, leaning against the jamb, arms crossed. He now wore a brown duck jacket and a baseball cap with the NFS logo. "Did he tell you that most of them will only make minimum wage cleaning toilets and making beds and selling moose key fobs in the gift shop? While he and his partners reap the profits."

"Buzz, please."

"No, let's tell the whole story, Dad." Craig Junior entered the room, approaching them where they bunched around the resort model. His eyes never left his father's. "If they're writing a story on the economic development the resort will bring to Grand Marais, let's tell the truth about what that means. It will create jobs that will attract immigrant labor because they're the only ones willing to work for those wages. Maids, house cleaners, groundskeepers, retail, all unskilled labor. Most on a seasonal basis. In with the thaw and out with the frost. That's about three months in Grand Marais, four in a good year. That's of little value to the folks of Grand Marais. I should know. I live there. I'm not a carpetbagger coming in to take their land and give them trinkets in return."

Nettles glanced first at Martha and then MacAuliffe. "Here, my friends, is my most vocal critic. Now you don't have to seek out the other side of the story. It's come to you."

Craig Junior saw MacAuliffe's phone sitting on the corner of the model, the Record light on. "Are you recording this shit?" He grabbed the phone. "Just pick up a brochure, read the website. All the same bullshit's there."

"Craig, please give the phone back," Martha said and held out her hand. "It's private property. It contains information important to our story. You don't have the right to steal it just because you don't like what's going on."

MacAuliffe watched Martha slide between Craig Junior and the door. She was patient, her hand stretched out. Her mismatched eyes focused only on Craig. He punched the Stop button on the phone and tossed it at her feet.

As she knelt down to pick it up, he bent with her and grabbed her hand. She immediately had his thumb angled backwards to the point of breaking. They rose together slowly.

Craig Junior leaned toward her, against the pressure she was exerting on his thumb, and hissed, "You need to drop this. He's not who he pretends to be. You don't know what you're messing with here."

"Then tell me," she whispered.

Instead of answering, he snatched at her with his free hand. She twisted away from his grasp, causing him to turn with her. A sharp push against his thumb sent him stumbling out the office door.

EIGHT

"Well that didn't end as planned," Martha said. Night had fully descended on Duluth during the interview with Nettles. Cars were streaming out of downtown Duluth while she drove toward it. The classical music station out of Wisconsin played something heavy on the brass and drama. Rachmaninov. The First Symphony, maybe.

"It was perfect," MacAuliffe said. "Life's messy. Family relationships are complex. Outcomes are never certain, despite what Nettles thinks about the upcoming auction. And people are irrational most of the time. We just got to witness all of it in real time. The north woods' version of reality TV. Duluth Dynasty. Mad Men of the North Shore. And we escaped unscathed with some good information. Unscathed if you're okay."

"I'm fine."

She turned off the radio. How did she explain to MacAuliffe that no confrontation left her unscathed? She took a deep breath, willed herself to relax, and allowed the distaste of the confrontation to flow up her spine and escape into the darkness. Repeating the process, the image of Craig Junior evaporated like a boat sailing into the mist. It helped a little.

MacAuliffe was studying her. "You're not okay. I'm sorry to be so flippant." He touched her forearm, his voice tender. "Is there anything I can do?"

"No." She softened her tone. "There are consequences to a fight, any fight. Even one avoided. I'll be fine." She moved her free hand to the steering wheel, breaking the touch between them. "What was your read on Nettles?"

"A bloviating prick. If he added God to his spiel, he'd be an old-fashioned white-man missionary saving heathens from themselves. The Arrowhead's seen plenty of them. I do think, however, *he* thinks he's sincere, that it's not just a marketing ploy. Missionaries are always believers. I doubt it's as draconian as Buzz makes it out to be, that the truth lies somewhere in the middle, but I do think Buzz is right that the people who will benefit the most are his father and his investors."

"That's obvious, Mac. You know that. They're also the ones taking the most risks, investing millions that they could just as easily lose if the project fails."

"Capitalism at work. It's just that the little guy is increasingly shut out of the process. His labor feeds the luxury lifestyle of Nettles and his ilk; yet the little guy gets fewer and fewer opportunities to rise out of poverty himself."

Martha saw him staring into the glare of oncoming headlights, remote, distant. An idealist trapped in a practical world.

"But I'm basically a socialist at heart," MacAuliffe added, with a touch of levity. "Lance was our capitalist. You saw what happened when they let the socialist play with the capitalist's cash box." He shrugged. "Let the folks of Grand Marias decide. It's their backyard. But I do think he was telling the truth about Rose Bumgarten."

"But the best liars stick close to the truth," Martha countered. "It's so much easier to remember and so much better if someone goes digging. What if it's all true up to the point of not being threatened by Rose's recruitment of investors? He did have her investigated. Admitted it. He admires someone who fights for her convictions. Shows class and vulnerability. I'm not familiar with Wolf Ridge, but the Nature Conservancy can bring some serious financial clout. Rose might've been putting together a threat to the entire project that Nettles couldn't ignore. If he doesn't get that last sixty-five acres, he's got nothing."

"For everyone except Rose and Nettles, it'll ultimately be a business decision," MacAuliffe said. "Her investors are going to set a limit on what the land's worth to them. They value preservation and know it comes with a cost, but they will not come to the auction with an unlimited pocketbook. They have a ceiling on what they'll pay. For Nettles, it's business, certainly. Remember, he's likely sunk millions of dollars into the development already. But it's also emotional. You heard him talk about family. The only time he came off his soapbox was when he talked about his daughter, how he longed for Buzz to join the family business. Now Nettles feels compelled to finish the project—for his daughter's sake, if nothing else. I believe him when he says he won't be outbid. Rose Bumgarten isn't going to prevent him from breaking ground."

"So if he wasn't worried about Rose, he wouldn't be worried about her daughter. So who put the bomb in your truck yesterday?" Martha squinted against the glare of someone driving toward them with their headlights on bright. The car passed before she could figure out how to flash her lights. "He also managed to work in an alternative motive for what happened to Amelia. She was a pothead, maybe a dealer. Left it there for us to make the connections."

"Yeah, that was a little too convenient," MacAuliffe said. "And I never trust things when they seem too convenient."

His gaze directed out the window, MacAuliffe paid no attention to the halos of streetlights passing by. His mind worked through the one evening with Amelia, from the time he met her wet and cold on the dock to flicking off the boat lights and hearing her soft voice whisper in the dark, "Thank you. Sleep well."

"Goodnight, Amelia," he'd replied, feeling both sincere and silly, as if he were starring in an episode of *The Waltons.*

Was Amelia running from a drug deal gone bad? Was she just a junkie hiding behind good manners? He'd seen no signs of it. Experience in conducting hundreds of interviews had given him confidence in his ability to read people.

He also remembered times when he'd been wrong. Martha had been one. Maybe limping for a week after their first meeting had clouded his judgment. Had he also been wrong about the Bumgarten girl?

Lance had never hesitated to challenge his ideas and opinions. It forced MacAuliffe to dig deeper into his reasons and convictions. The deep loss he felt about his friend's murder snuck up on him when he least expected it, grief slamming into him like an exploding airbag. But that was how grief manifested itself once the rawness of his death had passed. Boom, it was there, overwhelming and intense; then it was gone, leaving only a profound sadness.

Martha didn't fill the silence with words; she didn't attempt to take the place of his old partner. They were moving in parallel, but different, universes.

Or, he realized, maybe that last encounter with Buzz had left her more disturbed than she let on. He felt clueless about how to reach out to her. "Sure you're okay?"

"Yes. It was just something Craig Junior said. I'm trying to make sense of it." Martha repeated the brief exchange.

"Wow, 'You don't know what you're messing with,'" MacAuliffe exclaimed. "Now, that's the kind of threat I'm used to. Drop the story or else. Of course, no one ever says what the 'or else' is."

"But was he threatening us or warning us?"

"You think it might have been a threat from Buzz? That the old man ain't what he pretends to be seems pretty obvious."

"Craig Junior knows something. Whether it's about his father or something else wasn't clear." Martha braked for a stop-light. "How much do you think he heard?"

MacAuliffe hesitated before replying. "Buzz joined us near the end of the conversation. When Nettles was telling us about the drug problem in Grand Marais and how Amelia had been caught with pot. But Buzz talked only about the resort. He certainly made his position known. I'm surprised Rosie hadn't teamed up with him."

"Why not, is the question?" Martha asked. "Where am I going, Mac?"

His head hurt from searching for answers that weren't there. His stomach growled. It had been a long time since Amazing Grace this morning. He wondered what his mother was making for dinner and whether she was expecting him to make an appearance with Martha.

"Want to continue this over a beer and dinner?" he asked.

She left MacAuliffe at the bar nursing a Bent Paddle stout while she ran across the street to check into the hotel. During the time alone, she called Ray Palmer.

"All's quiet on the Western front," the Seattle police detective said. "Ate a soggy sandwich standing in the rain outside your place. Nothing coming or going. Emily and the kids are sitting tight. You can relax. You *really* live over a garage?"

"It's a Carriage House," she said, recalling the name Olivia Heiden had given her apartment over the now nearly empty three-car garage. She didn't tell him she also owned the large house on the property.

"Whatever. Still just a fancy name for a garage."

"Thanks, Ray. I owe you one."

When she walked into the 310 Pub, the noise and heat and the bustle of people assaulted her like Ballard Avenue on a Friday night. The bar was crowded except for an empty stool on one side of MacAuliffe. The place was starting to fill up with couples on dates, young people seeking dates, and the after-work crowd who were in no hurry to go home. Overhead, televisions showed reruns of old hockey games. Off in one corner, a small screen was showing the Twins game. The pub had an industrial warehouse decor— refurbished brick walls, industrial conduits left exposed, a well-worn floor of wide pine planks.

She slid in beside MacAuliffe and sipped the chardonnay waiting for her. He must have stepped outside. She could smell the cigarette he'd smoked while she was gone. Neither one said anything for a while.

"I think it had to be a warning about his dad," MacAuliffe said. "Nettles didn't get where he is by always playing nice. He's used to getting his own way. He welcomed us to the house because he thought we were doing something to help him and his resort. But if I write something he doesn't approve of, he might make other plans for me. He might have a reputation for burying unflattering stories and journalists—figuratively, of course."

"Or not," Martha replied.

"You always so cheerful after a glass of wine? No, 'he isn't what he pretends to be'? Buzz was talking about dear ol' dad. I need to do more research on Nettles."

"It might have been a threat from Craig Junior to discourage you from writing a pro-resort story."

"He and a couple of thugs from the Nature Conservancy gonna bust my chops? Doesn't feel right. I mean, after all, Nettles was right—there's a whole lot of trees in the woods up there. Three hundred acres, even a thousand acres of scrub forest, is like a tick on a dog."

"At least consider it, James." She stared at him until he looked up from his pint. Eyes the color of a clear summer sky gazed back at her as if they could see into her soul. She was surprised at how uncomfortable and vulnerable she felt.

He brushed his long hair back behind his large ears and nodded. "Okay, I'll consider it."

Both returned to sipping their drinks. Eventually, MacAuliffe said, "Amelia didn't give any indications of being a pothead. Besides, don't all kids smoke a little weed? I know I did. She didn't smell like one. Didn't light up and didn't ask if I had any. No one kills someone for not paying their pot dealer. Unless the street rules have changed since I was a kid, you can't even get a baggie unless you pay first."

"What if she was the dealer?" Martha said. "And didn't pay her supplier?"

"Yeah, I thought about that. But she was sixteen, in Grand Marais, population of about fifteen hundred, and even if she was dealing and didn't pay up, would she be a big enough player to be worth killing? Wouldn't someone have slapped her around a little and found another dealer? It doesn't add up."

"Do you think Nettles was lying?"

"Or given bad information. I mean, when I was sixteen, I certainly knew how to roll a joint and chug a beer, but that didn't make me a pothead or an alcoholic. It meant I was a normal teenage kid. You remember what it was like."

"Actually, I don't," Martha said. "I didn't do either when I was in high school. I didn't have my first glass of wine until I was in graduate school."

"Graduate school? Really?" MacAuliffe looked at her as if she'd just grown wings. "Wow, that's pretty incredible. They call you Saint Martha?"

"Saint Marti. Gran had always called me Marti, so my sisters would call me Saint Marti. It was *not* a term of reverence, I can assure you."

She could tell he didn't know whether to believe her or not. She didn't feel inclined to elaborate. She continued, "So how do we discover if he's lying or was given bad information? We can't exactly deposition him."

"I've got an idea. A couple, actually. What do you say to a trip to Grand Marais? The drive is beautiful this time of year. We're a week or two off peak fall colors but we should get plenty of burgundy and gold, and the lake is always gorgeous. There's a lot I miss about being home—though don't ever mention that to my folks."

"That'd be nice," Martha said. Home. She'd noticed Mac spoke of home in much the same way she thought of home. Where you're from and where you live, both are home, not two contradictory ideas but two places that hold memories and value to the person you've become. You love to visit home and are anxious to get back home when you do.

It'd be good to see her dad. The former Marine sergeant now kept a running tally of his Jeopardy! score and challenged her with questions when she called every Tuesday night. Maybe when this was over, she'd drive across the UP to Sault Ste. Marie for a visit. The twins were anxious about his growing memory lapses. She was more anxious about his drinking and smoking. The morning smoker's cough, the declining effort to get out of his chair. Following an afternoon of drinking beer and an evening of sipping bad whiskey, he'd often pass out with a lit cigarette in the ashtray. The end tables and nightstands had telltale burn marks from cigarettes that had fallen from an ashtray and been left to smolder out. If a cigarette dropped onto his La-Z-Boy or bedsheets, he probably wouldn't know it until too late.

"How is your dad?" MacAuliffe said.

It was obvious he was repeating the question. How did he know she was thinking about her father? She wasn't comfortable with mind readers, and replied, "You should really stop smoking."

That may have been the first time she'd ever said that to anyone. Not to her dad, not to Gran, not to her sisters or brothers. Adults made adult decisions. And she was fine with them if they accepted the consequences of those decisions. Why did it bother her more in MacAuliffe than in people she loved?

"Yeah. You noticed, huh?"

"Hard not to."

"You ever been addicted to anything?"

She sipped her wine and gave a brief nod. How did she explain to MacAuliffe that she'd pursued karate, tai chi, judo, kendo, all so she'd never be victimized again, but that the violence inherent in the martial arts had become an addiction for her? Yoga had been her attempt to break the adrenaline rush of doing the *Bassai Dai kata*, but she too had relapsed. Before she could explain, he stood up and waved.

A large African-American man strode toward them, scanning the room as he moved. A large man, he had a certain grace to his movements, a precision and lightness to each step, obvious in the way he twisted to avoid a waiter passing with a tray of drinks. She knew he must have studied dance or one of the martial arts. He also looked like he'd dressed out of a dirty laundry basket. A skinny black tie carried some of his lunch and hung askew down the front of a wrinkled white shirt that was open at the neck. Khaki slacks had dirt on the knees and around the pockets. The toes on his loafers were scuffed, as if he'd spent the day kneeling on concrete. His face was stern as he approached. "Got your text." His voice was a surprisingly pleasant tenor when he spoke.

MacAuliffe introduced him as Mark Monahan from the Duluth Police Department. She felt all her barriers instantly go up, shutters slamming closed before a storm.

Her eyes narrowed, and she edged to the seat of the bar chair, her body squared off to face the police officer, feet planted firmly on the floor. MacAuliffe suspected it was a mistake to invite Monahan without telling Martha first. Chalk up another faux pas to his growing list.

"So what you got?" Monahan asked.

"Buy you a beer?" MacAuliffe replied. "Unless you're still working, of course."

Monahan scanned the bar a second time, glanced at his watch, and then back at them. He pulled over a bar stool. "Sure. I'm off duty. But I buy my own. I've spent half the day under your frigging truck with forensics."

MacAuliffe signaled the bartender, and Monahan ordered a Surly Furious. An order of hot artichoke dip arrived, followed by wings, then deep-fried cheese curds. He invited Mark to join them. Standing hunched over at the end of the bar, the police officer dug in. Business could wait while he sampled a little of everything. MacAuliffe noted the grime under his fingernails and saw Martha begin to relax a little. She slid back in her chair and took her time spreading the dip over a piece of bread.

"We talked to Craig Nettles this afternoon," Martha said.

"Is that supposed to mean something to me?" Monahan replied. Half his beer disappeared with one long gulp.

MacAuliffe filled him in on how he'd come up with Nettles' name and the connection to Rose Bumgarten.

"How does any of this relate to Amelia Bumgarten getting blown up in your truck?"

"We're not sure if it does," MacAuliffe said. "But Nettles described Amelia as a pothead heading for trouble. Said someone's growing weed in the woods there and selling it to kids who're selling it to other kids. Claimed Amelia might be one of them. I'm not buying it, at least the part about being a dealer."

Monahan looked at him with weary eyes, shaking his head. "Dude, you even been in a small town lately? There's meth, there's pot, there's heroin again. Goddamn opiates. All of them killing people. This time of year you got all the tourists flocking up north. She'd have no shortage of clients. There's plenty to kill over if she was involved in any of it, especially if she was dealing the harder stuff and not playing straight with her supplier."

"Why was she working nights at some school sweeping floors and locking the doors?" MacAuliffe asked. "Why steal the money from my wallet? If she was stiffing her source, she didn't need gas money from me."

"Habit?"

"Say you're right, Mark. I only spent a few hours with her and could be misreading this completely. Maybe. But the important question is, where did Nettles get his information?"

"He said he was having Rose Bumgarten investigated because she opposed his resort development," Martha said to the detective. "Who did the investigation? Could that person tell us more? What was his source of information? You're in a position to ask Nettles for a name, to investigate what that person knows. Mac's already paved the way for you to drop by. He told Nettles that it might be relevant to a police investigation into Amelia's death. Nettles won't be surprised to hear from you."

"I didn't mention that it happened to be my truck that blew up," MacAuliffe said. "Must've slipped my mind."

"Yeah, must've," Monahan said. "Okay, I'll check into it. By the way, the girl was alive and breathing when the truck went up in flames. The ME found smoke in her lungs. He also didn't find any reason for her to be unconscious. No puncture wounds that reached the internal organs. No dents in her skull from getting whapped—a tire iron, rock, anything that'd leave some evidence. The skin was pretty much gone, obviously, but the rest was intact. Like she just got in the truck and kaboom. I reached out to this Rose Bumgarten in Grand Marais, but I haven't heard anything back yet. Till we know more, you should be watching your back. If the person on the trigger couldn't see who got in, they might've blown it up assuming it was you."

"But, Mark, there's got to be someone who wants Mac dead for that theory to make any sense," Martha interjected. "There're people who aren't particularly fond of him. Journalists have that way with people. But he was an investigative reporter for a small newspaper with limited circulation best known for a rather tawdry sex column, and he couldn't pay all his bills in the end. Hate him maybe, but those aren't reasons to kill him."

"Thanks for the support, solicitor," MacAuliffe said. "I think. We just have to figure it out. We have an eyewitness. Ester Petrowski saw Amelia leave the boat and walk across the parking lot. We know both of them came back. Ester P had to get the leftover bread from Amazing Grace. Amelia, we're not sure where she went but Caribou Coffee makes sense. It's the only place open that time of morning."

"But Mrs. P didn't see anyone else, just the girl," Monahan said. "And for some reason she thinks you're a frigging hero."

"You feed her cat and you'd be a hero, too. But the timing works, Mark. Amelia didn't go straight to my truck and leave.

My guess is she went over to Caribou to get coffee, maybe some food for the road. It's the only place that would've been open that early. Have you shown her photo to the baristas over there?"

Monahan shook his head. "Need a picture to show."

"Ester always walks the same route with her dog. By the time Amelia had returned, she was back and starting to feed the birds. Right in front of where I park. She would've seen Amelia get in the truck. But she doesn't recall seeing anything else. Traumatic amnesia?"

"Certainly possible," Monahan said. "Even likely."

"So what happened between the time Amelia walked across the parking lot and the time she got back?"

"Or the truck was already rigged to blow, and they just blew up the wrong person."

"Or she gave some indication that she was taking the truck," Martha added. She rose from the stool and stood facing Monahan. "That would've given someone time to plant the bomb and retreat."

Standing beside the police officer, she appeared small and insignificant. If Monahan gave her a bear hug, MacAuliffe thought, she'd disappear completely.

"Okay, boys, this has been more fun than anyone ought to have in one day," Martha said. She threw a couple of twenties on the bar. "I've been up since one o'clock your time. I'm bushed; I'm turning in." Turning to MacAuliffe, she added, "Don't forget to tell him about Craig's warning—or threat."

NINE

Morning fog hung still and heavy on the lake, hiding water and sky. Majestic old trees lining the street dripped moisture off leaves just starting to hint at autumn colors of orange and red. The Forester crept past the trees and mansions hidden along the shore. Somewhere lost in the mist was Nettles' lakeside house with its sweeping lawn and idle boats. Traffic approaching the city was light, the occasional glimpse of blurred headlights appearing and disappearing.

Martha enjoyed driving in the fog. It was a chance to slow down, to concentrate fully on driving. It was also a chance to let her subconscious work on problems, seeking solutions buried deep in the fog of her psyche, waiting to be revealed to the light.

Beside her, MacAuliffe seemed lost in thought. He watched the waterfront glide by in images obscured by fog. They spoke little. Nothing about a dead girl or what they might uncover in Grand Marais. Even what they might be searching for.

Martha watched her rearview mirror. She took Monahan's warning seriously. The fog made identifying anyone following them impossible. And it made it nearly impossible to be followed, as well.

In Two Harbors, a small town whose port was lost in the heavy marine air, they pulled into roadside coffee house. MacAuliffe stayed outside to smoke. Once they left town, the coastal Highway 61 dwindled down to two lanes, and they went long stretches not seeing any traffic either coming from behind or approaching. Coffee and nicotine seemed to bring MacAuliffe alive. Now, as the fog begin to lift with the morning sun, he sipped his latté and began to talk.

"Mark Twain had the Mississippi River. Bob Dylan had Highway 61. Runs all the way to New Orleans. It's this symbol of freedom for him. He's from Hibbing, Minnesota, but he was born in Duluth, you know. He had Highway 61. I had Interstate 90. I went west as far as it'd go, my ribbon of freedom. 'Gotta think about your pension,' Dad always told me. 'Good benefits, gotta think about that when you have a family.' Hell, I didn't even have a girlfriend. What twenty-something thinks about family and benefits and pensions?"

He sipped his latte. "I drove I-90 to the very last exit, and when I crested the hill into Seattle, I had on Dylan's 'Like a Rolling Stone.' Elliott Bay opened up in front of me like heaven on earth. Mount Rainier loomed over it all like the magic mountain in a fairytale. Last time I saw Mount Rainier for two months, but I knew it was there. I knew I was home. Everything had been stripped away. I was on my own, free to fail or succeed, a complete unknown."

MacAuliffe bowed his head, and in a voice that made Dylan sound like Elvis, he croaked out the chorus of "Like a Rolling Stone." It was so bad she admired his willingness to sing. It was something she would never attempt. If she didn't do it well, she didn't do it at all.

"Don't give up your day job," she said, when he finished. "Dylan never appealed to me. I never bought into that great poet crap. He's too cynical. Dylan sneers at a woman who's fallen from grace and finds herself in a hostile world."

"But that's just the beginning of her journey," MacAuliffe replied. "Everything has been stripped away. She's free now. She's got nothing left—no false glitter, no secrets, no fears. That's so liberating. Besides, it's a metaphor."

"Don't talk to me about metaphors. Dylan's not living in the back of a van with a two-year-old kid. That's one of my clients, by the way, a woman beaten up enough until she snapped and she felt her only options were to kill her abusive husband or run. Fortunately, she ran. Poverty is romanticized by poets, but it is not romantic. It's a downward spiral to despair, depression, and crime that few people have the means to escape."

"See, you just called Dylan a poet."

"I did not."

For the next hour, through heavy woods and small communities, along the lakeshore and over rolling hills of scrub forest, they argued back and forth about poetry and music, with periodic gaps to appreciate the beauty of the lake in the few places it appeared between the trees as the curtain of fog lifted over the scene. A streak of sunlight now hit the lake, splintering into thousands of tiny golden fragments that glinted off the water. Names of places that had little meaning to Martha slipped by—Castle Rock, Gooseberry Falls, Split Rock Lighthouse, Beaver Bay, Tettegouche, and Tofte. The scrub forest of conifers mixed with birch and poplars and maple trees—all seen against the backdrop of Lake Superior—reminded her of home.

The drive could just as easily have been from Sault Ste. Marie through the Upper Peninsula toward Duluth, hundreds of miles of shadowed forests all set against the backdrop of this same inland sea, a drive west she'd made just once—when she moved to Seattle, a place she now called home.

It had been on a trip in the opposite direction, driven by the family friend Walt Boudreau, that had changed her life forever. Martha had no regrets, no remorse about killing Boudreau. Nor did she ever wonder if her lack of remorse made her a monster. There is a monster in everyone, she knew. Hers just sat a little closer to the surface.

MacAuliffe studied her as she drifted off in thoughts that she didn't share. A beautiful woman, in an exotic way. A studied intensity had settled across her brow. Her blue eye was startlingly clear, like the lake on a bright summer afternoon. But her face always seemed touched by a hint of sadness. A little of it he knew about, most of it he didn't. That courage and inner strength didn't come from ordinary, everyday experiences. It came from struggles, even tragedies. It came from times that had challenged her soul.

And still, she remained steadfast in her friendship. He could do no less.

"What's the plan for Grand Marais?" she asked.

"A plan might be overstating the situation," MacAuliffe replied, still watching her. Beyond her face, a gondola could be seen running up the hillside. They must be approaching Lutsen, what passed for a ski resort in the Minnesota hills. It also had the golf course for duffers, as Nettles put it. "I did some more digging into Nettles when I got home last night. Mom says hi, by the way."

"Thank you. I thought she was delightful. Find anything new, anything interesting?"

"Mom's an artist and works a lot with the local nonprofit community. She remembered when Nettles' wife died. It was maybe fifteen years ago. I found a long obituary about her in the *Duluth News Tribune*. One of the cancers. She'd fought it off once, but it came back. She was only forty-four. Seems she'd been a stalwart on the boards in the nonprofit community. Mom said there were some ugly rumors at the time, that Nettles didn't visited his wife in the hospital because he was too busy dallying with a new girlfriend."

"Rumors sometimes carry an element of truth," Martha said. "That had to leave an impression on the kids. Might explain Buzz saying, 'He's not who he seems to be.' Anything else?"

"The Duluth social pages love their rich people. After his wife died, there were lots of photos at fundraising galas of Nettles wearing a tuxedo and holding a drink, usually with someone half his age draped on his arm. Preference is for busty brunettes, it appears. Never the same woman twice until a few of the photos showed him with his daughter Bess. They were from at least ten years ago. After that, nothing. Appears he stopped attending the events or the newspaper lost interest in him."

"That'd be a blow to his ego."

"Or he got it stroked in other ways. The Chamber voted him Man of the Year, can't remember the year. A favorable article on the resort ran in the *Minneapolis/St. Paul Business Journal* last year. He told them the same things he told us, down to his daughter being listed as MIA in Afghanistan."

MacAuliffe pulled a notebook from his coat pocket and flipped through some pages. "He didn't make the Forbes list of richest people—who knew Minnesota had six billionaires living here? But he did make the *Business Journal*'s list of wealthiest Minnesotans. Number nineteen, it seems. He got lots of press when he donated enough money to start the capital campaign for a new business center on the UMD campus."

"Sounds like a few of my former clients. A man accustomed to getting what he wants."

"Not always it seems. One story buried on the second

page of the already small business section of the *Duluth News Tribune* was of his being charged by a former employee with sexual assault. Nettles denied the accusation. Said it was all consensual. The woman—married at the time—admitted to the affair but countered that being raped wasn't consensual. It was well before the MeToo movement and it took a lot of courage for the woman to bring charges. Still does."

"Which usually means there're others who didn't bring charges." Her voice carried a certainty that would brook no objections. "What happened?"

"No further mention of it in the papers. I didn't dig into the court archives."

"Had to be settled out of court with a gag order not to talk to the press."

"Nettles is a powerful man accustomed to getting his own way," MacAuliffe said.

"Rich men usually do. Any more thoughts on Monahan's concern that you were the real target?"

"He's just doing his job. I understand. But none of the facts add up. No, they're not after me. They were after Amelia. And they found her."

"So back to my original question—what's the plan?"

"We start asking questions and see what falls from the trees. Heaven knows, there're enough of them up here. At least it's not winter. Then you'd understand why people say Ullr, the Norse god of winter, lives in northern Minnesota."

Martha laughed, the intensity and sadness temporarily lifting from her face. "You forget I grew up in the Soo. We had no shortage of trees or winter in the UP."

They passed Cascade River State Park and drove a couple of miles. "Slow down," MacAuliffe said. "Someplace in here is where Nettles plans to locate his resort and golf course."

Highway 61 followed the lakeshore. Boulders and a rocky shore edged the lake until in the distance he could see the road ascend to bluffs with trees growing right to the edge. They crested a hill, and it felt like they were dropping directly into the lake. The fog was nearly gone. A hazy blue sky and milky blue waters were replacing it. Leaves from poplars and white-barked birch trees fluttered golden in the wind. The occasional maple was just beginning to turn orange. They contrasted with the evergreen forest that predominated further back from the road.

MacAuliffe knew the conifers were not the towering white pines found in a virgin forest. Once this area had supported an active lumbering industry with centuries-old pines right to the water's edge. Trees were harvested and floated to mills further south. The timber barons of a century ago—like the Nettles family—had brought the first wealth and prosperity to the region, much of it centered around Duluth. Now the road ran through a haphazard growth of species fighting for survival in a harsh climate.

"Want to stop?" Martha asked.

"Man, I guess you need more imagination than I have to see this as a thriving resort and golf course," MacAuliffe replied. "Let's keep going. I was never good at interviewing trees."

Grand Marais soon announced itself the way most small towns did in the north woods. Martha recognized the signs and knew they could be anywhere in the conifer forests from Maine to Minnesota. In clearings in the woods, clapboard houses of white and red and tan became more frequent and moved closer to the road. Accompanying barns and outbuildings were replaced with two- and three-car garages. Lawns grew larger, as if pride of ownership required a riding lawn mower and acres to mow—a peculiar pastime that she found fraught with ennui. Roadside billboards, often homemade, announced places to stay, food to eat, a list of the Ten Commandments in case anyone required a reminder about a particular sin. An old cemetery appeared off to the right.

The Gunflint Ranger Station for Superior National Forest appeared on the side of the road.

"A thought," she said, making a last-second turn into the parking lot. "Let's talk to Buzz again. If he knows you're not writing a story on the economic development associated with his father's resort, he might actually be an ally in finding out what's really going on up here. He knows the community; he probably knows Rose Bumgarten."

"And you thought I brought you along just for your good looks."

"Don't be a sexist jerk with me. Ever." Before he could protest, she added, "Even in jest. That's your one mulligan."

"Apologies."

She nodded. "Accepted."

As they walked toward the building, MacAuliffe said, "He might be a little upset about yesterday."

"Then we've wasted ten minutes on what's turning into a beautiful morning. It was time for a break anyway. But I'm guessing he'll get over it if he knows you weren't planning on promoting the resort."

From behind a counter, a stick-thin woman with long red hair worn in a French braid turned as they entered the Ranger Station. She was dressed in the Forest Service uniform of khaki shirt and olive slacks. She set down a stack of papers. A summer spent outdoors had freckled fair skin, and too many summers spent outdoors had left her skin dried out and leathery. Creases formed around her mouth as a warm smile radiated out from the thin, freckled face.

"May I help you or you just being polite before asking for the restroom?" she said.

"Yes, on both accounts," MacAuliffe said, leaning on the counter. "Do you have any good maps of the area? This is my first time back in Grand Marais in nearly twenty years or so. Wondering if you could recommend a good hiking trail?"

"Welcome back. We've missed you," the woman said. A name badge was pinned over her left breast, Marlena Berglund. "What you thinking of? A stroll along the beach, or you got some real hiking boots tucked away someplace? The trails can get pretty rugged out there."

Boat shoes with socks, Martha noted for the first time. Berglund had spied it right away. Not that MacAuliffe exactly oozed outdoorsman with his jeans, Oxford shirt—today, white—and a tweed sport jacket.

"I think you're just the person to talk to," MacAuliffe replied. He introduced himself and said he was working on a feature story about the drug problem affecting small towns in America. "I was in Duluth yesterday. Detective Mark Monahan from the Duluth Police Department implied Grand Marais would be a good town to profile. You're observant, you're part of law enforcement up here. I suspect you're local to the area. I was wondering what you knew about the problem."

"Yeah, you can tell Detective Monahan if he'd do a better job on his end, we'd have less drugs on ours," Berglund replied. "Most of the stuff comes up from Duluth. Have any ID?"

She studied his driver's license and then his face; she glanced at his business card. She tossed them all on the counter. "Never heard of *The Ballard Gazette*."

"This is freelance. I'm home visiting my parents for a few weeks—they're in Duluth. Thought I'd make it a business trip so I could write it off with the IRS."

"Not real keen on people scamming the federal government. That's how I pay my cable TV bill—if not much else. How do I know you ain't here just to score some good weed?"

"Would I walk up to a law enforcement officer and announce my intentions?"

"There's a reason they hand out the Darwin awards."

"Good point. Give Mark a call." He handed her the card for the Duluth police officer.

Berglund glanced at it and stuck it in her shirt pocket. "Yeah, there's a drug problem in Grand Marais. But it's not different than any other small town in America. Heroin's back. Sold mostly to the teens. We've got unemployed miners cooking meth in the backwoods. We've got our prescription addicts to complete the Triple Crown of drugs. Pot never goes away. Most of law enforcement looks the other way—at least at pot."

"Including yourself?"

"Off the record—including myself. If you print anything otherwise, I'll sue you for libel, slander, whatever else I can bring against you."

"Defamation of character," Martha said, joining MacAuliffe beside the counter.

"Thanks for the help," MacAuliffe said. He made introductions.

"Did you know Amelia Bumgarten?" Martha asked.

"Sure, it's a small town. Amy's a year younger than my oldest, Anna. They're in band together. Plays the violin. First chair. My daughter's an oboist. They're both in the school play this year. They're doing Thornton Wilder's *Our Town.*"

"A high school classic," MacAuliffe said. Martha couldn't tell if he was being sarcastic or not.

"Why you asking about Amy?" Berglund asked, her voice suddenly cautious.

"There was an incident in Duluth a couple of days ago," Martha started.

"'Incident' encompasses a multitude of sins," Berglund said. "And none of 'em any good."

"Do you know her mother, Rose?" MacAuliffe said.

"Yeah. We're both single moms in a small town. Hard not to gravitate toward each other. We shared problems of raising teenagers. They're good kids, don't get me wrong, but, well, teenagers are still teenagers. They get in trouble and you just hope they survive it. We had some common interests. Sometimes Rose joined me in the woods."

"Have you seen Rose in the last few days?" MacAuliffe said. "Detective Monahan hasn't been able to reach her."

She pointed a quivering finger at MacAuliffe. "Stop jackhammerin' me with questions and tell me what the hell's going on with Amy."

"There was an explosion in Duluth," Martha said. "Amy may have been involved."

Berglund pulled a phone out of her back pocket and thumbed through her contacts, pushed a button. The disappointment on her face made it clear she got voice mail. She said, "Rosie, it's Lena. Call me right away, honey. It's urgent." To Martha and MacAuliffe, she added, "Amy'd no more blow something up than this lake'd go dry. Now, talk to me!"

Neither Martha nor MacAuliffe responded. The ranger darted looks of increasing panic back and forth between them. "Oh no. Oh no." It came out as an extended moan. "Is she hurt? How bad? Where's she at?"

The questions came out in a flurry. Again, neither Martha nor MacAuliffe answered.

"Oh my God," Berglund gasped, and sagged into a chair. A freckled hand came to her mouth.

Martha said, her voice quiet, "We believe Amy might've been killed in the explosion." She hastened to add, "There hasn't been a positive ID yet."

Deep brown eyes welled with tears, and Berglund swiveled her chair around. Martha studied the map of the national forest under the glass counter. Berglund sniffled, daubed her eyes with a tissue she took from her pocket and blew her nose. She turned back. "I'm so sorry, so sorry. Amy was such a talented girl. Rose must be beside herself."

Berglund had gone pale, as if in shock. Which she probably was experiencing right now, Martha knew. Small towns went years, even decades without a tragedy.

"We're hoping to contact Rose if you could help us," Martha said. "She isn't answering her phone."

"She must have found something," Berglund said. It was almost a whisper. More tears ran down her cheeks. This time she didn't wipe them away.

"Must have found what?" MacAuliffe asked. His voice had grown quiet, gentle.

Between sniffles, she said, "Rose hated the idea of this resort they were planning to build just south of town. Down Highway 61 a few miles. Had plans for a bunch of condos and a large hotel, even a golf course. They were talking to the tribe about adding a casino. We're sitting in the middle of God's paradise and they wanna put in a fucking golf course and casino, excuse my French. None of us could stomach the notion, but instead of just whining like a barroom lawyer, Rose actually tried to do something about it."

Berglund sobbed again, found another tissue under the counter, and blew her nose. "That's why Rose joined me sometimes on patrol. She was testing the water quality and sending it down to someone at the U, searching for—praying for, really—

environmental pollution, an endangered species whose habitat would be destroyed. Anything to shut down development."

"Did she uncover anything?" Martha asked.

Berglund shook her head. "Not that I know, but she didn't share her results with me. She must have. Must have."

A bell jingled and a man and a woman entered the Ranger Station. They were dressed for a serious hike on the Gunflint Trail. Berglund stood up and said, "I'm sorry. We're closed for lunch. Could you come back in half an hour?"

"Early lunch," the man quipped. "Another cushy job working for the feds."

"Come back in half an hour, please." The slow, precise enunciation revealed a steel in her voice that had the two hikers pivoting on their heels and leaving with an exaggerated huff.

MacAuliffe waited until the bell jingled a second time. "Would she have shared any of the results with Amy?"

Berglund shrugged. "I don't know. Not that she ever talked about, but Rose was pretty tight-lipped about all of it."

"I'm sorry to keep pressing you, Marlena," MacAuliffe said, "But we're trying to get to the bottom of who killed Amy. Any possibility she was dealing drugs?"

This time it was Berglund's turn to snort. "And I'll be the next pope. Rosie was upset at first about Amy going Goth. Everything black but her hair. But I told her, pick your battles, honey. This one ain't worth the fight. Rose was lucky to have a daughter like Amy. She's on the honor roll; she's a good violinist; she's in the school play. Works a job and won a scholarship to the U. Let her paint her fingernails black and dye her hair purple or green or whatever the color of the week is. Yeah, she got busted for smoking a joint. BFD. And Craig can be a righteous asshole at times. Amy's not the first one to have a toke or two after a stressful day."

Maybe it was her choice of words or the images they invoked but Berglund went into deep sobs, her chest heaving as if it wasn't big enough to hold all the pain that consumed her.

When the sobbing stopped and she blew her nose again, Martha said, "You mentioned that 'Craig' busted her for smoking dope. Is that Craig Nettles?"

"Yeah." Berglund nodded. "He can be a real prick about his territory at times."

MacAuliffe jumped in. "Detective Monahan said we should contact him. Is he working?"

"Nah, called in sick again. Craig tends to get the sunshine flu. Sun came out on Wednesday and Craig's been sick ever since. Probably why he turned down the offer to go full-time. Doesn't seem to care. Ain't living on his paycheck, I suppose. From the lucky sperm club. After Rose, he's probably the biggest opponent of the resort here in Grand Marais, and his father is leading the development. Craig Nettles, Senior, from Duluth, from one of the old-time timber baron families. God bless their souls for raping and pillaging our forest."

"What did you mean about Craig being a prick about his 'territory'?" MacAuliffe asked.

"We're all assigned a territory to cover. It's hard in-season when we're up to our eyeballs in campers and hikers and folks heading to the Boundary Waters, but we still gotta respond to calls when they come in. Mostly mundane stuff—illegal camping, fishing without a license, a fight between a couple of ugly drunks at the campgrounds. But we're each responsible for a section of the Gunflint District. Just to keep an eye on it. It's a big area with very few people. Someone can take out a couple of trucks of logs and no one'd know about it for months. Most of the time it's just local yahoos cutting firewood for winter. A tree here, a tree there. Go in, get it quick, get out. Federal land, they feel it's theirs to use as they please, I guess. We've shut down a couple of meth labs. A couple of years back we had a squatter living in the woods that Craig had to boot out."

"But how do you cover an area this large," MacAuliffe asked.

"We mostly patrol in vehicles," Berglund said, "but sometimes we hike through the back woods. Rose enjoyed coming with me when it was my day to patrol. I enjoyed the company. Craig sometimes brings up his old man's yacht and drives the coast up to Grand Portage, even though most of the shore's private property. Claims it helps him see better back into the hills for fires or logging. Yeah, and I'm Katherine Hepburn. One day last spring the kids were having a party in the woods, out at Woods Creek Camp. School was just out. Someone brought a keg; someone brought some pot. They had a big bonfire. Craig found out about it, and since it was in his territory, he went in and busted 'em, Amy included."

"Was your daughter one of them, as well?" Martha asked.

Berglund shook her head. "Would've been probably, but she was already grounded. My house, my rules. She broke them and got grounded for it. I got a grandbaby out of it."

"Where's Craig's territory?" MacAuliffe said.

Berglund spread out a topo map on the counter and drew an arc northwest of town that encompassed everything north of Grand Marais to Grand Portage on the Canadian border.

"That's huge," Martha said.

"Yeah, welcome to the National Forest Service, caring for the land and serving people with little budget and less staff. We all have similar territories to cover."

"He's not south of town, down where his father is proposing to build the development?" MacAuliffe said.

"The Supe saw that as a possible conflict of interest. I cover south."

"How did he even know about the party?" Martha asked. "I can't believe he just drove past it on his way home from work. Kids aren't that stupid."

"Tip. That's how we get most of our information on illegal activities. Have to. Area's just too big otherwise. It may be sparsely populated but we've got our share of busybodies and cranky old farts who think they're the only ones who should be allowed to piss in the woods."

"Like Rose Bumgarten," MacAuliffe said.

Her thin, freckled nose now red, Berglund glared at him. "What do you mean?"

"Some people've said she didn't want Nettles' resort for the same reasons. Didn't like him pissing in her woods."

"I thought you were writing a story on our drug problems."

"I am, but Amy's tragedy brought up some concerns about her mom."

"Rose is a decent, hardworking woman, a good mom and a concerned citizen," Berglund said, her voice a low growl. "That resort was bad news. Gonna destroy what makes this area great. A lot of us agree with her."

"Marlena, we're not here to argue with you about this," Martha said. She'd moved closer to the counter, leaned forward, softened her voice. "What reason did someone have to kill Amy? We're wondering if it might be related to her mom's effort to stop the resort. Mac's a journalist by profession so he might write a story, but that's not our real purpose. He could've been killed in the explosion that killed Amy. Another woman almost was. A schoolteacher out walking her dog."

Berglund swore. "Should've known. Played me like a cheap fiddle. And I fell for it, hook, line, and sinker."

"We didn't mean to deceive you," MacAuliffe said, resisting the temptation to point out her mixed metaphor. "Well, okay, maybe we did. I did. But we're serious about looking for information. And a young woman *was* killed in Duluth two days ago. I know it was Amelia Bumgarten. Call Officer Monahan. Text him. You've got his card." When she didn't reach into her pocket, he added, "You're law enforcement, Officer Berglund. Go to the Bumgarten house with us to check on Rose."

"I have no authority outside of NFS boundaries," Berglund said. "We play at being cops."

"A young woman is dead," Martha said. "And no one can reach her mother. Who is a friend of yours."

"You should call the Cook County Sheriff," Berglund said.

"Then we have to explain ourselves all over again," MacAuliffe said. "You could be stopping by as a concerned friend."

Martha recalled her first meeting with MacAuliffe and realized what he had in mind. She added, "And it'll keep Mac from doing an illegal B&E." MacAuliffe just shrugged. "We have a history and despite my best attempts as his attorney to keep him out of trouble he always seems to find new way to circumvent me."

"Damn city folks," Berglund said. "Rules don't apply to you, I know. Okay, let's go."

TEN

A small white rambler with peeling paint sat up against the trees on the edge of town. Green shutters and a neat lawn of trimmed shrubs and mowed grass surrounded the house. An older Subaru Outback station wagon sat in the driveway. Berglund parked along the street and jumped out of the Forest Service SUV, striding toward the front door.

Martha had the door open and one leg out to follow when MacAuliffe said, "That's not right."

"What's not right?" she said.

"Amelia said her mom wasn't home. No car, no kitchen light, no mom. And she wasn't answering her phone. Now the car's home."

"Have you considered that maybe Amelia was lying to you? Or that maybe her mom just wasn't home yet. Or that maybe she really did run away from home for reasons she wasn't comfortable sharing with a stranger?"

"Every time I try to make sense of this."

He studied the scene again. Berglund was on the front porch, pushing the doorbell. Everything seemed quiet, tranquil. A lazy autumn Sunday morning in small-town America. This wasn't right. "Did Marlena's description of the girl sound like someone who was troubled and had run away from home?"

"Maybe there was more tension between mother and daughter than anyone knew. Maybe it was more than teenage rebellion, maybe she was using, even dealing. Maybe she was pregnant. Maybe she was a spoiled princess who didn't get her way. She wouldn't be the first good kid to fall from grace with her mother. And still be a nice kid to other people. God knows I run into them as potential clients all the time. For every young woman who's genuinely in trouble, I get ten who just need to make a phone call home."

"I get that. Any and all of it's possible. My dad didn't talk to me for two years when I was in high school because I grew my hair long and smoked a little pot. Dad thought I was on the expressway to perdition, and I took every opportunity I could to rub it in his face. I was a horrible teenager, a know-it-all, narcissistic brat. But I was still on the honor roll, played basketball, and edited the student paper—a trend-setting bastion of radical liberalism, if I do say so myself. I was still kind to small dogs and polite to my parents' friends. You weren't there when Amelia lectured me about being nice to my mom. Guilty conscience? I don't think so. It sounded genuine, like someone who had a real love and appreciation for her mom. And none of this explains the disappearance of Rose Bumgarten."

"Let's go see what we can find out."

As they approached, Berglund was on her tiptoes, peering into the window atop the front door. She held her hands to either side of the visor of her NFS baseball cap. She rapped hard on the door again and shouted, "Rosie, it's Lena. You home? Put your panties on, honey; I'm coming in."

She tried the door handle. It was locked. "That ain't normal. Not around here."

"I'll check for other doors," Martha said, stepping off the porch and heading toward the driveway.

"I'll check this way," MacAuliffe said, going in the opposite direction.

The side door under a small awning was also locked. Martha pounded on the door. No other sounds were heard. The Thermopane windows wouldn't be easy to break. She peered in the window looking for Rose Bumgarten, for any signs of life. A galley kitchen extended away from the door. The place was a mess—dishes stacked on the counter, a couple of open boxes of cereal, a coffee pot. Oak cabinets lined the walls, both top and bottom, one with the cabinet door left open. Photos covered the front of an old white refrigerator. Two chairs were thrown back from a small table in a corner nook.

Suddenly, she caught a shape flit by out of the corner of her eye. She banged the door again. MacAuliffe walked through the kitchen and unlocked the door.

"Bathroom window," he said in response to her unasked question. "No one ever remembers to lock their bathroom window."

A row of small hooks by the back door held a series of keys of various sizes and shapes. MacAuliffe took a keyring off the hook and flipped through the keys.

"I'd appreciate it if you didn't touch anything till we can figure out what's going on," Berglund said, her thin frame standing in the doorway.

Martha hadn't realized back at the station how short she was. Maybe five one, five two at the most. And small. The boyish figure. The face full of freckles. She could easily have passed as a teenager in a baseball cap. Berglund must have fought not being taken seriously as an officer of the law her entire career. She now wore a gun on her hip and rested her hand on it. The safety strap was unhooked.

No one spoke. Martha noticed the profound stillness that filled the house. No radio, no ticking clock, no dripping sink. Just an unearthly quiet. A hint of something permeated the air. Coffee, rotten food, unwashed dishes? It could have been any of it—and all of it. The kitchen resembled a refugee camp deserted on short notice.

MacAuliffe flipped various light switches, and lights blinked on and off.

"Don't touch anything," Berglund barked.

"Sorry. Wanted to check. Amelia said her mom left the kitchen light on. Always. Twenty-four seven always. They're all working. Somebody turned off the kitchen light."

They found Rose Bumgarten sitting upright in bed wearing a practical nightgown of robin's egg blue flannel. She leaned against the headboard, her eyes closed, her skin a waxy greenish-blue. Her mouth drooped open and a blue tongue hung over her bottom teeth. The television flickered across the room, the sound muted. A sliver of light streamed through a crack in the curtains. It reflected off a glass of water that sat on a dresser, creating a ghastly halo above the dead woman's head.

On the nightstand beside the bed was an overturned vial and a used syringe.

Suddenly, Berglund was all cop. If she grieved for her friend, it was being done in private or it would come later. "Clear the room and don't touch anything," she ordered. Her phone was in her hand and she was talking to the 911 operator.

Martha bumped into MacAuliffe as she backed out of the room. He was glancing around, so she did the same. Observe, catalog, process later. A blouse, sweater and worn jeans lay tossed over a chair. Undergarments were piled on the floor beside the chair. The closet door was open. A jewelry box on the dresser had the lid flipped up, and various earrings, bracelets and necklaces were visible. A set of earrings and a bracelet sat on the dresser in front of the box. A white sheet was pulled up to the dead woman's waist; a comforter cover of green with flowers and weaving vines came to her knees. A simple necklace around her neck glinted shards of gold. Blue hair hung limply to slumped shoulders. A remote control peeked out of a folded edge of the blanket. A bowl rested on her lap and contained a few remnants of popcorn.

"Clear this room now!" Berglund ordered.

MacAuliffe was already in the hall, stepping around furniture and an overflowing laundry basket. His shirt untucked, he used the lower hem to turn a doorknob. A closet. He eased the door shut again. An open door revealed a bathroom. An electric toothbrush sat charging on the sink counter along with a bar of soap. A small hand towel had been thrown in the sink. One towel was draped on a hook. Another lay piled on the floor. The shower curtain was half-closed, the toilet seat up. A corner cabinet revealed a disorganized jumble of makeup, tubes of lipstick, cotton balls, girl stuff. Lots of girl stuff.

Again using his shirt hem, he opened a door across the hall. A spare bedroom was being used as an office. The couch now served as a bookcase with books, loose papers, and binders piled on top. A desk, with a small clear spot in the center, and two file cabinets lined a wall. Four topo maps, joined at the seams to show all of Superior National Forest, were tacked to a wall. Red, blue, and yellow pins with numbered tags were pushed into various places on the map, mostly in the sections south and west of Grand Marais. A stack of manila folders sat on one corner of the desk. A series of spiral notebooks lined the back. A computer printer served as the bookend on one side. A closed laptop sat on the desktop. He knew he didn't have time to investigate the room before the police arrived.

He found Martha in the last room down the hall. She stepped further inside when she sensed his presence. He slid in beside her, neither speaking. This had to be Amelia's room. In contrast to the rest of the house, the room was neat and tidy, organized, free of clutter. Walls were navy blue with glittery stars on the same blue ceiling. The bed was made, covered with a handmade comforter with a geometric design of turquoise blue and fractured silver, an abstract representation of the moon over the lake. A couple of ornamental pillows—those tiny useless ones—accented the blue of the comforter. A poster of some young hunk holding a violin adorned the wall over the bed. It was autographed. Some dude named Joshua Bell. The room had a dresser topped by photos and other mementos, a desk, and some books neatly stacked on the desk.

In the background, wailing sirens were fast approaching.

"Time to go," Martha said.

They stood out on the street as patrol cars from the Cook County Sheriff's Office converged on the little white rambler. The house was cordoned off, the street blocked, an attempt to minimize the lookie-loos, Martha was sure. It was too late to prevent the gossip. Enough people had stood on their front porches or driven past before the police barricade went up, attracted to the sirens and lights. People drawn to the macabre spectacle of a tragedy. This had to be big news in the little town of Grand Marais.

Soon, Berglund joined them on the street. She'd aged a decade in the past hour, the creases around her mouth and eyes, the furrows in her brow all more pronounced. Her eyes were swollen and bloodshot. She'd gone someplace for a good cry.

"They'll want to talk to you next," she said, wrapping her arms around her chest. "Cook County's lead, but they're calling in somebody from St. Paul. They're not set up for this kind of investigation."

"I hope they didn't miss the little details."

Berglund nodded, her gaze focused on some distant point in the trees. "The necklace. I saw it right away. A woman doesn't take off her earrings and her bracelet before bed but leave her necklace on. I pointed it out, but the Sheriff wants to do his own investigation. Build his conclusions from the evidence. Said we're jumping to conclusions. Maybe she was just in a hurry to get in her pjs and shoot up."

"Understandable," Martha said. It felt good to be standing in the sun, feeling the warmth soak into her bones. "Eliminate prejudice and let the facts speak for themselves. But they've got so many people in there now, they can't share the same experience of first walking in."

"All the more reason to trust the people who found her," MacAuliffe said. "We all saw the signs, especially the necklace."

"They're good folks and conscientious officers," Berglund replied. "They'll do the right thing. I told 'em what we all noticed. But right now Sheriff Gould won't assume it's anything other than what it seems—an overdose."

"She and her daughter just happened to die within a day or two of each other by coincidence?"

"The police are on it," Berglund said. "I told 'em about Amy. Everyone in there knows Rose was consumed with stopping the resort, and Nettles had made it clear nothing was going to keep him from building it. They'll connect the dots. And it might just be what it seems. Rosie had a history of battling demons."

"You believe she resumed her heroin habit?" MacAuliffe said. "Why? Because Nettles had already beat her? Because he had. He'd out-lawyered her, out-moneyed her, and out-lobbied her. She wasn't going to be able to prevent the resort from happening. And she had a sixteen-year-old daughter. She may have hated losing to Nettles, but she wouldn't have jeopardized Amy's future by throwing away her own."

"That prick doesn't own all the land yet," Berglund retorted. "Without one last parcel he wouldn't be able to build."

"Which comes up for auction next month. Who's going to provide the unlimited funds to outbid him for the land? The Nature Conservancy? Wolf Ridge certainly doesn't have that kind of money. Did Rose have someone else lined up to join her team?"

"How do you know about that?" Berglund barked.

"Because Nettles told us, Marlena," Martha interjected, her voice soft. "We interviewed him yesterday when Mac discovered a link between Rose and the proposed development. He's been two steps ahead of Rose and the anti-resort movement the entire time. He made it clear that he wouldn't be outbid for the last sixty-five acres. It's personal. His father started this project nearly fifty years ago. He owed it to the memory of his daughter to finish it."

"He's not doing it for his daughter," Berglund snorted. "He's doing it because it'll make him more money—as if the asshole needed more."

"And now two people are dead," MacAuliffe said, the argument gone from his voice. "We might be wrong about Nettles, but it's got to be something more than what we've found so far."

For a while, Martha watched the police come and go, and still no one came over to interview them. MacAuliffe leaned against the front fender of the car, hungrily sucking on a cigarette. He barely exhaled before taking another deep drag. A white panel van drove through the street barricade and parked on the street. "Be sure to sweep the car, too," she heard Berglund yell at the two people who jumped out.

MacAuliffe smoked a second cigarette, this one with less urgency, while thumbing his phone. He crushed the smoke on the street and walked back.

"Just heard from Monahan. They confirmed that it was Amelia in the truck. Pulled her dental records."

Martha stiffened her spine and drew her shoulders back. One deep breath. A second. "I'll let Marlena know."

She marched back toward the house.

They walked the tree line around the house, slowly, not saying much. They stayed in the sun and remained visible if someone from the Sheriff's office decided to interview them. The edge of the lawn was full of light and warmth and hinted at the summer days that had slipped away. The front row of trees was mostly birch, with different kinds of evergreens deeper in the woods. The trees were thick and prevented light from penetrating to the forest floor. Martha fingered the paper-like quality of the birch bark.

"When I was young," she said, "we used to go out into the woods and peel birch bark with Gran, my dad's mother. She helped raised us after my mom left. She sold it to have a little extra money. Now I realize how much she had to sacrifice to take us in. She made up in love what she lacked in money."

MacAuliffe reached out and rubbed the bark. It was white and ridged beneath his thumb. He rubbed it several times before pulling his hand away. "I wonder if that's what Rose was doing here. A place where she always kept the light on so Amelia could find her way home. Her currency was love."

"Maybe." Martha took his arm and they continued to stroll. "You know you're not responsible for her death."

"Oh, I know, but every time I tell myself that my stomach turns to molten lead. I liked her. I had nothing going on. I could have offered her a ride to the Cities. If I'd been with her that morning, she might not be dead."

"Or you both might be."

They continued to walk through the grass. It felt soft and luxurious under her feet. She wondered if Rose Bumgarten ever walked barefoot through the yard just to feel the grass in her toes, to smell the clean, crisp air, to feel the warmth of the sun on her shoulders. She breathed in the air, the fragrance of flowers and grass, the scent of pine needles crushed under their feet. And the freshwater lake. So different from the saltwater of Puget Sound. Sharper, rawer, cleaner.

They rounded the corner of the garage. Two people in white hazmat suits had all the doors open to Rose's station wagon.

"Good," MacAuliffe said. "The car wasn't home when Amelia went on the run. It may tell us something."

"Do you always get like this?" she asked. "It seems, I don't know, so personal. Think about the good that you did. You trusted Amy and offered her a warm place on a stormy night. You fed her; you listened to her. You didn't know someone would follow her to Duluth. You didn't know she was going to steal your truck. You just saw a person in trouble and helped. That speaks volumes about who you are. Remember the bigger picture."

MacAuliffe offered a wan smile. The sun lay on his shoulders, on the top of his head. His blonde hair seemed streaked with gold and white. He said, "I really don't believe in the bigger picture. There's just the here and now. This is where we live. These are our lives. They're fragile, they're precarious. They're miraculous. They're all we have. And someone I met—even if only for a brief time—had hers taken too soon. I owe her discovering who and why. I can't quit because it gets difficult or people won't talk to me. I have to dig a little deeper, work a little harder. I feel responsible to people so their stories are told, that the truth is known. I've always seen it as the one thing I can do to make a difference in the world; it's my way of helping them find peace. I owe that to Amelia."

"Lance said you were going to get into trouble someday because you cared too much."

"So did he. It's why we made a good team, why we started the *Gazette*. To make a difference, to tell the stories that other people weren't willing to tell."

"And it's why he's dead."

"Martha, it's fine if you want to call it quits, go home. I understand. You ain't got a dog in this fight. But I have to see this through to the end. For Amelia's sake. And my own."

And her own, as well, Martha realized. Life had changed when she'd fallen in love with a man who cared too much. He'd been snatched from her in an instant with the firing of a bullet. She still felt the loss every day with the same intensity she had experienced in loving him. Yamamoto-*sensei* had been reminding her that she needed to move beyond grief and loss, not be consumed by the anger that emanated from her violent past.

She again tucked her hand in MacAuliffe's arm. "My dad loves that expression. 'Ain't got a dog in that fight.' Well, it seems that I do. And I was wondering what plan that dog had for digging deeper, working harder?"

MacAuliffe smiled. From the pocket of his jacket he pulled a set of keys and palmed them, so they were visible only to Martha. “Let the police do their job today, and we come back tonight to see what they missed.”

ELEVEN

A man in the tan and brown uniform of the Cook County Sheriff's Office lumbered in their direction. For all his size, his uniform looked like it was cut for a larger person. The shirt was doubled over down the sides where it tucked into his pants. The belt was cinched tight and created puckers around the waist. He introduced himself as Sheriff Steven Gould and said he had a few questions, informing them in a manner that brooked no argument that the interviews would take place at the Angry Trout Café.

"I have to keep my blood sugar regular or I might faint in your lap," Gould said. "That wouldn't be pleasant for either of us." To Martha, he added, "No offense intended, miss."

"None taken," she replied. "As you won't take offense, I hope, at my inherent distrust of all police officers. Personal experience."

"Feisty and honest," Gould laughed. "We'll get along just fine. You can ride with me." To MacAuliffe, he added, "If you haven't been to the Angry Trout before, son, you're in for a treat. Best fish on this entire lake and it's a big lake, in case you hadn't noticed."

On the short ride down the hill, Gould started his interview. "Was this a social visit? Or why'd you hitch your pony at Lena's frontier outpost asking about Rose Bumgarten?"

The questions surprised Martha. She assumed he'd start by verifying the account Berglund had given of discovering the dead woman. "We suspected her daughter Amy had died in an explosion in Duluth under suspicious circumstance. No one had been able to get in touch with Rose. We were here to find her."

Gould pulled the car into a gravel lot. The Angry Trout Café was an old warehouse with cedar-shake siding that sat half on the gravelly shore and half on pilings out over Grand Marais Harbor. A vintage schooner with tanbark sails reached across the harbor, making for a point past the lighthouse on the end of a concrete jetty. The big lake where blue water blended seamlessly with blue sky was its destination. A half dozen sailboats bobbed on mooring buoys inside the harbor, and a small fishing boat followed in the wake of the schooner. On the distant point a white building with a red roof flew the flag of the US Coast Guard.

MacAuliffe pulled the rental car in beside them.

Stepping out of the car, she inhaled deeply. Like drinking a glass of clear, purified water. She was jarred back to the present when she heard Gould say to MacAuliffe, "Now you'll wanna just keep quiet until I'm through talking with your sweetie."

MacAuliffe glanced at Martha. She just shook her head in response.

The lunch crowd had mostly gone, and Gould requested a table overlooking the harbor. To the waitress, he said, "Anna, honey, we're on official business here. If you'd be so kind, and I know you always are, to keep the touristy types away from us, I'll be sure to make it worth your while when settling the tab."

"No problem, Sheriff. Start you off with a Mesabi Red?"

"You know it, sweetie. And a glass of water. I'm on duty today. Ms. Whitaker, Mr. MacAuliffe? No need to refrain from an adult beverage while we chat. Since you two'll be doing all the talkin', might consider a little something to wet the whistle. If God's willin' and you're as blameless as the saints, this'll be the only time Cook County's giving you a free meal."

"The same," Martha said. "And water too, please."

"I'll have the milk stout," MacAuliffe added.

Without further preamble, he continued his interview of Martha. "Now, Ms. Whitaker, Rose and Amelia were two of our own, and we take care of our own here in Grand Marais. You were telling me about your interview with Craig Nettles."

Which she hadn't been of course. Berglund had filled him in well. For all his folksy demeanor, he was determined to suss out what they knew and how they came to know it.

"Mac made the connection that Rose was leading the fight against the development of the new resort led by Nettles," Martha started.

Over beers and an appetizer of fish fritters—which no one had ordered but to which no one objected—Martha laid out events just as they happened, down to mentioning that Nettles had followed through and sent her the recipe for his homemade butternut squash soup. She pulled out her phone and opened the email of the soup recipe to show Gould.

He studied it. His round lips formed a circle and he exaggerated the first syllable, "Oh my, Honeycrisp apples and nutmeg. Never would've thunk it. Have to mention it to the missus." He handed the phone back. "I may have to confiscate that later for further study. Crucial evidence, of course."

"Of course," Martha replied.

"Okay, Ms. Whitaker, back to Craig Nettles before you so conveniently changed the subject. We all assumed she didn't have a snowball's chance in a hot oven of preventing the bulldozers from leveling those trees. Did Nettles indicate otherwise?"

"No," she said. "Unless Rose had a deep-pocketed benefactor who was willing to sign a blank check, she wasn't going to stop Nettles. He needs that last piece of property and is willing to pay whatever it takes to get it. It's part of a family legacy for him."

"Family legacy? Craig Junior's like a bear with its foot in a trap every time he talks about his old man's resort."

"It's for his daughter," MacAuliffe interjected. "The one who died in the war."

"I see—" Gould was interrupted by the waitress bringing lunch to the table.

Martha started salivating at the sight of her smoked trout salad and realized how hungry she was. The smoked trout smelled divine, and the chef certainly understood the art of presentation. Local carrots, cherry tomatoes, fresh strawberries and sliced beets contrasted with the greens of lettuce, arugula, snow peas, and cucumbers. All topped with a fillet of smoked lake trout. Hard-crust bread and a homemade maple-mustard dressing were on the side. At least she could enjoy lunch.

MacAuliffe didn't hesitate to ponder the presentation of his fish and chips but dug in. It had been a long time since their coffee in Two Harbors this morning. The sheriff bowed his head and closed his eyes. His lips moved without speaking. He crossed himself, and pursed his lips as if he planned to lean down and kiss his lunch.

Gould took a bite of his trout and set his fork down, chewed slowly and carefully. He noticed her watching him. "That, ma'am, is the definition of perfection. Not even a Lutheran could complain about this. Well, on second thought . . ."

He took another bite, this time of greens and set his fork down, chewed slowly and carefully.

"How much weight have you lost?" Martha asked.

"Forty pounds. That much and a little more to go. I was setting a bad example for my officers. Couldn't ask them to pass the fitness test if I couldn't do it myself. Ran two miles this morning without a break. Slower 'an molasses in January, I'll grant you, but still two miles nonstop." He took another bite. "And that's all the sharing we're gonna do. Right now, my job is to find out who killed Rose Bumgarten and her daughter, and you two nosy Nancys can help me do that."

Gould's phone rang and he excused himself to take it. When he returned, he said, "By the way, kiddos, I'll be needing your whereabouts over the past few days. ME figures Rosie died three days ago. Not official, of course. Also, he sent the vial off for a toxicology analysis. His guess is fentanyl, might be heroin. He'll wait for the lab to confirm."

"Self-administered?" MacAuliffe asked.

"Doc didn't opine one way or t'other. Now you were about to tell me where you were three days ago. We call that an alibi."

"Three days ago?" MacAuliffe said. "Amelia only died two days ago."

"And you were where?" Gould insisted.

"With my family in Duluth," MacAuliffe replied. After a moment studying the wall over Gould's shoulder, he added, "Mom made beef stroganoff. I came over earlier to help her in the kitchen. After dinner, I cleaned up while Mom beat Dad in a game of euchre. My sister Katie dropped by with her kids, and we all played push rummy. I left the house about ten o'clock and returned directly to my dad's boat where I'm staying. Alone."

"Dinner?" Gould replied. "Never quite figured out 'dinner.' Now, supper, I know exactly what and when that is. Never was too comfortable with folks who have dinner instead of supper. I'll have to verify all of this, of course. How about you, ma'am?"

"I was still in Seattle, meeting with clients during business hours," Martha said. "Wednesday evening I went to the gym where I teach and did some weight training. Detective Ray Palmer, of the Seattle Police Department, is one of my students. He'll be glad to verify all this for me. Or I can just show you my plane ticket?"

"Ticket will do for now." He nibbled on his salad. "You were telling me about Craig Nettles."

"What reason does Nettles have to kill Rose or her daughter?" Martha said. "If she couldn't prevent him from building the resort, he's won." She hesitated. "Of course, maybe someone's framing him."

"Or it's got nothing to do with Craig Nettles and the resort at all," Gould said.

This time it was MacAuliffe's and Martha's turn to set down their forks. They waited expectantly as the sheriff finished chewing. He wiped his mouth on the napkin.

It was MacAuliffe who asked what they both were thinking. "And what else might it be?"

"No idea," Gould said, shaking his head. "But Craig Nettles has been playing in my sandbox for a long time. I don't really care for the sonofabitch. I think he'd cut down every last goddamn tree if there was a profit it in, and he'd put a big ol' Ferris wheel in the middle of God's Eden on earth if he thought someone'd pay to ride it. But I don't think he'd kill a mother and a daughter to make it happen. He'd out-hustle them, outsmart them, out lawyer them, certainly out spend them, but in his own way, he's an honorable man."

The sheriff glanced out the window before returning his attention to the two across the table. "A decade or so back he could've evicted ol' Mrs. Hokanssen when he was well within his rights to do so. He'd bought her property at auction when she couldn't pay her taxes, but he let her live rent free on the family homestead till she moved into a nursing home. He owned the property, but he wasn't ready to start digging yet, so he didn't cause the ol' Norwegian widow any more grief by throwing her out on her keister."

MacAuliffe leaned across the table. "Even if Nettles didn't kill Rose and Amelia, it doesn't mean he's not the central figure here. What if someone's trying to frame him, Sheriff, to make it appear like he's involved? Why? I'll bet you dollars to doughnuts that the coroner will confirm that Rose Bumgarten died of a massive overdose, too massive even for an experienced addict. What's the population of Grand Marais? I saw thirteen hundred when we drove into town. Is there a drug dealer in town that you don't know about? Doesn't mean you've been able to catch him or pin something on him, but don't you have a pretty good idea who's pushing dope in the community and who's using?"

"We know who most of the perps are," Gould said. "But not all of them. We got some small-time pot dealers. We've busted a few out-of-work rednecks cooking more than their daddy's moonshine out in the woods, but it's a lot of woods and we know there're others. Opiates are mostly coming up from Duluth. Someone's brought heroin back. We've flagged some of the dealers, busted a few, but not all of them. Getting evidence that'll stand up to a judge and jury can't be anecdote or rumor."

"Heard any rumors that Rose was using?" MacAuliffe asked. "She had a history of addiction problems."

"Nada."

"Did she have any known enemies?"

Again, Gould shook his head. "Nothing that's come across my desk. But it's possible. Tommy Brooks—that's her boss—is the legal equivalent of a family doctor. He takes care of most of the legal needs for the locals. Only practicing attorney in

GM. Wouldn't represent the meth heads when we busted 'em. Thought they were guilty."

MacAuliffe fiddled with his fork, stirring the remnants of ketchup left on his plate. "And have you heard that Amelia's a user and possibly one of your dealers?"

He snorted, causing the last of his Mesabi Red to come out his nose.

While Gould wiped himself clean, Martha jumped in. "Nettles told us Amy was using and implied she might be dealing. When he had Rose investigated—which he does for all his opponents, by the way. Might even have a file on you. Anyway, when he investigated Rose, he was told that in addition to going through treatment herself, she had her hands full with a drug-using daughter."

"Where'd that cockamamie story come from?" Gould said.

"Nettles Junior busted her and several other kids at a party in the woods last spring," Martha said.

"That? Holy mother of our savior Jesus. Craig said they were smoking weed. But there was no evidence. The kids said they just had some beer. Probably a little of both. But it was a goddamn graduation party and most of the kids were members of the frigging National Honor Society. I got the kids to apologize for trespassing on National Forest land, commit to raising money for an interpretive plaque, and give a lecture at the school about underage drinking. Craig agreed to let them all go with a warning."

"That's not the story that made it back to old man Nettles," MacAuliffe said.

"Where's he getting his information?" Gould asked.

Martha and MacAuliffe shrugged in unison.

Gould flagged down the waitress and requested coffee, "black and strong, honey. Gonna be a long day."

MacAuliffe ordered a coffee with cream. Out the window he saw the schooner *Hjørdis* sailing back toward Grand Marais Harbor, its tanbark sails full on an easy reach about a mile offshore. The lake shimmered now with the full sun, a coruscation of gold fragments against the blue water. Other than the schooner, the lake was empty all the way to the horizon.

After the waitress departed, MacAuliffe said to Martha, "They had to be expecting Amelia to come home. Probably even at the house waiting for her."

"That's just wild speculation," Gould said.

Martha said, "No, it's not, Sheriff. They wouldn't have pursued her to Duluth if they didn't need her dead, too. Easiest place to find her would have been at home. How'd they know to pursue her if they hadn't seen her bolt? They had to see her approach the house. Only she ran when she saw the kitchen light off. What did Amy know that made her vulnerable?"

"They had to believe her mother shared her work with her," MacAuliffe said.

"What did Rose discover that was worth killing over?" Martha asked.

"That is the question. I don't know."

"Would you two frigging amateur detectives please talk to me," Gould said. "We don't know that they were waiting for Amy. We're not even sure she was killed. Our dear Rosie might've started old habits again. Maybe she did have a dirty secret that we didn't know about. You're speculating without any evidence."

"Sheriff, really?" MacAuliffe said. Exasperation was clear in his voice, the sagging of his shoulders. "You're not troubled by the coincidence that Rose OD'd right before Amelia is killed in Duluth?"

"Of course, I am," Gould began.

"Mac's right, Sheriff," Martha interjected. "There are some reasonable and logical assumptions we can make from what we know to date. Mac, explain what Amelia told you before she was killed."

MacAuliffe recounted how he'd come across the runaway on the Duluth waterfront and what she told him—about the kitchen light being off, how she'd known someone had been in the house, how her mother had warned her not to trust anyone. He added, "We know now Rose died three days ago and Amelia two days ago. Those are facts. Because of the kitchen light, we know they had already been to the house. I checked—the kitchen light hadn't burned out; it'd been turned off. Something neither Bumgarten *ever* did. Twenty-four seven, three-sixty-five *ever.*

"Rose was probably already dead inside," MacAuliffe continued. "Yes, we're speculating that someone was waiting for the girl when she got off work, but it's a logical extension of the facts since we know someone went to great lengths to kill Amelia. Why make Rose look like an overdose? Someone knew her history of abuse. Who? Nettles and whoever investigated her. They had to know Rose would be discovered, which means they were doing it intentionally. If you want to hide a murder, it's a whole lot easier to take the body out to the woods, create a little blood, and let the wolves and bears remove the evidence. Was the plan to have Amelia overdose, as well? Mother and daughter caught in the duo tragedy of drug addiction? It'd fit well with the rumors that Amelia was dealing. Only no one suspected her mother was one of her clients."

He interrupted his narrative to sip his coffee. "But like the magician on the stage, it's all fake. By staging Rose in her bedroom, they guaranteed that someone would eventually find her. Neighbor, concerned colleague, cleaning lady—okay maybe not the cleaning person. But someone. They wanted the body discovered. Why? One obvious reason is to frame Nettles. Everyone knew Rose was after his pet project."

MacAuliffe gave a slight shrug of his shoulder and said to Gould, "If you have better theory, I'd love to hear it."

"In my experience, theories only lead to wrong conclusions," the sheriff replied.

"If it's wrong, Sheriff, we start again," Martha said. "But we've got to begin somewhere."

"Yeah, it's called evidence. Evidence leads to provable facts."

"We've given you facts, Sheriff," MacAuliffe said. "What do the facts mean? Why were they both killed? Who had means and motive? Isn't that still part of the triumvirate of standard police work? At some point you have to start to connect the dots. Amelia threw a spanner in the spokes when she bolted. That changed their plans. And if they staged Rose's death to be found, they couldn't very well just drop Amelia in the harbor. What if her body's carried out into the lake on the river current before anyone noticed it? The explosion eliminated that problem. It drew attention to her death. Again, it all points back to Rose and that points back to Nettles. But what's his motive? There isn't one, that we know of today." He hesitated. "Oh, shit."

"What?" Martha asked.

"Nettles was in a demolition unit in Vietnam. They had to know that."

"But he's got an artificial leg," Martha countered. "How's he going to get under your truck to plant the bomb?"

Gould pushed himself away from the table, spilling the last of MacAuliffe's coffee in the process. MacAuliffe and Martha jumped back.

"You may be right," Gould said, standing up. "But it still ain't evidence. Just more theories and speculations. Suppose that's the difference between police work and fake news." He ignored MacAuliffe's sputtering protests and waved a hand. "Why don't you two kids play like a hoop and roll away. I've got your numbers if I run short on wild ideas about the demise of the Bumgarten ladies. But don't go too far. You're still on my list of possible suspects."

"While you're ignoring evidence, Sheriff," MacAuliffe snapped at him, "I'm sure you'll ignore the fact that in a house with two women someone had left the toilet seat up. Or is that just more fake news?"

TWELVE

In the parking lot, they stood on either side of the rental car. Martha soaked up the warmth of the sun, on her shoulders, on her extended hands, on her face as she tilted it skyward.

It lasted just a few seconds before she glanced at him across the car top. "I've missed you. Don't ever cut and run on me again. Ever. Friends don't do that." Before he could reply, she added, "And you might cut Gould some slack, Mac. He's two hours into discovering one of his residents is dead. He's just doing his due diligence and he's has to do it by the book or everything can be thrown out in court. And I completely missed the toilet seat. Good catch. Women don't do that."

"I just remembered it because I had to pee. So who was visiting?"

"Good question." She beeped the car unlocked. "What's next?"

"Get rooms for the night, I guess. I'll start by talking to the folks where Amelia worked. If you're up to it, maybe you could go talk to Rose's boss? Gould mentioned Tom Brooks, a lawyer here in town. If you talk to him, just be open to anything. Don't assume; don't lead him on. Just—"

"Mac, I know how to interrogate a witness."

"Right. Good point. Let's rendezvous for dinner, compare notes. Let's make it early. I want to go see what Rose might have been investigating."

"Is that how you and Lance worked?" she asked.

On the lake, Martha saw the green-hulled schooner motor toward the marina. Its sails down, it approached the slip slow and easy. That's how she'd rather be spending time in this quaint, picturesque lakeside town. A sail aboard the *Hjørdis*. A leisurely hike. Then a massage and maybe some ice cream, a guilty pleasure. A dinner by candlelight, a book by the fire. Shared with a lover and a friend. She'd been single and independent for so long the ache of loneliness surprised her. Was true loneliness the realization that you were on nobody's mind?

"When we worked together," MacAuliffe said, turning to see what she was watching. "But that wasn't often. I was better at investigating and writing the stories. He was better at editing and running the paper. Made for a good team. Besides, he was usually too busy writing the sex advice column."

"That sneaky sonofabitch," Martha laughed. She remembered being sequestered with him and Corvari, their chaperone from the Seattle Police Department. Corvari pressed him on the frank, occasionally titillating—and in both her and Corvari's opinions, disgusting—sex column. The entire time he went on about consenting adults and freedom of the press, but never even hinted at that he was the one writing the column. A shudder ran through her at the memory of how well he'd taken his own advice.

MacAuliffe seemed lost in his own reflections, whether about Amelia Bumgarten or his late friend, she didn't know. She said, "I'll get us some rooms and go talk to Brooks. I'll text you with the hotel. Can I drop you somewhere?"

"Nah, Amelia worked at the North House Folk School. It's that yellow building right next door. Later."

Hjørdis approached an empty slip. MacAuliffe trotted in her direction and grabbed the bowline while a deckhand stepped off with a stern line. What sailors around the world did when seeing one of their fellow mariners approaching the dock.

Martha had texted that she was running late. MacAuliffe nursed his stout under the unblinking gaze of John Wayne at My Sister's Place. Skis last used when Hiawatha paddled the shores of Gitche Gumee made an "X" on the wall over his head. Out the window, the sweet light of evening slanted sideways across the parking lot.

From a lifetime of habit, MacAuliffe had opened his computer and was organizing the day's information—facts of Rose's death, the conversation with Gould, quotes from the interview with Amelia's coworkers, reflections, observations. He never knew what might be required for a story—if he ever wrote a story again.

The interviews at the North House Folk School hadn't shed any insights into who or why someone wanted Amelia dead, but they had confirmed his growing belief that a vibrant and passionate life had been tragically snuffed out. The executive director broke down in tears upon hearing the news of Amelia's death and passed him off to the program director. The pockets of her Norwegian cardigan filling with used tissues, the program director showed him the cedar-strip kayak Amelia was building for her mother for Christmas—though "Amy always laughed that since they were much the same size, it was really a present for both of them." The room with its stacks of dried cedar slats, sawdust, and wood shavings smelled like a walk in the woods. Amelia's project sat off against the far wall, out of the way of the classroom space. The ribs and the cockpit had been shaped, and the bottom planks had been attached.

In the bright yellow building facing Highway 61, the gift store manager, a white-haired woman in her fifties, had been the only dried-eyed one, though MacAuliffe suspected it was personality, not lack of affection for the dead girl, that had kept her emotions in check. She seemed to be the type who'd organize the community into work details if Grand Marais were ever swept over by a forest fire.

MacAuliffe glanced around at the potpourri of items tacked to the wall with Hiawatha's skis—John Wayne, a beer sign, some brightly colored old miner's wash pans, an animal skin from a fox or a beaver or some such north woods creature. How did they fit together to tell the story of the tavern?

How did the pieces of Amelia's story fit together with her mother's? There was so little information to work with. He reminded himself that some investigative reports took him weeks, even months, to develop, finding people willing to talk on the record, analyzing documents, searching for the one crucial piece of information that would be the cornerstone for all the other pieces.

He knew Amelia's story was there. If he could just piece together the clues.

His identity as an investigative reporter depended on him unearthing the answers. He had to find out who murdered Amelia Bumgarten and her mom.

And then he had to write her story. For her. And for himself.

So much had been stripped away. Loss and failure had piled up until he now sat jobless, homeless, a man without purpose; he'd be defined only by his character. And that scared him.

Martha spied him at a table in the back corner. MacAuliffe was doing what she most often pictured him doing: typing on his computer, peering intently at the screen as if he knew all the right words lived in there, and like a giant jigsaw puzzle, it was his job to put all the pieces in order. John Wayne peered over his shoulder to assess his progress.

She slid into the opposite side and took a drink of his stout. A foam mustache lingered on her upper lip and she licked it off, all under his watchful gaze.

"Let me know if you need some help with that," he said.

She ignored his remark. "What'd you learn this afternoon?"

"That Amelia was making a cedar-planked kayak for her mom. That she was late to work at the gift store twice last month, and one Ms. Ingrid Johnssen, the gift store manager, questioned the work ethic of Amelia's entire generation and the parents who raised them. One time it meant she was late to her book club. They were reading a novel by someone named Duffy, called Cartographer something, but she doesn't know what the fascination is with all these war books. But she couldn't complain—even though she did—because Amelia was a natural salesperson—had 'the gift of gab'—always got people to buy something. Also thought Amelia was a little too free with the center's copy machine, as if ink and paper were free. Spent more time doing her homework than stocking the shelves. But, hey, Johnssen didn't run the place, as she reminded me. She's a go-along, get-along kind of gal. Told me herself."

"She sounds cheery," Martha said.

"Ms. Johnssen knew nothing, however, about who or why someone wanted Amelia or her mom dead," MacAuliffe said. She took another sip of his stout and licked her lips again. He shook his head. "Would you stop doing that."

"Come on, Mac, I'm teasing you. Lighten up."

"Martha, you don't tease. You're the last person in the world I'd expect to tease anyone."

"Good. I'm not too predictable then." The waitress arrived at the table, and Martha added, "Bring my friend another stout because I'm going to drink his, and what pizzas would you recommend?"

They settled on a thin crust chicken pizza with green olives, artichokes, spinach, sun-dried tomatoes, and feta cheese. Martha said, "And make it a large; I'm starving, and I may get hungry later."

"The large comes in six quarters," the waitress said. "The extra large has eight."

"Six quarters?" MacAuliffe asked.

"Bring us the extra large and ignore anything he says," Martha said.

MacAuliffe shook his head and rolled his eyes. When Martha laughed, he reached over and took his beer back. "How'd the interview with Brooks go?"

"Come on, Mac, weren't you ever young and stupid once? It's six pieces versus eight. Not quarters. But you know that, asshole." She reached for the beer again, and he pushed it back. "I discovered that Grand Marais is still in the height of tourist season this weekend. We may have the last room in town. You can sleep on the floor. Like in your Boy Scout days. And I found out where Nettles got his information about Rose and her daughter."

"Really. From whom?"

"Rose's boss, Tom Brooks. Seems not everyone shared Rose's views on the development. Brooks bought into Nettles' argument that the resort would bring jobs to Grand Marais. And they need jobs, he said, even if they aren't all the best paying. Didn't hurt that he's a committed golfer."

"People don't live here to golf. They live here to hike in the woods and fish and shovel snow and be closer to God and nature."

"Which Brooks' wife is very much committed to. All of her family lives here. Five siblings, aging parents, enough nieces and nephews to repopulate the Catholic Church. His words, not mine."

"And I always thought this was Lutheran country."

"Well, not entirely it seems. Nettles did a couple of land deals through Brooks over the years. When he approached Brooks about putting together a profile on Rose, Brooks accepted. Seemed money's been tight at the law firm, Nettles paid well, and promised to run all the real estate deals through his law firm.

"Ethics always evaporate with enough money," MacAuliffe said. "The only question is what's enough."

"I'm surprised you're surprised by that," Martha replied.

"I suppose I'm not. Just disappointed—again—at seeing how the real world works. Did Brooks say anything else?"

"He tried to justify it by saying he wasn't going to divulge anything that wasn't already public record. He didn't think it'd hurt. He was pro-resort anyway and it seemed to him that Rose had run out of options. So he took Nettles' money to give up Rose's life secrets."

"Wow! Betrayed by those who know you best. An attorney and her boss, no less. That's gotta hurt more than if it was just some creepy private investigator poking around the edges of her life for Nettles."

"Yeah," Martha said, her voice quiet. The image of Hewitt came to her unbidden, his long white hair pulled back in a ponytail, his long white beard shaking with laughter. She had loved him like a father.

As if he could read her mind, MacAuliffe reached out to take her hand. "I'm sorry, Martha. So sorry. That was thoughtless."

"And true," Martha said and tried to smile. It didn't work.

She pulled free of his hand and began pushing aside the condiments, Mac's computer and notebook. The waitress placed a hot pizza and a fresh round of beers on the table.

The aroma wafted up, and Martha decided to serve MacAuliffe first—otherwise he might not get any. Talking to the backstabbing partner had left her famished.

She devoured the first piece of pizza without looking at him or saying anything. When she did glance up, she said, "Sorry, I was hungry."

"No problem," MacAuliffe said.

He couldn't help but focus on the blue eye, startlingly clear. Her thick hair was raven black and had begun to curl over her ears. It gave her a smart, feisty appearance. Ebony eyebrows arched over those startling eyes. He shook his head to rid himself of the image and where his mind was taking him.

"How did Brooks take the news of Rose's death?" he asked.

"He seemed genuinely upset. He knew about her drug history when he hired her. She'd been completely forthright about her previous problem. Heroin. Brooks never saw any signs that she had started using again. He was shocked that her death was an overdose."

She grabbed another slice of pizza. "Brooks knew she was a licensed attorney, but he couldn't afford to pay her as an attorney, so she hired on as a paralegal. She worked a second job as a waitress during tourist season at the Angry Trout. She didn't talk much about her efforts to shut down Nettles; she knew his position on the resort."

"Did you call bullshit on him? From one attorney to another, of course. Giving up personal information on an employee to win the contract from Nettles."

"Of course. When I told him there was a concern that the report may be instrumental to the police investigation, he got real talkative. You know, the general CYA things we attorneys say when we're afraid to say anything. He got all defensive. Said he never meant Rose any harm. Nettles swore he wouldn't reveal his sources."

"What a backstabbing creep."

"Yeah." Martha flagged the waitress. She held up two fingers.

"I don't think I can eat another two pizzas," MacAuliffe said.

"Sometimes you're so funny you make yourself laugh. I'm surprised your sister didn't kill you growing up." She rolled her eyes and shook her head.

"What'd he say about Amelia?"

"Brooks said he included the incident from last summer when she and a bunch of other kids got busted for the party in the woods. It was public record, so he mentioned it. Apparently, Amelia was the only one there who Craig Junior found with pot. And she had several baggies of it. Brooks said speculation was the other kids had given her their pot because she was underage and would get off with only a hand slapping. Probably not unexpected but it all disappeared by the time the police arrived."

"So Buzz gets a little free pot, and Nettles interprets the facts in a way that's convenient for him." Frustration edged MacAuliffe's voice.

Martha took a bite of pizza. "Still doesn't explain why someone would kill them. Rose wasn't a threat to his development. Amelia wasn't involved. So why? There's something going on with the Bumgartens that we haven't uncovered yet."

"Did Brooks have any ideas?" MacAuliffe asked. "A disgruntled ex-husband? Someone she filed an abuse charge against? Someone who didn't like the way she wore her skirts or who she invited into her bedroom? The mob?"

"You watch too much television."

"If it's on TV, it must be true." MacAuliffe smiled. "It's how I get all my history."

Martha shook her head.

"Rose seemed to be on good terms with her ex," she said. "He's an attorney doing social justice work in the Cities. Sometimes he sent money when he had it; most of the time he didn't. She didn't seem to care. She let Amy decide if she wanted to see her dad. Sometimes she did. Most of the time she didn't. Brooks said his firm covers what lawyers always cover in small towns—estate planning, wills and power of attorney, an occasional divorce, a couple of delinquent fathers not making child support. They got an illegal logger off with a fine. He didn't know of anyone disgruntled enough to threaten her. She hadn't mentioned anything."

"So what did she uncover?" MacAuliffe asked. "Who did she offend?"

"Or maybe it was Amy who discovered it. And she shared it with her mom."

"Good point. We've been assuming that Amelia's murder was the byproduct of something Rose uncovered. Maybe it was the other way around."

Martha didn't respond, her attention drawn to the front of the restaurant. MacAuliffe followed her gaze. Silhouetted against the Leinenkugel's sign behind the bar, Craig Nettles Junior stood paying for a pizza. His baseball cap was pushed back and showed a friendly, animated face as he chatted with the cashier. A bag rested on top of the pizza box. Beside him stood a young girl of eight or ten, cheerful brown eyes scanning the room as if she were seeing Disney World for the first time. She wore faded jeans with rolled-up cuffs and a tee-shirt with pink sparkles. Her brunette hair was tied back in a ponytail.

Martha tossed MacAuliffe the car keys. "Slide out the back and see where Craig goes. I'll meet you at the MacArthur House. Google it. We're out back in the Spruce Cabin. It's blue with a purple door."

Before he could respond, she rose and wove her way between the tables until she stood beside them. Only then did Nettles notice her.

"You," he said, his voice stone cold.

"Hi, Craig," Martha said. "Marlena Berglund said you called in sick again today. Like yesterday. Called it the sunshine flu. Hope you're feeling better. We thought we should let you know we really aren't writing a story on the economic benefits of your father's resort. It was a way to get in to talk with him."

"So what're you doing in Grand Marais? Other than keeping me from my supper?"

"Enjoying the fall colors." She gave her best fake smile. "And investigating who killed the Bumgarten women. You did know Rose Bumgarten was found dead in her house this morning?"

"Yeah, small town. News travel fast. It's too bad."

"A friend?"

"I didn't know her. Met her a couple of times was all."

"Really? Seems the two most vocal opponents to your father's resort would know each other better, maybe even be allies in the good fight to save the wilderness."

"Do you have a point, or do you just like to hear yourself talk? Our supper's getting cold."

"I was also curious about your warning. Or was it a threat?"

"Just a fact. Nettles doesn't take to people who get in his way."

The use of "Nettles" startled her, and the young girl used the opportunity to tug on Craig's sleeve. "Can we go? I'm hungry."

"We're going right now, sweetie," Craig said.

Martha dropped to one knee. A red splotch like the remnants of someone's kiss or strawberry ice cream adorned the girl's cheek. "Hi, my name's Martha. What's your name? Are you and your dad picking up some pizza for supper?"

The girl nodded her head but added in a shy, high-pitched voice, "He's not my dad. He's Buzz."

Dimples formed in her cheeks when she smiled. A missing front tooth was visible with the smile.

"Well, I hope Buzz knows the tooth fairy."

"My mom says the tooth fairy doesn't exist."

"Lizzie, remember we don't talk to strangers," Nettles said.

The girl inched behind Nettles, still giving Martha the gap-tooth smile.

"Nice to meet you, honey," Martha said, standing up. To Craig, she added, "You know Amelia Bumgarten was killed in Duluth two days ago?"

"We're leaving," Craig said, to the girl. "Take my hand, sweetie." Balancing the pizza box in one hand and the holding the little girl's hand in the other, he stepped toward the door. Turning back, he said, "It's a tragedy what happened to the Bumgartens. It's too bad, but I didn't really know either of them personally."

She took a leap. "So what happened when your mom died, Craig?"

He seemed to hesitate before responding. "You don't know what you're getting into here. I told you before—leave it alone."

"Then explain it to me, Craig."

He pushed the door open and stepped out into the evening.

Martha hoped that MacAuliffe had had enough time to get

to the car. She watched from the front window as Nettles settled into his truck. The pizza box and bag went on the backseat. Through the windshield she could see him help Lizzie with her seatbelt. He laughed at something the girl said and fastened his own seatbelt. Buzz. The girl had called him Buzz. Curious.

A few moments after his truck exited the parking lot, she saw the rented Subaru pull out after them.

THIRTEEN

MacAuliffe had run out of the bar with his phone still on the tabletop, tucked back behind his open computer, both of them pushed against the wall with the arrival of the pizza. Martha had found them when she was picking up his things.

Three hours later there was still no sign of him.

Martha had been aware of the wind most of the evening, listening to it blow steadily from the southwest as she waited to hear from MacAuliffe. In front of the cabin, she sat in an Adirondack chair and watched the treetops sway and dance with the breeze. The trees were mostly birch with leaves just starting to turn golden. She waited outside as the oranges and reds of twilight faded to gray and then to charcoal.

With an extra blanket wrapped around her shoulders, she watched stars start to pop out against the arching black dome of the sky, becoming visible as if a mystic star keeper went from spot to spot and flipped a switch. Soon the keeper's nightly task was complete, and she gazed upon a heaven of brilliant pinpricks of light. The Milky Way, never visible against the man-made aura of a Seattle night, swept across the sky like a flowing river of silver stars. It reminded her of other times and other places.

A late-night car ride with Lance Trammell as he reminisced about how his father had taught him the constellations at the family cabin on Neah Bay, as far west as a person could go without wading into the Pacific Ocean. And he held her hand in silence as she told him how she'd first killed a man—without regrets, without second thoughts.

Waiting required patience, something she had little of tonight. She threw off the blanket and kicked off her shoes. Her toes planted in the cool grass she began to stretch—calves, hamstrings, thighs, back. Then she began to move. From the mountain pose she dropped to a downward dog. Rising she held the tree pose until she felt her leg begin to quiver. Her breathing flowed in and out. Her focus remained fixed on a dark spot in the trees out in front of her and the breaths filling and emptying her lungs. She repeated the pose balancing on her other leg. The warrior stance brought her into a fighting position, but she wasn't ready.

Since being shot, her left shoulder and arm required more stretching to loosen up. She grasped her left elbow and slowly worked her arm across her body until it rested tight against her chest. The pose lasted for a count of ten, twenty, then thirty. She shook out her arm and repeated it until she felt ready to again adopt the warrior stance. The movements of the *kata* started slow and flowing, and picked up speed with each twirl and thrust. Her shoulders and hands followed her legs. A kick, a twirl, a jab, and soon she was completely lost in the dance. Sweat began to form. Her breathing became jagged and gasping. Still she continued the dance of death.

Each time she envisioned Trammell dying in her arms she heard Yamamoto encouraging her find a new reason to use her talents, to discover a way through her pain and loss. Tragedy is part of being human, as you well know from the young women who seek your counsel, she heard her teacher say in his quiet, wise voice. Feeling pain and anger and frustration only makes you human. But it also leaves you open to the possibility for joy and happiness.

How do you move forward? Why do you move forward? What do you do next?

Yamamoto and his questions faded as she whirled to a stop. "I don't know," she shouted. "I don't know."

Yelling into the dark sent someone from the neighboring cabin scurrying back inside. The thought of dancing to an unseen audience forced her to smile at the absurdity of it all. She was now just some crazy lady screaming in the night. Which wasn't far from the truth, she supposed.

The cool grass under her feet, the sweet smell of the big lake, the breeze against her wet skin, the domed sky with its twinkling lights expanding to infinity, the song coursing through her body after the *kata*. She couldn't appreciate any of them.

Goddamn you, Mac, how could you not take your phone?

Earlier, when worry was just a mote beginning to worm into the back of her mind, she'd talked with her father, who informed her he had won four out of five days on "Jeopardy!" this week. I'm up forty-three thousand dollars, he announced, as if the check were in the mail. The twins were hovering around him like mother hens, and he'd visited Eddie in prison this week. Don't like the way he's getting all tatted up. He sends his love. Chippewa County has an opening for an attorney, honey. Love to have you home. Thanks, Dad, she said. Any chance you'll come out to Seattle for a visit? Don't really care for travelin' no more, Marti, you know that, he replied. Done enough of that when you were kids. And I ain't got no one to feed the damn cat if I take off like your sisters every time a north wind blows.

Might as well rent out their houses for as much as they're home. God knows they could use the extra money.

Martha knew they now coordinated their trips so both of them were never gone at the same time, but she hadn't called to argue with her father. Thank goodness they were there and concerned about him. Gotta go, Dad. Expect some lutefisk to show up in your mailbox. You save your money, honey. I'll be just fine eatin' pickled herring. Love you so much, Dad.

On her phone she made an entry in her tasks: Dad Lutefisk

A second call to Ray Palmer in Seattle went to voicemail after a couple of rings. "Just checking in, Ray. Let me know if everything's all right with Emily and the kids."

Her phone chimed with a text message. "All fine here quit worrying im on it cant talk Got a drunk in the car subdued w/ Byobu dashi – sp? – u taught me much thanks"

Now it was over three hours and no word from Mac.

Martha had been through all the scenarios—Craig Junior had driven to Duluth; the rental car had broken down someplace; MacAuliffe had been discovered and now lay dead or dying in the woods. Each possibility was worse than the previous one.

She sat, paced, worried, and fretted until the cold air began to seep into her bones, and she wrapped the blanket tightly around her and paced some more. The cabin light from the voyeuristic neighbor blinked off. She opened Mac's cell phone, planning to call Craig Senior to inquire where his son lived. Password protected! She swore under her breath, and tried to calculate the number of possible permutations in a five-digit password. She jammed the phone back in her pocket.

How did people survive before cell phones? Martha felt like a helicopter parent whose kid was late coming home from their first date. Every tragic possibility ran through her mind—again. How could Mac have run off without his cell phone? No one forgot their phone. People were more apt to run off without their shoes than their cell phones.

Goddamn it, Mac, talk to me.

The only responses were the chirping crickets and the rustling of the trees. Silver starlight flickered and danced through the fluttering leaves. The breeze off the lake had brought a chill. She pulled the blanket around her shoulders and up under her chin.

She jerked awake when something cinched around her neck and began cutting off her airway. Eyes flicked open to pitch black. She blinked to make sure they were really open. The boa constrictor wrapped around her neck coiled tighter and tighter. She struggled to sit up, but the blanket she'd earlier cocooned her body in for warmth now restricted all attempts to free her hands. The Adirondack chair creaked with her efforts. Someone was behind her, something around her neck, a bag over her head. Her attacker was silent, strong, strangling her, intent on killing her. She was close to passing out.

She snapped her head back, hard. It hit only chair. But the grip loosened just for an instant, and she gasped air before the cord tightened again. If not for the blanket that she'd tucked up high under her chin, the cord would've garroted her. Even with the blanket it would strangle her. It twisted tighter, and she thrashed and wiggled. Flogging about had worked her legs free of the blanket. They touched the ground.

Martha feigned giving in, giving up, allowing her body to go slack, all while her feet found purchase on the ground. And she knew she had only one chance. Her feet planted solid for leverage, she lunged backwards, screaming out in *kiai*, a scream that declared her fighting spirit, as much a weapon as her hands and feet. She screamed long and loud. Her hands suddenly free she clawed at the cord around her throat.

Her assailant was prepared for the move. They rolled backwards together, both flipping from chair to ground with an audible thud. The assailant, now on top, slammed her face into the dirt, the cord constricting again. She kicked and torqued her body and shifted her weight to no avail. Knees pinned her shoulders to the ground, hands wrenched tighter on the cord.

About to pass out, she heard a scream.

Something crashed into her, and the weight on top of her vanished. Suddenly breath came back to her lungs in long, ragged gasps. She tore at the hood over her face. Years of training had her up and in a fighting crouch in an instant. Flickering dots of light passed before her eyes, but soon they began to focus in the darkness. She spun to catch sight of anyone, anything. Someone lay on the ground, curled in a fetal position. The obscure silhouette of someone ran for the woods behind the cabin and disappeared into the trees.

A loud groan and a long string of curses escaped the fallen person. Mac.

Martha knelt beside him, a hand on his shoulder. Still her eyes scanned the woods for their attacker. Ready, alert. Blood and adrenaline coursing through her. Begging the person to return, she shouted a *kiai* challenge, this time a war cry. Let's finish this here and now. They'd quickly learn that Martha didn't fight fair either. Only the wind blowing through the trees responded.

"Mac, can you move?" she said, slowly moving around him, scanning three-sixty for any sign of attack, any shadow out of place. She forced her breath to slow down into long inhales and exhales. Don't focus on the sweet luxury of still being able to breathe. Focus on staying alive.

Mac rolled over to his knees, his head touching the ground. "Fucking kicked me in the balls. Oh, that hurts." He began to stand up and quickly collapsed again. He lay there curled in the fetal position, moaning.

The Adirondack chair lay on its side, the blanket strewn across the ground beside it. Under the blanket she found a cell phone and punched in 911.

FOURTEEN

"You two certainly know how to spoil a good weekend," Sheriff Steven Gould said, pulling up a chair in front of Martha, their knees almost touching. He flipped through the report taken at the scene by one of his deputies. Dressed in a navy-blue tee-shirt and khaki pants, he'd been waiting for them at the Cook County Sheriff's Office when they arrived by squad car to the new red brick building on the edge of town. "Tell me again what happened."

"I'd fallen asleep outside," Martha began without preamble, and proceeded to tell of the attack as clearly and concisely as she could. A short, sharp declaration of the facts, as best she knew them, laid out in a straightforward chronology of events. Simplicity without ambiguity. Gould listened without interrupting. Her voice remained quiet, soft. It hurt too much to speak above a whisper. A mug of hot tea helped a little, and she sipped from it frequently. She concluded, "Mac saved my life when he tackled the guy. I was about ready to pass out. The guy was skilled. He anticipated my reaction and rolled with the backflip without ever losing his grip. Just like I would've done if our positions had been reversed."

"Let me look at your neck, honey." Gould leaned forward, and a finger traced a line around her throat. "That's a nasty l welt you got there. Sure you're okay? Maybe have the doc examine it? Might wanna put some antibiotic cream on your nose, as well. Got a good raspberry there."

"I'll be fine," she said.

Gould sat back. A gray stubble lined his multiple chins. His hair was cut short in the manner of police officers around the world. Only a hint of thin, wispy angel hair remained on his crown, a fact that had been hidden earlier since he'd never removed his hat. Turning his attention to MacAuliffe, he said, "And you? How come you weren't with your sweetheart from the beginning?"

MacAuliffe shifted uncomfortably in the chair. Gould's hands were clasped across his stomach, and he waited. Her friend's lips moved but either there were too many words tripping over each other to get out or there were no words at all. Martha could see him composing himself.

"I'd asked him to tail Craig Nettles, Craig Junior, out of the restaurant," she said, giving Mac time to gather his thoughts.

"Please, Martha, you just sip your tea and rest that voice of yours. It's your boyfriend's turn to natter away on this and that." He turned back to MacAuliffe. "So you weren't there to protect your sweetie 'cause you had a bee in your bonnet about Mr. Forest Ranger. Wanna tell me all about it, son?"

"We ran into Craig Junior at the pub, My Sister's Place," MacAuliffe said. "He had a young girl with him."

"Craig called her Lizzie," Martha said. A scowling Gould cut her off from saying anything else.

"They were picking up a pizza to go," MacAuliffe continued. "I thought it'd be a good idea to follow them. I ran out of the restaurant but forgot my phone. Maybe a mile outside of town, to the northwest, I think, they stopped at a little house backed up to the woods."

"Yeah, that'd be where Craig lives," Gould said. "Lizzie. Probably Lena Berglund's youngest. She's adopted, and sometimes Craig will babysit her when Lena pulls the weekend shift. Craig probably needs the babysitting money." He chuckled. "What were they doing?"

"They ate the pizza, then some popcorn, and watched a movie," MacAuliffe said. "*Frozen*, I think."

"People are getting killed, and you're peeking in the windows? Do you just do stupid things or are you really that stupid?" Gould shook his head in disbelief.

"The jury's still out on that one," MacAuliffe replied.

"Don't be a smartass with me, young man," Gould barked. "And I'm dead serious on that. Both of you could've been killed out there tonight. It's not gonna happen on my watch. No more going rogue."

Martha held her head in her hands and shook her head at the image of Craig Junior and the young girl. Memories of another late night watching television came flooding back to her. That's how it started. A motel, some whiskey after a long day of driving, Johnny Carson and a scared young girl who didn't know how to prevent the wandering hands of her father's best friend. Her voice soft, she asked, "Did you see . . . see anything inappropriate?"

"Nothing," MacAuliffe said. "They sat on opposite ends of the couch, the pizza and then a big bowl of popcorn between them. She fell asleep during a second movie, and Buzz picked her up and carried her off. To bed, I presume. Buzz came back and started turning off lights. That's when I headed back to town. But because I forgot my phone, I couldn't Google directions to the MacArthur House. I asked for directions at the Holiday station on Broadway. The guy working didn't know the place, but he Googled it on his phone. His name was Russ."

Gould nodded and made a note.

"When I arrived the place was dark except a nightlight on the front porch of the office," MacAuliffe continued. "But Martha had told me we were in a cottage out back, the Spruce Cabin, purple with a blue door or blue with a purple door. I couldn't remember. I figured I'd be able to find it. When I came around the corner, I saw them wrestling in the grass. I didn't know what was going on, but then I heard Martha scream and knew she was in trouble. I rushed over to help. You've heard the rest."

"So you've told me what you did, son, but you failed to mention why you did it. Why is usually so much more interesting, don't you think? So how about you open that reporter's notebook and tell me what prompted you to follow young Mr. Nettles in the first place?"

"How is that relevant, Sheriff?" Martha asked. "Two people are already dead, and someone was determined to make me the third victim less than an hour ago."

"Ma'am, did you ever consider they might all be related? But of course you did. You're too smart for your own good, it seems. Word is all over town about Rosie and Amy being dead. ME confirmed it was fentanyl, by the way. Only a few hundred times more potent than the big H. Also found some of it in Amy's room, along with a nice supply of weed. All tucked away in a dresser drawer under her privates. So had Rosie fallen into bad habits again and was being supplied by her goodie-two-shoes daughter? Or had someone given Rosie a deadly dose of this nasty fentanyl shit and set up our dead local honor student for the fall? Now, I'm inclined to believe the latter, as you journalistic types say, but till we get our inquiries done, we won't know."

Gould's false smile never left his face. "The Cook County Sheriff's Office and our friends in Duluth are doing due diligence and checking out all possibilities. Now have you considered the possibility you might've brought the attack on your sweetie here 'cause you been a little too fast and loose with your questions and opinions? You ain't exactly been secret about your inquiries. Lena, the North House, Tom Brooks, even Junior. Did I miss anyone? Probably, but it's a small town, I'll hear about it eventually. Everyone knows each other, everyone talks. Some to me, some to my officers who talk to me, some to their neighbors. But people know. If someone did murder the two Bumgartens, they sure as hell know you're in town searching for 'em. Maybe they were following you, eating their pepperoni pizza right beside you at My Sister's. You split up and that gave 'em an opportunity. It almost succeeded."

"It would have succeeded if Mac hadn't jumped in," Martha said. She reached over and quickly squeezed MacAuliffe's hand. To the Sheriff, she added, "Does anyone in Grand Marais call Craig Junior 'Buzz'?"

Gould didn't respond at first to the change of topic. Finally, he said, "Heard him called a lot of things. Not all of them I can repeat to the church choir, but never heard him called Buzz."

"I talked to the girl briefly at the restaurant," Martha said. "Mac wasn't there. She said Buzz wasn't her father, but she called him Buzz. That's his family nickname."

"Well, solving that mystery doesn't seem real high on my list of priorities right now."

"He also warned me again about not getting involved. He told me, quite emphatically, to 'Leave it alone.'"

Gould studied Martha with intense eyes. "Why would he warn you like that?"

"Who stands to benefit if the old man goes down for killing

the Bumgartens?" MacAuliffe asked. "Nettles made it clear Buzz was the only remaining heir in the family."

"So your thinking is," Gould started, "the son is setting up the old man for the fall for the murders of Rose and Amy Bumgarten? The problem with having a good imagination is you can imagine all kinds of wrong things. Would Craig kill Rose and set up the old man over this development? Why would he risk the gravy train to stop it?"

"Maybe it's not about the resort at all but about the family money," Martha said.

"So why not wait until it's developed?" Gould asked. "Then there'd be even more to inherit. Right now, it's just a whole lotta forest. And murder? Two murders? Craig already stands to inherit the old man's millions so why risk it by killing two people? That seems to require something more. I'm thinking we should be peeling back the covers to find that one raw emotion, something so hurtful that it's worth killing over. That's what can lead to murder. And I'm thinking that's not someplace where duffers can spoil a good walk by whacking a little white ball around."

Gould turned his attention to MacAuliffe, "Was that Craig you took a lick at for attacking your sweetie?"

MacAuliffe shifted uncomfortably in his chair. "No. No, it wasn't Craig's. He's a big dude. Easily larger than Martha. This guy wasn't. He was smaller, lighter than that. When I hit him, he moved. If I'd remembered my football drills about wrapping them up after a tackle, we wouldn't be having this conversation. I hit him but didn't get my arms around him. That gave him a chance to get away. But it wasn't Buzz."

"Don't beat yourself up, son. You might've washed out on the football field, but you saved your honey. That's worth a score in my book any day."

"Sheriff, please," MacAuliffe sighed and shook his head. "We're friends and colleagues, but we're not 'sweeties.' Two people are dead. Martha could've been next. We're friends, got it? Just friends. Christ almighty!"

"Yes, Christ is frigging mighty," Gould said, making the sign of the cross. "I apologize for upsetting your delicate sensibilities. Didn't know you were such a sensitive kind of guy. But how about helping me out a little here. Did you get a peek at the other guy? See anything that might help us identify him?"

MacAuliffe shook his head again. "It was dark. He wore dark clothes, a dark jacket. I remember grabbing the sleeve as we tumbled. Maybe a nylon windbreaker. But he was up fast, and it slipped out of my hand. Then he kicked me. I think he wore boots." He shifted in his chair as if trying to sidestep the memory of the kick to the groin. "After that I was seeing stars. Not much help, I'm afraid."

"Maybe this has nothing to do with the resort," Martha said. "Murdering Rosie was just the opportunity to take him down. We don't know anything about Nettles' past or other business dealings. He has to have made some enemies along the way."

Gould's head nodded as he caught the line of Martha's reasoning. "The old man ain't always been an altar boy on the way to fattening the golden calf of his northern Minnesota fortune, I'm sure."

"Might not even be about money," Martha continued. "A pissed husband? A scorned woman? How long's he been a widower? There were rumors of a girlfriend when his wife died. There was one sexual assault charge that must've been settled out of court. Were there others? Could someone be framing him or blackmailing him?

Gould shifted under their unceasing attention. A thick hand wiped his brow, and he shook his head. "Not much, not really.

He's Duluth, we're the North Shore. The two get together only when we wait on their tables. I've met the man a few times over the years. Town meetings, a couple of times in the office. He was a damn war hero, saved some buddies. Of course he pulls that patriotic pile of dung when he's working the crowd. Never knew his wife. Craig Junior's lived up here for better part of a decade so most of us eventually found out that his sister didn't come home from this latest damn forever war. Losing a kid's a mightier test of the soul than any father should have to endure. Know how I'd feel if one of my kids didn't make it home."

For a time nobody spoke.

"But Amelia?" MacAuliffe asked. "How do you account for her? She believed someone wanted to kill her mom. If Rose was targeted as a way to get to Nettles, why did they have to take her out, as well? She was too hard to track down; the act was too intentional, too violent to be collateral damage."

Gould sat back in his chair, arms crossed. "You got a different theory?"

"I think we don't know enough right now. Better to gather facts and then develop a theory than have a theory and only gather the facts that support it."

"Seems I've been saying that since we met. But I suspect you've got a theory anyway."

"What if Rose really was the target?" MacAuliffe said. "What if this has nothing to do with Nettles at all? What if she stumbled on something else while out in the woods? Something that our midnight ninja wants to keep very quiet? Rose was the target and Amelia was a necessary casualty because of what she *might* know. And her running just confirmed it."

"Still doesn't explain why they attacked your sweetie."

MacAuliffe let it go. Against fools the gods themselves struggled in vain. It was the only thing he remembered from

Schiller, but it had been a touchstone of so much of his reporting. He also recalled something that Lance had once said when they were investigating the gang-related activity that had moved into Ballard. MacAuliffe said, “Violence is a heavy wheel that spins of its own momentum.”

A deputy entered and gave the sheriff a quick nod. The sheriff stood up. To Martha and MacAuliffe, he said, “You kids get some shut-eye now. Deb, here, will take you back. If I have any more questions, I got your numbers. And I have every expectation you’ll be back in Duluth before I talk to you again. If you’re not, I can’t tell you how disappointed I’ll be.”

FIFTEEN

She found MacAuliffe outside, his face lit by the faint ember of a cigarette as he took another drag. Treetops bent and swayed with the increasing wind. Lightning flashed in the distance, a spidery streak of bright white against the black sky. MacAuliffe sat in an Adirondack chair beside the cabin door, positioned so no one could get in and no one could approach him from behind.

"Couldn't sleep either?" she asked, her voice quiet. "Or standing guard?"

"The former probably led to the latter," he whispered back. "You?"

"Must've dozed off because I didn't hear you leave, though I swear I've been awake the whole time."

"You know you snore?"

"No wonder you've been single this long."

"So who's the girl? His daughter? Spending the weekend with dad?"

"I don't know," Martha said. "She said she was having pizza with Buzz, not her dad. Little kids aren't usually as adept at lying to adults."

"Buzz. Interesting. Throughout history, fathers have hidden behind other names—friend, uncle, pope."

Lightning again splintered across the sky, a thick bolt descending from the heavens to earth. They were silent, each counting Mississippi one, Mississippi two, Mississippi three before thunder rumbled through the night.

"I still love a Midwest thunderstorm," MacAuliffe said, crushing out his cigarette and placing the butt in his pocket.

"Seems late in the season for a thunderstorm," Martha said.

"Late, I suppose, but not unusual. Weather's all out of whack everywhere."

"At Gran's in Sault Ste. Marie, my sister Rachel and I slept in the attic, and the thunder and lightning scared her. We'd curl up together and make a game out of counting the time between lightning and thunder. Gran had an old metal roof on the house. I loved to hear the rain on the roof. The sound varied so much—steady drumming to sudden crescendos. I thought it was magical and imagined the gods fighting in the heavens." After a pause, she added, "Rachel was afraid of a lot of things."

Another bolt of lightning had them both counting for a moment. When the thunder passed, MacAuliffe said, "I can't imagine you afraid of anything."

"I was afraid of dying here tonight. He was good and he caught me by surprise. When I did manage something, he expected it. He's been trained. I didn't think I'd make it. Thank you for not letting that happen. That took a lot of guts."

"Ignorance is bliss. I didn't know what I was doing, just that you were in trouble. Your scream scared me into action."

"It was supposed to scare him, but obviously it didn't. Another few seconds and I would've passed out." She leaned down and kissed MacAuliffe on the cheek. "Thanks. Nice to know you've got my back."

"Hey, don't let that country bumpkin of a sheriff see that. Might think you're sweet on me."

"Let him. I don't care. But don't believe for a moment that he's a country bumpkin. That's all an act. He's sharp, curious. He's trying to figure this out just like we are. He's spot on about identifying someone whose raw emotions are twisted out of balance. Only he got started two days later than we did, and he's got to play by the rules. If he doesn't, the whole case can be thrown out in court. But we don't have to play by the same rules."

He held out the keys that he'd palmed to the Bumgarten house. "You thinking what I'm thinking?"

"Can't sleep anyway."

They sat in the car and peered down the street at the Bumgarten house. A front porchlight cast a feeble halo upon a cement pad. The windows were all dark. The kitchen light that MacAuliffe had turned back on was again off. No movement came from the house or along the street, except the whipping tops of the trees that bent and rose. An occasional gust buffeted the car.

Over the top of the trees, the sky suddenly lit up with a flash of lightning, a fractured windowpane of bright light. He counted the seconds before a boom of thunder shook the air. It was close and coming closer.

"Let's get inside before the storm hits," he said.

"First, put on these," Martha said, holding out a pair of latex gloves.

"What else you got in your Hermione bag? An umbrella? A truth wand would be useful right now."

"It's lonely being an adult," she said. "I stopped at a drug store on my way to the B & B. I also bought you a toothbrush and a pair of pajamas—just in case you had any ideas about sleeping in the buff."

"You thought of everything." He slipped the gloves on and snapped the edges at the wrists. The first drops of rain smacked the windshield like bugs on the freeway.

"I could lose my law license for this, you know. Felony breaking and entering, at a crime scene no less, are grounds for revoking my license."

The risks Martha might be taking to investigate this story had never occurred to MacAuliffe. The attack at the Spruce Cabin had almost cost her her life. Now she was willing to take the chance she could be disbarred? He said, "I'm sorry. It never dawned on me. Why don't you sit this one out? You've risked enough. I'll go in, do a quick reconnoiter, and get out."

She pushed open the door. "No way. If someone's waiting in there for you, you'll need me. 'In for a penny, in for a pound,' as Gran used to say. Of course, she usually said it when she was playing blackjack at the casino. Let's go."

They sprinted down the block, coming in out of the rain at the side door. He peered through the partially open curtain into the empty kitchen, seeing and hearing nothing except his own shallow gasps. He slowly inserted the key and waited for the next flash of lightning. It came in short order. The thunder rolling across the landscape drowned out the snap of the deadbolt unlocking.

They paused in the mudroom, their eyes growing accustomed to the faint light that filtered in from the kitchen window. They crept through the cluttered kitchen and down the messy hall. Outside of the bedroom that doubled as an office, Martha placed a hand on his arm, and whispered, "Something's different."

"It should be. People have been here all day."

"No, it doesn't smell the same."

They both sniffed the air. MacAuliffe said, "The toilet's backed up or something."

"Yeah." She crept to the door of the office and flashed a quick light inside. She jumped back. "Berglund's in there, slumped over the desk."

"Dead?"

"I don't know," Martha said. "But some people's sphincter lets go when they die. It's a natural reflex of the body. We discover another dead person and no one's going to believe we aren't involved."

"But we're not."

"Tell that to Gould."

"We can't walk out if she's in trouble."

Suddenly, they were blinded by light. MacAuliffe squinted at the glare and blinked several times before the thin, gaunt face and thick red hair of Marlena Berglund came into focus. She rubbed her neck, rolled her shoulders, and yawned. Her face contained the contradictory expressions of a bemused parent who knew that she, too, had once broken the rules, and anger at their having broken the rules. She just shook her head.

"You two make more noise than teenage girls at a sleepover," she said. "I expected you a couple of hours ago. Left the bathroom window open for you, but you must've stolen a house key. Smart."

"What's that smell?" MacAuliffe said, by way of greeting.

"A dirty diaper," Berglund replied. She disappeared back into the office.

"Seems we crashed your party," MacAuliffe said through the open door. "I'm afraid I should've taken Martha's advice. She insisted this was a really bad idea."

Berglund appeared in the doorway holding a baby against her shoulder. "Oh, stuff it."

She bounced the baby and cooed softly to her. Bald and smiling, the baby was fascinated with Berglund's ear, grabbing it with fingers that resembled the tentacles on a tiny squid.

"I've got no jurisdiction here," Berglund said. "This is Gould's crime scene." To the baby she added, "Come on, honey, let grandma change your diaper."

Berglund disappeared with the child into the bathroom.

Martha directed her voice toward the unseen forest ranger. "You want to explain what's going on here?"

"Keeping the two of you out of trouble," Berglund shouted back. "You made it pretty clear this morning at the office that Jimmy Mac here was pretty skilled at a little B&E. All in the pursuit of journalistic truth, I'm sure. But the question is, what are *you* doing here?"

"Trying to establish a connection between the deaths of Amy and Rose," Martha said. "Have you found anything so far?"

"Nothing."

The toilet flushed, and Berglund reappeared with the child strapped to her chest. He, she, it? cooed softly around a pacifier in its mouth. Berglund continued bouncing the baby while she talked, making it seem as normal as Gould interrogating them over lunch.

"Talked to Mark Monahan in Duluth," Berglund said. "Told me Amy was killed by a homemade bomb, some C4 wedged between fuel tank and frame. Would've taken about ten seconds to put in place if you know what you're doing. Used a simple electronic switch to trigger the blasting cap, detonated by remote control. Could've been a phone or a control for a wireless car or airplane. They're tracking down the C4, but everything else's available at any Radio Shack or hobby store. Rose died of an overdose, but you already suspected that, I'm sure. No one's acting like it's a suicide. I've been going through her notebooks. She's got books of field notes and graphs and water quality tables, and none of them are close to problematic."

"Well, we're missing something," MacAuliffe said.

"A regular Sherlock Holmes," Berglund said. "Even us trail jockeys can see that. No wonder you big city folks can't ever see the forest for the trees. You see the obvious and announce it like God tattooed it on your pecker. Why don't you take your coonskin cap and magnifying glass back home if that's all the help you're gonna be."

"You know, Sher—" MacAuliffe stopped, figuring this was probably not a good time to point out that Sherlock Holmes wore a deerstalker hat. "I'm just saying—"

"Well, quit saying it," she snapped. "At least when Hunter shits her diapers she does it because she doesn't know better. You oughta know better."

Her sun-weathered faced glared at them, eyes intense, determined and, yes, kind. When neither responded, she said, "Okay, here're the rules—we're a team. Full disclosure. You come up with something, anything, you tell me. I'll do the same. Rosie was a friend of mine. This is personal."

"What am I searching for?" Martha asked, joining Berglund at Rose's desk.

"Whatever you were planning to look for when you broke in," Berglund said.

Topographical maps of Superior National Forest were pinned to the wall, edges of one map trimmed so it seamed perfectly with the next. Red, white, yellow and blue pins, each with a corresponding number, dotted the maps. They were mostly clustered south of town. All of the pins were in the Gunflint District of the national forest.

"Is there a legend?" Martha asked.

"Volume one of the notebooks," Berglund said, tapping one of the three-ring binders on the desk. "Red pins are places where she took her baseline readings and initial water quality samples; white are second and third water quality readings; blue are farms and residences; and yellow are notes and observations. Mostly wildlife sightings—bear scat, an eagle's nest, a moose and calf, that kind of thing."

Berglund stood and pointed at a yellow pin that seemed to be in the middle of the forest. "Here, Rosie noted that someone's been doing some illegal logging, near Rosebud Creek between Seven and Birch Drive. Small clearing, probably someone cutting firewood, maybe a little extra to sell. Gonna have to check out the tree poachers."

Martha rose and pointed to an arc of red and white pins that ran north and northwest out of Grand Marais. "Why did she stop here? The map continues up to Grand Portage and the Canadian border."

"She's posted all of Superior National Forest here. That line is the Gunflint Trail, County Road 12. One of the main roads into the Boundary Waters. In the summer it gets so busy you'd think you were still in the Cities. We've issued about a hundred and fifty thousand permits this year for our good citizens to take to the backwoods where we have to be ready to rescue them at any time. Each permit can include up to nine people. The reason the locals tolerate it and Nettles is interested in his resort is folks spend money here, lots of it. Gonna be upwards of sixty million of their hard-earned shekels this year to recreate in God's little green acre. Gives jobs to folks like me and outfitters and resort owners and grandmas selling homemade wild huckleberry pies. Nettles wants a piece of the action. The way I figure it is since Rose was attempting to put the brakes on the resort, which'd be down here—" she pointed to the stretch of waterfront along

Highway 61 south of town—"that she didn't need to monitor further north."

"Methodology to her research?" Martha asked.

"All I know is what I just told you. Rose didn't share much with me. Wasn't real trusting with what she was up to."

Martha recalled how Amy had told MacAuliffe that her mom had insisted she trust no one. Rose had to know that not everyone agreed with her position opposing the resort. Did her suspicions include her forest ranger friend? Berglund's tanned, gaunt face studied the map. Did Berglund have another interest in investigating what Rose had discovered? Was her interest more personal than she let on?

"She was an attorney by education but worked as a paralegal," Martha said, coming back to the maps, trying to make sense of it all. "Did she also have a background in environmental sciences? Did she have a lab set up somewhere? She could take the water quality samples, but did she also analyze them? It's possible; most folks in law school start from other backgrounds. I studied archeology and cultural anthropology. Rose could've been a science major in her undergraduate days, but someplace there'd be evidence she was doing her own work. Does the National Forest Service have a lab? Was she using a spare bedroom, the garage? What equipment would you need? It'd have to be more than just a microscope, I'm sure. How do they even do water quality analysis? And where are the water quality samples? She wouldn't just flush them down the toilet, would she?"

"Told me once she was sending them down to the U, but what department, what professor, what campus, wouldn't have the foggiest."

The extended conversation had disturbed the baby Hunter who let out a couple of small whimpers. That quickly evolved into a series of choked cries. Soon she was in full meltdown, deep wails coming from her tiny body that were only partially muffled by being projected into Berglund's chest.

In a quiet soprano, the ranger began to sing, "Hush little baby, don't say a word, Mama's gonna buy you a mockingbird." When she'd finished the lullaby, she started all over, replacing Mama with Grandma. Soon the baby was asleep again.

"That was lovely," Martha said, offering the woman and child a faint smile. Still, Rose hadn't told Amy to run to Berglund if there was trouble. She'd advised her daughter, Trust no one. "Maybe you could sing me to sleep, too. After tonight, I could use a lullaby."

Martha hummed the familiar melody.

"Storm keep you awake? Just an old-fashioned thunderstorm. Didn't picture you being afraid of a little spat between Odin and the missus."

Of course Berglund didn't know about the attack. How long has she been here studying charts and graphs on water quality? At least a couple of hours. Martha sucked on her lower lip. She also knew that with police officers, there was never such a thing as full disclosure. Rose hadn't trusted the woman who now claimed to be her friend, and Martha would be wise to follow the woman's lead. Still, the attack was public record. This was a time to earn some trust.

"A few hours ago, someone tried to kill me," Martha said. "He was good, and he was serious. I'd be dead right now if Mac hadn't heard us fighting."

For the first time, she assessed the NFS officer. Her long hair could have been worn up under a stocking cap. Smaller than Nettles certainly. Would she have had the specialized training? Police officers often did, but National Forest Service officers? They carried guns and had to take care of problems with the public, with poachers, with illegal camping and logging. They must have some training. But did it include hand-to-hand combat? Her attacker had been skilled—and trained. Was Marlena a vet with Special Forces training? She would've had plenty of time to get over here while they sat with Gould at police headquarters. Had MacAuliffe's counterattack left any visible clues? No grass stains on the knees of her faded jeans. They weren't freshly laundered. No sign of fresh dirt on white but well-worn sneakers. Mac thought the person who attached her had been wearing boots.

Of course, none of it meant anything.

"What happened?" Berglund said, after the awkward silence.

"I was outside waiting for Mac to return. I had dozed off. Someone threw a bag over my head and was trying to strangle me." Martha proceeded to relate the main points of the past couple of hours. When she finished, she smiled. "That's why we were late breaking in."

"Wow, just glad you made it at all. Had no idea. You've told Sheriff Gould, of course?"

"Yeah. We were with him for over an hour."

"You've scared someone," Berglund said. She softly bounced from foot to foot for the sake of Hunter. "And it seems the God-fearing, outdoor-loving folks of Grand Marais have a murderer in our midst."

"Anyone come to mind?" Martha asked.

"Ain't seen no one walking down Broadway with a Glock strapped to his hip and a garrote in his hand, if that's what you're wondering."

"They're not usually that obvious," Martha said. When she noticed Berglund rolling her eyes, she add, "Sorry."

"Leave the mansplainin' to the men. They just take a little longer getting to where you and I already arrived."

Martha smiled for the first time all evening.

She quickly turned somber again. "Unless it was a crime of passion, murderers tend to be smart, devious, manipulators. It's probably someone else's fault, never their own. Paranoia and cold-hard fear may play a part. My guess is it's someone who's really angry, full of rage. They're just skilled at hiding it."

"Sounds like you've known a few folks that fit the bill."

Now was not the time for full disclosure. She didn't trust Berglund enough to bare her soul and give her a possible weapon. Martha said, "Read about them in a book. Opening my own firm left me with few clients and lots of time."

"Yeah, bet it was called the Book of Life."

Martha ignored the probe. "Most people never see through a murderer's façade. So who's only pretending to be normal?"

"And what did you and your boyfriend uncover that scared him so much that he had to kill you next?"

SIXTEEN

MacAuliffe leaned against the doorjamb as he watched and listened to the two women talk. Martha was on edge, her taut body and tight voice communicating an underlying intensity that Berglund wasn't picking up on as she rocked the baby nestled against her chest. Someone had tried to kill her mere hours ago. Finding Amelia's killer had now become personal for Martha, as well. It was one thing to take out an unsuspecting couple of reporters, as she had done to him and Lance on the Lake Union houseboat, but MacAuliffe had sat through the trials and heard the stories of what had happened in Utah before Martha returned home to take down an armed police officer, leaving him with a broken jaw, ruined knee, and pinned to the floor with a nail gun.

Who better to see through the tricks of a murderer than someone who already knew all the tricks? He studied Martha with fresh eyes.

MacAuliffe made some noise as he entered the room. "I've been wondering if something else might be going on, as well."

"Like what?" Berglund asked, turning to face him. She held a notebook in hands that were lean and sinewy from a lifetime of work spent in the woods of northern Minnesota. Her deep brown eyes held him.

"Well, I've been searching Amelia's room. Gould told us they found some drugs—most likely fentanyl and a stash of marijuana—in her undies drawer. Not a particularly good hiding place—unless you want to ensure someone's going to find it. But I'm puzzled by what we're not finding, or at least what we're not *seeing*. There's nothing that might explain or even hint at why someone killed the Bumgartens and decided to attack Martha. Amelia's room is too neat and tidy. Where're her schoolbooks, her homework? There's no sheets of music for the avid violin player, no scripts to read for the theatre student. Nothing that screams here was the life of an active and engaged high school junior. Nothing. The police wouldn't have confiscated all of it and tidied the room up behind them. So where are the missing pieces?"

"Wonderful powers of observation, Sherlock," Berglund said. "But how does that tell us anything about what happened to Amy or her mom?"

"I don't know," MacAuliffe said. "When I talked with Ingrid Johnssen at the North House Folk School, she complained Amelia spent more time doing homework than restocking shelves. She had to have her schoolwork with her to do that. But Monahan told us there was nothing in the truck besides her body and her cell phone. He said everything leaves some residue. A nylon backpack would've melted but it would've left some residue."

"That missing backpack's still bothering you," Martha said.

"Yeah. It only makes sense that if Rose told Amelia to run if anything happened to her and said that her father would know what to do, she had to be taking some kind of information to him. It had to be in that backpack. She didn't go home to change clothes or even pick up her toothbrush. She had to be carrying her schoolbooks—and she had to be carrying something to her dad, something she already had with her."

"You're thinking they had to take her backpack before blowing up your truck," Martha said.

"It fits the evidence," MacAuliffe replied. "Or the lack of it, anyway."

"But the schoolteacher didn't see any of that and she was there feeding the birds when Amy got in the truck to leave."

"I know."

"They stole it before she got in the truck," Berglund said.

"But why get in the truck then?" MacAuliffe said.

"She could've been unconscious."

"But Mark Monahan said there was no physical evidence of assault, and Ester P would've seen them dragging a body to my truck. If Amelia was conscious when she climbed into my truck, she would've raised holy hell in the parking lot when they were stealing her bag. Again, Ester would've heard that."

"They had to know she was going to your truck," Martha said. "Mark said it was an explosive attached to the fuel tank. Even if quick, it would've taken a minute or two to do it. Ester didn't see anyone else besides Amelia."

"If her school bag's like either of my kids," Berglund said, "she'd need a forklift to move it. She had your keys. She might've dropped it off rather than carry it with her."

"Of course," Martha said. "They could've stolen the bag and planted the explosive while she was gone. They had time, while neither the schoolteacher nor Amy were there. They didn't know what her mom had told her, so they felt it necessary to silence her and do it in an obvious way that led the police back to discover Rose's body. So they waited and blew up the truck when she got back."

"Makes sense," MacAuliffe said. "Now I'm wondering if somebody didn't find what they were after. If Amelia had the information in the backpack, why attack you?"

MacAuliffe let Martha reach the obvious conclusion.

"The midnight attacker thought you and I now have the information," she said.

"But we don't."

"But they don't know that. And the possibility exists that we do. So we become liabilities. Ones to be eliminated."

"A lot of 'ifs' and 'maybes' and 'could'ves' that lead to a pretty shaky conclusion," Berglund said.

"You come up with anything better?" MacAuliffe said. "We'd love to hear it."

"It wasn't your neck being garroted," Martha added.

Berglund shook her head. "Not yet, no, but I got a lot of notebooks to go through yet."

The baby whimpered in her sleep, a tiny thumb creeping toward its guppy mouth. Berglund gently shooed it away.

Martha breathed a sigh of relief. MacAuliffe didn't believe in full disclosure either. If the bag had been taken from the girl after departing the boat and before the truck explosion, and if the perps believed they now had some vital information—two big ifs, she realized—then the logical place to search for the missing evidence was aboard the *Virginia V*. If it had been emptied by the frightened teenager before attempting to steal Mac's truck. She knew Mac had come to the same conclusion and wasn't sharing the idea with Berglund. The missing information tied the two deaths together. Mother and daughter, two murders, one person hiding something worth killing for.

"You didn't bring any wine by any chance, did you?" Martha asked. "I could use a glass about now."

"No, but I helped myself to a bottle Rosie had stashed in the pantry," Berglund said. "Raised a toast to old friends. May they rest in peace. A dry Riesling from out your way. It's not bad."

"Probably a Chateau Ste. Michelle. That's a good vintage. Not too sweet for a Riesling. Mac, you want one?"

Martha glowered at him from behind Berglund's shoulder.

Even for a guy who was still single, he understood *the look.* He said, "Sure. Let me help. Okay if we grab a couple of glasses?"

"Yeah, Gould's crew is done in here, or so he told me."

"He knows you're here?" Martha said.

"They wrapped up the crime scene that fast?" MacAuliffe added.

"Course he does," Berglund responded. "Unlike you two vigilantes, I asked for permission, not forgiveness. Ain't worth losing my badge, my job, and the only source of income I have for my kids, granddaughter, and me. Good jobs are hard to come by in Grand Marais, and I appreciate having a roof over my head and some food on the table. And so does my little Hunter Bunter." She cooed at the baby in her arms, who responded by drooling on her shoulder.

MacAuliffe just looked at the ranger as if she were an alien from outer space. But that's pretty much how he felt about all grandmothers of infants. He also noted that if Berglund had an opinion on the speed with which the local sheriff finished his investigation, she didn't offer it.

In the kitchen, MacAuliffe grabbed glasses from the cupboard. Martha found the wine. As she poured, she whispered, "Remember Rose told Amelia not to trust anyone."

"Way ahead of you, counselor," he said, his voice hushed. "Good thing Gould ordered us back to Duluth. Amelia had to be taking something to her dad. If they didn't find it in her backpack, she might've stashed it on the *Ginny.*"

Martha poured a third glass of the dry Riesling, handed one to MacAuliffe and carried the other two back to the room. Berglund had her head bent over one of Rose's notebooks. Martha pulled up a second chair to join the ranger. She grabbed a notebook and opened it to the first page.

"I'm matching case numbers from the field reports with the numbers pinned on the wall," Berglund explained. "I'm scanning the reports to see if anything jumps out. Not sure what it might be until we find it. Rosie's done a good job of flagging anything unusual, like the illegal logging at Rosebud Creek."

"Got it," Martha said. The first page of the notebook was marked "43." She studied the chart until she found it. A red pin marked 43 was pinned where a blue streak entered Lake Superior. Further up the blue streak was a white pin marked 43W2. She leaned forward. It was a spot about a mile up Fall River. The next page in the notebook was marked 43W2, a water quality analysis dated four months after the date on the first page. A glance at the maps revealed dozens if not hundreds of pins, most south and west of the little town of Grand Marais where Nettles was planning his resort.

It was going to be a long night.

A second, more thorough search of Amelia's room had produced nothing. Now, he set down a another bottle of wine—a Chateau Ste. Michelle's Indian Wells cab—this time with a platter of Colby cheese, green olives, and a couple of pieces of old bread he'd scavenged from the kitchen. At least Rose had good taste in wine.

Martha had dozed off in her chair, and MacAuliffe nudged her in passing. Long fingers, unadorned with jewelry or polish, rubbed her face, her eyes, her temples. She yawned and flipped to the next page in the notebook.

"It's like she didn't exist," he said. "Or maybe it's someone's romanticized notion of a young girl's room—a teddy bear on the pillow, perfectly matched and folded socks. And why was the toilet seat left up in a house with only two women?"

"Maybe it's a reaction to her mom," Berglund said. "Housekeeping was clearly not one of Rosie's strong suits. So Amy overcompensated. What do you mean about the toilet seat?"

"When we discovered Rose, I noticed the toilet seat was up. Did she have a boyfriend? A weekend guest?"

"She could've reclaimed her virginity for all I know," Berglund said.

Martha ignored them and scanned the wall charts. "Do either of you see a red 281?" Her notebook was opened to the last page. She stood up, rolled her shoulders and stretched.

"Notes say it's a base reading at the mouth of Devil Track River," she added. "Here's the lake, here's Devil Track. But no number 281." She put her finger on a blue streak north-northwest of the town and began to follow it south. "Rose indicates the nitrate reading is high."

"That usually means someone's using too much fertilizer too close to the watershed," Berglund added. Musing aloud, she said, "Opel's is down here, Ella's Inn is further up Highway 61." Her finger traced the road. "Neither one farms. That's not an area where you get much livestock or farming. Old man Corker might be running a few cattle. Craig shuts him down if he's letting his cows graze on public land. He'd know this area better. It's part of his territory. Maybe it's just the resorts using too much fertilizer to keep their lawns pretty for tourists."

MacAuliffe leaned forward, pointed. "Here's the mouth of the river. Didn't Rose normally take base readings near the mouth? No pinhole in the map. If she took the reading, why not put it on her board?"

"Getting too far from the development?" Berglund offered.

"It's the last page of her notes," Martha said. "You're right, it's probably just too far from her area of focus."

Investigating stories, MacAuliffe knew, was often about uncovering the facts that people were trying to hide. They let you see what they wanted you to see—like Nettles with his promo pitch about the development. All true—or mostly true—just shy of all the facts. Buzz provided his own set of facts. Classic salesmanship from both father and son. Here, someone knew the police would find Rose, and they staged the scene so the police would see a victim of a drug overdose. Once they looked closer, however, the police would discover murder. And that would lead them back to Nettles.

But what was here that someone didn't want the police to discover? What details were being hidden?

MacAuliffe carefully lifted the bottom corner of the chart. He dropped the map back down, studied it, and lifted it again. "Someone's replaced the chart. The pinhole is there in the wall, just not on this map." He raised the edge again. "There are more pinholes." He pointed to the river on the chart. "There's one more here and then the pin holes split. One side runs up this tributary that enters Devil Track. She took readings along both."

"That's Woods Creek," Berglund said. "The Superior Hiking Trail follows it there near Lindskog Road for a few miles. That's north of town, nowhere near the resort."

The ranger studied the map. MacAuliffe wondered if she was seeing features and details that only one intimate with the area would recognize. She was quiet for a long time.

"No field notes?" the ranger asked finally.

"Just the one page, number 281," Martha replied.

Together, they started flipping through the binders again, volumes one through eight.

MacAuliffe slowly peeled the map off the wall. "There're at least a half a dozen pinholes in the wall that aren't on the map," he said. "Maybe book nine is what Amelia had in her backpack."

"Woods Creek," Martha said. "At least we know where to start searching. The haystack just got a little smaller."

"Yeah, but remember, Gould ordered us headed back to Duluth this morning," MacAuliffe said. "Demanded we stop playing in his sandbox. I'm not real keen on seeing the inside of his jail."

"Didn't get the impression you two were much good at following orders," Berglund said. She ran a finger down the thin blue line, as if memorizing its bends and curves. "At least *I* know where to start."

SEVENTEEN

MacAuliffe and Martha were headed back to Duluth by mid-morning. MacAuliffe slept most of the way, his head leaning awkwardly against the side window as forest and lake glided past. The thunderstorm had blown through with the night. The elements that remained had a piercing beauty. The sky was high and pure, a deeper blue than Martha had ever seen. The vast lake gleamed a lighter, luminous blue. The water shimmered streaks of gold with the rippling of the breeze. The rain had freshened all the colors of the woods. Hillsides were ablaze in reds and golds interspersed with rich, dark greens.

He woke once—at a roadside pullout in Tofte—when Martha stopped for coffee and a bathroom break. He requested his usual large latté but was sound asleep again by the time she returned with it. She drank his latté as they wound their way back south. She realized she'd been humming "How does it feel, how does it feel . . ."

Dylan ear worms. Myths about dropping out and being free got trampled under the reality of losing everything—as Mac had to be discovering. Lance, his boat, his profession, his business.

And now his truck with a teenager inside, a young woman with a name, she reminded herself. Amy. Amelia, Amelia Bumgarten.

At least he had a loving, caring family. No one ever died of hockey-puck muffins and bad coffee. She knew so many who didn't even have family and for whom paying the rent was a source of constant anxiety.

She glanced over. Drool flecked the corner of his mouth and his long hair had fallen across his face. Grass stains on the shoulder of his white Oxford told the story of how he'd tackled her assailant. Despite the danger to himself, he hadn't hesitated.

And he'd saved her life.

It was an act that happened outside the framework of past and future, good and bad, right or wrong. It was an act of loyalty—to their friendship, to Mac's idea of what it meant to be human. She didn't know if she could have done the same. Oh, maybe in a fight; she knew how to fight. But in an area where she had no expertise, where she had to risk—and maybe lose—everything. She knew she would've wavered.

And she felt disgusted with herself.

He awoke with a start that scared her with its suddenness. His eyes zipped from side to side. "Where are we?"

"Coming into town. Something Harbors."

"Two Harbors. Great."

She had a sudden desire to reach over and wipe the drool off his beard. "Did you remember something?"

"Yeah, Mom loves the wild rice from Buddy's Mercantile. It'll be up here on your right."

MacAuliffe had her pull off the road at a blue storefront that resembled part antiques store and part junk shop. A large wooden barrel with an undersized door in it captured her attention as he jumped out. She wondered what it could possibly be. A hobbit sauna? A kid's outhouse?

While she waited, Martha replayed again how she'd almost died last night. Her attacker had crept up on her. She'd been unprepared. She'd forgotten Jonesy's first lesson. Her first martial arts instructor, Marcus Jones, a retired Marine on Okinawa, had taught that scared and determined young girl that she never knew when someone might attack. She had to round every street corner, stroll through every park, browse the bookshelves in every library as if it was an opportunity for someone to attack. He'd taught her to always be ready—and to never fight fair.

And that was how the midnight attacker had fought. It wasn't about being fair. It was about fighting to win—at all costs. And that meant Martha should be dead. Except for Mac.

Why had he rushed to help her? Love and trust, friendship and loyalty. Emotions and values that opened the door to being hurt so profoundly that sometimes, in the deepest part of your soul, you couldn't breathe. And sometimes they killed you. Like Rachel. Like Lance. Was Mac to be next? The thought left her devastated. A single tear escaped down her cheek.

MacAuliffe returned to the car carrying a small brown bag. "Wild rice and maple syrup—real maple syrup, of course. Not even Mom can ruin these. She loves them. It'll put me in her good—You okay?"

"I was just thinking of how much Lance would've enjoyed working with you on this," she lied.

He touched her hand for a brief instant. "Yeah, I miss him. I'm sure you do, too." He held up his bag. "But this would've prompted him to make a new list of his favorite things. He was a regular Julie Andrews with his lists. When you're feeling down, just remember wild rice and maple syrup and—"

"I never thought of wild rice and maple syrup going together," she interrupted.

"The Native Americans mixed them together all the time for some great desserts. Rice pudding with a twist." He buckled in. "You know, maple trees will explode from a buildup of too much sap if you don't tap them," he said.

"Really? I didn't know that." She merged back onto Highway 61.

"Oh, yeah," MacAuliffe said. "Little known fact from the north woods." For the next several miles, he told her about how the buildup of pressure from the sap running in the spring could cause a tree to literally blow its top. Martha didn't believe a word he was saying, but she enjoyed the sound of his voice. After a sleepless night, it helped keep her awake on the last part of the drive back to Duluth.

They were interrupted when her phone rang. Berglund.

"Hang on," Martha said and pulled off Highway 61. The first curve brought her right to Kitchi Gammi Park. A verdant expanse of grass, interrupted only by a couple of picnic tables, a bench, and a lone Charlie Brown tree, led to a narrow beach and a vast expanse of blue lake. "What's up?"

"You asked how Rose handled the science," the forest ranger started. "I just knew it was through the U. Tucked into volume two of this blasted omnibus of pure boring bullshit of enviro reports was a quick note from one Bryan Barnes. Missed it the first time through. Seems he's a prof of environmental sciences at UMD. Since you're in the 'hood, which I assume you are by now, I thought maybe you'd swing by to talk to him."

"What did the note say?" Martha asked.

"Not much. Just 'Finished the labs for Cut Face. Nothing unusual. BB.' It was an email that Rose printed, but it included a signature box with his info. There's no history of it on her computer. Damn fool for not having her computer password protected anyway. Might as well invite 'em to steal from you.

Cut Face Creek is south of town near Terrace Point. Some of the watershed certainly includes the planned resort."

"Can you text me his phone number?" Her phone pinged.

"Way ahead of ya, darling. Let me know if he's got anything interesting to say."

"Will do. Get some sleep. It was a long night."

"Good advice, but I'm a little wound up. Might take a hike up Devil Track before getting my beauty rest. Lord knows I've missed enough of it with this grandbaby. Missing a little more ain't gonna change the truth. My face looks like a cracked egg every time I see it in the mirror. So I took down all the mirrors. But I promised Anna one mistake wasn't going to ruin her life like it did mine."

"Be safe, Marlena," Martha said. "I'll let you know what BB has to say."

Across the water, she realized the distant shore was now visible, a low, dark line that could only be Wisconsin as the lake narrowed to it western-most point. How could a place with so much beauty hide so much evil in its shadows? She rolled her tired shoulders and realized it was the same question she asked herself each time an abused woman walked into her office seeking help. Berglund was one of the good folks who found a way to appreciate the beauty and care about the people around her without giving in to so much evil.

MacAuliffe reached for his latté. It was empty, so he got out and stretched, at first barely able to touch his knees but moving and stretching until he finally was able to grab his ankles. "Who's BB?"

"You may be the least flexible person I've ever met. You should take up yoga. That was Marlena. She said BB is a professor at the local university, Bryan Barnes, who may have been doing the lab testing for Rose's environmental work."

"Do you trust her?"

"Probably. She's certainly not the one who tried to strangle me. She's going to take a hike up Devil's Track."

"What is she thinking?" MacAuliffe said. "There's a killer on the loose, and she's going for a walk in the woods by herself?"

"I'm sure she'll take her gun—just in case."

"How much good would it have done you last night? She doesn't know what she's dealing with. Hell, we don't know what we're dealing with. But if he got the best of you—"

"He caught me by surprise."

"And he's not going to catch Berglund by surprise? Makes sense, I'm sure. He'll just walk out onto the trail and announce his intentions to kill her before doing anything."

"Sarcasm doesn't become you, Mac. I'm not infallible." Flint was in Martha's voice.

"As my friend Friar Lawrence once said, 'Go wisely and slowly. Those who rush often stumble and fall.'"

"You have a friend who's a priest? I thought there already was a saint for lost causes—Jude the Apostle."

"No, Friar Lawrence from *Romeo and Juliet.* Berglund needs to be more cautious."

MacAuliffe shook a cigarette out of the pack and struck a match. He inhaled the welcome nicotine. Getting a read on Martha was vexing. One moment she was open and playful. The next he feared she was going to do one of those karate things to him. Yeah, asshole, he reminded himself, someone had just tried to kill her—and almost succeeded. That'd be enough to put anyone on edge. She had to be scared. He knew he was when he charged across the lawn toward the fighters struggling in the dark. His legs had never felt so heavy, his pace so slow. All he could think was he wasn't going to make it in time. Another friend dead. Another failure. Lance, the paper, Amelia, Martha—he remembered her struggling, the scream. He thought it was a death scream. It scared him so. A kick in the balls was a small price to pay when he heard that first deep gasping for air coming from her.

He crushed the half-smoked cigarette under the sole of his boat shoe.

"God, I could use some coffee—and some breakfast," he said. Martha sat with her eyes closed, her head resting on the steering wheel. "Hey, I'm sorry. I was just concerned for her."

Martha's eyes opened, and she nodded. MacAuliffe couldn't help but think how incredibly sad she seemed. He loved her heavy eyebrows and the short black hair curling around her face. Like a blackbird with a broken wing. God, he was a writer by trade. Couldn't he think of a better simile to use than that tired old cliché? But there it was: a cliché, and an appropriate one at that.

The estates along Congdon Boulevard, with their circular drives and perfectly manicured green lawns, whizzed by as they drove into town. The large home of Craig Nettles, Senior, appeared off to the left in flashes of white barely visible through the towering trees and thick hedge. MacAuliffe leaned toward Martha, peering through the driver's side window.

"Go around the block," he said.

She did, and MacAuliffe asked her to park. He ran across the street and peered over the fence. Nettles' backyard was an immense stretch of freshly watered green grass between the branches of the arborvitae. Squinting, changing locations up and down the fence, taking the time to linger with another cigarette—God, he was smoking too much again—he could just make out the backyard.

Back at the car, he said, "Thanks. 'Daddy's yacht' is still at the dock. I can't figure out why Buzz uses the boat for cruising up the coast. Shouldn't that be the job of the Coast Guard?"

"But Marlena said she did the same, only in a kayak," Martha said.

"Okay, but with a kayak, you can poke into the river mouths and coves. You're also quiet, in case there is any unusual activity. And there's no fuel consumption. This is no yacht, but it's probably forty-five, fifty feet. It needs fuel the way a newspaper needs ink. Has to suck it down by the gallon."

"What kind of boat is it?"

"Ah, a power boat, mostly white."

"To ragbaggers, they're all the same, I'm sure."

MacAuliffe smiled. This was the playful Martha he'd come to enjoy. "Pretty much. I don't know. It's not a trawler. It's not a fishing boat like your little rig. It's the kind of boat you see middle-aged men driving while younger babes wearing handkerchiefs sit on the deck sunbathing. A Bayliner or a Sea Ray or one of those kinds of boats."

"My little rig?"

"Well, it is little."

"It's a Grady White 23, the best fishing boat ever designed. Handles like a dream, sturdy enough for most any weather, practically points its bow toward the salmon."

"Divining rod and all, it's still little."

"You're hopeless. How far is it to Grand Marais? By boat?"

"Highway 61 follows the coast so it's the same as a car. Maybe a hundred miles or so."

"That's five hours of cruising time, say four if you're in a hurry. Probably consumes around 25 gallons per hour at mid-range speeds. Do the math."

"It's another thirty-five, forty miles farther up to Grand

Portage," MacAuliffe said. "Maybe a hundred fifty miles total. Six, seven hours. Then back to Duluth. Wow. I can't imagine the National Forest Service footing the bill for that, and a seasonal forest ranger certainly can't—unless he's paying with daddy's credit card. Playing in daddy's yacht, indeed."

"So what's that tell you?" Martha asked.

"Nothing really, but it sure leads to more questions."

EIGHTEEN

They walked up the sun-dappled sidewalk toward Heller Hall, a two-story red brick building that housed the University of Minnesota Duluth's environmental sciences programs. MacAuliffe noted the young adults laden with backpacks and tote bags who hurried into and out of the building and past the green lawn without glancing at the trees that were starting to turn, one already having morphed into a blazing red. Earbuds and smart phones distracted their attention from the changing seasons. School being back in session was reminder enough that summer was over and autumn had arrived in the Northland.

Brick and glass, functional designs in squares and rectangles with hard corners, two and three stories, the buildings of the UMD campus reflected modern utilitarianism and budget constraints more than architectural flourish.

Inside, Dr. Bryan Barnes rose from behind his desk when they knocked on the open door. Tall and lean, he dressed like he'd never heard of an iron and couldn't afford the drycleaners. A French striped shirt, slightly rumpled, hung from his sinewy frame. A solid burgundy knit tie was loose around his neck. Black chinos with a hammer loop and frayed edges along the pockets contrasted with a light linen blazer hung that on the back of his chair. A thin face lined from years of too much sun was topped with thinning gray hair, teased up with a little product.

MacAuliffe suspected from the different shades of tanning on his face that he'd cleaned up recently to get himself ready for school. Whiter patches around his eyes spoke of lots of time in the sun wearing sunglasses, and the different shade along his jawline and long chin hinted at a beard that had only recently been removed.

"Dr. Barnes?" Martha asked.

"And you'd be Whitaker and Mac-something?"

"MacAuliffe, James MacAuliffe," he said. "Thank you for agreeing to see us on such short notice."

He extended a hand. The man's small, brown eyes were hard, wary. "It's a busy day. How may I help you?"

Since he didn't sit and made no offer for them to sit, they stood.

"It's about the untimely death of Rose Bumgarten," Martha began. "We got your name from Marlena Berglund, an officer in Grand Marais, as someone who's worked with Rose. You did some analysis of field samples she was collecting."

It was a statement, not a question. During her legal days at Carey, Harwell and Niehaus, it had been drilled into her: Don't give a witness the opportunity to deny—even when you're unsure. Confirmation will be the lack of denial.

Neither Martha nor MacAuliffe, however, anticipated his reaction. MacAuliffe saw him stagger, as if hit by one of Martha's open-hand jabs.

"What?" he said, his voice barely audible.

"Rose was found dead in her home yesterday morning," Martha said. "The police are investigating it as suspicious."

"That can't be," Barnes said, stumbling backwards into his chair. "I talked to her just a few days ago. What happened? Is Amy okay?"

His hands covered his face, his head shaking back and forth.

MacAuliffe pulled up a couple of chairs and they sat down, neither of them talking for a time. Barnes grieved behind rough, calloused hands.

"I'm sorry, Dr. Barnes," Martha said, when the professor wiped away the tears. "I take it you were close?"

His thin face reappeared, eyes now puffy and brimming with unshed tears. He sat up, squared his shoulders, daubed his eyes with his shirt sleeve. A hand swiped his hair in a well-practiced habit that appeared unconscious.

"Excuse me," he said. "I hadn't heard. Yes, Rose and I were close. And yes, I was doing the lab analysis for her field work. But, please, do you know if Amy's being taken care of?"

Martha never hesitated but leaned forward, her hands clasped as if in prayer. "I'm sorry, Dr. Barnes. Amy is dead as well."

She proceeded to give him the bare facts of the case.

"I'm so sorry," Barnes said, wiping his eyes again with his shirt. "I'm so so sorry, but what's this got to do with me?"

"Officer Marlena Berglund was going through Rose's field reports to see if there was anything suspicious. She found your name among the reports. As you know, not everyone shared Rose's opinion on the development in Grand Marais. She asked us to talk with you."

"Did Rose mention any concerns to you?" MacAuliffe asked, taking a notebook from his jacket pocket and flipping it open. A pen had been hiding in his long hair. "She'd mentioned to Amelia that she wasn't to trust anyone. Why might she have said that?"

"She never said anything directly, but she knew Nettles' resort had its backers in the community. It created a rift with her boss at the law firm, I know. Rose wasn't naïve enough to think everyone took her side on the argument. She was just being cautious."

"Did anyone ever threaten her?"

"Not that I know of."

"So why did you do the lab analysis for her?" MacAuliffe asked, dropping his head to scribble notes.

"First, because I believed in what she was doing. Putting a resort and a golf course on the North Shore will have devastating consequences. The long-term environmental degradation to the area, despite what Nettles tells everyone, could be, will be profound. I've read the EIS and I know they say otherwise, but you can't build a championship-caliber golf course without using a ton of water and fertilizer, and you can't pave over the rest of the land with buildings and parking lots without flushing way too many of the chemicals into the surrounding watershed or directly into the lake. It just won't work."

"But it seemed to have convinced some folks. The state's Department of Natural Resources for one."

"They're idiots," Barnes snapped. "They're also the ones who allowed open-pit mining on the Range."

"So why approve it?" MacAuliffe persisted.

"It's politics, pure and simple. The promise of jobs up north creates a short-sightedness that will win out over sound environmental practices every time. Sign a promise for environmental cleanup that becomes null and void with the first bankruptcy, and you're good as gold. Politicians don't care that it's a hollow promise. And they know that it is. Companies create shell holding companies that shield them from the liability of bankruptcy, and then they walk away scot-free, leaving the public to clean up the mess. The politicos are just pandering to voters. And the land and water are the casualties. They're treated like there's an endless supply, so sacrificing a small percentage of them won't hurt. Rose knew what she was up against."

"But who'd be willing to kill her to stop that fight?"

"I'd start with Nettles."

"But he'd already won the fight," MacAuliffe said, shaking his head. "Nettles had no reason to kill them. He just needs to purchase the last remaining tract of land so he can begin digging. It makes no sense. Amelia, Rose, none of it."

Barnes placed his palms on his desk. "I have no idea."

After a brief interlude, Martha said, "You said, your 'first' reason for helping Rose. Is there more?"

"That's private." His voice was quiet.

"And the police are investigating her death as a homicide," she said. "We got your name from them. They'll be calling soon, I'm sure, if they haven't already."

Barnes scanned his bookshelf, as if seeing the titles for the first time. When his eyes returned to his guests, he found Martha and MacAuliffe both still there, waiting.

"We've enjoyed a summer romance the past few years. I'm married, and I'd prefer my wife didn't learn about it."

"That will be for the police to decide, not us."

"But mostly, as I stated, I believed wholeheartedly in what she was doing. We shared an interest in protecting the land. And that sparked a relationship that proved enjoyable for us both the past couple of summers. We liked being together, camping and hiking, listening to the Twins games on the radio. We were both a little lonely. We hit it off. I was able to help her out, so I did. When I returned to campus in the fall, I ran the tests on her samples. Some we took together. Others she took on her own. It's good for my students to get lab time with actual field samples, to learn the methodology of handling specimens, to prepare the materials and results. For a career in the sciences, they have to learn how to do proper research."

"Why did it end?" MacAuliffe asked. "The affair?"

"It didn't. As I said and will say again, it was just a summer romance."

"You'll excuse me," MacAuliffe said. "But you hardly seem the age to call an affair a summer fling."

"Well, that's what it was. Literally. We both knew going in and both accepted the arrangement. Companionship, intellectual stimulation, good sex, no commitments. I'm in Duluth most of the year, and as long as Amy was in school, Rosie was committed to Grand Marais. But my research in the region put me up north during most of the summer. My wife stopped joining me in the field years ago. One thing led to another."

"When did you last see Rose?"

"Last weekend. School begins at the end of August, but I was going up on weekends to wrap up my research for the season. We got together. I spent the night."

"Amy knew about the affair?"

"Yes, but we didn't flaunt it. She'd gone to a friend's house for a sleepover. They were thinking of starting a bluegrass band and wanted to practice. She plays the fiddle. Quite well in fact."

"Pity the poor parents of that house," MacAuliffe said. He flipped back a couple of pages in his notebook. "Dr. Barnes, some of Rose's notes are missing. We only started to suspect this when we ran across a single page for the field results from Devil Track River. It didn't have a corresponding entry on her maps. We suspect other results may be missing, as well. Do you still have the results from the lab work you performed for her?"

"Of course." He consulted his computer, his hand busy clicking the mouse. His head nodded. "Devil Track. The first reading was from two years ago, July 12 to be exact. Near the mouth of the river, but far enough back so the waters of Lake Superior didn't influence the water sample. I have the GPS coordinates if you want them. Preliminary analysis showed an unusually high concentration of nitrates in the water. A second test, a month later, confirmed the results."

"So what does that mean?" MacAuliffe asked. "And since Devil Track River is well north of town, it's not near the location where Nettles plans to build. Why take samples there?"

"What does it mean? Someone's probably using too much fertilizer near the river. Maybe a farmer who's pasturing cows and who doesn't have the proper setbacks. Could be a resort that fertilizes its lawns to resemble a golf course. Why? I encouraged Rose to take readings up and down the North Shore to establish a baseline. She's not a scientist. I advised her on how to conduct a proper scientific study that would stand up to scrutiny. If you don't know what normal is, you won't know what's abnormal."

MacAuliffe leaned forward, his head nodding. "Rose was playing a long game, wasn't she? She knew she couldn't stop Nettles now. He'd won this round. But if she continued taking samples, she hoped to shut down the development in the future. She was establishing the baseline so she could measure the deviation from it in the future."

"Of course," Barnes said. "It was an action of last resort. She knew she was out of options for preventing the development. She hadn't been able to raise the money to buy the last parcel, so she'd adopted this rearguard action, hoping it'd pay off down the line. She knew it was a long shot, but it was the only one she had left. And it gave her a purpose to go tromping around in the woods, I suppose. She was always so happy there."

Both remained quiet until MacAuliffe turned to Martha. "But this is still north of town."

Martha asked Barnes, "Would the resort development drain into this watershed?"

"I'd have to study it more closely," Barnes equivocated. His thin lips completely disappeared as he chewed on them.

"Come on, Dr. Barnes," MacAuliffe said. "Two people are dead. This isn't a trial where you're under oath. Give us an educated guess."

"Unlikely. Though some of the northern edge may drain into Devil Track Lake, which'd then be noted further down the river. I'd have to study the topo maps to get a better idea."

Martha met MacAuliffe's eyes. "What if this isn't about the development at all? What if Rose found something else?"

MacAuliffe turned back to Barnes. "You said you kept your analysis for Rose. We think she investigated further up Devil Track River, but those records are missing. I don't have the GPS coordinates, but could you find the results of her field research, say, north and northwest of town? We're focused on Devil Track because we know she took water quality samples there. The rest we're just guessing at."

"Give me a little time," Barnes said. He stood up, cinching the tie around his neck. His hands automatically smoothed his hair. He grabbed the sports jacket off the back of his chair. "My files are sorted by date, cross referenced with GPS location. Rose would've taken samples up Devil Track on different days from her original samples. It won't be hard to pull the information, but right now I have students hungry to learn about whether the Canadian Shield has hindered or helped the water quality of the Arrowhead over the past millennium and how that impacts the larger environment of the North Shore."

MacAuliffe couldn't tell if he was being sarcastic or serious.

NINETEEN

Martha and MacAuliffe waited in the car. Sunlight and fresh air wafted through the windows as they sat parked in front of the *Virginia V*. The damaged roller furling jib was down, the sail gone, the furling unit lying on the deck. Beside the *Ginny*, another boat had disappeared from the marina, and a slight breeze had halyards tinkling against masts like distant spoons being dropped onto a tile floor. In another month or so, they'd all be gone, parked on the hard or, masts down, inside large sheds, waiting next spring's thaw.

"I wonder if you're right," MacAuliffe started, "that maybe this has nothing to do with the development of the resort at all." He pushed open the car door.

Martha's short-cropped hair ruffled slightly with the breeze. "So what else might it be?"

MacAuliffe smiled. "No idea."

"So what do we do now?"

"We take the next step. It's all we can do. Where does the story lead us? Wait to hear from Barnes. Right now, I'm going to see if Amelia left me any hidden messages." He glanced at the boat. "Seems Dad's already begun the repairs."

Just then, a bald head popped up out of the companionway. It was followed by a large man, his belly extruding over his belt. He hoisted a garbage bag to the deck and then swung it over the lifelines to the dock where he tossed it beside two others.

"Hey, Dad," MacAuliffe called out.

The man squinted against the bright sun. He hitched his khaki trousers up as MacAuliffe approached and said, "I been cleaning up your mess. You left me a real doozy this time. Just when I was thinking of selling her. Isn't worth much now, not in this condition."

"Doing fine, Dad, thanks. Glad to see you, too."

The older man ignored the remark. "You must be Martha. Ginny told me all about you." He grabbed a handrail before stepping cautiously to the dock and extended a hand. "Sorry to miss you at the house."

"Nice to meet you, Mr. MacAuliffe." Martha took his hand and held it longer than necessary. Though of much the same height, his bulk made her feel as unsubstantial as clothes on a hanger. A gray stubble lined both of his chins, and his broad forehead and bald pate were covered with a fine layer of perspiration. What remained of his hair was white and needed a trim. Faded gray eyes remained fixed on her. Mac resembled his mother more than his father with the exception of his father's strong nose, straight and perfect, a nose she'd love to have adorning her own face. Oh well, she'd long since come to terms with her oversized nose with the crook in it—except when she ran into perfection.

"Ted. Please, call me Ted. You keeping Jimmy out of trouble? That's a fulltime job itself."

"Actually, he's keeping me out of trouble. Last night, someone jumped me in the dark and Mac drove them off with a football tackle Earl Thomas would've been proud of. Probably saved my life. Don't mention it to him, though. We don't want him getting a big head. You know how those writers are. A grain of truth and a lot of hyperbole."

The older man chuckled with a deep rumbling that grew from his belly. "Well put, well put, indeed. A grain of truth and a lot of hyperbole. Ha, I'll have to remember that one. Earl Thomas? Had to be sorry to see him leave. That wasn't pretty."

"No, it wasn't."

"I'm right here, you know, listening," MacAuliffe said. "Earl Thomas? The same one who gave the finger to the crowd on his last play as a Seahawk? Didn't know you were a fan."

"I'm a woman of many tastes and many secrets."

"Well, don't reveal them all at once," Ted MacAuliffe said. "Keeps those boys guessing." Turning to his son, he added, "Glad to hear you been making yourself useful for a change."

Martha wondered if MacAuliffe was hurting more or if he was exaggerating his limp as he came down the dock.

"You come across anything unusual, Dad?" MacAuliffe said, nodding toward the garbage bags piled on the dock.

"That's just wet bedding and cushions to take home so your mom can dry 'em out properly. Put a couple more bags in the dumpster but didn't see anything unusual. Didn't find any of your girlie magazines, if that's what you're wondering."

Martha intervened before things escalated between father and son. "Ted, the young woman who was killed in James' truck may have left some critical information behind. Be okay with you if we looked around? And in the garbage bags, I suppose?"

"Sure. I'll go grab a bite to eat. I been starving for the past hour." In an aside to his son, he added, "And you plumb eaten everything there was to eat on the *Ginny*. Ever think of restocking when you run out of someone else's food?"

"I didn't know you were coming for lunch or I would've

restocked the Spam. Had a lot going on the past couple of days, in case you forgot." MacAuliffe pulled out his wallet and offered his father a twenty. "Here, get yourself a sandwich over at Amazing Grace. Keep the change."

His father ignored the money. "Notice you found nothing wrong with Spam."

"Might I suggest some family counseling?" Martha said. She offered a faint laugh that no one else joined in on.

Ted MacAuliffe hitched up his pants and grabbed the twenty. He stalked away with a parting jibe. "It's probably my money anyway."

They watched him march down the dock and follow the boardwalk toward town.

"Dealing with him is enough to drive a saint to suicide," MacAuliffe said.

"Maybe it wouldn't if one of you decides to be the adult," Martha replied. "Because he pushes your buttons doesn't mean you have to react."

"That's about the parenting technique he knows. Other than sarcasm, of course."

"You don't always have to have the last word, Mac. I read recently the road to wisdom is paved with four statements—I don't know, I'm sorry, I need help. And I can't remember the fourth."

"And you can't go home again."

"Mac, your father's not going to change. Why don't you be the adult?"

"Thank you for intervening," MacAuliffe said. "I'm sorry you had to see that. I need help. With my father, of course, but right now if you'd take the garbage bags, I'll take the inside of the boat."

"Of course."

The *Virginia V* was cool and still inside. The teak trim and table glowed gold in contrast to the white lockers. Most of the forward cushions were gone, the water-soaked vee-berth empty. MacAuliffe just stood in the center of the salon. The leaves of the table were dropped and locked into place, just like they had been when he'd offered the runaway girl a place to crash for the night. Amelia had slept on the settee in a sleeping bag—also gone—while he slept in the vee-berth. Books that had once lined the shelves over the settees were gone, whether home to dry out or thrown into garbage bags, MacAuliffe didn't know. The lockers had been emptied of anything damp, leaving behind a pair of binoculars, an air horn for the bridge, and a few cans of beans, a jar of Kalamata olives, and an unopened bag of basmati rice.

He thought they constituted an acceptable lunch.

MacAuliffe rolled his neck, then his shoulders, and took a deep breath. The verbal bickering had been the one constant in his life with his father. Let it go, let it go. He whispered it like a mantra. Martha was right, his father wasn't going to change. Why did he have to be the adult in the room? It was so hard trying to raise your parents.

He scanned the boat again. The old man had washed the dirty dishes in the galley, now drying on the small countertop. Papers, charts, and books were piled on the nav station. Sail bags, the spinnaker sock, and extra lines and fenders still lay stuffed in the aft quarter berth.

If Amelia had left anything behind, where would it be? What would it be? Something small, probably a thumb drive, maybe papers. The nav station was the logical place to hide something. He started flipping through the books and charts, setting them off to one side when he was convinced they hid nothing of importance. Inside the nav table, they had remained dry from the dousing from the fire hoses. Charts of Duluth harbor, the North Shore to Grand Portage, the Wisconsin shore from Superior out past Bayfield and the Apostle Islands, a large chart of the entirety of Lake Superior, from the Arrowhead past Isle Royale over to Sault Ste. Marie—all lay neatly folded and in order heading east from Duluth to Sault Ste. Marie, over four hundred miles away. There was a handheld compass, a pair of dividers, a parallel ruler, all essential for navigating the big lake without electronics.

MacAuliffe rifled the well-worn pages of the 1983 edition of Bonnie Dahl's *Superior Way*. The lake hadn't changed since the last ice age, so apparently there was no reason to spend money on the latest edition.

He reached the bottom of the papers. Nothing. He put them all back and closed the lid.

Next, he raised the cushions on the settees and peered into lockers. Nothing. He popped up a teak floorboard. Fuel tanks and water tanks but nothing that shouldn't be there. In the galley, pots and pans and dishes were in their places. A tea kettle sat on one of the two burners, the plastic funnel for his drip coffee off to one side. The small refrigerator was still cold and empty except for a little remaining half-and-half for his coffee. The lockers behind the oven held coffee, his French press, and a can of evaporated milk, emergency backup if he ran out of cream. A banana, just this side of going bad. A loaf of whole wheat bread, which had gone bad, now growing green spores along the crust. Apparently his dad hadn't finished cleaning when they interrupted him.

He continued his search. The quarter berth was chock-full of extra gear, and he began extracting it piece by piece—fenders thrown up to the cockpit, spare lines he recoiled and tied off before tossing them up beside the fenders. A storm jib, nothing hidden in the bag; the spinnaker, the same; the spinnaker chute, again nothing; a spare water pump, still in the box; a set of oil and fuel filters, with a date written in his father's tight, backwards scrawl noting when he should replace the old ones.

Maybe Amelia had taken everything with her.

With the quarter berth empty, he lifted the cushions and checked the compartments under the bunk. He removed the companionway ladder and peered into the engine room, the odor of diesel fuel expanding to fill the main salon. Nothing in the toolbox, nothing in the crevices beside and behind the engine except sound-board insulation.

"How's it going down there?" Martha asked. She crouched in the companionway opening, hands shielding her face from the sun, peering down. Her hair shimmered with a tinge of gold.

"Nothing so far. And I'm running out of places she could've hidden anything."

"It was only a guess that she left anything behind." Martha dropped into the main salon. "Let me help you put things back together."

"I take it you didn't find anything either?"

"Oh, I found lots of things. I'm always surprised what someone will throw away. But nothing that might lead us back to Amy. I got a full set of foulies out of it, though. Fit perfectly. From what I can tell, there's nothing wrong with them. I hope they fit in my suitcase."

"Dumpster diving. How low we've gone. If your friends at Carey, Coleman and Frick could only see you now."

"Carey—oh, stop it, Mac. You're just like your father. They probably wouldn't be surprised."

She reached back up into the cockpit. "Your dad dropped this off." She handed him a Pyrex container. "Some mac and cheese from your mom for lunch. She sent it with him, and he added some sausages from the Smoke Haus. He said to warm it in the oven for half an hour at three seventy-five."

"He had lunch the whole time." MacAuliffe swore under his breath. "I hope you like your mac and cheese with Velveeta."

"Are they still making Velveeta?" When she was a little girl, Gran would make a Mexican *queso* dip with Velveeta cheese and a jalapeno. With a bag of tortilla chips, it was a complete meal. "Sounds great to me. But maybe that's because I'm hungry enough to eat my boots." Her voice grew serious. "He just wants the best for you, you know."

"I know. For him that means getting a 'real job'—defined as a doctor, lawyer, postal service worker—with good benefits, a decent retirement package, and season tickets to the Bulldogs hockey team. 'Jimmy, gotta think of your future.'"

"Well, right now your future is telling me how to warm this up. I'm starving."

He found the lighter and handed it to her. "I've got to turn the propane on in the cockpit. Then light the oven. There's a pilot light on the front of the right-side element. Easy peasy."

MacAuliffe clipped the companionway steps into place. He opened a hatch in the rear of the cockpit, opened a valve, and yelled down, "All set." Sitting back in the cockpit, he lit a cigarette and sucked deeply of the nicotine while he thought about how much he missed home and missed the thrill of investigating a good story and missed his business partner and friend Lance and missed the life that he'd created for himself away from here. But with everything lost, what did his future hold?

The harbor water coruscated gold with the bright sun and rippling wind. Only a few days ago he'd pulled Ester Petrowski from these chilly waters. He wondered how the retired math teacher was doing and whether Newton had returned home or if the old golden retriever was still staying with his folks out on

Park Point. He wanted to talk to his mom anyway. He should swing by and feed Leibniz the terror cat and visit Ester P in the hospital. She might have remembered seeing something the morning of the explosion.

His cigarette smoked to the filter, he flicked out the remaining ember and tossed the butt into the water. He tried to snatch it back before it hit the water. When he wasn't smoking, he hated people who just tossed the butts wherever they happened to be. He leaned over the gunwale but couldn't reach the drifting filter. It swirled in the harbor waters, where it'd take a millennium or two to decompose.

Martha's voice made him forget his contribution to environmental catastrophe. "Hey, Mac," she called up. "I found Amy's papers."

He jumped down the companionway without using the steps. He found her sitting on a cushionless settee flipping through papers. "What the . . . Where?"

"In the oven," she said. "There's a note for you." She pointed to a folded piece of paper with "Mac" scrawled in beautiful cursive.

He sat down beside Martha and began to read:

Hey, Mac,

Sorry again about 'borrowing' your truck but I needed wheels to get to my Dad's. No one'll expect the National Honor Society kid to steal a truck. Dad's in St. Paul and he'll know what to do with my Moms papers. At least I hope he will. I'm taking him the papers and a thumb drive, but I made an extra copy too. Here they are in case something happens to me. Your a newspaper guy, you should be able to figure something out. I know something happened to Mom. I almost wish it was a relapse, but I know its not. I just hope she comes out of this okay. (I hope I come out of this okay too for that matter). I don't know what they mean but Mom said I'm supposed to take these to Dad if anything happened to her. One time I overheard her say, "All's not right in the woods". Like no shit. It's the woods in northern Minnesota. Mosquitoes and trees. And more mosquitoes. But Mom loves the woods and loves being away from the temptation of her junkie friends. (And I'm working on not being too sarcastic, not always successfully BTW. I guess it means I'm growing up. Oh shit, that's a horrible thought.) BTW2 Mom didn't trust anyone in GM so you shouldn't either.

Thanks for taking me in when I needed a safe place to stay. And thanks for not being a creepy old dude.

Stay safe,
Amelia Bumgarten

PS. Be nice to your Mom. Tell her I loved her lasagna.

MacAuliffe placed the paper on his lap. Why hadn't he taken her concerns more seriously? If he had, they'd both be dead, he reminded himself. That didn't seem to help, and he felt as impotent to help Amelia now as he'd been when she was alive. Only sixteen. A life cut short. And for what? "All's not right in the woods."

"Anything?" Martha asked.

"I'm not a creepy old dude."

"Wow, 'old dude'. That must hurt. I mean not as much as being a creepy one, of course."

"Sometimes you're so funny you make yourself laugh," he said, repeating her line. He tossed her the note, gave her time to read it. His eyes began to water up at a life not lived and a horrible death. At least, he hoped it had been painless.

"Pretty much confirmed what we already knew," Martha said. "She sure doesn't think her mom fell off the addiction wagon. And it's always good to know that you're not a perv with young women."

He reached over and tapped the papers on her lap. "Anything interesting here?"

"It appears to be the missing volume from Rose's field notes. It's a little hard to tell. The copies are out of order and all done in black and white, so I don't have the color coding of the originals, but I saw Devil Track River appear once or twice."

"You want to take them up to Barnes? He should be able to confirm them for us and maybe tell us what they mean."

"Sure. You?"

"I've got to talk to Mom and feed Ester P's cat. But we should eat that mac and cheese first."

Life's expectations were better set under a low ceiling and on a full stomach.

Lunch over, MacAuliffe placed the dishes in the galley sink. "Why would they attack you if they had the thumb drive?"

"Maybe they didn't find it," Martha said, reclining on the cushion-less settee. "We're only speculating that they took her backpack. Or maybe they were worried that Amy had told you what her mom was investigating, and then we showed up in Grand Marais asking troubling questions. It'd be a logical assumption."

"Possible." He started washing the silverware. "Or maybe once you've killed the first person, killing just becomes the easiest solution to any problem."

He glanced over the counter when Martha didn't respond. Her eyes were closed, her breaths shallow and regular. He let her sleep while he finished the dishes.

TWENTY

Martha dropped him off at the Park Point bungalow, and he began lugging garage bags toward the house. They had put the boat back together as best they could and left his father fussing over the fuel tank, worried that too much water had gotten in for the engine to run properly.

"Hey, Mom, it's me," he called out as he opened the front door. His voice was greeted by a deep woof. Newton slid off the couch and bounded into the foyer, expecting MacAuliffe to scratch his wiggling butt of gray and red hair.

"In my study, Jimmy," came his mother's voice, faint and distant from a speaker on the kitchen counter.

MacAuliffe dropped two garbage bags off in the laundry room before exiting the house through the open kitchen door. In the small garage out back, he found his mother hunched over her workbench with her welder's hood flipped up, examining a piece of Cor-Ten steel welded into a rectangle. It was joined to a smaller square box with a short steel rod. The whole piece was about two feet tall. The air smelled of burnt metal, and a tack weld at the base of the rectangle still glowed red. Seeing him, she lifted the hood off her face, blushed red from heat. Her hair was held back from her face with a red, sweat-soaked bandana, a damp ring showing where the hood's headband had clung to her head. She tossed her thick work gloves inside the mask.

"What you working on?" he asked.

"A maquette of the piece I was commissioned to build for the park in Mankato," she said. "The one I told you about for the memorial to the Lakotas that Lincoln had executed."

"The one that'll resemble wind chimes, only they'll never chime?"

"Thirty-eight of them. Full size. With a name etched on each one."

"That'll be a powerful display," MacAuliffe said.

"It's meant to be." Newton had joined them in the garage, lying down near her feet, and she reached down to pet him. "We must never forget how we've silenced the voices of people who are different from us. It's important to keep their stories alive."

Like he felt compelled to tell the story of Amelia Bumgarten.

"You should mention your work to Martha. She was raised in part by her Chippewa grandmother on a reservation near Sault Ste. Marie."

"How interesting. Of course." She stroked Newton's ears, prompting the old dog to lick the sweat off her hands. "When'd you get home?"

"Just now. I brought some stuff from the boat that needs to be cleaned."

"Put it in the laundry room," she said.

"Already did."

"How's Martha? How did things go up north?"

"Didn't go the way we expected." He told her about the death of Rose Bumgarten, the attack on Martha, the missing field notes. His mother was a patient listener. She had that singular ability to make each person feel like they were the only person who mattered and that their story was worth all her attention. His father, in contrast, always gave the impression of just letting someone talk while he formulated his next comment—usually a sarcastic one if the conversation involved his kids.

She let him finish with the discovery on the *Ginny* of the missing notes.

"Is Martha okay?" Virginia asked. "I can call Dr. Malcolm if you think she's hurt."

"If anyone should see her, it's me."

He downplayed the heroics of his Earl Thomas tackle but did mention he'd been kicked hard in the, um, in the gonads for his troubles.

"Goodness, you've had quite a week being back in sleepy ol' Duluth. First, Mrs. Petrowski, then Martha. You'll be in the running for First Citizen Award if you save many more people. Should I call Dr. Malcolm for, um, this injury?"

"First Citizen of Duluth? I'd have to decline. Of course, I'd rather have to decide if I was going to accept or decline the Pulitzer. No, I'll be fine, Mom."

"Jimmy, you don't have to be the rebel on everything. It's okay to just say 'thank you' sometimes."

"You sound like Martha."

"Tough being surrounded by smart women, isn't it?"

"Yeah. But right now I've got other things to worry about. Have you heard anything from Ester Petrowski?"

"I took her some brownies yesterday," his mother said. MacAuliffe felt sorry for Ester P but knew she'd be too polite to decline chocolate hockey pucks. "She asked me to watch Newton a while longer. She's going to be released soon but said it'd be a while before she'd be able to walk him again. I fed her cat yesterday. I see what you mean about put out the food and run. Next time I'm taking these with me."

She picked up her heavy leather gloves.

MacAuliffe chuckled. His mother often made him laugh. "Any chance I can borrow your truck for the rest of the day?"

"Of course."

"And do you still have your kayak?"

"It's hanging behind the shop. Paddles and life jackets are over there." She nodded toward the far corner of the garage. "Where you going?"

"Just something that's bothering me." He started to leave. "Thanks, Mom. Thanks for everything."

Her head already covered with the welding hood, she mumbled, "You're welcome."

Martha had been sitting outside Bryan Barnes' office for two hours waiting for the professor to return. The door was closed so she found a chair in the reception area and carried it down the hall and plopped it down outside his office. An older man—another professor she guessed from his threadbare tweed jacket and clashing tie—asked if he could help her with something, an offer she declined. Students passed back and forth, and Martha gathered they had been back in school long enough that quiz and test results were the current topics of the day, expressed with pronouncements of joy, outrage, surprise.

She meandered up and down the hall. At one open door, a female professor sat, head hunched over, with a male student, her pen flicking across a paper on her desk. The contrast was stark—a student in gym shorts, tee-shirt and flip flops against the crisp ironed blouse, linen jacket, and brightly colored scarf of the professor.

How come the female professors had the resources to dress with style and care while their male counterparts dressed like they'd just come from the thrift store? Apparently, gender equality at the university hadn't extended to some unspoken dress code.

Still no sign of Barnes. She sat down again outside his office, flipping through Amy's papers until all the numbers began to move like spiders across the pages. A text to SPD officer Ray Palmer went unanswered. A phone call to Emily Reilly went straight to voice mail. She left a message.

A passing student in cargo shorts and pink rubber flip flops complained to a buddy that it was unfair to have a test right after the Bulldogs upset victory over someone called Bemidji. The victory kegger had seriously limited his study time.

Another student explained to a friend how it was obvious that the formation of massive sulfide deposits had to come from the heat and fluid flow of magma in submarine volcanic terrains.

Had she been such a totally boring student in college? She knew the answer—and then some, she thought.

Dr. Barnes woke her with a gentle nudge on the shoulder. She had his hand twisted inside out before she fully woke, pushing him away. He stumbled across the hall and didn't end up on his butt only because he slammed into the wall first. An armload of books thudded to the floor, papers fanned out in a cascade of white sheets. His mouth gaped open.

She blinked herself fully awake.

"I'm sorry," he replied. "I didn't mean to startle you. Please don't misconstrue anything."

Barnes quickly scanned the hall, whether hoping for a witness to verify his benign intent or worried that someone might view the incident as inappropriate behavior, she wasn't sure.

Martha didn't believe in apologizing for something she wasn't sorry for, so she offered only, "Of course." She set Amy's notes on the chair and added, "Let me help."

In his office, he dumped the books and papers on a desk already piled with books and papers. Barnes dropped into his chair, shaking his head. “Why can’t they learn to put their name on every sheet? I’ll never sort these out.”

“Or you could put yourself in the running for Teacher of the Year award,” Martha said. “Throw them all out. The big win against Bemidji might’ve distracted a few from studying this weekend.”

“A few? You don’t strike me as the football type.”

Martha offered a thin, tight smile. “I’m sure I’ve got a few more surprises in me.”

“That’s for sure,” Barnes said. “I’ve never understood how academics could be completely subverted by the quest for winning the big game. Now it’s football, but that’s just the minor leagues compared to hockey. Listen to me—talking in sports metaphors.” He held up his hands as if divine intervention might put the quizzes back in order. When it didn’t, he added, “I’ve been in class since you left this morning. I haven’t had time to gather the information for you.”

“I understand. But we’ve found some new information that I was wondering if you could look at for me.” She pushed Amy’s notes across the desk. “We think these are the pages from the missing volumes of Rose’s notebooks.”

Barnes fanned through the pages. Soon he was organizing the pages like he would a deck of cards. Martha didn’t interrupt him with questions or chit chat, and he worked as if she weren’t there. He booted up his computer. After it came to life, he studied the computer screen. “You think these are important?”

“We think the originals were stolen from Rose’s office. We’re hoping you can tell us if they’re important.”

He studied the papers, compared them to something on his computer screen, made a check on the paper, flipped to the next.

Noting the volume of pages he had to go through, Martha sat back and let him work. She texted Ray Palmer and Emily Reilly again.

A text from Officer Palmer came back shortly: "Stpped at garage on way to work. No one home. ER not answering phone. No sign of ER or JO. Ill stp by again soon"

She remembered Jerome's angry outburst at the house after being served. A restraining order wouldn't prevent a drunk and angry Jerome Olsen from beating up his girlfriend again. Or worse.

Or? Oh, Emily, have you done something stupid? Martha feared Emily had lost her resolve to push forward with a permanent separation. She knew most women did. So many factors came into play—love, power, economics, fear. All of them tangled in a muddled mess.

Martha could only hope. But hope was not a plan to bet your future on.

She texted Palmer back. "Keep me in the loop. Thanks, Ray. MW"

Would anything be different if she'd remained at home in Seattle? Was it her job to shepherd Emily if she wasn't ready to let go of her abusive high school sweetheart? Before Martha could decide, Barnes interrupted her.

"I'm sorry, but if you want my help maybe you could put your phone away." He glared at her from across the desk.

Martha scowled back at him, wondering what he'd said. "I had a work issue come up. Please, you have my full attention now."

He was muttering something about kids and their fucking phones and how they didn't know how to read anymore when Martha slapped the table with an open palm. The resounding smack sent him flailing back in his chair. "Dr. Barnes, I really don't appreciate your attitude. I had an important work issue that required my attention. I have asked you for a favor, I understand, but the police certainly won't be asking. They'll be confiscating all your computers, and you'll be having these chats in a ten-by-ten gray room with nothing but a clock on the wall and a two-way mirror. I know. I've been there. If you're lucky, you won't be handcuffed to the table. They won't care if you have classes to teach or quizzes to grade. They won't care if your name is sullied, if you lose all academic credibility, or if it costs you your precious tenure. They'll also want to know when you last saw Rose Bumgarten, and they'll be contacting your wife to provide your alibi on the night she was murdered."

She let that sink in, before adding, "And since you've missed the obvious, kids are reading all the time. The delivery system has changed but people are reading more than ever. Because they get the information on their smart phones or iPads or computers doesn't mean that they're not reading, not thinking, not learning. You're the one who's in danger of becoming extinct if you don't recognize that and adapt to it."

Again, she said, "Now please, you have my full attention."

It took him a moment to compose himself. "I was saying, I compared the notes in chronological order. I have the analysis for all but the last four. Two of those are in my lab now. Rose gave them to me last weekend when I was in Grand Marais. The final two I have no record of. From the GPS readings, however, all four were taken north of town somewhere in the vicinity of Devil Track River and Woods Creek. Here, take a look."

He pivoted the monitor around so they both could see the screen. He opened a different page that immediately filled with a sea of green. His cursor hovered over a point where flat green met the robin's egg blue Google Maps used to indicate water. "Are you familiar with GPS readings?"

"Yes," she nodded.

"Good, you know that it can be accurate to within about ten feet of actual. Usually it's spot on, but the margin of error is built into the system. Here's where Devil Track River empties into Lake Superior. That was the site of the sample she took two years ago on July 12." He moved the cursor to a point upstream. "Here's where Woods Creek enters Devil Creek. I've already done the analysis on the sample taken from this juncture. Let's see, in September of last year, it produced an even higher reading of nitrates, meaning she's moving closer to the source. From the GPS readings, the last four samples are taken also from this area, probably further upstream. I'll have to confirm the locations, but I'm guessing from the slight variation in the GPS reading two were taken up Devil Track and two up Woods Creek. My methodology is to pinpoint the exact location when I complete the lab analysis, which I can do for the first two but not the last two."

Martha studied the page. "But even without the samples, you can pinpoint the locations from the GPS coordinates?"

"Of course." He glanced at the papers and added, "Her notes indicate she took them on the Monday after I was there last weekend. Did you come across any water samples when you were going through her place?"

"Monday?"

"That what her notes say. You're sure you didn't see any labeled plastic containers in the house?"

"You've seen her house?"

"Okay, point taken. Still it'd be easier to know what she found if we could analyze the samples."

Martha sat quietly. In her mind, she worked the calendar forward and backwards. Monday. The Cook County coroner had placed the time of Rose's death sometime Wednesday evening, before Amelia blew up in Mac's truck early Friday morning. Rose must have known she'd stumbled on something important if she had made copies of it for Amy so quickly. Within two days of taking the water samples, she was dead. But the samples hadn't even been analyzed yet. Had she discovered something else?

"I'll ask Officer Berglund to search again," Martha said. Monday. What secrets had Rose discovered under the forest's shadow? She stared at the raccoon eyes of the professor. "But I'm not sure it matters. Who knows you're doing the lab work on the field samples?"

"Just Rose. My students think they're running reports on my summer research."

"You should keep it that way. The two other people who knew about them are now dead. Can you expedite the two samples you have in your possession?"

That left the professor visibly shaken, his face paling. "Of course."

Martha stood up. "Good. And I'll need those GPS coordinates, Dr. Barnes. It's time to go take a hike in the woods to see what Rose discovered."

But first, she had another visit to make. With luck, Nettles was still out of town.

TWENTY-ONE

In a hospital waiting room replete with soft music and soft pastel prints, MacAuliffe tried to make sense of life. And death.

Why had he been spared the same fate as Amelia Bumgarten? Now she was dead. A young woman with a lifetime of opportunity in front of her. Her mother had moved them to some rural burg in the northland surrounded by trees and big water where she hoped to escape her own addictions and offer her daughter the chance of a better future. She loved her daughter and was willing to work two jobs to give her a decent home and a normal life. Now she was dead because she believed the environment in which she raised her daughter was something worth fighting for.

And Ester Petrowski had dedicated her life to teaching. In retirement she walked her dog, nursed her ornery cat, fed the seagulls, and heaped praise on former students like Mark Monahan, who had flourished under her tutelage. When the truck had exploded, MacAuliffe hadn't been the one tossed into the water like yesterday's fast-food wrapper; it had been Ester P, an innocent bystander.

Now she lay in a coma. The ICU nurse had informed him earlier that she had been doing well, that they hoped to let her go home today. Then, without warning, she'd experienced a severe stroke. CPR and a defibrillator had brought her back from the dead. The next twenty-four to forty-eight hours were critical if she was to have a chance of recovering.

Martha pulled into the circular drive in front of Nettles' lakeside home. She rang the doorbell and waited, swatting away first one mosquito, then another and a third. She'd forgotten about this part of living in the northland. No one came to the door. Catching Sophia at work with Nettles down in the Cities had been a long shot. She rang the bell again.

A city bus rumbled by. It disappeared behind the front hedge. Martha heard the airbrakes hiss as it came to a halt.

She rang the bell a third time and stepped back from the door. The front lawn could have been a putting green at Nettles' new golf course. The driveway was a herringbone pattern of red bricks. Not a single weed sprouted between the bricks.

Sophia came around the corner from the sidewalk into the driveway. A grocery bag hung from each hand. She wore faded jeans and an oversized white shirt with a light blue sweater draped over her shoulders. Sneakers adorned her feet. Her hair was pulled back in a ponytail. A wisp of gray hair had escaped and dangled beside her ear.

"Ms. Whitaker," Sophia said, coming to a stop. "Mr. Nettles isn't expected home for another couple hours or so."

"Good," Martha said. "I'm here to see you, Sophia."

"I can't imagine why."

"May I help you with those?" Martha pointed to the grocery bags. "I'd like to talk with you if you have a few minutes to spare."

"I'm fine, thank you. I can't imagine we have anything to discuss. If you'll excuse me."

"Sophia," Martha said. The woman paused midstride, turning her head sideways. "Two women are dead. We're trying to figure out if Craig Nettles is involved or if he's being framed."

"I wouldn't know, ma'am." She took another step toward the house.

"And you're not curious to find out?" When that elicited no response, Martha asked, "Were you working for the family when Elizabeth Nettles was alive?"

"Yes."

"So you've been here fifteen, twenty years?"

"It'll be nineteen in September."

"So you knew Mrs. Nettles?"

"Of course. She's the one who hired me. I started as an afternoon nanny and tutor for the children."

"Oh, what subjects?"

"Is there a point to this, Ms. Whitaker? I'm sure my history in education can't be that interesting to you."

Sometimes, Martha knew, the best way to reach a reluctant witness was to be forthright and honest. If that didn't work, you walked away. "You're right, Sophia, I'm sorry. James and I want to understand what kind of person Craig Nettles is, and if he's connected to the deaths of the two women. They were both murdered, Sophia. And we think it was to shut them up. About what we're not sure, but one was quite vocal in her opposition to the NorthShore Resorts in Grand Marais."

A long silence followed.

Finally, Sophia said, "Why don't you come in? I have food to put in the freezer."

Instead of leading her to the main house, she took the sidewalk around the side of the house. A small brick building was set back near the hedge. Martha recognized it instantly as a former garage. The main door had been filled in with bricks, but the shape, size, and location all spoke of her home, the Carriage House. Beyond it, the manicured backyard stretched to the lake, where the large boat bobbed at the dock.

Sophia unlocked the door and invited Martha into a small kitchen that could have been laid out and decorated by Martha Stewart or some such doyenne of décor. Sophia said, "May I bring you an iced tea?"

"Yes, thank you." Sophia took a pitcher from the refrigerator and poured two glasses. Martha said, "I live in Seattle over a garage. It makes for a great apartment."

"Ms. Whitaker, please. You're not here to chat. We're not going to be friends. How may I help you?"

Okay, direct and to the point. She could do the same. "Do you think Nettles would've killed someone if she stood in the way of his resort being developed?"

There was no hesitation. "Rose Bumgarten posed no threat. And if she had, it would've just been a whole lot easier to pay her off. It's amazing how principles vanish with enough money."

"So you know about Rose?" And you didn't answer the question, Martha thought. What a person doesn't say can often be as interesting as what she does say.

"I read the news. I'm Craig's personal assistant, schedule his meetings, write his checks. I knew Ms. Bumgarten opposed the resort. She didn't pose a threat. If she did, she would've been offered a healthy sum to go away. It's a lesson Craig's learned well through the years."

"The sexual assault charge against him, for example?"

"Of course."

"How about the judge who decided the land use case? Quid pro quo, maybe?"

"That one I'm not sure about, but I'd be surprised if it didn't involve some kind of mutually beneficial agreement. Under the table, of course."

"Of course. Sounds like a nice guy."

"He's not—at times. He likes to get his way."

"Like when his wife was dying."

Sophia just nodded. "I sat with Beth for days, weeks, sometimes with the children, usually alone. First at home and then in the hospital. Ovarian cancer. It wasn't pretty. Whereas the young woman that Craig was fucking was. I saw how much it hurt Beth and the kids. They all knew."

"Why did you stay?" Martha asked.

"It's amazing how principles vanish with enough money. A young woman from a dirt poor family from Ely with little formal education. But I was smart. I made myself indispensable to Craig. And I didn't have to fuck him to do it, if you're wondering. I was also worried about young Craig and Bessie after their mother died. I had grown to love them as if they were my own. They needed someone to care for them, and it was never going to be their father."

"How'd they take it? Their mom dying, their dad not being there?"

"Not well, of course. Buzz took it the hardest. He was older, he knew better what was going on. He was very close to his mom. He didn't get along well with his father even then. Bessie was closer to her father. Father and daughter, they were so much alike. Ask Buzz sometime how he lost a kidney and two ribs."

Sophia stood up. "You'll have to excuse me. I have to change and prepare supper. Craig wants supper served by six o'clock."

Martha stood up. "What happened to Craig Junior?"

"Please, Ms. Whitaker. I've said enough. As I'm sure you're aware, I could lose my job for talking with you. I'm not that indispensable. But he didn't kill Rose Bumgarten." She stared at Martha. "I can assume none of our conversation was on the record? I also assume nothing will ever reach Mr. Nettles about our talk?"

"Of course," Martha said, and showed herself out.

Martha had showered and changed into blessedly clean clothes. She was inhaling the lingering scent of lavender and toweling off her still damp hair when she heard her phone beep. A text from Mac read: "Can you create reason to go see old man Nettles and keep him occupied from say 6 to 7? Best if you can get him out of kitchen and into front room office? LMK. Cheers Mac."

"LMK." Her brain flashed through possible meanings until she figured it out. She glanced at her Fitbit. That would be in less than an hour. She texted back: "I'll see what I can do."

Now what? And what excuse did she have to call Nettles? Ask him to let her see the investigative report the lawyer Brooks had done? Possible if she framed it right, but not likely. Maybe ask him how Craig Junior had lost a kidney and two ribs? She'd promised Sophia.

Her phone beeped. Mac included a phone number and, "Thx. Maybe interested in job offer?"

Of course. Mac was good, but would Nettles believe it? Only one way to know. He picked up on the third ring. "Hi, Mr. Nettles, this is Martha Whitaker. We met a couple of days ago regarding that story on your resort development in Grand Marais. I'm wondering if you're back in town yet."

"Almost, Martha. Driving through Moose Lake now. Did you get the recipe for my butternut squash soup?"

"I did. Thank you. I'm anxious to try it."

"Good." He paused. "What can I do for you this afternoon?"

"If you have time, I thought you could buy me a drink and tell me more of what you had in mind about that job offer."

From his immediate silence she knew he either didn't believe her or didn't remember he'd made her a job offer.

Nettles recovered quickly. "After the way Buzz treated you and your reporter friend, I didn't expect to hear from you again."

"It was just a little misunderstanding. No harm, no foul. I can be a skilled negotiator."

"I saw that."

"And I'm an even better attorney."

"Interesting. You have my attention. But I thought you were pretty emphatic that Seattle was home."

"Well, it was. I mean, it is. But Mac is interviewing for a job with the *Duluth News Tribune*, and we're considering staying here for a while. Mac is from here, you know, and I grew up in the UP, so the upper Midwest means a lot to both of us—roots, family and with the lake we both get our water fix. But for us to consider a permanent change, we both need to secure jobs."

Where did that come from? She almost had to sit down, the lie had slipped so easily off her tongue.

"I didn't realize you were a couple."

"Let's say we're exploring the possibility. Why don't you buy me a drink and we can discuss the job. Assuming of course you were serious about it. Maybe I assumed wrong."

"Oh no, I always have openings for talented people, and I could use a friendly voice at the paper. They're not always as enthusiastic as I'd like them to be."

"Well, I can't promise anything. Mac has a strong professional ethic when reporting on the news, but I can always put in a good word."

"Okay, I'm intrigued. But it's almost my supper time. We're not like you city folks who have supper *after* going to the opera.

Six o'clock is fashionably late around here. Instead of a drink, why don't you join me for supper? Want to come over to the house? I'll call Sophia and let her know you're coming. She said she's making a chicken and mushroom Marsala; it's quite good, one of my favorites."

"Thank you, Mr. Nettles, but I'd prefer to keep this more professional." And it'd be easier to keep him out of the kitchen if he wasn't home. "I know you understand. Let's meet someplace for dinner. I'm sure you have a favorite restaurant that you'd recommend."

"Of course. Do you like Italian? We can meet at Va Bene on Superior Street. Say, in forty-five minutes?"

"That sounds nice."

"Good. I'll call ahead for a reservation. Dress casual but the food is superb, and they have a nice wine list."

"I look forward to seeing you then."

After she hung up, she texted MacAuliffe. "You so owe me. Dinner reservations at 6pm. Place called Va Bene."

"Gr8, yes, owe u. Bring me doggy bag. Antipasto superior is good starter. Love filetto di manzo."

"What are you doing?"

"Going for a paddle"

She went through her entire wardrobe in seconds, flipping one hanger to another. A pair of jeans, a pair of slacks, a couple of blouses. A sport coat that had served for a multitude of occasions from weddings to funerals. She was glad Nettles had specifically noted the restaurant was casual. An iron nestled on the top shelf in the tiny hotel closet. She spread her damp towel on the bed and began ironing jeans, a white blouse. The black silk sport coat added a touch of class. Light makeup, earrings, and her Fitbit completed her preparations. What to do with her hair? What did women do with short hair? No time to ask Mac's sister for a fashion consult. Instead, she used a little mousse, combed it a couple of time with her fingers and decided that tonight she'd go with the slightly wild, definitely casual style.

Google maps showed Va Bene was less than a mile away by car. Plenty of time. What was fashionably late in Duluth? But you're never supposed to be late to a job interview. She decided to be late.

She called Emily again and left another message, this one with a clear tone of concern and urgency. A text to Ray Palmer brought an almost immediate response. "Working W Sea near White Cen right now. Will swing by garage later or when go off shift at 11."

West Seattle near White Center was a rough part of town, a place where poverty and drugs and unemployment collided in often violent results. "Okay, thanks. Be safe," she texted back. Her phone rang almost immediately. Caller ID identified the number as Barnes' mobile. "Yes, Dr. Barnes?"

"I took your advice and threw out the first quiz results. In glancing through some of the answers it's probably for the best. Never good to start the semester with half the class failing. A couple of my better students will be upset, but they'll be fine."

"They usually are. The football crowd will be happy, however. But I'm sure that's not why you called."

"A couple of my graduate students completed the analysis of the two samples that I hadn't logged. I thought if you weren't busy, I could go over them with you during supper."

"Thank you, Dr. Barnes, that's very kind of you. I appreciate the invitation, but I already have a dinner engagement." What was this thing about supper instead of dinner? "Maybe you could just give me the synopsis for a non-scientist. I've got a few minutes."

"Sure," Barnes said. "The short version is, I located them from Rose's GPS coordinates as being on Devil Track River, upstream from the location where Woods Creek joins in. They had some trace pollutants, but all in all they were clean enough that you could probably drink from the river at that point without doing any harm. What's of note is what isn't there. There's no high concentrate of nitrates like we found in the lower portion of the river."

"Even negative results tell us something."

"All good science is learning how to understand negative results," he said, as if lecturing to his undergraduate students. "I also pinpointed the other two GPS coordinates from Rose's notes. As we suspected, they're both on Woods Creek, one about two miles upstream from the confluence with Devil Track, the second another two to three miles upstream from that. If you could get me new samples, I could analyze them in the lab."

"I guess we need to make a trek up Woods Creek," Martha said. "Any chance you're available to help?"

He stuttered and stumbled over his response. "Not anytime soon, I'm sorry. Classes all week, sorry, and my wife has . . . has a family reunion in the Cities next weekend. Sorry, but I can't help."

"Of course. Okay, thank you for calling me, Dr. Barnes. I appreciate the update. Be safe."

TWENTY-TWO

When she walked in, a waiter directed her to a corner table in the back room. All-glass windows overlooked Lake Superior, making it feel as if they were perched on the lake itself. Nettles was sipping a cocktail when he saw her and immediately jumped up. His limp was noticeable as he stepped toward her. He too had dressed casually, if not wearing a tie constituted casual in his world. Gray slacks with a crease sharp enough to give paper cuts; a pressed band-collar shirt in pale pink with two buttons open, a tuft of white hair showing; a classic blue linen sports jacket—with a very high thread count. It was topped by that crew cut of white hair, the red face with pale eyelashes and a broad smile.

"Goodness, you look stunning," Nettles said.

"Not the usual greeting for a job interview," Martha replied, her voice carrying a hint of frost. She offered him a hand.

"The MeToo movement kind of missed me. But true, none the less. Please, please, have a seat." He held out a chair with the best view of the lake.

He quizzed the waiter about the wine list, but Martha interjected. "Thank you, Mr. Nettles, but—"

"Please called me Craig."

"Of course. Craig, it seems you already have your drink."

Lawyering 101. Take control of the situation. Once given up, it's damn near impossible to get back. Nettles nodded, as if to say, point ceded.

She ordered a mid-list chardonnay by Kendall Jackson. A safe if not particularly inspired choice.

While they waited for her drink, he remained silent, giving her time to appreciate his choice of locations. Someplace over the hills of Duluth the sun had set, washing the lake and the distant shoreline of Wisconsin in soft pastels of pink and gold.

MacAuliffe gave a passing nod to the beautiful evening. The water steadily slipping under the keel of the kayak had changed to an inky black. The dark red of the kayak's upper hull and the navy jacket he'd borrowed from his dad's closet would soon be indistinguishable to all but the most keen-eyed observer. The rhythm of paddling quickly came back to him. Shoulders square with the boat, he pushed the paddle through the water. The easy motion propelled him down the shore. He had to trust Martha to do her part to keep Nettles occupied and resist the urge to paddle harder. Working harder didn't mean going faster.

He paddled south from University Park, passing the estates and luxury houses of Duluth's elite, their large lawns now swathed in deepening shadows. In the background, he saw people sitting down to dinner, a television flickering. A couple of houses were totally dark except for security lights. Outside one house someone—man or woman he couldn't tell—stood on the deck, the ember glow of a cigarette visible when they sucked deep. He resisted the urge to stop paddling and light up himself. It'd be a foolish way to draw attention to himself.

He trusted he'd recognize his destination when he reached it. The large boat moored at the dock with the ski boat on the lift should be easy enough to spot. Still, with the growing darkness, he inched closer to shore with each stroke. Passing one dock, a motion-triggered light flicked on. What if Nettles had a motion-sensitive light on his dock? What if he had a security system rigged to the boat? All problems to worry about when he got there. Right now, he was just a solitary kayaker out for a late evening paddle.

Nothing could be better.

After a while of steady paddling, he paused to catch his breath. The clock on his phone was visible through the plastic bag. It was taking him longer than he thought. He hoped Martha could keep Nettles occupied.

Nettles was on his second bourbon by the time the antipasto superior showed up. The prosciutto was sliced so thin she could practically see through it. With a rich taleggio cheese, it made for a mouthwatering appetizer. Their hands brushed as they reached at the same time for a another helping. Martha drew her hand back.

"Please," she said, "after you."

"I'm sorry, you're my guest. Please."

"So tell me what it's like to work for you," Martha said, cutting a wedge of the taleggio. "Do you oversee all the details of your projects or do you give an assignment expecting your staff to have the competence to do the work with minimal supervision?"

"So am I a micromanager?"

"In essence. But also do you have good people working for you? People who take the initiative and who have the expertise to follow through. I very much appreciate the creative energy that comes with working and collaborating with other smart people."

"You're smooth."

"And you didn't answer the question."

"You're direct. I like that."

"And you still haven't answered."

Nettles smiled. Was he playing with her like a wolf with its food? If so, he'd quickly learn this food could bite back.

"Yes, I'm a micromanager," Nettles said. "My name is the company. Things have to be right or it reflects badly on me, not you."

"That's fair," Martha nodded. "How big is your legal team?"

Nettles finished his bourbon in a large gulp and signaled the waiter. "I have a real estate attorney on retainer, and I have my personal attorney. I hire other attorneys as I need their expertise. Sophia has the information."

"So what expertise do you require from me?"

The waiter appeared and Nettles ordered another bourbon, one ice cube this time, not two. Martha declined a second glass of chardonnay.

"Maybe with dinner," she said, and turned her attention out the windows. The sunset was slowly giving way to the darkness. She felt as if she was at dinner with a prospective client for CH&N. That was a life she'd left behind without regret—other than occasionally missing the paycheck. Mac so owed her. What was he doing? Still, she might as well enjoy the food. To Nettles, she added, "Are you ready to order? I'm starving."

The boat appeared as a dark silhouette against a distant yard light. MacAuliffe eased the kayak alongside the stern. No flood lights announced his arrival. He remained still, scanning the surrounding yard, the neighbors, listening for any alarms. A chorus of crickets created a distant white noise, water lapping against the boat's hull an occasional interlude. Freshly cut grass scented the night air.

Across the boat's transom he saw the name, *Executive Suite*, and groaned at the bad puns that frequented powerboat names. He was also sure Nettles claimed the boat as a second office, qualifying it as a tax write-off with the IRS. MacAuliffe rolled out of the kayak onto the swim step, knowing his mother would be embarrassed at his ungraceful exit of the small boat. The front pocket of the life vest produced a pair of latex gloves taken from his mother's cleaning closet. He tugged them on, finishing with a tight snap.

In the cockpit, he slid into the shadows and leaned against the combing. He remembered to breathe. Nothing unusual troubled any of his senses. The crickets chirped. There was the faint sound of distant road traffic. The gentle lapping of water. No activity from the big house, none from the neighbors. On the starboard side of the spacious cockpit, steps led up to the flybridge where there had to be a second helm station. From under his life vest, he removed his phone and a small crowbar from his mother's shop. The flashlight on his phone shone bright for an instant, just long enough for him to locate the door handle. He had the crowbar positioned to pop the door when he decided to at least try it.

The door slid open.

Why not lock the door? Wired to security? Carelessness? Forgetfulness? No alarms sounded, so MacAuliffe proceeded as if it were one of the latter.

Inside, he closed all the curtains before turning on his phone light again. The salon lit up as he slowly rotated around the room. Teak paneling and cabinetry with a satin finish contrasted with light gray or cream carpeting. On the port side, a built-in settee of leather the color of caramel curved out on either end. MacAuliffe studied the interior. Something wasn't right. The starboard side of the salon was empty, as if they had forgotten to put in all the furniture. And the curve of the long settee begged for a coffee table or something—a place to put drinks, to hold a platter of cheese and crackers. He examined the carpet and saw four holes, right where he'd expect a coffee table to be bolted to the floor.

Past the main salon was the inside helm station to starboard and the galley to port. Beyond that and down a couple of steps, an open door showed one of the staterooms. He was sure the boat had two or three. At the helm station, he found the battery switches and turned them on, and then went to the electrical panel and started flipping switches for the boat's navigation systems. He systematically went through each electronic device and turned them on. They began to power up.

A plaque beside the helm seat informed him the boat was an Ocean Alexander, not a boat usually found on the lake. It was several steps up from the Bayliners and Sea Rays that proliferated like nautical roaches. Lifting the helm seat, he found charts of Lake Superior, many the same as his father carried on the *Ginny*. He scanned them. Nothing of interest had been scribbled on any of the maps of the North Shore. Under the charts were boat pamphlets and warranties. *Executive Suite* was an OA Altus 48, built in 2006. That was a big boat for the lake, an expensive boat. It would have to be hauled out soon for the winter.

In the galley, the carpet morphed into a teak-and-holly floor, but it had the same teak paneling and cabinetry as the main salon. It too was sparsely furnished. Only an espresso maker sat on the speckled brown-and-silver countertop. The lockers were bare of everything except coffee and a coffee-bean grinder. Puzzling. Even he couldn't live on coffee alone.

On the lower deck, he found three staterooms, each with a head. One cabin was empty—the one with bunk beds—with no sign of having been used since the boat first slid into the water over a decade ago. In the master suite, a sleeping bag was rolled up on the king-sized bed, and a bare pillow rested beside it. Nothing hung in the closets; lockers were empty. In the third stateroom, located to port, he found the first signs that anyone had used the berths. Bedding had been casually thrown over a double bed. Foul-weather gear and a squall jacket hung in the closet. Boat shoes and a pair of rubber boots were tossed on the closet floor. In a drawer, he found some essentials—men's underwear, socks, tee-shirts. Another locker had a sweatshirt, a sweater, a couple of pairs of faded jeans, all clean and folded, all sized for Buzz, not his heavier father. Nothing appeared to be hidden between the tees or briefs, nothing rolled up in the socks or jacket pockets.

On one side of the bed was a copy of *Bob Flowerdew's Organic Gardening Bible: Successful Growing the Natural Way*. Why did Buzz have the organic gardening Bible? Curious. Puzzling. It told him nothing.

In the engine room, MacAuliffe found a couple of large Yanmar diesel engines, a generator, the basic tools and filters and spares one would expect on a boat this size. Things were clean and tidy, with only a hint of diesel permeating the air. He closed the engine compartment and returned to the helm station.

The caprese salad had been awesome. The tomatoes were like eating liquid sunshine, the basil so fresh it must have been picked right before being added. The sweet balsamic reduction and olive oil didn't overpower the salad. Now, Martha sat back while the waiter placed the filetto di manzo in front of her. If the aroma was any indication of the quality of the entrée, there'd be none left to take to Mac when she was done.

"You still haven't told me anything about the job, Craig."

"I know you're running your own shop for homeless and battered women," he replied. His entrée was seared scallops and Martha almost offered to switch. Almost. He continued before she could decide. "That's commendable, very commendable indeed. But I'm more interested in knowing what you did for Carey, Harwell and—"

"Niehaus. You've done your homework. Corporate law. Mergers and acquisitions. Big market real estate. I worked through most of the departments until I became more of a generalist, doing whatever was required to aid the client. Sometimes we had to use the law to protect them in court. That's where I excelled."

"Getting crooks off the hook," Nettles said.

The tender cut of beef topped with gorgonzola cheese was delicious. Martha didn't respond as she savored the beef, cooked to a perfect medium rare. Every bite was to be treasured. She chewed slowly, swallowed. "That's one way of putting it, I suppose. It's also one of several reasons why I quit."

"Quit or forced out after the incident with the Seattle police officer?"

"I quit." Her voice harsh. She had no intention of sharing with Nettles all that led to the incident with Harry Callison. She added some levity to her voice. "You're amazingly adroit at avoiding answering direct questions, Craig."

"A skill that I perfected in the military, I'm afraid." He rapped his artificial leg under the table. "See what good it got me."

"Which you're still doing, I see."

"A lifetime of practice."

She remained quiet, concentrating on her food. Because she didn't enjoy the company didn't mean she couldn't enjoy the exquisite dinner. A glance outside told her night had swallowed the last remnants of the day. City lights reflected off the black water in glimmering silver streaks. She sipped her chardonnay, alternating between wine and water. Nettles barely touched his water, preferring the bourbon, now his fourth, one ice cube, not two. She returned to her food. Still she said nothing.

Nettles wasn't skilled in the subtleties of letting silence linger. He said, "I need a generalist."

"Someone who can get a crook off the hook?"

White teeth gleamed as he just shrugged. A smile or a snarl, she couldn't tell. He gulped the last of his bourbon.

Back at the helm station, all the electronics were now live and ready. Mostly MacAuliffe was interested in the chart plotter. Like all computers it had a history feature, and he pressed a few wrong buttons before he found it. Three times this summer Buzz had patrolled the North Shore on the boat, each time plugging in the same coordinates. They took him up the coast from Grand Marais to Grand Portage. The plotter had dozens of coordinates, all of which kept him close to shore, almost as if he were following Highway 61. Buzz had let the autopilot do most of the work of steering the boat. A set of coordinates took him between Marr Island and the shore. There was no way of telling how often Buzz had disengaged the autopilot and investigated something unusual or suspicious on shore.

MacAuliffe followed the plot points up the coast and then noticed each ended with the same wild deviation. The next-to-last way point was south of Grand Portage, just miles from the Canadian border, then the next point was twenty miles out into Lake Superior. He tapped the screens back and forth. Each of the three trips ended in the same place. The chart plotter told him it was north-northwest of Rock of Ages Lighthouse off Isle Royale. What the hell?

He dug through the charts and pamphlets again. He removed everything from the cubbyholes around the helm station, careful to place each item in order so he could return them exactly as they had come out. Nothing. Next he went over to the galley, and there in the top drawer he found the log for *Executive Suite*. Each trip was recorded in the log, with all the normal log information of time, weather, sea conditions, any unusual sightings—truck parked on the beach near Brule R., a large tree floating off Hollow Rock—"pulled to shore"—illegal camp on Deronda Bay. Each patrol took two days and ended with a trip twenty miles out into the lake so he could anchor in Grace Harbor on the southwest point of Isle Royale. Why?

Using his phone, MacAuliffe confirmed the distance between Grand Marais and Grand Portage. Thirty-five miles up Highway 61. It wouldn't be much different by boat. Two days? Even at a leisurely pace, a round trip between the two towns was an easy day trip in this cruising machine. And, then, why run the extra miles out to the island? A fishing trip? A mini-vacation or catching up on some comp time? But three times? Did he take company on these patrols, a special friend, a romantic getaway? But the log indicated that Buzz hadn't lingered at the national park. The next morning, he made a bee line from Isle Royale to Grand Marais, often arriving before eight o'clock in the morning; once he took the boat back to Duluth after stopping to refuel in "GM." So why motor twenty miles out to Isle Royale to spend the night in Grace Harbor if he planned to be home early the next morning?

Some story was being told by the bare facts of the log and the points on the chart plotter, each with the extended side trip to Isle Royale duly noted. But MacAuliffe didn't know what it was. With his phone camera, he took screen shots of the plotter so he didn't have to write down all the coordinates and photographed pages from the logbook. A puzzle wrapped in an enigma shrouded in a mystery. Or something like that.

He took extra time making sure everything was exactly as he'd found it and slipped out into the night. Right before he dropped his phone into the waterproof bag, he texted Martha. "Heading home."

Martha's phone chimed just as she pulled into Nettles' driveway. A motion-sensitive light suddenly cast a pool of light around the front of the house. The drunk developer sat in the passenger's seat, appearing way more sober than he had any right to. The ease with which he'd agreed to her insistence that she drive him home had surprised her. Experienced with designated drivers? Or for another reason?

"Excuse me, Craig," she said. "I've been dealing with a work problem back in Seattle." She checked her phone. "Heading home." Okay, time to stall. She turned to Nettles. "Thank you again for a lovely dinner and the insightful conversation. That's quite a yacht you've got docked there on the lake. I'm a bit of a boat nut. It certainly dwarves my Grady-White. You get out on her much?"

"Nah, not much, mostly Buzz uses it. Thinks it's his private toy. A good way to impress the gals. Makes quite an entrance in Grand Morass, I'm sure."

"So no luck getting him to join the business? It must be hard to build all of this and then not have anyone to hand it off to."

"That was supposed to be Bessie. She would've brought her brother around. They were close. He's hated me ever since their mom died."

"I'm sorry. I can't imagine how difficult that must be. I was just wondering if I might be working for him someday. We didn't get off on the . . . the best of terms, shall we say."

"Nah, you've nothing to worry about there."

"What happened?" Martha knew it was a risk, but she needed to give Mac time to slip away.

"His mom and I weren't getting along when she got sick. It happens, but kids are always the last to understand. Buzz blamed me for her death. There wasn't anything I could've done to change the outcome. It was the big C. But he didn't see it that way. He was pissed, probably drunk. Tried to run me off the road one night. Missed me but didn't miss a big ol' elm tree."

"Wow, that's hard."

"Yeah, that tree was hard all right."

Listening closely, she heard the words slur. She'd be passed out in the backseat if she'd had five—or was it six?—bourbons. Instead, he makes a joke about his son attempting to run him off the road, an accident that most likely cost his son a kidney and two ribs. She found Nettles disgusting. Okay, Mac, I'm running out of patience here. I hope you're gone.

MacAuliffe pulled himself out of the water onto the swim step of *Executive Suite*. When his eyes cleared of lake water, the first thing he saw was a gun pointed at him; the second was Nettles' housekeeper Sophia behind it.

"You?" she said. The gun never wavered. "I see why journalists have earned their bad reputation."

"Sophia, I can explain." He automatically raised his hands.

She lowered the gun and the phone she held in her other hand. "I already told your friend, Ms. Whitaker, that Craig had nothing to do with Rose Bumgarten being killed. What're you guys after?"

MacAuliffe inched his hands down. That was unexpected. When did Martha talk to her? "I'm sorry, we haven't spoken this afternoon. How do you know?"

She hesitated, her shoulders sagging. "I know Craig. I know how he operates. I also write the checks. He would've attempted to pay the woman off first. He would've made it hard for her to refuse. He can be very generous."

Looking at the wrong end of a gun probably wasn't the time to ask how she knew so much about Nettles' generosity. Instead, he asked, "What's Buzz got to do with all this? He's the one using the boat."

"Other than he hates his father, I have no idea."

"What keeps him coming back then?"

"Like I said, Craig can be very generous. But it always comes with conditions."

The sound of an engine revving and a car door slamming drifted across the backyard. Sophia looked in the direction of the noise. Turning back, she said, "That's gotta be Craig getting home. Go. Now. And if I see you or your partner around here again, I may just accidently shoot a prowler in the kneecap. And believe me, I will not miss."

"I'm glad you were able to reconcile," Martha said. "That must've been a horrible time."

"Talking to shrinks and the threat of losing his inheritance has an amazing effect on a kid," Nettles said.

Martha could almost see the smirk on his face. Time to lie again. "I'd love to go fishing. See what lake fishing is all about. What're you doing tomorrow? Maybe you could tell me more about the company and why you think you require a generalist with my expertise? It'd give me time to think about the job—and talk salary. Some expertise comes at a higher cost than others."

"Sure those battered women got lots of dough to cover your *expertise.*" Nettles managed after a couple of attempts to get his seat belt unfastened. "Sorry, can't take you out. Buzz called this afternoon. Going on final patrol of his territory. Tomorrow. Before winter. Another six hundred gallons of fuel on the old man's credit card. Just another contribution to Uncle Sam and my silver-spoon sperm. Gotta love 'em both." He leaned closer and placed his hand over hers. "Wanna come in for a nightcap?"

Martha deliberately picked it up and placed it back in his lap. "Thanks, Craig, but you've had enough for both of us tonight. I'll make sure you get in the house safe."

His hand touched her leg, much too high up for any mistake about his intent.

"Of course, we can just skip the Pappy's. You didn't call about a job. You're too sexy and smart for that little newspaper boy. Maybe wonderin' what a—"

"If you don't remove that hand by the time I finish this sentence, I will break your hand, probably your nose, leave you bleeding on the driveway—and don't assume I can't or won't. It would give me great pleasure to do both. Then I'll have a report filed with the police for sexual assault by the time you figure out how to unlock your front door. I will be very, very expensive to buy off. Time's up."

The hand was gone. She reached across and opened his door. "Good night, Mr. Nettles. Thank you for dinner. It was, well, an insightful evening."

He groped her breast. "Come on, honey. You're after a little taste of real power—"

She snatched his thumb and bent it backwards and shoved. He thudded onto the concrete, his artificial leg hitting with a sharp smack. "You have no idea what real power is, you arrogant, self-centered, small-town drunk."

He staggered up, his right palm bloody from the landing. "You ungrateful bitch. You fuckin' led me on with your flirting and Craig this and Craig that, and Craig take me—"

Martha jerked the car into reverse, then hit the brakes. The passenger door slammed shut from the momentum.

Good to her word, she waited until Nettles had let himself into the house. It gave her plenty of time to text MacAuliffe: "You so owe me."

TWENTY-THREE

When the truck pulled into the driveway of the Park Point bungalow, the kayak sticking out of the bed, Martha came out of the house and stood in the door, arms akimbo, the silhouette of a spider waiting for its prey. When MacAuliffe emerged from the truck, he was soaking wet; his long hair, tucked behind his ears, lay plastered to his skull. Martha was unsure whether to bite his head off or laugh.

"You're all wet," she said.

"Brilliant deduction. Thought I should check the underside of the boat before I left."

"How'd that go?"

"'Bout like you'd expect. It was dark. My phone light didn't work too well underwater, though I can endorse the waterproof qualities of Ziplocs."

"I'm sure they'll be glad to hear it. What happened?"

"Mom should get a more stable boat."

"Nothing to do with operator error?"

MacAuliffe laughed and Martha joined him.

"Oh, it was all operator error. I saw the headlights when Nettles pulled in the driveway, and I was hurrying to get away.

Didn't quite make the recommended entry into the kayak."

"Glad I gave him time to grope me in the driveway. Gave you time to escape without getting caught."

He grimaced. "Sorry about that. But why were you there too?"

"He was too drunk to drive. I took his keys away from him?"

"Did you leave him in one piece?"

"What?" she hissed. "What about me? Am I okay? Did I appreciate getting sent on a job that I was clueless about, only to be harassed by some drunk who thinks he's a regular Lothario. He knew the only reason I called was to go to bed with him. Asshole. Fucking asshole. And that goes for you, too, James MacAuliffe. How dare you ask me if *he's* okay."

She stormed back into the well-lit house.

"Martha, I'm sorry," MacAuliffe called at her back and followed her inside. He ignored Newton, who had bounded out despite his arthritic hips, wagging his tail in expectation. "Martha. I'm sorry, okay? It was a bad joke. No one I know is more capable of handling some lecher with wandering hands than you. I didn't mean to be insensitive."

Martha spun around. Her voice was a hoarse whisper. "I accept your apology, asshole. But just because I *can* take care of myself doesn't mean I'm okay. And it doesn't mean I appreciate being put in a position that I have to put some wannabe Romeo on his knees."

MacAuliffe reached out and took her hand. To his surprise, she didn't pull it away. "I'm sorry. I hope you didn't hurt yourself kicking that wooden leg."

"Goddamn you, Mac." She pulled away and stormed into the kitchen.

By the time MacAuliffe had showered and changed into dry clothes, his mom and Martha were sitting at the kitchen table drinking wine.

"The hanging of the Lakotas has become a forgotten blot on the myth of Lincoln," Virginia said. The scale mock-up of her sculpture sat on the floor between them. Her head popped up when MacAuliffe entered the room. "Ah, the little newspaper boy."

"What?" MacAuliffe said. "Little newspaper boy?"

"I'll explain," Martha said.

"And I'm off to bed," Virginia said. "Just wanted to make sure my truck and kayak got home safe."

"What about me?"

"I quit worrying about you a long time ago." She patted Martha's hand. "Thanks for being interested in my work, hon. Remember, the guest room is all made up if you prefer to stay."

She kissed MacAuliffe on the cheek. "Good night, honey. I'm glad you're home safe, too."

MacAuliffe studied the wine, a red Syrah from 3 Horse Ranch. All that remained was a finger or two after he poured himself a glass. He sat down. "You still mad?"

"I'm not mad," Martha said. "The last time someone assumed I could take care of myself—and them—they ended up dead. I've almost died once on this investigation of yours. But mostly I don't like being taken for granted, and I really don't like being left in the dark about what's going on."

"Imagine my surprise when Sophia mentioned you guys had already talked today."

"I don't do tit for tat, Mac. You could've told me what you were doing."

"That sounds a lot like being mad."

"I'm getting there, Mac."

They sat still and quiet, sipping wine and listening to the ticking of the wall clock, an old fashioned analog model with a van Gogh sunflower motif.

MacAuliffe broke the silence. "How'd it go with Nettles?"

"You were right about the food. I had a nice dinner."

"That bad, huh?"

"He's in some kind of trouble and requires an attorney who's good at, as he puts it, getting crooks off the hook. He didn't say what it was. Even with five or six bourbons he wouldn't talk. Or he doesn't need an attorney at all and just thought I'd jump into bed with him because he's rich and powerful. I dispelled him of that notion."

"Five or six bourbons? I'd be on my lips."

"So was he after he groped me. I warned him once, but he's not a man who understands no. He does now."

"What kind of trouble? You think he's involved in this after all?"

"He's involved in something, but I'm not sure it's killing the Bumgartens. He may be worried someone's setting him up. It may have nothing to do with the resort. He's pretty tightlipped about his business, even when drunk." She swirled the wine in her glass and drank the last of it. "Yes, I dropped by to talk to Sophia this afternoon. She's his personal assistant and insisted he didn't do it."

"Yeah, I know," MacAuliffe said. He reached across the table and poured her the last of the Syrah. "She greeted me after I missed the kayak. With a gun pointed at my face. She said you guys had talked. You buying her idea that Nettles would've paid off Rose rather have her killed?"

"Yes, I am. When I worked at CH&N, I had several clients like Nettles. It's what they would've done. It's how they operate. Paying someone off isn't necessarily illegal. And it's only money.

That's what they have a lot of and know how to use. Money is power. They understand that. To them it's a good or bad day on the stock market. To you and me, it's a lifetime of opportunity. Yeah, he would've paid off Rose, and after a little negotiation, including the very real threat of a mountain of legal bills, she wouldn't have been able to refuse." She picked up her glass, realized it was empty, and set it back down. "Did you uncover anything?"

"Just more weirdness and some strange plot points on the chart plotter. If Buzz is using that floating piece of Tupperware as an orgy palace, he does a really good job of cleaning up the mess."

"What were you searching for?"

"I don't know. It just didn't feel right that Buzz'd use a million-dollar boat to do unnecessary shore patrols. Why not by car, by foot, by canoe or kayak like Berglund, or by small boat. Hell, daddy would probably buy it for him."

"Nettles figures it's like taxes—just another of his many donations to the federal government. He thinks Craig Junior uses the boat to go play, impress girls, be the big man in a little town. The old man's trying so hard to bring his son back into the family fold that he can't say no."

"I don't think Buzz is playing. No sign of it on the boat, in the log, on the chart plotter. He runs up the coast, zips over to Isle Royale for a night at anchor, and leaves early the next morning."

"Isn't Isle Royale out in the middle of the lake?"

"It's not that far, twenty, twenty-five miles offshore."

"That sounds like the middle of the lake."

"It's a big lake, remember."

"Yeah. Well, it's probably good that you broke into it tonight."

"I didn't break in. It was unlocked."

"It's still breaking in, Mac," Martha said in her best lawyer voice. "As Sophia with her gun well understood. Anyway, you wouldn't have been able to after tonight. Craig Junior is picking the boat up tomorrow." She peeked at the clock over his shoulder. "Well, today actually, for a final patrol of the North Shore before winter."

"Today?" MacAuliffe repeated.

"Nettles said he called this afternoon and is using the boat for his final patrol up the coast before winter. He'll be on the water by first light."

"Or we've stirred up something that has him panicking."

"What? Running over the border to Canada won't do him any good. We have good extradition agreements with them."

"I don't know. He's using the boat for something more than patrolling for forest fires, I'm sure. Maybe he's cooking meth in the woods, and we're getting too close to finding it. Hang on, I've got to go talk to Dad."

When MacAuliffe returned, he carried another bottle of wine. He uncorked it and poured more for each of them. "What'd Barnes have to say this afternoon?"

"Goodness, I almost forgot about that. At least that was productive. We might have something."

Martha was halfway through recounting her afternoon with Dr. Barnes when Ted MacAuliffe appeared in the kitchen. An old bathrobe draped his heavy frame and bare, thick legs extended to bare, hairy feet. The fringe of white hair that surrounded his bald dome stuck out in all directions as if he'd grabbed an electric fence on the way to the kitchen. Seeing Martha, he tightened the belt on his robe.

"Jiminy Cricket, Jimmy," he grumbled, "what's so goddamn important it can't wait until morning? I been asleep for an hour and you come shaking me like the house's burning down. I'll be awake the rest of the night now."

"It's important, Dad," MacAuliffe said. "Any chance you'd call Uncle Chuck and ask to borrow his go-fast boat?"

"What? You woke me for that? Coulda called him yourself if it was so goddamn important. See how he takes being woken up in the middle of the night from some wet—" he stopped midsentence, glancing at Martha. "Sorry. What's so important about taking out some stinkpot? As a kid you took to fishing like a turkey to Thanksgiving. You suddenly found religion?"

"Dad, I've got to get to Isle Royale in the next day or two. The *Ginny* isn't in any shape to do it."

"You made sure of—"

"Dad, please. This is important."

Martha swirled her wine without taking a drink. "Actually, James, you should follow him on the lake. I've got to take a hike up Woods Creek. I'll get Marlena to go with me. You should have someone with you."

She gave her widest smile. "Great time for some father-son bonding, Ted. Maybe you could help us out? A young woman and her mother are dead. James has found clues the police missed. He's really good at scaring bad guys into doing stupid things. This might be one of them. But I can't be there to protect him, and you know better than me he needs someone. I'd be more comfortable knowing someone he trusts has his back."

Guilt and praise, some cajoling and more guilt had the desired effect. The older MacAuliffe shook his head and waved a hand in dismissal. "All right, save the shill for the circus. I'll call Chuckie in the morning. But I'm driving. I can't afford to fix two of 'em after your shenanigans. Chuckie loves that boat more than he loves Marie." As he left the kitchen, he was heard muttering, "Blow up Chuck's boat and I'll sure as hell . . ."

When it was just the two of them again, MacAuliffe contemplated the bottle of red wine. He thought about raiding his father's liquor cabinet for the good stuff—as he'd done as a teenager. He thought about getting seriously drunk. The last time had been with Lance. They had just won the Best Investigative Feature at the annual state journalism awards, besting the uppity- nose boys from the *Seattle Times* and *Spokesman-Review* for their story on a veteran who got lost in the system of an overworked and underfunded VA, and drank himself to death under the Ballard railroad bridge.

Reaching for the bottle brought the kitchen clock into focus: nearly one o'clock. He couldn't afford to be hungover if he hoped to follow Buzz up the coast in a few hours. What game was he was playing with his dad's million-dollar toy? His hand extended past the bottle and patted Martha's. "Life with the MacAuliffes. Now you see why I live in Seattle."

"That's just your father being a normal father, James. I like your family. They're weirdly nice, loving, concerned about you."

"Yeah. Right." No, he couldn't get drunk tonight. Maybe when this was all over, he'd drink to Amelia, to her mother. Maybe this beautiful woman who let him hold her hand at the family kitchen table would join him. He remembered Lance joining him in obliterating—if only for an evening—the memory of the vet Tommy Morse with too much cheap whiskey. "I'm calling it a night. I've got a busy morning if I'm going to be ready to follow Buzz on the Big Gitche Gumee. You want to stay?"

"Yeah, I think I will," Martha said. She drained the last of her wine and stood up, removing dirty wine glasses to the sink. "Your mother's gone to all the trouble of making me a bed. She offered me some clean clothes that she thought would fit."

"She's good at guilt."

"James, come on. What's the matter with you? It's not guilt. It's being kind and decent."

"Yeah. Right."

Night surrounded her in a darkness so deep it was like a dream of what the night was like. Something around her neck tightened, garroting the breath out of her. She struggled to escape, thrashing from side to side. She thrust backwards into the unseen assailant. Her fingers clawed at her neck, trying to pry the noose from her neck. Trying and failing. Her movements only caused it to tighten more. She was close to passing out, close to losing consciousness, close to dying. With her last thoughts she saw a light—bright as a headlight in the night—focus on her face, on the face holding the garrote behind her. Walt Boudreau grinned at her from beyond the grave, his face twisted in maniacal glee, one eye missing, the eye where she'd pushed an icicle into his brain. His laughter filled her ears. The noose grew even tauter. With a final push, she drove backwards, her head hitting his with a loud crack.

And she was awake. Gasping for air. Flailing in the sheets that had wrapped around her like a mummy. She sat up and took one deep breath after another, willing the nightmare away, willing her body and mind to calm. While her breath soon returned to normal, nothing she did drove away the image of the grinning Uncle Walt, her tormentor, her rapist, the man who had quietly murdered her sister.

She slipped out of bed and out of the house, following a sandy trail over the hill, to where the big lake opened before her in all its shimmering beauty, starlight rippling in tiny flecks. In tee-shirt and panties, she began to move—at first a simple pose with arms stretched before her, legs flexing and moving, her mind focused only on her breath, her body, each following movement precise, each one a faster, a little more violent, a shadow leopard in the night, performing the ritual dance of the *Bassai Dai kata*.

Sometime later, half an hour, an hour, two, she didn't know, exhaustion kicked in. She whispered to the sleeping MacAuliffe, "Move over."

She could see him curled on his side, a misshapen lump under a fluffy comforter, his soft breaths coming at slightly less than a snore. He grunted in response and scooched over. She slipped under the covers and spooned into his warm body. His arm draped over her, and he cupped her breast. Within moments, the gentle sounds of sleep returned. She left the hand, liking the touch of a friend, of someone who would risk his life to cover her back.

Twenty-Four

When he awoke, he was alone. He remembered enough to know that he hadn't spent the night that way. At some point, Martha had joined him, warm and soft and oh so attractive wearing nothing but—he couldn't remember what she wore. He also didn't remember anything else. The image of her face, the high cheekbones, the large nose, the perfect skin, all framed with short curly hair, came to him. The memory of her slipping into his bed and her image left him with a throbbing erection.

Water from the shower sounded like distant morning rain. His morning consciousness hadn't raised the carefully constructed barriers between friends and lovers, between reality and desire. He closed his eyes again and indulged in the fantasy of joining her in the shower.

Over bad coffee and worse bran muffins, they sat across the kitchen table in awkward silence. Outside, the morning sky over Wisconsin was beginning to lighten. In these early days post-autumnal equinox, that meant they were getting a later start on the day than planned. Virginia hovered over Martha and her son, mustering all the motherly devotion at her disposal—and that was a lot.

Martha enjoyed her homey chatter. "Some honey with that muffin?" "More coffee? I know you enjoy your morning coffee, Jimmy." "Jimmy, you have to eat to keep up your strength." "My jeans fit you nicely—if you wanted to wear capris. But supposed to be warm again today. Good idea to roll up the shirt sleeves." "I can fry up some eggs and bacon. Good protein. Have it ready in a jiffy. Maybe some homemade raspberry jam, honey?"

Not sure who she was talking to, both replied.

"Thanks, Mom. I'm fine."

"Me too, Virginia. Don't go to any trouble."

"Let me go check on your father." In plaid pajama bottoms and a Minnesota Gopher sweatshirt, she padded out of the kitchen.

"Bad night?" he asked when they were alone.

"Not all of it," she replied. "You?"

"Not all of it." A shy smile peeked out of his blonde beard. Wet hair was tucked behind his ears and fell to shoulders covered by his traditional Oxford button-down—this one blue.

She held his hand for a moment. "Thanks for having my back again. I appreciated it."

"Any time." He pushed a half-eaten muffin away. "God, that's awful."

"Give her a gift to a cooking school. A thank-you gift or maybe a Christmas present. Heaven knows she needs it."

"Needs what?" replied Virginia as she popped back into the kitchen. "Anthing I can do to help? Getting your father out of bed in the morning is like having teenagers all over again. Not even Katie was this difficult to get going in the morning."

MacAuliffe marveled at how fast Martha shifted stories and how well she lied.

"Marlena Berglund," Martha said. "She's the Forest Service officer we've been working with in Grand Marais. She needs me to go with her to investigate some strange water quality readings in the woods outside of town. Which means, I've got to hit the road."

"You be careful, honey," Virginia said, placing a hand on her shoulder. "You be very careful."

"I'll be fine. Berglund's a good officer—and she carries a gun."

But Martha knew guns were overrated.

By the time the younger and older MacAuliffes motored Uncle Chuck's Tiara 31 past the Nettles residence, the dock was empty except for a couple of mooring lines tossed across the planks.

"Fuck," MacAuliffe muttered.

"So living on a boat taught you to talk like an old salt," his dad said.

"Knew it long before. Learned it as a kid from an old sailor." He studied the electronics displayed along the dash. "You know how to turn the radar on?"

"Oughta be able to figure it out."

While his father fiddled with knobs and dials, MacAuliffe studied the shoreline. The backyards of Duluth's elite spread out before him in verdant swaths that were only possible with built-in sprinkler systems and lots of fertilizer at the end of a long, often dry summer. He stared at the empty dock. How much of a head start did Buzz have?

"Isn't that the Nettles' place?" Ted MacAuliffe asked.

"Wouldn't know, Dad. Never got to hang out in the Congdon area when I was a kid. You delivered the mail. You should know this area."

"Only saw it from the other side. Wanna tell me what's going on? Noticed you ain't getting any fishing gear ready. You think Craig Nettles has something to do with the death of those two women?"

"The less you know right now, the safer you'll be."

"And the less I'll be able to help."

The radar flashed on, blinked a couple of times and then showed the North Shore as it ran northeast from Duluth toward Two Harbors. MacAuliffe adjusted the setting from two to five miles, then ten miles.

His dad pointed to a green blip that had appeared on all the settings. "That one's southbound, probably a freighter steaming for Duluth." A smaller blip hugged the shore. Ted took out binoculars and focused ahead of them toward shore. "Small, probably not twenty, twenty-five feet. One, maybe two people onboard. Going slow. Probably got a pole or two down."

"That's not it."

"What're we looking for?"

MacAuliffe didn't answer but scanned the horizon. To the northeast, the deep blue of Lake Superior extended as far as the eye could see, calm and motionless under a bright morning sun. A spec on the horizon was probably the freighter steaming south. To the east-southeast, the Wisconsin shoreline stretched out like a distant, fallen tree on the horizon. No other boats came into view, nothing else blipped on the radar. There was only so much he could do by himself. He required more than a driver. He needed another pair of eyes—eyes that knew what to watch for. He said, "An Ocean Alexander 48. Called *Executive Suite*. It's probably already half-way to Grand Marais by now."

"God, I hate stink potters," his father said. "Better sit down, son. We're gonna make our contribution to environmental catastrophe."

And he opened the throttle to *Mac's Place* to full, throwing MacAuliffe into the portside pilot's chair.

"You got any bug spray?" Marlena Berglund asked. The Forest Service truck sat on the side of the road, parked in front of someone's house.

"Isn't it a little late in the season for bugs?" Martha replied.

"Don't see any snow," Berglund said. After filling the truck with toxic fumes, she handed the can to Martha. "Don't skimp and don't forget your feet. Ticks love to crawl up your legs, make little nests in the ol' pubes and live there sucking blood 'til you're so sick with Lyme disease you'll wish you were dead. Then the doctor's gotta shave your privates balder than a newborn baby. Scratches worse than the clap when it grows back."

"I take it you're sufficiently recovered?"

"Never fully recover from Lyme disease. Stays in your joints so you always feel like an old dog hobbling to the finish line. Ain't a pretty sight—in dog or human."

Martha gave extra attention to her feet and ankles.

They entered the forest where the bridge on Highway 61 crossed Devil Track River and scrambled down the road grade to the riverbed. Berglund plunged forward without a glance back. She set a quick pace, seemingly not bothered by boulders or bugs—of which there were many, mosquitoes and deerflies the most plentiful and ticks rising up her pant legs, Martha was sure, from the thick underbrush. Steep hills rose on both sides of the river. The highway was quickly left behind. Devil Track River raced through the woods in this section, over rocks and under fallen trees, only occasionally slowing to whirl in backwater eddies as it wound its course to the big lake.

After getting smacked in the face a couple of times with rebounding branches, Martha gave the ranger some space as she bushwhacked a trail along the river's edge. A wide-brimmed floppy hat adorned Berglund's head, with her long auburn hair pulled back in a French twist that lay off to the side of her backpack. She wore her duty uniform of a long-sleeve khaki shirt and olive slacks. Leather hiking boots protected her feet from ticks and the uneven ground. Martha took comfort in the sight of a gun strapped to her hip. She wondered if the ranger knew how to use it and hoped she wouldn't have to on this trip.

For a time, highway noise filtered through the trees, but soon even that was gone. She wasn't sure what kind of trees made up the forest. Some deciduous, with leaves in various stages of gold and red and orange. A lush carpet of leaves and pine needles covered the ground and crunched with every step. The only tree she could identify with any confidence was the birch, with its white paper bark peeling from the trunk in large sheets with curling edges.

Martha hoped Berglund had lunch packed in her backpack. She knew better than to come into the woods unprepared, and here she was, completely unprepared—no food, no water, no bug spray. Enough mosquitoes swarmed around her head to make her really regret not having any bug spray. But Berglund had been in a hurry to begin, said she didn't plan to wait for her if she wasn't at the ranger station by nine o'clock.

"Days're too short and the area too wide to treat it like a Sunday stroll after the preacher says 'Amen,'" she had informed Martha. "We should be putting boots on the ground by seven and eating our granola bars as far into paradise as we can travel in an hour."

Paradise? She brushed a swarm of mosquitoes away from her face, but so far they were just buzzing, not landing and biting. Oh, f—, she brushed one into her eye, where it either died or sat there sucking blood from her unprotected eyeball, feeling like a boulder in her eye when she blinked. It took some furious blinking to clear the predator.

Still, she'd been late. She'd overslept after finally falling into a deep, dreamless sleep with Mac's arm wrapped around her. A quick stop at the hotel had been required to get some full-length jeans and a sun shirt. Sneakers were the closest she had to hiking boots, but they'd have to do. Caribou Coffee had provided a triple latté for the road. God, how did Mac's folks drink that vile-flavored brew they called coffee? No wonder Mac had run as far away from home as possible.

While she waited for her coffee, her phone pinged. Ray Palmer's text read: "No emily or kids at garage issued APB on Olsen. ideas?" Martha texted back, "Ballard house? Parents? Where's Olsen staying?" Martha knew Emily had failed in her resolve to leave her abusive boyfriend. It wasn't the first time it had happened with one of her clients. It wouldn't be the last. Still, it hurt, and she wondered if she could have prevented it if she'd been home taking care of business. Two thousand miles away, she had to leave the problem to Palmer to solve.

Now, she hurried to catch up with Berglund, hoping she had something more than just granola bars in her backpack.

Broken sunlight flickered and danced in playful games through the canopy, but the heavy shade kept it cool along the river. Even so, Martha was soon working up a sweat as she scrambled over blown-down trees and boulders strewn along the path. The music of the river as it rushed down the hillside became a contrasting lullaby to the mosquitoes' angry buzz.

After an hour or so, Berglund came to a halt where the river was joined by a large creek. She found a flat spot and shrugged out of her pack. Patches of sweat lined her back and ringed her underarms. She offered her water bottle and Martha sipped gratefully. Berglund stepped carefully on a moss-covered rock and bent to dip a bandana into the cool river. She wiped her face and her neck before tying the soaked cloth around her neck. Then she gave herself another dose of bug spray, including renewing the application around her ankles.

"Figure we've come about a mile," Berglund said. She pointed to the large creek. "That's Woods Creek."

A mile? One effing mile? How was that possible? Suddenly the enormity of their task and the vast wilderness of the north woods came home to her.

"Any idea what we're searching for?" Martha asked, sitting down on a fallen log.

"Nothing yet. Might wanna pick another spot to sit. That log's full of termites. How the forest takes care of its downfall. A real nuisance if they get in your undies."

Martha made a point of not jumping up, but slowly rising and brushing off her butt. Had she become such an urbanite that bugs now bothered her? Sault Ste. Marie sat on the edge of a forest very similar to this. Gran had taken her and her sisters into the forest to chop firewood, cut Christmas trees and boughs for wreaths, and strip birch bark for extra spending money.

She'd killed her first man deep in the woods of the Upper Peninsula. Uncle Walt hadn't visited her dreams for a long time. Why last night?

Berglund interrupted her thoughts. "Rose'd tie a ribbon to a tree to mark the spot she took readings. That way she could come back and find 'em if she needed. This is where we begin searching in earnest. We got the GPS coordinates so we should be able to locate the spot, but we don't know what she found there that bothered her. We can take a new water sample, see if anything obvious jumps out at us."

"She ended up dead," Martha replied. "So the probability is high that she found something."

"There you go splainin' the obvious again. When we find the first ribbon on Woods Creek, we start moving upstream from there. Gotta believe it's something different, unusual, something out of place. Might be a clearing, might be an unauthorized cattle herd grazing on public land, might be an illegal logging camp. Not sure if any of 'em are worth killing over."

"Depends on how much someone's got to lose."

They found *Executive Suite* tied to the fuel dock at the marina in Grand Marais.

If MacAuliffe hadn't been so anxious that they'd missed Buzz, he might have enjoyed the day powering along in Uncle Chuck's go-fast powerboat. The lake was calm with barely a ripple across its broad expanse of crystalline blue water; the day was warm under a bright late summer sun that moved across a cloudless sky. A couple of times they had slowed down to check out a boat, but each time found themselves approaching someone out for an end-of-the-season fishing trip. They quickly veered off and throttled up again.

Five hours later, they saw *Executive Suite* well before they entered the harbor at Grand Marais. The lighthouse sat on the end of the breakwater. At the nearby Coast Guard station, the flags all hung limp in the breezeless air. *Executive Suite* was visible over the outside breakwater and a smaller inside rock jetty, its high white sides motionless at the fuel dock. MacAuliffe automatically noted they must be at high tide, with so much visibility over the rocks. Almost instantly, he chided himself—they were on a lake, even if a really big lake. It had no tide.

Mac's Place came around the breakwater and entered the protected harbor, which today mirrored the placid waters of the lake. Buzz stood near the stern talking to the dock attendant, a fuel hose running from the pump past their feet and into the side of the boat. The forest ranger wore his duty uniform of greens and khakis and the battered NFS baseball cap with the brim bent into a tight U shape. He held a couple of bags of ice in one hand.

"Plan now, Jimmy?" Ted MacAuliffe asked, as he shifted *Mac's Place* into neutral. MacAuliffe had ducked out of sight into the boat's cabin at the first sight of Buzz on the dock. His back was to the boat drifting off the fuel dock. His father continued, "We oughta fuel up, too, but you go pulling up beside him and you might as well announce you're hot on his tail."

MacAuliffe studied the scene from a porthole. Buzz wore dark wrap-around sunglasses, held around his neck with red croakies. He glanced in their direction but quickly returned his attention to the attendant, laughing over something the young woman had said. Maybe explaining the sleeping arrangements to the attractive blonde in mini shorts. More likely laughing about how the ol' man was paying for another few hundred gallons of fuel.

"See a guest dock or an empty slip?" MacAuliffe asked.

"Got one in sight."

"Can you dock her by yourself?"

"Shiiittt, with twin screws and a bow thruster, I could park this baby in the back of your mama's truck with the wind blowing thirty knots. You just sit back and take yourself a nap. It's what you do best."

Apparently the old sailor was taking to this environmental destruction.

He didn't have to park it in the back of Virginia's truck. He didn't even have to park it alone. A young man came out the marina dock and lent a hand, grabbing the bowline as Ted MacAuliffe brought *Mac's Place* gently to an open spot on B dock.

"Sweet as a girl's first kiss," he chortled, stepping off with the stern line. To the marina attendant, he said, "Just waiting for that plastic pleasure palace to get off the fuel dock."

"First hour's free," the man replied. "After that I have to charge you a night's moorage."

"No problemo."

But it was a problem. Buzz left *Executive Suite* parked on the fuel dock to make the long walk around the harbor, before disappearing into the Coast Guard office. They waited for him to reappear but whatever he was doing took longer than an hour.

"Damn government employees are never in a hurry to do anything," grumbled the retired postal worker. Once the sixty minutes had passed, the marina attendant gave them a grace period long enough to finish his text before walking back down the dock with a clipboard.

"Tiara 31, nice boat," the young man said. He'd nicked himself shaving his three chin hairs this morning, giving him a raw and bloody appearance. "Buck and a half a foot. With swim step, bowsprit and anchor, call it an even fifty bucks."

"Come on, man. We're leaving as soon as *Executive Suite* moves," MacAuliffe protested. He noticed his father had walked away to fuss with the spring line, untying it, making a small tug, and retying it again.

"Cash or credit card?"

MacAuliffe handed over three twenty-dollar bills. "I'll need change. And a receipt, of course."

"Change? Ah man, you yachties are all the same. Cheap as the day is long."

"Change and a receipt," MacAuliffe repeated. "Make it free and I'll teach you how to swear at customers properly."

The pimply-faced kid sulked away. Before he could return with the change, Buzz reappeared and hopped aboard *Executive*

Suite. The blonde threw off the mooring lines with a wave and a smile, and he eased away from the dock as easily as if he was pulling away from the curb. From the helm on the flybridge, he did a U-turn in the narrow basin and gave the blonde a final nod.

So what are you up to, Buzzie boy? What game are you playing on daddy's yacht?

TWENTY-FIVE

Now following Woods Creek, the two women scrambled up one long continuous hill. The forest canopy filtered out most of the sunlight, and their pace slowed. Every fallen tree was an obstacle to get over; every standing tree had a ring of spear-like, dead lower limbs they had to maneuver around. They found one of Rose Bumgarten's ribbons about a hundred yards up Woods Creek from their lunch spot—if a granola bar and a couple of sips of water could be considered lunch. A pink plastic ribbon was tied to a tree at about head height. Berglund stood beside it, using the break to catch her breath until Martha joined her.

"From her notes, this should mark Rose's first reading up Woods Creek," the ranger said, touching the fluttering tails of the ribbon. "We know nitrates in the water are way too high, but we don't know why."

"This and Devil Track were the last two places Rose took water quality samples," Martha said. "What's the watershed for Woods Creek?"

From her backpack, Berglund pulled a National Forest

Service map, like the one taped to Rose's office wall, without the pin holes in it.

"We're here." She pointed to a thin blue line on the map. "To the south, we have Devil Track, quite close actually. If the problem's that way, I'm thinking some residual readings would show up in the river. Since it didn't, I gotta believe the problem is here to the north, between Woods Creek and Durfee. Here." She pointed to another thin blue line on the map.

"God, that's miles," Martha said.

"Right. Welcome to my world. And now you start to understand the magnitude of the problem."

"What about a helicopter, ATVs, or horses? This will take weeks to explore on foot."

"You've gotten a taste of the search so far. No way you could do this on a horse or ATV. You got a helicopter in your back pocket and the money to pay for it, I'm all for it."

"Two women are dead, maybe a third. The feds can't muster any additional resources to hunt down a killer?"

"A third?" Berglund asked.

Martha filled her in on Ester Petrowski, the retired schoolteacher in Duluth.

"Jesus, I had no idea," Berglund said, shaking her head. "Not good news when the unsung heroes of the world get caught in the crosshairs of someone else's shit. But the trouble is, honey, we can't tie any of these deaths to Rose or her work up here in the north woods. My esteemed employer has a hard-enough time paying its staff a living wage. He certainly ain't gonna authorize the use of a helicopter on some harebrained theory that a backwoods conspiracy nut job is responsible for all this murder and mayhem. We ain't seen a budget increase in so long we have to haul water from the creek just to flush the goddamn toilet when we're done tweeting. That don't leave a lot of room for helicopters to support some notion that the Minnesota woods is harboring the next Ted Kaczynski."

"So we're on foot?"

"You catch on fast. Must've gone to college, you're so smart. We're on foot."

The plan was simple: follow the creek and every hundred yards or so, or at the sight of anything unusual, hike east into the woods to investigate. Simple in theory, hard to execute as it entailed scrambling through a thick woods with obstacles at nearly every step. They took turns, one continuing up the creek, the other venturing into the woods, clambering over or around downed trees, getting slapped in the face with branches, and wading through thigh-high ferns and whip-like saplings. Berglund had brought a hand-held compass. Following the compass was the only way Martha stayed on course heading into the woods, and she needed it to bring her back to the creek.

Over the course of the afternoon, they found glades and meadows opening in sunny patches that through the woods hinted at a possible spot of interest. On Martha's trips out, she discovered a nesting spot for a deer or moose, a recently killed white-spotted fawn, the blood just beginning to dry, though whether killed by wolf or bear or cougar, Martha had no idea. She just knew it was best to leave the area as quickly as possible. There were more bugs than oxygen molecules. They swarmed her head constantly, and the braver or suicidal mosquitos flew into her eyes and mouth. The deerflies ignored the bug spray, landing on exposed skin and taking out chunks of flesh when they bit. She couldn't even think about ticks crawling their way up her legs.

Her admiration for Rose increased with each trip out and back. But nothing in any of their discoveries hinted at why Woods Creek might have a higher-than-normal level of nitrates.

She hesitated by the creek while Berglund ventured out. The sting of bug spray mingled with sweat dripped into her eyes. This is crazy, just crazy. There had to be an easier way.

Martha had always believed in trusting people with professional expertise. If she required tax advice, she went to an accountant. To sell Hewitt's houseboat, she signed up with a broker who specialized in Lake Union houseboats. When she'd been suspected by the police of doing harm to her old friend, she hired the best attorney she knew in criminal law. Now, she was searching the woods. And who knew how to search the woods better than a ranger with the National Forest Service? Given enough years, they might, and in her mind she emphasized *might*, uncover something of interest. Even then, it might have nothing to do with the deaths of the Bumgartens. She had to think of something else if she ever hoped to help MacAuliffe solve this case—and get out of these woods.

She started climbing up the hill, the creek continuing to murmur in that babbling nonsense that held all its secrets.

"Thought you got lost," Berglund's voice shouted from upstream. She sat on a log beside the creek.

"Just slowing down, I guess," Martha said. The effort to smile seemed too much to attempt.

Berglund appeared as exhausted as Martha felt. Her body sagged on the log, shoulders slumped, eyes closed in fatigue. Her face had a nasty red welt—probably from a limb that smacked her across the face—and blood trickled from a scratch across her forehead. A couple of deerflies fought for the right to land on the blood.

She opened her eyes. "Gonna call it a day. Running out of daylight anyway, and I just ran into Lindskog Road. Called Anna to come pick us up."

"You got cell reception?"

"Nah. Sat phone. Only thing that works out here in the woods. Have to pay for it myself, of course. Come on, she'll be along in a few."

"You live near here?"

Berglund shook her head. "We're townies. Honey, we've only covered about two creek miles today." Rising, she added, "Only another twenty or so to go. Tomorrow we get to do it all over again."

Moving from marina to fuel dock, fueling up, topping off the water tank, getting ice and beer, some munchies to go with Virginia's leftover spaghetti took the better part of an hour. By the time *Mac's Place* rounded the breakwater, there was no sign of Buzz and his floating pleasure palace.

Ted brought the radar back online, increasing the distance covered with each push of a button. The machine recalibrated while the two men studied the monitor.

"Where'd your boy go?" his father asked. He pointed to the screen. "That's a freighter coming north. That boat's behind us. You think Nettles might've turned around?"

MacAuliffe thought back to the logbooks he'd seen aboard the boat during his midnight visit. The afternoon was growing short, and the sun would be setting in a couple of hours. "What's the weather supposed to do in the next twenty-four hours?"

Ted steered the boat northeast up the shore. He tuned the VHF radio into NOAA weather. Both listened, but while the father watched the radar, MacAuliffe scrolled through the image gallery on his phone. Page after page of Buzz's logbook flicked by. He occasionally paused to read an entry.

"Clear and calm through the rest of today and tonight," the disembodied voice of NOAA radio reported. "Clouds building tomorrow with possible thunderstorms in the evening and into the following morning. Winds from the southwest will be five to ten knots with occasional gusts of fifteen."

"Swing closer to shore, Dad," MacAuliffe said. "His territory begins north of Grand Marais and runs up to Grand Portage. If he's still heading north, he's started his patrol."

"I thought the Coast Guard patrols the water?"

"They do. And most of the shore is private property. Buzz does it this way so he can go play in the boat, I suspect. At least that's the opinion of one of his colleagues. Just be glad you didn't have to deliver mail up here."

"Yep, would've made your momma right unhappy, I'm sure." Ted increased boat speed a knot or two. "Your girlfriend is a really nice young woman. Your mom likes her."

"And you don't?" MacAuliffe said.

"That's not what I said. You gotta twist everything into an insult?"

"She's not my girlfriend. She's just a friend."

"Right. I seen how you look at her. I heard the doors creaking last night. If you didn't want me to know, you shouldn't've woken me up. Warned you I'd never get back to sleep. But I'm telling you, Jimmy, oughta think about that one. A good woman doesn't come along every day and she's a damn fine woman, I'd say. Lawyering is a good profession, chance to make some decent money. But . . . you know . . . maybe encourage a little help in the, you know . . ." And he cupped his hands in front of his chest.

MacAuliffe didn't know what to do or say so he just laughed, shaking his head as he laughed harder. "Better be careful what you say, Dad. Martha's killed men for less."

That had the intended effect of shutting his father up. Damn fine woman, indeed. MacAuliffe wasn't sure how much truth there was to it, but he knew about Callison and the men on the

Utah mountainside who'd killed Lance. Only one came off of the mountain alive, and he'd forever hobble around the prison yard on his breaks. He knew she harbored secrets that were never too far from the surface, dark secrets that manifested themselves in bad men getting hurt. It wasn't too hard to figure out that something evil and violent in her past triggered that kind of response. It wasn't hard to figure out what. He just didn't know the specifics. Still, she'd crawled into his bed last night. Maybe his father had seen something that MacAuliffe had missed. Not that that'd be unusual. At thirty-five, he was still clueless about women.

God, he wished he had a cigarette. Do I have to always turn back into a teenager around my father? How do I have an adult relationship with him? Or maybe talking about the size of a woman's breasts is an adult relationship between men. If so, he wanted to jump off the boat now.

To change the subject, he said, "Now I understand why Nettles takes two days. He drives up from Duluth in the morning, refuels and then begins his patrol in the afternoon. The visit to the Coasties' office had to be to let them know he was cruising this afternoon. If he follows his usual pattern, he'll run up the coast, keeping an eye open for anything unusual. I remember from his log he found some illegal campers on the beach, a fire back in the hills. He'll have to slow down to do that. Then, he anchors out for the night and finishes the patrol on the second day."

For half an hour, they powered northeast along the coast, staying within a mile or so of shore. Late afternoon unfolded like images from a Winslow Homer collection—pastels in yellow, blue, and green replaced the bold primary colors of the morning. Sun, water, and forested shore. Interruptions came in a gliding seagull, a distant freighter steaming toward the Soo Locks, the flash of a car speeding up Highway 61. The steady rumble of the diesel engines became white noise to the shifting colors of the afternoon. It was easy to forget that this Lake Superior was the same lake that held the remains of countless wrecks, from the *Bannockburn* to the *Edmund Fitzgerald*, with all their crews still entombed in the big lake.

"Might have him, Jimmy," his father said.

MacAuliffe slid over to the helm station, following his father's finger as it pointed at the radar.

"At ten miles, I couldn't find him, but when I dropped it down to two, I noticed that Marr Island had a strange bump on the far side. Hadn't heard any reports of the island splitting in two so I thought that might be where he's anchored."

With the radar set on the two-mile sweep, Marr Island was coming up fast on the port beam. Ted eased back a little on the throttle, dropping their speed from twenty knots down to twelve, thirteen.

"Not too slow, Dad," MacAuliffe said. "Don't want him becoming suspicious if he's watching."

Through the binoculars, he held the island steady in his view. Rocks were the only things visible on the small pancake splat of land. A couple of other rocks, one with a scraggy tree trying to take root, were visible behind Marr Island. As they crept along, the back side of the island came into view and with it, *Executive Suite*. "Got him. He's dropped a hook inside the bay. He's in the dinghy taking a stern line to shore."

"Smart. In case NOAA's wrong. Been known to happen. If the wind picks up early, he'd be exposed to a northerly. What you want me to do?"

MacAuliffe hesitated. He couldn't very well go up and anchor beside him. What was Buzz doing? Of course, smuggling people or drugs was the most likely answer. MacAuliffe remembered the boat's salon table had been removed, better able to carry more cargo. But would Buzz risk a million-dollar boat if he got caught? Would he even care? Oh right, it was his father's boat, and he pushed Craig Senior's buttons every chance he got.

That sounded familiar.

If he was smuggling, where was he picking up his cargo and to whom was he selling? And how did it all relate—if it did—to the deaths of Amelia and Rose Bumgarten? Maybe it had nothing to do with Rose's work in the field.

Maybe in her work as a paralegal she'd interviewed an illegal alien who came clean about how she entered the country—smuggled through Canada via boat to Grand Marais. Most of them ended up in the sex trade in the Cities or elsewhere, but a surprising number were used as household help or farm laborers—all working as indentured servants.

MacAuliffe had no idea. Throw enough shit at the wall and some of it was bound to stick.

Still, he could think of no way to observe what was happening behind Marr Island. The one advantage he had was he knew where Buzz was going. Tomorrow he'd finish his patrol of the North Shore and then zip out to Grace Harbor on Isle Royale. But what was he doing between now and then? He could think of no way to observe him and be inconspicuous.

"Let's go to Isle Royale. Might have some time for fishing tomorrow."

TWENTY-SIX

Showered, dressed, and properly caffeinated, Martha texted Berglund. "Ready here. Meet at the office?" The clock said six thirty; the new sun said it was time to get started.

Despite being more exhausted than she could ever remember, she hadn't slept well again. Only, MacAuliffe wasn't here to slip into bed with to help turn off the nightmares. A text in the evening to Mac said she'd booked the Spruce Cabin again. The one with the purple door. The message had gone unanswered.

Now, she tugged on the laces of her new hiking boots. Martha had had time yesterday evening to get better prepared for another day of trekking into the deep woods. New socks and boots, a backpack, a handheld compass of her own, a sunhat and gloves, a couple of water bottles, bug spray—lots of bug spray—moleskin for the inevitable blisters from the new boots, ibuprofen, and sunscreen. She also picked up some high protein munchies, granola bars, ham and cheese slices, fruit, and cauliflower florets. Packed and ready to go with the new backpack, she waited to hear back from the ranger.

Already she'd eaten two yogurts and sliced Havarti cheese with a Honeycrisp apple. Three ibuprofen topped off breakfast, in part to ward off the aches from yesterday and in part to prepare for the ones to come.

Martha hoped Berglund had had time to recover from yesterday's hike. She had looked as exhausted as Martha felt by day's end. Would she have made time to take care of herself with Hunter strapped to her chest for the evening? Babysitting probably precluded a long hot bath.

Her phone rang. Berglund opened by saying, "Got a serious kink in the plan, honey. Goddamn Craig decided to go playing on daddy's yacht and he was supposed to cover the office today. Betsy is down in Duluth. That leaves me and an intern to smile nice to flatfooters and city folks—no offense, of course."

"None taken," Martha replied.

"So, sorry to tell you, girl, you're on your own today. I'd recommend you start on Lindskog Road where we came out yesterday. The Superior Hiking Trail follows Woods Creek north of there and should give you an easy reference point."

On my own. She suddenly felt Rose's killer slipping further and further away. God only knew what he planned to do next.

MacAuliffe watched the sun rise over the trees of Isle Royale National Park until it slowly started to warm him in the cockpit of *Mac's Place*. The boat drifted at anchor in Grace Harbor on the southwest end of the island park, not enough wind or current to hold it taut on its anchor. He was drinking bad coffee. Apparently Uncle Chuck had no more appreciation of good coffee than did his folks. So he settled for Folger's, brewed cowboy style in a pot on the boat stove, strong and bitter. His father still slept, the door to the vee berth closed, which was as much privacy as a person would ever get aboard a boat.

They had passed Rock of Ages Lighthouse last night with only an orange sliver of twilight still in the west. Grace Harbor was inky black by the time they motored slowly into the cove. A Keystone Kops routine followed as they figured out the boat's anchoring gear and system by flashlight, with more than a little yelling back and forth between father and son. Suddenly a beam of light flooded the bow. His father had found the boat's spotlight. They had drifted too close to shore and had to start the process all over again. Fortunately, they were alone.

He texted Martha, updating her on their location. After much debate, he decided to add, "Hope you sleep well." The message beeped back as Failed. No cell signal on the island and nothing from shore reached this far.

His uncle had obviously never been to the island. The only chart onboard that included the park had it on such a scale that Grace Harbor wasn't even an indent on the shore and the long inlet of Washington Harbor resembled a creek. He might as well be using a road map.

Buzzie boy would spend the morning patrolling the coast before heading over to the island, but MacAuliffe didn't know if that'd take him two hours or eight. He didn't want *Mac's Place* here when Buzz dropped hook in Grace Harbor. While Buzz had no reason to suspect the Tiara and its crew of following him, he must have noticed it motoring by yesterday while fueling *Executive Suite*. MacAuliffe needed to see what was happening aboard *Executive Suite* once it dropped anchor, but he had to do it without *Mac's Place* being seen.

"You save any coffee for the ol' man?" came his father's voice, his bald head gleaming from the companionway. In white tee-shirt and whitey-tighty briefs, his white-haired fringe standing out in clumps and tufts, he could've been a polar bear with a bad haircut.

"That I did," MacAuliffe said. "On the stove. Pour easy and most of the grounds will stay in the pan."

He reappeared with a cup in hand. He was either sure they were alone or unconcerned that the neighbors might see him in his underwear. He took his first sip. "Oh, Jiminy Cricket, when did you make this? Use it to peel the varnish off the teak."

"What happens when you sleep in. You get burnt coffee. That's been simmering for nearly two hours."

"Couldn't sleep, huh? Missed the little missus, I bet."

"Dad, don't start today, please."

Any further retort was left unsaid either out of respect for his son's request or because he was preoccupied with the first attack of the mosquitoes. He slapped a bare leg, then his ear. "What the hell? Need a good breeze to blow these bloodsucking bastards away."

"Supposed to get one tonight."

"That'll be too late. I'll be sucked dry by then."

He disappeared below, and MacAuliffe returned to his problem of how to spy on Buzz without Buzz knowing he was being spied on. Was he smuggling people, drugs, ancient Greek artifacts? Or just taking some time off, a little R and R on the island after a strenuous day patrolling the coast? MacAuliffe didn't believe that, given how he never lingered the following morning. But what did bring him so far from the coast?

He pivoted in the captain's chair. The tree-lined shore wasn't far off, but in a place devoid of all ambient light, he wouldn't be able to tell much of what was happening on the water after dark. Anchoring beside Buzz would certainly prevent any illegal activity from taking place. With the press of a button, the chart plotter came to life.

"You ever dropped the hook in Washington Harbor when you cruised through here?" he asked his father when he reappeared fully dressed and smelling of bug spray.

"Time or two," he replied. "Mostly up toward Windigo."

The far end of the inlet was home to one of two Visitor Centers for the park, Windigo, named after a cannibalistic giant in native myth. That was too far in to hike back and forth. MacAuliffe pointed at a spot on the chart plotter. "What about this little cove here? Might be large enough for one boat, if there's enough water."

"Possible." He mused aloud, "She draws about three feet. Oughta stern tie to keep her from swinging too much. Might work. Thinking you'll come back in the dinghy?"

"Shit, does Uncle Chuck even have a dinghy?"

Digging through lockers revealed a blow-up inflatable and a foot pump in the aft lazarette. It had stubby little oars made for grade schoolers. Rowing a baby's wading pool would be easier. But it might work. MacAuliffe started making a mental list: boat, oars, binoculars, something warm to wear and something to keep him dry—NOAA was calling for a storm tonight. He'd need a lifejacket, maybe a little food, a flashlight.

"Think there's a walkie talkie set on board?"

They found one in a locker off the main salon, but it was dead and there were no spare batteries on board.

"I'm going to take the dinghy to shore here, Dad. You take the boat around and anchor in this cove. I should be able to hike back in pretty good time in the morning or when Buzz leaves. I don't know when he's going to get here, but we should be gone by noon at the latest."

"Problem with your plan, son," Ted MacAuliffe said. "I won't be able to stern tie without the dinghy and that cove ain't big enough to swing on a hook."

"Good point. All right, let's get you secure, and I'll portage back or row around."

"On it," his father said and fired up the engines. "Get ready to haul anchor."

Martha waited outside the office of Sawtooth Aviation, LLC. At nine o'clock sharp, a woman arrived to unlock the door and welcome her into the office.

"How may we help you this morning?" the woman said, thumping her oversized purse on an oversized desk. "We being me, of course."

A short efficient haircut, a cute face, a lovely smile, and pleasantly plump, the woman reminded Martha of what Emily Reilly might look like in twenty years. A cheerful Emily, not the Emily who had walked into her office last month with the broken nose and eye socket. Martha wondered if Ray Palmer had had any success in locating Em and the two children. Where would Jerome go if banned from returning home by the restraining order? She hoped Ray found them before someone got hurt again.

"Or I can just talk to myself." She showed no sign of being impatient. "I'm gonna start the coffee. Care for cup?"

"Sorry," Martha said, with a smile. "You remind me of a client of mine. Back in Seattle. I'd love a cup if you brew it strong and have some cream."

"This is not a truck stop, darling. Of course I brew it strong. Anything else we can do for you besides a good cup of coffee?"

"I want to book one of your tourist flights."

"You're two for two for the morning. Good start to a beautiful day in my book."

While she waited, Martha circled the small office. Photos and framed certifications lined the available wall space. A few of the photos were of small airplanes, several were of animals in the wild—a big bull moose standing knee deep in a lake, a mother and her calf wading through snow so deep only the calf's head and top of its back were visible, a herd of deer crossing an opening in the autumn woods, the trees gold and burgundy.

Sawtooth Aviation had popped up immediately on Google when Martha had entered "Grand Marais scenic flights." Located about eight miles outside of town north of Devil Track Lake at the Grand Marais/Cook County Airport, the company offered tourist flights of the area. And that was exactly what she wanted. On her own, on foot, she required a miracle to discover the source of Rose's nitrate readings. And she'd stopped believing in miracles a long time ago. She could only hope an overview from a plane might give her a starting or ending place to begin her search.

The woman returned carrying a perfect cup of coffee and sat down at the desk and gestured for Martha to join her. "So what can I do for you today? I'm Char, by the way, Char Lumsden. Finnish if you're into your genealogy."

Martha introduced herself. She wrestled with how much to tell the woman about her true purpose. She couldn't pretend to be a tourist and ask the pilot to focus on Woods Creek. "I'm investigating the murder of Rose Bumgarten, and we've trailed a clue to the woods but it's too vast an area for me to cover on foot. I'm hoping to get a bird's eye view of the area east of Woods Creek."

"Police? Feds? Private detective? I heard Rosie died of a drug overdose. Wondering what your interest is."

"None of the above. A friend and I found Rose in her house. She did die of a drug overdose, probably fentanyl, a street drug that's a hundred times more powerful than heroin. She had a past history that makes it credible that she'd resumed old habits and died as a result of it. That's the premise on which Sheriff Gould is conducting his investigation at this time."

She let the little lie sit there to be contradicted.

"Sounds like maybe you don't believe the conclusion of our good sheriff," Lumsden said. "You shouldn't let that roly-poly exterior fool you; he's a sharp cookie up here." She tapped her temple a couple of times. "Even got a bunch of those initials after his name. Like P, H and D. Noticed you still didn't answer my question. Wondering about your interest in our local tragedy."

"This is personal. As you may have heard, Rose's daughter Amy was recently killed in a truck explosion down in Duluth."

"Yeah, heard that, too. Damn shame, damn shame."

"That truck belonged to my friend. He's visiting his family in Duluth, and we were troubled by the coincidence of mother and daughter dying so close together. We wondered if it was related to some work Rose was doing."

"Her obsession with the NorthShore Resort?"

Martha nodded.

"Not a soul in GM didn't know her position on that. She's been going door to door asking people to sign her petition. I wouldn't sign and I told her so. Told her why. Area's short on jobs, and if they aren't the best, who gives a flying fuck, as we say in the biz. They're at least jobs. Hell, half the town works for minimum wage during peak season. But that's only three months long, not even that some years when summer arrives late or winter comes early. You ever tried to pay the mortgage or buy groceries working three months a year? The resort promised to stay open year-round—hunting in the fall, skiing and snowmobiling in the winter." Lumsden shook her head again. "Nosirreebob, wouldn't sign it. But the resort was planned for several miles south of town and Woods Creek isn't anywhere in the vicinity."

"That's why I've got to get up in the air. Rose was working the Woods Creek area right before she died. Have you got a pilot who can take me?"

"Yeah, I can take you, honey, but might be wasting your money."

"It's my money."

"Then I'm glad to take it from you. It's two sixty for an hour. Gratuities always appreciated."

Martha pulled a credit card from her purse. "Take plastic? Add ten percent."

Lumsden ran the card, poured two to-go cups of coffee, grabbed some sunglasses. "Might wanna pee now because once we're up in the air your option will be a paper cup. Boys get an orange juice bottle. Ladies room is the second door on the left. Says 'Ladies' on the door."

As they left the office, Lumsden flipped the Open sign on the door to Gone Flying and locked the door.

"Work here alone?" Martha asked.

"Nah, the guys'll start drifting in in an hour or two. I come in early because I do the books, get caught up on the paperwork, track who needs to renew their FAA certifications, office manager stuff. The boys don't know it, but I get paid better than they do, and it gives me job security when we start the seasonal layoffs. And we're starting to slow down. Peak tourist season is over and now we're dealing with mostly hunters scouting good locations for the fall and folks without kids who dream of seeing the lake at sunset. All best done in the afternoon and evening. I prefer getting out of the office early and into the air. Day's crisp and bright. Don't have to argue with the guys about leaving the toilet seat up."

After an hour of rowing, MacAuliffe wished he'd portaged this inflatable bathtub across the spit. The dinghy didn't track worth a damn and it glided about half its own length with each stroke, making for a lot of pulling on the stubby oars. The headwind didn't help either, mild but steady from the southwest and right on the nose. Already blisters formed on his palms, and he kept pausing to splash cold lake water on his face and neck, afraid he'd get heat stroke in the afternoon sun. That of course brought the rubber tub to a complete stop, forcing him to get its momentum started all over again. With no hat, he took off his shirt, dunking it in the clear lake. Below, he could see rocks deeper than his paddle could reach. Okay, that wasn't all that deep, but the water was crystalline for many feet. Rocks, a tree snag, and darting fish. He draped the soaked shirt over his head and started rowing again.

The hour of rowing felt like it had stretched into a week until he rounded the point into Grace Harbor. The gentle breeze now pushed him toward his destination, rather than thwarting him. Right where the rock-strewn shore changed to a sandy, pebbly beach, he reached the spot he'd identified this morning as a potential hiding place. It was a place to launch the dinghy without having to drag it over the rocks. Heavy underbrush and pine trees came down to the water's edge, offering ample places to hide it and him. He hauled the dinghy ashore and into the trees, turning it around before he began cutting ferns and evergreen branches to drape over the boat. One of Aunt Marie's boutique boat bags held most of his gear. In a plastic grocery bag, he had a Ziploc bag for his wallet, phone, flashlight and binoculars, another with some food. He moved everything well back into the trees and covered them with a layer of greens.

He walked up to the high point of the beach and stood scanning the surrounding water. The lake was empty as far as he could see to the south and west, the direction Buzz'd be coming from, and to the east where the lake opened up into its oceanic expanse and to what he could see to the north. A distant line of clouds gathered in the west, a gray edge on the western horizon in an otherwise cloudless sky.

NOAA might be right about that storm.

TWENTY-SEVEN

Her only experience with flying had been commercial jets. Cruising at thirty thousand feet, the large farms of Eastern Washington took on the appearance of Gran's patchwork quilt. Flying in a prop plane, a Cirrus SR22, made with pride right here in Minnesota, in Duluth, in fact, according to Lumsden, was a whole new experience. One that both thrilled Martha and left her clutching the seat in a death grip.

After takeoff, they circled wide, flying in a large loop north of the airport where forest and lakes quickly swallowed up any sign of civilization. An occasional road cut through the woods. She saw a woman hanging out laundry in a small clearing. The elderly woman's face, her white hair and pink-and blue-apron were all visible. She was hanging sheets on a line, the first one already flapping in the wind. The woman waved, and Lumsden wobbled the wings back and forth, causing Martha to grab her seat again.

"That's Alvin Furiel's wife, Elmira," came Lumsden's voice into her headphones. "She's gotta be seventy-five if she's a day. Alvin died a couple of years ago. Heart attack while splitting wood. We check on Elmira when we fly over. She waves if everything's okay."

"Nice," Martha said. She wondered who would check on her when she was seventy-five.

"There's a moose," Lumsden said. "In that swamp about ten o'clock off the left wing."

The plane altered course, and she had a camera out with a long telephoto lens. The moose stood on a bog island and raised its head at the noise of the plane. Lumsden snapped off several pictures. "A young bull. You can tell by the small rack, probably getting ready for his first winter away from mama. Imagine he's feeling the hormones kick in about now. Gonna have to lose a few battles with the big bulls before he gets himself a little moose tail." She laughed into the mic. "The boys will want to know about that one. Racks have been pretty scarce—at least on the moose."

She chuckled again.

The plane continued its big arc. Lake Superior came into view in front of them, glistening under the morning sun, deep blue in color, as large as an ocean. No distant shore was visible across the lake, only an endless expanse of blue water. The near shore appeared below her. Highway 61 was a gray ribbon up and down the coast, traveled this morning by several cars. Two boats were visible cruising up the shore, a white tail of water coming in their wakes. To the northeast, Martha decided, consulting her mental map of the area. She wondered if one of them might be Mac and his father. Be safe, my friend, she whispered, be safe.

Another boat cruised south, closer to shore, its wake barely visible. The sight of the boats triggered the memory that Jerome Olsen worked on his grandfather's fishing boat, a crabber or a longliner, she couldn't remember. It was moored at Fisherman's Terminal. Surprised she had cell reception, she texted the message to Ray Palmer. It might prove useful in his search for Emily Reid and her kids.

As the plane continued its turn, Martha saw a freighter in the distance, steaming northeast toward the far end of the lake. Would her father or the twins be at the Soo Locks to see it transit through on its way to ports south? Watching the freighters lock through had become her father's second favorite pastime—after winning at Jeopardy!

Now flying south, Grand Marais appeared in front of them, its inner harbor dotted with boats. Arms of an artificial breakwater extended from both directions, like the jaws of a carabiner held open. The lighthouse was visible near the endpoint on the northern arm. The white Coast Guard building sat behind it near the end of Artists' Point. As they flew nearer, she could see the flags outside the building. They ruffled in the breeze.

The plane started a wide turn and slowed down.

"Okay, darling, this is Woods Creek." Lumdsen's voice came in clear over the headset. "We're going to fly over it as low and slow as I can make this buggy go. Now, don't worry if you don't see everything on one pass. We can do this till we run out of fuel, and this beauty comes with its own parachute. Always wanted to try it." She gave her familiar laugh again.

A few seagulls circled and cawed overhead, noting his presence, hoping for food. His only companions, rats with wings. How appropriate in some ways. If Ester P were here, she'd be feeding them stale breadcrumbs. He wondered if she'd survived the night. If she hadn't, it would be a trinity of murders. Amelia, Rose, and Ester P.

MacAuliffe took his bearings with a hand-held compass and headed off into the dense forest. The pines were thick in number and big in size. MacAuliffe didn't know the park's history to know whether this was first or second growth. Second, he guessed, knowing loggers had been through the area long before the national park system. No tree was sacred to a lumberjack with a crosscut saw. The mosquitoes and deerflies on the island, however, had no trouble navigating the forest to find him. His bug spray had washed off long ago from sweat and lake water. He did his best to ignore the swarms.

He reset his bearings and worked around a fallen tree. With the lake still visible through the trees, he ran into a wide clearing, then a trail, whether human or animal he didn't know. He spiked a white paper towel on a dead lower branch. A little farther, the charred wood of a long-extinguished fire and the flat site for a tent told him the trail was probably human. The campsite wasn't listed on any of the park maps.

A thrashing noise in the woods caught his attention and he came to a sudden halt. He saw nothing. Had they reintroduced wolves onto Isle Royale? That was a thought best left unexplored. The only comfort came in knowing a wolf, or a pack of wolves, wouldn't make noise if hunting in the woods. It was more likely a deer or a bear. That didn't comfort him any more than a noisy wolf.

He checked his phone. It had taken him fifteen minutes to reach Washington Harbor. Within twenty, he grabbed the stern line of *Mac's Place*. His father lay stretched out on a bench in the cockpit, a boat fender as a pillow, a hat covering his face, his hands clasped across his round belly, sleeping as soundly as if he were at home in his recliner watching one of Virginia's Masterpiece programs. MacAuliffe could smell the bug spray and desperately wanted to wake him to get a refresher dose.

Let the old man sleep, he decided. Who knows what he's got in store for him in the next few hours. He tied a piece of white line to the tree with the stern line to let his father know he'd made it back.

Backtracking, MacAuliffe marked the trail as best he could, tying more white line to trees, spiking paper towels on tree limbs. He needed to be able to retrace his path if he were running back in the dark with only a flashlight. He had no intention of rowing that bathtub back around the point.

Back at the beach, he started setting up camp. He laughed to himself at the thought. No tent, no sleeping bag, no way to cook, and little to eat. Some camp. Uncle Chuck didn't even have a book onboard *Mac's Place* to borrow for this lonely stakeout.

MacAuliffe brushed away rocks and broken limbs from a couple of sitting spots where he could lean against tree trunks and see the cove. He cut more pine branches. Last, he donned a navy knit stocking cap and began to fumble with several large black garbage bags they had found in a galley locker.

"Won't take any light at all to see that shirt you got on," his father had said. With scissors, he cut holes in one garbage bag for his head and arms. In another, he made holes for his legs so he could step into it like a pair of bathing trunks. Others were to wrap around his arms, held in place with some blue painter's tape from the engine room. "And might be windy and wet tonight. This'll be better than wearing nothing but your skivvies."

Outfitted as best he was going to be, MacAuliffe leaned against a tree trunk. Okay, now the waiting began. He could only hope Buzz stayed faithful to his previous shore patrols.

"That's Woods Creek to your left," came Lumsden's voice. "And that's Devil Track River branching off to the left."

The woods she and Berglund had spent all day yesterday tromping through went by in a flash.

"That path you see occasionally through the trees is the Superior Hiking Trail."

Martha kept her focus to the right of the trail and creek. Neither appeared often through the dense canopy. What was she looking for? Anything unusual, anything out of place, she heard Berglund's voice say.

An open space in the forest revealed a green meadow, drenched with sunshine. Martha said into her mic, "Right, about two o'clock. What's that?"

"Make a note of it," came the response. "We're doing an overview now. We'll fly closer on the next pass."

Two more open spaces drew Martha's attention, and she made a mental note to check further. No signs of cattle illegally grazing in the public forest appeared, but they could be hidden under the forest top. Then she remembered seeing Elsie Furiel waving at the plane. No, if they were down there some sign should be visible. She thought she saw a rooftop appear.

"There, is that a cabin through the trees, just off your wing?" Martha could see no road in or out, but she was sure she saw a rooftop. It was quickly swallowed by the trees.

"Yeah, that's the crazy lady's place. She was living off the grid in the woods. Don't know if anyone ever saw her. Craig Nettles from the Forest Service discovered it on one of the patrols he flew with Brandon. He came back and evicted her freeloading ass out of Uncle Sam's backyard."

Any mention of Craig Junior put her on full alert, but she needed to concentrate now on the land passing quickly under their wings, despite the plane flying just over stall speed. Another open patch came into view. The land flattened out into a large open space with a large knoll on it. They passed over a road.

"Woods Creek starts in that swamp there," Lumsden said. "Not too far north of County Road 60. Another trip over?"

"Yeah, please," Martha said, taking a deep breath and letting her eyes relax. "Woods Creek is how long?"

"Probably twelve, fifteen miles total." She banked the plane in a sharp turn this time. "Let's come at it from the north this time. You get different openings through the trees and see different things."

Flying over it a second time revealed some of the same open spaces. This time the cabin wasn't visible through the treetops. An open spot became visible along the Superior Hiking Trail.

"There, where the trail and creek run side by side," Martha said. "What's that?"

"One of the Woods Creek campgrounds. That's where Nettles busted a bunch of high school kids for having a party in the woods last year. A nice trail running in from the road to the camp. Easy to walk in, better if you got an ATV. The keg can get kinda heavy in a hundred yards." Martha heard that hearty, frequent laugh boom into her headphones. "Got drunk and screwed there a few times myself when I sowed a couple of my wilder oats."

They were back over the lake.

"Again?"

"Yeah, can you circle some of the open spots, and maybe the crazy lady's cabin?"

"Got it."

At the first grassy meadow, Lumsden flew the plane low, and Martha saw a deer now grazing near the edge of the woods.

"Mother and twins from her spring dropping," Lumsden said.

This time, Martha saw two smaller deer, their heads raised in the direction of the plane, standing behind the larger deer and closer to the woods.

"Getting fattened up for hunting season. Good."

Martha didn't know if it was good, but she understood how some folks took to the woods every fall to kill wild animals. Her dad had been one of them until his best friend and hunting buddy Walt Boudreau had died in a cabin fire.

"This open patch seems different," Martha said, pointing to her right.

"Good eyes. It is different. A few years back, ol' Jonny Pressley ran cattle there. Illegally of course. Grazing on public land is frowned upon by the feds unless you got a permit and Jonny was a cantankerous ol' son of a bitch who wasn't paying money to graze his cows on land he was already paying taxes on. Not that he probably ever made enough money to pay taxes, but don't let facts get in the way. Forest'll fill it in eventually. Just takes time."

"We've got the same problem out west. Did Pressley take a gun to the federal agents?"

"He might've been ornery, but he wasn't crazy. He cut a deal. Gave up his herd in a year when prices were so low he would've lost money on them anyway. Paid a small fine and laughed that he got the better deal. After the grazing and all the cow shit for fertilizer, the meadow grew back covered in ferns. Strange to see them dying off so soon. Usually happens a little later in the season. Climate change happening right before our eyes."

By now they were too far to see the spot where Martha thought she saw the cabin. They flew over the other open meadows, the knoll near the top of the hill, and soon were again over the swamp.

"Had enough fun for one day?" Lumsden asked.

"Can we see that cabin again?" Martha replied. "Other than the open meadows, it's the only unusual thing in this whole area. It only appeared through the trees when flying north."

"Your wallet is my command, darling."

She banked wide and started working back toward the lake.

"You mentioned Craig Nettles patrolling his territory by plane," Martha said, as they circled back. "Do the Forest Service agents do that often?"

"All the time. They'd never be able cover this much territory otherwise. They're way understaffed up here. Feel sorry for 'em actually. Well, maybe not Craig. He comes from old money and has all the personality of a slap in the face with a wet mop. He usually flies with Brandon, one of our young bucks who thinks he can land a floatplane in a swamp. They talk hunting and titties and things that only underage males with penis brains find important. Betsy will fly with anyone, but she covers the area up in the Boundary Waters, often flies out of Two Harbors. I take Lena up a couple of times a year. Nice lady. Funnier than a hoot. Which you gotta be, I guess, if you live up here where it's winter most of the year and mosquito season the rest. Not easy being a single mom raising two kids and a grandkid on a ranger's salary."

Yeah, Martha thought, real funny. Funny enough to lead a city slicker on a hike through the woods because she knew of no way to search this area other than on foot. Why did Marlena lie to her? She remembered Rose admonished Amy not to trust anyone. What did Marlena know that she wasn't revealing?

Soon, they were flying north again up Woods Creek. Both were peering through the windshield as they neared the location of the cabin. Lumsden flew so low the treetops rustled with the passing of the plane.

"Got it," Lumsden said. "Eleven o'clock."

A cabin roof was definitely visible through the treetops. The green metal roof would blend in on the casual flyover. Martha peered down, hoping to see anything besides the roof—a trail in, a roof antenna, a truck, even an outhouse. A woodpile passed into and out of her vision behind the cabin. Just a momentary glimpse but she was sure it was a woodpile. Suddenly, she saw something blue, light blue, move toward the cabin. Then it was gone.

"Seems Craig has to make another eviction." Lumsden had seen it too.

"Or he didn't do such a good job the first time."

"Time to take you home?"

Martha just nodded. It was time to talk to Marlena Berglund.

To stay alert, he hummed Bob Dylan tunes and nibbled on crackers and peanut butter, sharing crumbs with the constant horde of bugs. When he was through his Dylan repertoire, he switched to old Ian and Sylvia ballads, one of his mother's favorites when she was in her studio. He was about to start on John Denver songs, also frequently heard coming from the garage, when he sighted *Executive Suite* approaching the harbor.

The boat was probably a mile off, approaching at a leisurely pace. MacAuliffe stretched out on his belly and covered his head and the end of the binoculars with pine boughs. Maybe they just did that in the movies, but it made sense to keep any sun from glinting off the binocular lenses. Buzz navigated from the upper helm station, glancing around on occasion. He appeared relaxed, confident, as if he'd done this hundreds of times. He brought the boat in along the shore of Washington Island and then Grace Island. MacAuliffe could have counted the hairs on his unshaved chin.

Near where MacAuliffe had stowed the dinghy, Buzz turned to starboard, straightened the boat out and steered her into the center of the cove. He bumped it into reverse and quickly shifted into neutral. While the boat drifted to a stop, he scampered from the upper helm to the bow. The large CQR anchor dropped with a splash, followed by plenty of chain, then anchor line. Suddenly the boat revved in reverse and came up taut on the anchor line. All standard operating procedure when anchoring.

Only. MacAuliffe sharpened the focus of the binoculars. Buzz would've needed a remote controlling the engine to make it surge in reverse like that. Or someone had to be at the helm. MacAuliffe didn't see a remote, though his view of the port side of the boat was obscured. The tinted windows prevented him from seeing inside the boat. Buzz checked the anchor line, wrapped the line around the windlass and cleated it off. Just as MacAuliffe would've done. Buzz disappeared inside, closing the door behind him.

So how did you pull off that nifty anchoring maneuver, Buzzie boy?

TWENTY-EIGHT

With Lumsden's help, she was making a crude map of their discoveries. "Start at Highway 61 and work north," the pilot advised. They sat on opposite sides of the desk back in her office.

Martha had never been good at art, and she apparently took too long to decide whether Highway 61 should be curved, winding, or straight.

"Oh, here, just give it to me." With bold strokes, she gave Highway 61 a wave on the bottom of the sheet and made Country Road 60 a straight line on the top. "Don't worry about anything north of there."

"County Road 58, that's Lindskog Road." Lumsden talked as she drew. A wiggly solid line became Woods Creek, a dotted line became the Superior Hiking Trail. A dotted circle with a three-pronged flame, the Woods Creek campsite. An open meadow in the shape of a figure eight, adding antlers for a deer—"though no horns on those three. Just for reference."

"Got it," Martha nodded.

The fern meadow, a large oval perched on a couple of oval legs with a plant in the middle. The crazy lady's cabin surrounded by trees. Another meadow, this one an irregular circle. The knoll at the top of the hill.

Lumsden pushed the completed sketch across the desk. As if in response to some unspoken question, she said, "Hunters are lost without a map. Gotta draw 'em a map just to get to the can." They shook hands. "Loved doing business with you, darling. Hope you find what you're looking for."

What was she looking for? Martha still didn't know. But sitting in the shade on the side of Lindskog Road, she radiated anger. She'd driven straight here, the point where Berglund's daughter Anna had picked them up yesterday. Martha needed to calm down before confronting Berglund. She also hoped to discover why the ranger had lied to her. Anger, frustration, and fear that a murderer was slipping away, hiding within the immense forest, hiding behind Berglund's lies. She stared at the trail that'd lead her to Woods Creek Camp. What did the forest ranger know and why was she deliberately misleading the search for the killer? Unless she was the killer.

But Martha didn't believe that. She remembered how genuinely upset, even horrified, she'd been that first day at the Visitors Center when they told her of Amy's violent death in Duluth. She wasn't a good enough actor to pull that off. And she had been stunned when they discovered Rose propped up in bed, dead of a habit that she had supposedly kicked long ago.

But what did she know and what was she hiding? Martha knew it had to be hidden in this forest. Otherwise, why the elaborate ruse? But when and how to confront Berglund? Right now Martha didn't trust herself to not seriously hurt the woman.

She wished MacAuliffe was here. Smart, clever, accustomed to seeing through people's lies and motivations, he'd have ideas on how to proceed. Her mind drifted off to the big lake, hoping her friend was okay, that he too hadn't run into lies and deceit and danger in his investigation. Get back safe, my friend, get back fast. She sent him a text with her plans and waited in vain for a reply.

So figure it out, girl. Put on your big girl pants and head into the woods. What she really wanted was to turn this information over to Gould and never set foot in this godforsaken forest again. Could she trust Gould and take him the information? Rose had said trust no one. Was that distrust limited to her friend, Marlena Berglund, or did it go further? Again, she didn't know.

The forest is not evil, she reminded herself. Not believing it for a moment, she opened the car door and leaned down to put on her new hiking boots, remembering to spray her feet and ankles and legs with bug juice. She'd packed this morning for hiking the woods, so she'd go for a hike in the woods. And now she had a goal and two targets—the fern meadow and the cabin. Lumsden's map placed the former cow pasture northeast of the campsite. With no scale, she didn't know if it was a hundred yards off the trail or a mile. But she had several hours of daylight to locate it.

Lumsden had been right about the easy stroll into Woods Creek campsite. It wouldn't be fun toting a keg of beer, but with only a backpack, ten, twelve minutes of leisurely walking along the Superior Hiking Trail brought her to the campsite. Planks for seating ringed a fire pit. Flat patches of dirt and pine needles indicated the tent sites, none of which looked like they'd been used recently. A path branched off to a small clearing where she found a pit toilet. No outhouse building, just a seat in the woods over a hole in the ground. That had to be special.

Back on the main trail, Martha consulted Lumsden's sketch and decided to hike for half a mile or so before branching out into the woods. The trail wound through the woods but required constant attention for rocks and tree roots that could turn an ankle or stub a toe before she blinked. At a brisk pace, a half a mile should take her ten minutes, fifteen at most. She decided on ten so she wouldn't overshoot the meadow. She sipped from her water bottle, checked her watch, and set out.

At exactly ten minutes, she paused only long enough to establish a compass heading and then took that first step into the shadowed forest. Tree limbs whipped back at her, dead lower branches poked at her. There was no sign of a path, and fallen trees were constant obstacles. She picked her way, working through and around and over, getting scratched and jabbed and poked. She paused long enough to sip from the water bottle and wipe the sweat off her brow. The back of her hand came away bloody, a feast for the mosquitoes that swarmed around her head. But so far the bug spray had kept them from biting, except for the ones that discovered she'd missed the inside of her ears. Their arrival sounded like Lumsden landing the plane inside her head and abruptly ceased with the prick of a mosquito's bite. She boxed her ears and quickly wiped them down, both inside and out, with more bug juice.

Fifteen minutes in, she stopped to get her bearings. The Superior Hiking Trail was lost from sight behind her, but nothing ahead of her hinted at the fern meadow. Thirty minutes in, the shaded forest and dense undergrowth appeared much the same in every direction. The air was hot and stuffy and carried the scent of decaying wood. No breeze penetrated the deep woods. She reset her bearings, stepped around some kind of evergreen, and ventured forward again, ducking low to avoid being stabbed in the eye and twisting sideways to miss being run through the side.

After nearly an hour, she was beginning to give up hope of running into the meadow. Had she missed it and was now wandering aimlessly through the woods? It wasn't aimless, she chided herself. And she wasn't lost. Turning around and heading due west would eventually return her to the trail.

Violent memories from another time in another forest came from the woods that now extended before her and behind her. Then, she knew where she was going and moved steadily with a purpose through deep snow. Now, should she keep going east or turn around and head west, head home? Turning around, she saw distant sunlight flickering through the green branches. The light grew brighter as she moved forward. Suddenly she was out of the trees and found herself in a wide circular space, with sky above, blue and clear. She stood on the edge of the fern meadow, surrounded by an almost solid wall of forest.

Martha had come onto the meadow at its eastern edge, in one of the oval legs from Lumsden's drawing. She'd almost walked past it; she'd been off in entering the woods by a hundred yards or less. Hell's bells, she hated this forest, as if it were a malignant character that had come alive.

Standing at the edge, she stared over the meadow and realized the ferns hadn't died off. They'd been cut down, mowed. She inspected the tailings of a cut plant and held it up. Maybe this hadn't been a fern meadow after all. She retreated to where she found ferns growing under the tree canopy and compared the two plants.

No, she hadn't found a fern meadow. She'd found someone's marijuana crop.

Inspecting the leaf, she found it was still green and springy despite having been trampled in the harvest. And the harvest had been recent, very recent. She tucked it into her backpack and walked out into the field. With the harvest complete, she didn't expect anyone to be guarding the cash crop, but all the same, she kept her ears tuned for voices, for the cocking of a rifle, the sudden revving of a motor. All she heard were the birds chirping, the mosquitoes buzzing, the wind rustling the treetops. An old cow pie was visible under the ragged edges of a cut plant, dropped long ago, worn flat with rain and snow but still visible, still fertilizing the crop.

She emerged from the oval leg into the larger opening that Lumsden had drawn in her sketch. The upper part of the field sloped gently toward her. Martha glanced around and realized this field was different. The rows that had once been marijuana plants were farther apart, with a different plant cultivated between them. Kneeling, she fingered the second plant. Faded red petals littered the ground around it. She placed them and a cut stalk in her backpack.

Here, the ground was damp.

The ground became wetter as she moved uphill until she found mud and boot prints in a bare spot. An artesian spring? She kicked around for the source, and soon uncovered a PVC standpipe with a bar lever faucet attached to the end. Soaker hoses ran from the faucet. A small red flag on a wire post had been pulled out and lay half-buried under some cuttings. The white pipe ran up the hill and Martha followed it between plants. She found another outlet, another series of hoses, another flag pulled out. The field had been engineered with a gravity-fed watering system. Someone had invested a lot of time in creating the site. Why pull the marker flags?

Unless they were abandoning the site.

Rose had gotten too close, and then she and MacAuliffe came nosing around, investigating her work.

She worked her way across the field until she reached the upper point where field met woods again. The tracks were easy to see now. Boot prints and truck tracks, or something smaller but still motorized, had trampled the cut stems of the marijuana plants and many more faded petals. She followed the tracks until they converged into one that led back under the trees.

Set back in the woods was a lean-to with a camouflage tarp covering it. The tarp had been staked down on the corners and had a flap for an opening. Martha peeked under. A few bags of fertilizer remained. Cow shit and fertilizer. The source of the nitrates Rose had discovered in the water quality sample. She must have discovered the meadow.

Next to the fertilizer was a nearly empty box of PVC parts, a pair of gloves. A dirty, well-thumbed binder on the feeding and care of Khyber Kush in Northern Climes. Khyber Kush? She remembered reading stories about US soldiers in the Khyber Pass. In the Afghan region of the world. Of course. The mountains would have similar problems with short growing seasons and extreme winters as northern Minnesota. A hardy variation of the plant for a harsh climate. Glancing through the manual, she read that Khyber Kush was a smaller variety of plant. More apt to resemble a field of ferns, she realized, than the larger, more tropical varieties of marijuana. The similarity would be enough to fool a pilot more interested in locating moose and deer.

Near the back of the binder, the pages were cleaner, the corners not as well-thumbed. They were hand-written pages of notes with crude illustrations on how to grow poppies and harvest the resin from the bulbs. An illustration showed how to plant them between rows of corn and gave spacing requirements and watering instructions. That explained the faded red petals. Only, the corn had been replaced with a different crop.

Martha pocketed the gloves and the manual, dropping them into her backpack.

Back outside, she saw the PVC pipe. At least two inches, maybe more, ran along the ground back toward Woods Creek.

Most of the way, pine needles had been swept over the pipe, but in a few places, the white pipe peeked through. Gravity fed from the creek? Why not, she figured. Buried in a deeper back eddy of the creek, covered with a few strategic rocks, it'd be nearly invisible. A natural incline from the hillside provided the flow.

The trail out of the field was narrow, clearly too narrow for a truck. Still, heavy tire tracks were visible. An ATV and a wagon? Maybe a small tractor. The path wound between trees and zig-zagged back and forth. Martha could never see more than twenty, thirty feet in front of her. Which was probably the whole point, she realized. It'd also make it harder to spot by the casual hiker or from the air.

The angle of the sun dropped, and the shadows grew long in the forest. Twilight came early in the deep woods. She followed the trail out. Despite its winding course, it ran uphill and to the west. Martha suspected she knew where it led. The pieces were starting to come together. She also suspected she knew who waited on the far end.

The cabin sat in the growing darkness. A few leaves high overhead still caught an occasional glint of sun. Martha sat well off the trail, wedged between two trees and behind a large growth of ferns. At least they really were ferns this time. Bugs swarmed her, and she tried to pay no attention to them, but that was like telling an acolyte to clear his mind of all thoughts before stepping on the *tatami*.

The cabin was small, maybe twenty by thirty feet, about the size of the other cabins she had known intimately. Walt Boudreau had built his in the backwoods of the UP out of white pine logs; Hewitt's family cabin in the Utah mountains was constructed of old, weathered planks a century and a half ago. This one was sheets of something, probably an exterior plywood, stained brown with a high-pitched green metal roof. One side of the cabin had a row of windows, another contained the door and a couple of windows. On one end a tank with a circular, domed lid sat perched on four posts. She suddenly realized how much she hated cabins in the woods. Give me a boat anytime, she thought.

She watched the door and the trail that led out from the cabin to parts unknown. She circled the cabin and found the woodpile. A strong odor identified the location of an active outhouse. A small shed attached to the back of the outhouse housed garden tools, a chainsaw, a small generator. An ATV was hidden under a green and brown tarp, a trailer sat parked off in the woods, again under a tarp. As the evening darkened, she noticed a faint light coming from a window near the door.

Distant headlights flickered through the trees. Was she nearer the road than she thought or was her patience being rewarded? It soon became clear that the headlights were winding their way in her direction. An NFS truck pulled up in front of the cabin and parked. Martha wasn't surprised to see Marlena Berglund get out and hustle to the cabin. Disappointed, but not surprised. Rose had been right not to trust anyone. It was a lesson Martha hadn't heeded, and she'd been played for a fool.

A quick knock, and Marlena let herself in.

Martha crept from her hiding place to the truck and opened the door. She removed the keys that dangled from the ignition. Glancing up, she saw baby Hunter watching her from his car seat, his round face and eyes visible in the dome light. Or was Hunter a girl? She couldn't remember. She pocketed the keys and closed the door.

Now she waited outside the door, pressed against the cabin siding. A can of bug spray sat on a small shelf beside the door, and she was tempted to dose herself but didn't only out of fear that the hissing of the can would draw attention to her before she was ready.

One eye focused on the door, she started to breathe deeply, to prepare herself for any and everything that was about to happen. She'd not be caught by surprise again. This time it was her turn to be dishing out the surprise. She reminded herself that the goal was to bring people in alive. Still she felt rage rising within her.

She heard Berglund talking but couldn't make out the words. A second, quieter voice responded. The light flicked off in the cabin. The door opened.

Martha burst through Berglund, sending her sprawling back into the cabin to land hard on her butt and with a thump of the head. A scream, high pitched and shrill, rose above the commotion. Martha spun in a roundhouse kick, bringing her foot within inches of striking the girl's head. Lizzie. Ignoring both, she crouched and twirled, seeking anyone else in the cabin, ready for an attack, ready to attack. No one leapt out at her, no one was visible in the dark corners of the cabin. She flicked on her flashlight, quickly shining it around the cabin, into each corner, toward the loft, into the kitchen. No one was visible.

"Where is she, Marlena?" Martha whispered through clenched teeth. "Where's Bess?"

Berglund struggled to a sitting position. Her hand crept toward the gun strapped to her side.

"Since you've reached the bottom of stupid, Marlena, don't do it. What would Hunter do without his grandmother? That was Hunter I saw in the truck wasn't it? Cut a deal and you might be out in time to see him graduate."

Berglund's hand dropped, and soon she was sitting on the floor, sobbing into her hands.

TWENTY-NINE

Dusk expanded across the evening sky. A slim yellow crescent of moon in the far west trailed the sun toward the horizon. MacAuliffe watched them both disappear in the west. It promised to be a dark night. That was good. The brightest stars were already visible, Cassiopeia in her crooked chair, the Big Dipper. Between them, the North Star was coming into focus. But they'd soon be shrouded from view. In the southwest, an impenetrable wall of thunderclouds appeared like mountains in silhouette. Someplace over Grand Portage or Canada, an occasional lightning bolt flashed out of the clouds.

It had been a quiet afternoon in Grace Harbor. From the shore, MacAuliffe had watched Buzz lounge in the cockpit of *Executive Suite* with a magazine, then a book, a couple of beers. The ranger disappeared once and returned in shorts and tee-shirt. He took a nap, the brim of his NFS hat pulled low over his eyes. Mostly he sat in the shade provided by the flybridge. A couple of times he jumped up to the bow and peered off into the distance where open, empty water was all he could see.

MacAuliffe dozed a couple of times, shifting from one tree to the other when he felt himself growing sleepy again. He nibbled on his remaining food. The boat drifted over the hook in the calm, not enough breeze to extend it out on the anchor rode.

This is about as boring as it gets, MacAuliffe thought. Had he misread Buzz's actions and he really was just taking a little R and R time before heading home? He willed himself to be patient, but for someone used to the kinetic energy of moving, typing, talking to people, he found the waiting and spying hard to endure. Endurance was the best word he could think of when he considered his improvised camouflage suit of unbreathable garbage bags in the hot afternoon sun. How many pounds had he sweated away? He took little solace in knowing he could afford to lose a little weight anyway. How long before he fainted from heat exhaustion? Well, at least then the mosquitoes and deerflies could attack undeterred.

As evening settled over the lake, the lights inside *Executive Suite* started to take effect. All afternoon the tinted glass of the windows had been an impenetrable barrier in the bright sun. But now with the sun gone, the lights inside started to illuminate what was happening inside the boat. Buzz was visible in the galley, prepping food. Once, he stepped over to the inside helm station. He studied something—radar? weather? his stock portfolio?—before going back to the galley. Eventually he carried two plates into the main salon and disappeared from view. MacAuliffe sharpened the focus on the binoculars. Yes, he was sure, two plates. But where had he gone? He didn't appear outside; he hadn't gone forward to his cabin. He'd stepped into the main salon and disappeared. Eating behind drawn curtains?

There was still too much ambient light to launch the dinghy. For now, all he could do was watch from shore. A distant bolt of lightning flashed, followed by Mississippi one, Mississippi two. He heard the low rumble of thunder.

One of MacAuliffe's questions was answered soon after. A head and body stepped into the light of the galley, carrying a plate. He fiddled with the focus, but it was as sharp as it was going to get. The posture seemed different from Buzz's, and the hat was off. Like most Minnesotans, Buzz ate with his hat on. When the person turned, he knew it was a woman. In silhouette, her bust was clearly visible.

"Ah, so you're not alone, Buzzie boy," he whispered. Is this just a romantic tryst? Somebody's wife, hence all the secrecy? In the dim light, he couldn't make out her face, but she appeared bald. He checked again: yes, the curve of her breasts was obvious.

A moment later, Buzz, his hat still on, appeared carrying his plate to the galley. MacAuliffe had studied him enough over the past few hours to recognize his posture, his poses, the way he tilted his head forward when talking. Side by side, he was also taller, broader in the shoulders. They gracefully slid around each other in the galley without touching. Buzz stepped over to the nav station again. They both disappeared into the blacked-out main salon. Buzz immediately appeared alone in the cockpit. He slid the door closed behind him and jumped up to the bow.

The red and green of a boat's running lights approached the harbor. A growing breeze had caused *Executive Suite* to shift slightly, its bow now facing to the southwest, the anchor rode now out of the water. Standing on the bow sprit, Buzz directed a flashlight toward the incoming boat, flashing one long burst of light and one short burst. The incoming boat answered with the same. MacAuliffe recognized the sequence as the safe-to-proceed signal from bridge tenders.

The boat crept into the cove, following much the same path as Buzz had navigated earlier this afternoon. A silhouette stood on the bow, another hugged the railing at the stern. A third person had to be somewhere driving the boat. As it swung close to him in his hiding spot on shore, MacAuliffe recognized the profile. A trawler, a big Grand Banks or maybe a Passagemaker. It was nearly as large as *Executive Suite* but carried its height more forward than the Ocean Alexander.

The trawler came up behind *Executive Suite* and slowed to a crawl. People on both boats scrambled with lines and fenders. MacAuliffe had seen the maneuver many times before. It planned to raft up.

It was now fully dark, the last of the western twilight gone from the sky. A few stars were visible to the east, but the incoming cloud bank had swallowed the night sky to the west. While they were busy grabbing lines and placing fenders, MacAuliffe dropped the binoculars into the Ziploc, checked his garbage bags, and eased the dinghy out of the woods and onto the beach. Soon he was rowing toward the boats.

"Hi, Lizzie," Martha said. The young girl who knew Craig Junior as Buzz stared hard at her, eyes squinted and jaw set. "It's nice to see you again. Did the tooth fairy find you?"

The girl stood behind the table and said nothing in response. She scowled at Martha as if she were a monster who had just burst into the cabin. Scowling but not afraid. Kids were so intuitive, Martha thought. Lizzie didn't know what kind of monster she was facing or the kind she was living with. But she appeared ready to face it head on.

Lizzie had lit a camp lantern and placed it on the small kitchen table. Berglund and Martha now sat on opposite ends of the table, while Lizzie stood near the ranger, against the wall. The child wore a loose denim shirt over a pink and sparkly tee, faded jeans, a knee starting to show through on the left leg, and bright lime-green sneakers. Her brown hair was pulled back in a ponytail. She clutched a backpack in her hands.

Berglund had sobbed for a long time, and Martha let her cry. When your life is passing before your eyes, when everything you hold dear is vaporizing like the earth beneath a bomb, it's worth a good, long cry. Nurturing and comforting weren't high on her skills list, but apparently they were for the young girl. Lizzie massaged Berglund's hand with gentle strokes. She brushed hair back from the ranger's face and whispered over and over again, "Don't cry, Auntie Lena, it'll all be okay. Really. I'll help fix it." She began to hum. "Hush dear Lena, don't you cry, Lizzie's gonna bake you a cherry pie."

Martha had taken Marlena's gun and now stepped outside long enough to throw it as far into the bushes as she could. She saw light flash through the forest canopy. A few seconds later it was followed by one long continuous roll of thunder.

Back inside, she asked Lizzie if Marlena could have a glass of water. The girl brought one from a jug that sat beside the sink and handed it to Berglund. "Just take little sips at first," the girl advised. "Don't want your stomach bloatin'."

The girl had obviously done this before.

"Hi, Lizzie," Martha repeated. "My name's Martha, and we met at the pizza place with your uncle Buzz."

The girl spoke to her for the first time, her voice thin and faint. "He never told you that."

"I know. I figured it out on my own."

"No one's supposed to know. You can't tell anyone."

Martha tried to absorb this. "Is he a good uncle?"

"He's the best in the whole world." Her tone brooked no argument on the matter. "He takes me to movies. *Frozen* is my favorite. He lets me sleep over. I have my own room. He lets me eat ice cream and pizza."

"That's great, Lizzie. I won't tell anyone. I promise." She wondered if it was a promise she could keep.

"Don't do this, Martha." It was Berglund, her first words since being sent sprawling to the floor.

Martha spit out her reply. "And why not, Marlena? I befriended you, I trusted you. We were a team, remember? Tell each other everything. And you betrayed me. Why should I trust anything you say?"

"Because she and Hunter are my family." Lizzie jumped to her defense.

If it could only be that simple, but it wasn't any longer. It was such a shame that the innocence of youth had to be dashed by the actions of their elders. But that's where kids learned to love and cherish and lie and cheat—and kill. Martha said to Lizzie, "So Lena and Buzz are both your family?"

The girl vigorously nodded her head.

"It's nice to have family, isn't it, Lizzie?" Again the girl nodded. "Not sure how much good that will do you in court, Marlena, but it's good to know you still have one person who believes in you." Berglund sat motionless, her hands folded in her lap, her head down. "I imagine you're surprised to see me here. You thought I'd probably be lost in the woods someplace a few miles south of here."

At first Berglund didn't answer. She sat back in the chair and wiped her eyes. "Thank you for the water, Lizzie. You're my girl. Love you."

"You're welcome. Love you too."

"Char called." This time she was talking to Martha though her gaze remained steady on the far wall. "Just wanted to tell Craig the two of you were flying this morning and you guys saw someone in the old cabin. Thought he might need to evict another squatter."

"Imagine my surprise when I find a young girl here, alone. Except she isn't by herself, is she?" Martha turned to the girl.

"Why do you live out here in the woods, Lizzie?"

Thunder rumbled first and then a loud clap shook the cabin. The girl looked anxiously around and then at Berglund.

"Martha, please don't," Berglund said.

"I don't live here," the girl said in her fiercest voice, the gap from the missing front tooth just visible between thin lips. "I live in town with Auntie Lena. She adopted me. I have to take care of mama sometimes. She needs me. Thunder scares her."

"Oh, what's wrong with your mom? It's Bess, isn't it?"

Suddenly, Lizzie stood tall and straight. A fierceness filled her. Her dark eyes shone bright and she held Martha in a hard stare. "Of course. She has PSTD. It's not her fault. She got hurt bad in Afagan and sometimes she's not right. Storms are the worst. They trigger the war in her head. Buzz and I have to take care of her. We protect her. Auntie Lena and Hunter help us sometimes."

Of all the strange surprises she'd encountered in the past few hours, this was at least one thing that Martha could believe.

Since the bathtub didn't move particularly well from any position, he sat the wrong way and rowed facing the boats. He kept his strokes deep and quiet and closed the distance to the two boats. He bobbed on the rippling waters of Grace Harbor directly off the sterns of the two boats. The black garbage bags and a gray dinghy would be difficult to spot if he stayed outside the halo created by the cabin lights.

While he rowed, they completed tying up the raft, and Buzz's companion greeted someone from the trawler with a big hug. She shook hands with the other two. Buzz stood apart, nearly lost in the shadows on *Executive Suite*.

In position, MacAuliffe took out his binoculars and zoomed in on the sterns of the two boats. The hug and the handshakes done, now the crews worked. He occasionally pulled closer as the wind pushed him back. They were moving bundles, each about the size of a large suitcase from *Executive Suite* to . . . he saw the boat's name was *Sea-cronicity*, home port Milwaukee.

God, he wished he had a pair of night goggles. They weren't passing suitcases from person to person, from one boat to the next. It was something wrapped in broad sheets of cellophane.

For the first time it registered with MacAuliffe. Buzz and his companion weren't the ones smuggling in, they were the ones smuggling out. He knew then what it was. The bundles were bales, and Rosie's nitrate reading had to come from fertilizer. They were growing pot in the north woods. The boys on *Sea-cronicity* were rendezvousing with their supplier.

If Buzz and his partner hadn't crossed the line to murder, MacAuliffe would've rowed away, admiring their entrepreneurial spirit. It was only a matter of time before Minnesota and Wisconsin legalized marijuana. But until then, there had to be a healthy underground market for the drug. As far as he was concerned, pot should be legal everywhere. He hated the thought that these folks risked years in jail for providing a product more benign than alcohol or tobacco.

But a young woman's future had been snuffed out in a fiery explosion. Her mother must have stumbled upon the operation and died for it. Then, they had to be afraid Rose had told her daughter, so the daughter had to die, too.

Working carefully, he removed his phone from the Ziploc. He didn't want to dump it or himself into the water. And he had to do it all without attracting any attention to himself. He rowed as close as he dared without spilling into the circle of light. He made sure the flash was off and flicked the screen several times until the camera was on full zoom. He photographed the boats and the hand-off of the merchandise.

With five people working in a chain, one handing off to the next, it didn't take long to empty *Executive Suite*. The transfer finished, the woman stood on the swim step holding an oversized shopping bag with strap handles. She talked across the boat to one of the men from *Sea-cronicity* and handed him the bag. With the wind blowing toward him, he caught snatches of the conversation.

". . . new product . . . requested," she said.

The man on *Sea-cronicity* took it and handed a suitcase to her in return.

". . . as always," the woman said. "We'll let you . . . up and running again . . . shut it down . . . now . . . fucking nosing . . . deeper into the woods . . . us a season."

His deeper voice carried better across the water.

"No problem, Major," came the reply. "Gonna have to find me a new supplier 'til then. Nothing personal, you understand."

"I . . . Sarge. Just . . . forget . . . when I call."

"Come see us sometime in West Allis, Major," the man said. "You and the little one are always welcome. Not so sure about sourpuss here."

"Fuck you, Benny," came Buzz's voice and he stepped into the cockpit.

"Any time you wanna give it a whirl, asshole." The Milwaukee man laughed. "And we can share a smoke afterwards." He reached across the transom and gave the woman a hug. Her reply was lost to MacAuliffe.

The engines on *Sea-cronicity* suddenly chugged to life. He'd edged too close. With his phone still in his mouth, he pulled with deep, strong strokes but the inflatable proved as sluggish as before.

A man on the bow yelled, "Ready, here."

From the stern, Benny yelled, "Stern's free."

Sea-cronicity, already facing out of the harbor, eased ahead, just as a bolt of lightning lit the way out. It was followed shortly by a long rolling thunder. The first rain began to fall. The first drops were hard and heavy but few. MacAuliffe scrambled to get his phone back into the Ziploc. Another round of thunder and lightning brought a sheet of rain and the first real wind.

Suddenly, he saw Buzz and his companion standing on the stern, peering in his direction. Oh, shit, what could they see? Had they gotten a glimpse of the inflatable in the lightning bolt? He couldn't hear her, but between rolls of thunder, he heard Buzz say, "There's nothing out there, Bess."

She ignored him and stood at the rail, scanning the horizon. Several times her gaze swept over him but never paused. MacAuliffe saw her pull something from behind her. Her arms came up. Oh shit, oh shit. He frantically worked to seal the Ziploc. He felt the seal close, and he slipped over the side of the dinghy into the water. It was so cold it took his breath away. Oh God, don't inhale it, don't inhale the water. The idea of becoming another victim to Sudden Drowning Syndrome flashed through his mind in time with another bolt of lightning. He tried to swim but his garbage bags began to fill with water, dragging him under. With only his stocking cap and Ziploc above water, he ripped one of the bags and could suddenly move. He kicked away from the inflatable, moving sideways as best he could, further from their direct line of sight, further from her aim. She stood patiently on the stern of the boat, arms raised.

Suddenly a lightning flash illuminated the sky. Before the thunder came, he heard three, four shots and a sudden hiss came from the inflatable. It started to sag in the water. He kicked harder and used one arm to stroke, moving sideways as quickly as he could. Don't thrash, don't make a sound, move, Mac, move. His legs churned until he thought they'd fall off. But he started putting some distance between him and the inflatable. The spotlight from *Executive Suite* suddenly lit up the night. It swept across the water until it settled on the sinking dinghy. Another two, three shots boomed out until they were lost in a clap of thunder. When it passed, he heard Buzz yell, "Stop it. It's just a kid's rubber boat. It must have broken loose in the wind."

She emptied her clip into it all the same.

Lizzie sat at the table in the glow of the camp light, eating a slice of bread with strawberry jam on it. As she licked her fingers, Martha said, "Lizzie, where's your mom now?"

"On a secret mission."

"Really? What is it?"

"It wouldn't be secret if I told you, dummy."

"When do you expect her home?"

The girl rolled her eyes, a sign of exasperation understandable even to a non-parent like Martha. "We don't talk about it. That's the rule."

At least she's well trained. The sound of rain pattering on the metal roof became audible overhead. Many times Martha had welcomed the sound, closed her eyes and just listened to the wind and the rain. But not tonight. "Lizzie, honey, Hunter's out in the truck. Could you go out and make sure he's not scared of the storm?"

"Hunter's a girl," she replied.

"Silly me. I forgot. Could you make sure she's okay?"

The girl's eyes darted to Marlena.

"Hunter'd like to see you, honey, I'm sure."

She got up and skipped out of the cabin. She shut the door behind her. The two women stared at each other from opposite ends of the table. Berglund's hand grasped the water cup and kept squeezing it.

"What do we do now, Marlena?" Martha asked.

"I knew nothing about Amy and Rosie," Berglund replied. "I had nothing to do with that. Rose was my friend. Really."

"That's convincing. So they'll only charge you with being an accessory after the fact, because you certainly knew who did kill them. You didn't come forward, and you deliberately misled us when we started getting close. I wonder if your fingerprints are on that map that was replaced on Rose's wall. Had to be you or Buzz."

"Yeah, well, I wouldn't leave the toilet seat up."

"Point noted," Martha said. "Were you searching her office to find information in her field notes, or were you going to destroy them? In case Craig missed it the first time through? And then there's the whole matter of the marijuana field. I'd say your days as a federal employee are probably over."

"You're a regular fucking Sherlock." Some of the ranger's former feistiness was returning. "I only started to figure things out when you guys found the map had been changed. Woods Creek. Then I knew. Knew it had to be her and Craig. You don't know Bess. You don't know what she's capable . . ."

Her voice drifted off.

Martha remembered with cold clarity the feeling of her last breath being choked out of her body. She remembered seeing Rose Bumgarten in her bedroom. More thunder accompanied this thought. The patter of rain changed to torrents beating on the metal roof. "Oh, I think I'm starting to get a pretty good idea of what Bess is capable of." She paused. "I thought she was dead. Nettles said she didn't come home from the war."

"And that's what Bess and Craig want him to think. She was ambushed and badly wounded. She was listed as MIA. Some villagers found her and nursed her back from the dead. Seems growing pot was a major part of the local economy. I don't know the full story. Only they never told their dad when she came home. Not sure she came back through the front door."

Berglund shook her head in weary resignation. The feistiness had come and gone.

Martha remembered Lumsden telling her about one of her air jockey colleagues who flew with Craig Junior and claimed he could land a float plane in swamp. And there were a lot of swamps and lakes along the Canadian-US border. Martha said, "Not sure she'd have to."

Berglund continued, "I was scared, okay. Partially of Bess, but also that I'd lose everything. Anna and Hunter. And Lizzie. I adopted her when she was a baby. Craig needed help. Bess had Lizzie while she was in the military, and asked Craig to take care of her while she finished her tour. He didn't have a fucking clue on how to raise a kid. We agreed it'd be best if I adopted her and raised her. It explained who she was, why she was in town, in school. She'd visit Craig on the weekends, and when Bess returned home, Lizzie'd stay with me during the week and one of them on the weekend. But when Bess came back, she wasn't right. Her wounds were horrific enough, but she wasn't right in the old noggin—and that's worse. Both Craig and me knew it, but she wouldn't seek treatment or counseling. In her mind, the government had tried to kill her once, and then left her for dead. She sure as hell wasn't going to give them a second chance. Craig did everything he could to get her help."

"Including letting her build a cabin in the woods that was within his patrol area."

"Yeah. So what? It's a fucking big woods, in case you've forgotten."

"No, I haven't forgotten."

"Craig wanted to be close to take care of Bess, and I needed to look after Lizzie. It was a good solution. I was able to continue raising Lizzie, give her a sense of home, normalcy, family. Lizzie now has two families who love her. And for all the times that Craig's a colossal jerk, and that's pretty goddamn often, he loves that little girl. We both do. And Lizzie's all that's holding Bess together. She has bad flashbacks and the PTSD can be pretty awful at times, but Lizzie seems to be able to calm her, bring her down, bring her back. She's really the only one. Her and Hunter. Bess's gentle as a lamb with the baby. God knows why. Craig can't calm Bess down when she's on a rampage. She almost killed him one time when she was in the middle of a really bad episode."

"Why the pot farm, Marlena?"

"Take a fucking guess, if you're so goddamn smart."

Martha just let the insult linger between them without responding.

"Money," Berglund said, finally. "Bess couldn't just show up at the local convenience store and ask for a job. She'd never ask the old man for any money. They hate the bastard. Mostly 'cause of what he did to their mom. Such a vain, narcissistic prick. The final tipping point came one night when he was drunk and crawled into bed with Bess, thinking she was her mother." She wiped some tears away from her cheeks.

"Oh, God," Martha said, her voice now quiet. "Is Lizzie his daughter?"

Berglund shook her head. "You don't know Bess. She beat the shit out of him before that could happen. He came to his senses when he found himself on the floor bleeding. Buzz said it was quite a sight. Pushed him in a taxi half naked and sent him off to the hospital. Someplace in Italy. Didn't even send his leg with him. Threw it in the dumpster. They packed their bags and left. Nettles tried so hard to make it up to her, but Bess was having nothing to do with him. One time the old man's money didn't buy what he fucking wanted. Bess hasn't seen him or spoken to him since she left for boot camp. If she did, she'd probably kill him."

"Or frame him with two murders."

Berglund shrugged, but didn't respond.

"Her love, her approval is the one thing he wanted more than anything else," Martha said. She dared not admit her admiration for the way Bess handled the unwanted assault. Maybe they weren't so different. That was a disturbing thought. She shook the thought away and added, "So she took to growing pot to raise money."

"Yeah. Bess heard from an ex-Army buddy. He was complaining about his supplier. Said he wanted someone more reliable, so she went into the pot business. We either turned her in, ignored her, or helped her. The first one wasn't really an option, not with Bess. So I ignored the whole drug operation. My only concern was Lizzie. Craig got wrangled into helping Bess. I'm not sure why. Help his baby sister, make some money that didn't come from daddy, another way to say fuck you. I don't know. Probably a little of all of 'em."

"Craig still sees his father. We met him at the family home in Duluth."

"Are you really so clueless? The old man's worth a mint. Craig stands to inherit all of it. He wasn't going to let that gravy train get away—not completely."

"But why pot? It's legal in half the states and all of Canada now."

"Well, it's not in Minnesota. And there's still an active black market for weed everywhere. Just ask my friends in California who work for the Forest Service. It's legal there, but there's still more illegal pot farms in the northern Cal woods than fleas on a barn dog."

"Seems Bess was starting to diversify," Martha said. "She was also growing poppies. The kind that you harvest for opium."

"Knew nothin' about that."

"I'm not sure a judge will consider that a convincing argument."

"It's the truth."

"The truth from you, Marlena, seems to be in pretty short supply." The ranger didn't respond. Martha added, "And Rose found it."

It was a statement, not a question.

"I didn't know Rose had even set foot north of town," Berglund said. "I really didn't. Her whole focus had been in shutting down the plans for the resort. I hated that fucking resort. And Craig did too. He didn't really give a shit about the resort; he just couldn't stomach his father anywhere near GM."

Berglund buried her face in weathered hands. "When Bess went off the rails and started killing people, I had to do something. But I couldn't risk losing Lizzie or that little girl getting hurt. Bess would've killed me if she knew I helped you. But remember, I called you with that info on the prof at UMD? Craig had tried to hide it with the new topo map but when you found it, I thought that might be a place for you to start. I set you on the right path."

"So why the false trail of searching the woods on foot instead of chartering a plane?"

"Knew you were getting too close too fast. I needed to get Lizzie out first. Bess'd asked her to stay with her a few days. It was odd for a school week. I didn't know they were delivering until Craig called in and said he was gonna do his shore patrol. I pretend I don't know what he's doing but I'd figured it out. I think you must've spooked Bess, and she was getting ready to run. Now, I see she was figuring to take my little girl with her. I couldn't move until they were gone on the delivery. Just had to have a little more time."

The kerosene lamp cast its yellow glow across the woman's gaunt face. She buried her face in her hands again. "Now I've really fucked it up."

"Yes, you have," Martha said. She took a long time thinking through her plan, weighing pros and cons, trust and betrayal. Yes, it might work. She started, "But I want your help. I don't need it, understand. But I want to meet Bess alone. It may also be the only way for you to keep your daughter. And I'm not trusting you, Marlena. If you betray me again, if you bet on Bess instead of me, I'll do everything I can to make sure you rot in jail for the rest of your life as an accessory to murder. Wonder what Anna and Lizzie and Hunter will think of you then."

Berglund sat stone faced and motionless. Then gave an almost imperceptible nod.

"Good," Martha said. "Here's how it's going to work."

When Martha had finished, Berglund leaned back without commenting. Lizzie came back into the cabin just then, holding Hunter in her arms. Hunter was wrapped in a blanket, but Lizzie was drenched. "Auntie Lena, Hunter has poo-pooed her diapers. Can I change her?"

"I'd really appreciate that, honey. Thank you. Her bag is behind my seat in the truck. But put your raincoat on first and then stay in the truck." The girl removed a coat that hung on a peg by the door, wrapped it over her shoulders and stepped back outside. "She really is such a good girl."

"We have a deal?" Martha asked. She rose and extended the truck keys.

Berglund nodded and stood up. "But if you lose, we'll both be dead."

"I won't lose."

THIRTY

Twice he sank underwater, pulling the Ziploc with him, as the spotlight swept the cove. He floated motionless, his body spasming as the little heat generated by swimming immediately dissipated. The bright beam passed overhead, and he resurfaced slowly, forcing himself not to gasp or suck in water as it beat against his face. He heard more shots being fired, but none of them seemed to be aimed in his direction.

Using part sidestroke, part dogpaddle, he crept toward shore. Through the water, the rumble of the engines throbbed clear and loud. He glanced back. The bright spotlight from the flybridge still swept over the harbor, forcing him underwater again until it passed. The chain rattled as it was pulled in. Buzz was leaving. The woman, heedless of the rain and unrelenting thunder and lightning, continued to scan the water. She remained motionless on the stern, her hand stretched out in front of her. Each time the dinghy appeared in the spotlight, she fired more rounds. None of them missed the rapidly deflating rubber boat.

Rain pounded the churning water of the harbor. Wind whipped it into a frenzy, making it harder for them to see him, making it harder for him to swim back to shore.

Oh, God, the water was cold. He knew he didn't have much time before hypothermia became a factor. He felt his strength failing.

The anchor clanged into place on the bowsprit, and the boat motored forward into the white caps. It began a slow turn until it again faced into the harbor, the spotlight scanning the rough water. The boat seemed to be heading right for him, and MacAuliffe swam faster, trying to keep low on the surface. He dove when the light swept in his direction. He felt the boat wake push him aside when it rolled over him.

Executive Suite stopped when it came upon the deflated dinghy, the spotlight now steady on Uncle Chuck's rubber boat. MacAuliffe could see the woman on the bow, scanning the surrounding water. He heard the boat engines back and fill, and the higher pitched hum of the bow thruster. Buzz was working hard to hold the boat in place.

MacAuliffe kept swimming to put more distance between him and the boat—and the woman with the gun.

Finally, the boat began to turn again. The spotlight snapped off, leaving him in sudden darkness. He heard the engines revving, taking *Executive Suite* out of Grace Harbor toward the open lake.

When he crawled onto the beach from Grace Harbor, MacAuliffe couldn't remember ever being so cold. The rain felt warm by comparison, and he lay on the beach like the lone survivor of a shipwreck. Overhead, the lightning flashed, and thunder rumbled.

In time, he stumbled down the beach to his hiding place in the woods. Two pieces of cheese remained in his lunch bag, and he ate those while ripping off the remnants of the garbage bags that clung to his arms. He groped through Aunt Marie's boat bag and located the flashlight. Finding that his legs still worked, he set off on a jog along the trail he'd made in the woods.

Jogging didn't last long, but it helped to get some warmth back into his body. He slapped his arms and torso to get more blood flowing to all extremities.

His flashlight found the first trail marker, and he plunged on through the woods. Soon, he stood panting next to the stern line of *Mac's Place*. The boat was protected from the wind, and rode gently in place on anchor and a stern tie. There was no sign of his father. MacAuliffe yelled but got no response. He yelled louder and longer, but the wind and thunder carried the sound away. He swore and waded into the water. The muck on the bottom sucked at his shoes. He stumbled over something, rock, deadhead, he didn't know. He grabbed the stern line and pulled himself hand over hand along. The water was chest deep by the time he hauled himself aboard the swim step.

A voice came out of the companionway. "Don't move. I've got a gun."

"It's me, Dad."

"What's the password?"

"We don't have a fucking password."

His father's bald head appeared. "Okay, it is you. What's up?" Holding the flare gun and wearing nothing but his skivvies, Ted MacAuliffe stepped topside but remained well within the dry spot of the cockpit cover.

"Time to go," MacAuliffe ordered.

"We're in the middle of a thunderstorm, in case the fact slipped by your apparently water-soaked brain."

"No shit. That didn't prevent Nettles from hauling anchor and leaving. We've got to follow him." MacAuliffe flipped the battery switch on and turned the key. The diesel engines rumbled to life. He found a knife and jumped back to cut the stern line. He yelled at his father but had to repeat it because it was drowned out by a clap of thunder. "You drive, I'll get the anchor."

Sitting in the captain's chair in his whitey tighties, the old man drove them out of Washington Harbor and into the storm.

One green bleep showed at the edge of the radar, set to its farthest range. It was heading south and toward the mainland.

The storm wasn't easing. *Mac's Place* handled the swells easily, taking them off her forward starboard quarter. An occasional rogue wave slammed into the boat, causing it to shudder, but she always righted herself and kept going.

Now wearing dry clothes, MacAuliffe relieved his father at the helm. Despite water washing over the bow, he sat protected from the spray, sheltered by the windshield and cockpit cover. For a time, he pushed *Mac's Place* to close the distance between them and the blip on the radar screen. When it was comfortably within the middle circle of the radar, MacAuliffe eased the throttle to follow at the same pace. On the chart plotter, he laid out the projected course and saw it took *Executive Suite*, if the blip on the radar was Buzz, directly back to Marr Island.

"He's picked up his passenger and the bales behind Marr Island, had to," MacAuliffe said, speaking to his father. He'd filled him in on the basic facts of what he'd seen in Grace Harbor and what he suspected was going on. For once, his father was a willing listener. "Now he's going to drop her off again. He establishes the routine, so the Coast Guard thinks nothing of his making his two-day patrol and anchoring behind Marr Island for the night. Then once or twice a year—how often would you harvest marijuana? Whatever. Once in a while, the night at Marr Island includes loading up the cargo and . . ."

His voice trailed off. And picking up whom? A woman. Someone with a good understanding of how to use a gun. The words partially blown away by the wind came back to him. Sarge. Major. Military ranks. The woman the officer. He recalled how the woman and Buzz had moved about the boat galley without touching. Certainly not the way lovers moved in a tight space. The memory of standing in Nettles' study and going through the family photos flashed through his mind. Elizabeth. Named after her mom.

An engineer who had been deployed in a demolition unit, first in to blow shit up. Blowing up a Ford Ranger truck had to be easy in comparison.

"And picking up his sister," he said.

A sister who isn't dead.

Now wasn't the time to try to figure that one out.

He was quiet, but his brain raced through possible scenarios and outcomes. They were all bad. The last communication from Martha said she was heading into the woods with Berglund. She didn't know it, but MacAuliffe was sure they were looking for Bess Nettles, a woman who had just emptied a full clip into a tiny rubber boat with mechanical precision. The person, he realized, who had nearly killed Martha in the midnight attack at the cabin.

"Shit, I've got to warn Martha what she's up against," MacAuliffe said. "Sit down, Dad. We need to get to Grand Marais as fast as possible."

He pushed the throttle forward again.

Rain pounded the cabin, and she found it soothing, almost peaceful as she sat alone at the kitchen table. The flickering yellow light from the camp lantern left the cabin filled with shadows and dark corners. Flashes of lightning illuminated the corners for brief moments. How easy it'd be to fall asleep. She increased the lantern wick and began to explore.

Finished, Martha refilled the kerosene in the camp lantern and dimmed it to a low yellow glow, set it back on the kitchen table. She turned off her phone, not wanting to risk an unexpected ring or the beep of a text. Mac would certainly be reaching out to her as soon as he had service again. She listened. The rain had eased, was now a light patter on the metal roof. The thunder had moved out over the lake. She'd scrounged a light meal from the cabin's pantry, enough to quiet the hunger pangs, not enough to put her tired body into a food coma.

"Bess always returns directly to the cabin after a delivery," Berglund had told her. "She'll be worried about Lizzie being alone. She'll get back anytime between six in the morning and noon, depending on how things go on the hand off, the weather, whether Craig drops her off at the pick-up point or has to bring her back to GM. It all depends. Each time is different."

Martha moved a chair to beside the door, where it'd conceal her if opened suddenly. Now she waited, only time and her thoughts for company. She remained standing, letting her body rest. Each slow breath brought her a little closer to a meditative trance. Her fatigued body welcomed the reprieve, but her mind wouldn't let go of the previous times she'd confronted someone in the woods. Walt Boudreau, the rogue Mormon cops. This time didn't have to end the same. No one had to die in a cabin in the backwoods. Not a woman haunted by who knew what demons, who had been held together by a young girl, her daughter.

Martha hated what Bess had done—oh, she couldn't care less about her venture into agriculture. But protecting it by killing the Bumgarten women, that was unforgivable. Bess Nettles needed to be held accountable for those crimes. And the attack that had nearly left her dead? Vengeance is not mine to give, she reminded herself. Revenge is an endless blood curse.

Like hell, part of her answered. This voice had been strong her whole life, had dominated her actions when confronted.

And Craig Nettles Senior? She could only wish that he'd be the one to walk through that door first. A pathological narcissist, certainly. He cavorted while his wife succumbed to an agonizing death. He used money to correct all his mistakes—he paid off mistresses, bought the loyalty of Sophia, and he believed, wrongly, that he'd bought the fealty of his son. The one person who refused his money was the one he wanted most to come back to him. Martha had seen Nettles' drunken behavior and was repulsed by the thought of him crawling into bed with his daughter. He had violated the most sacred trust between parent and child.

It made Martha's stomach churn.

It was also that sacred trust that Marlena Berglund had tried to preserve, even if it meant lying about everything except the most central truth—she loved Lizzie as a daughter.

Martha knew that she could have cracked and lashed out like Bess. No, she was lying to herself. She had. Only she'd found forgiveness and grace. From Gran. From Hewitt, for all his later sins. Most importantly, from Lance Trammell. How might all of this been different if Bess had had a woman like Gran in her life, who could take her hand and reassure her that she'd always be loved. What if Bess hadn't gone to war with these horrible nightmares already gnawing at her soul?

The world isn't always a fair and just place, came the voice of her *sensei*. Get out of my head, master. He continued anyway. You can start with Bess Nettles. Show her mercy. Give her hope.

It was going to be a long wait.

Mac's Place sped across the water as fast as MacAuliffe dared push it in the rough sea. He had to trust there were no logs or deadheads floating in the dark water. When the blip on the radar screen veered off from Marr Island and quickly changed course to Grand Marais, he knew it wasn't fast enough. MacAuliffe could only guess that the cove had been too rough for anchoring and landing a passenger.

Before *Mac's Place* turned the corner into the harbor at Grand Marais, he spotted *Executive Suite* already tied up at the guest dock at the Grand Marais marina. In the parking lot, an NFS truck was pulling away, two silhouettes seated in the cab visible against the streetlight. Morning light was still an hour or more away.

"Goddamn it," MacAuliffe muttered. His phone call to Martha had gone unanswered. She didn't reply to his text. Berglund. Marlena might know. He dialed. She picked up on the first ring. "Sorry to call so early, Marlena. It's James MacAuliffe."

"I was awake," the ranger said, her voice flat.

"Do you know where Martha might be? She's not answering her phone."

There was a long pause. "Yeah, I know where she is."

"I need to warn her about Buzz. I think his sister's still alive and she may be dangerous. I'm pretty sure she's the one who killed Rose Bumgarten. I know Martha went searching for her."

Berglund didn't sound surprised. "Martha's waiting for her."

"I've got to get there. Buzz and his sister just left together from the Grand Marais marina. I don't have any wheels." The only response was silence. He shouted, "Goddamn it, will you help me?"

The panic continued to mount for MacAuliffe as he waited.

Finally, she said, "I'll pick you up at the marina. I'm just a few minutes away."

While his father steered *Mac's Place* toward an empty spot at the fuel dock, MacAuliffe scribbled fast. "Sea-cronicity. Trawler, maybe a Grand Banks. 45-50 ft. Home port Milwaukee, WI. Last known location, Grace Harbor, Isle Royale." He dated it.

"Just get me to the dock, Dad, then you're on your own."

"I'll be fine."

"And call the Coast Guard. Don't call on the VHF. If they're monitoring the radio, which I'm sure they are, they'll hear the call and begin dumping cargo. Call on the phone. Or walk up to the office. Tell them about the drug smuggling operation. Here's the information." MacAuliffe handed him the paper. "Tell them I have photos. But I need my phone right now. Just in case Martha responds."

As the boat approached the dock, MacAuliffe hopped onto the swim step and spanned the three feet of water with a jump. He was off and running.

"Be safe, son," Ted MacAuliffe shouted after him.

"Lizzie. Lizzie, honey, I'm home."

Martha heard the voice call out. She stood up and slid the kitchen chair to the side, under the window. Odd, the rain no longer pattered against the metal roof. She must have dozed off during the long wait. She began to flex, stretch, awakening sleepy muscles and mind.

Bess called out again. The kerosene lamp sat on the table, its faint glow still unable to penetrate the edges of the cabin. Martha stood perfectly still, breath in, breath out, waiting, preparing for anything and everything that might happen next.

Once more the voice called out, "Lizzie, honey." She came through the door fast, gun raised and ready before the last word had died on her lips. But Martha was ready too. She slammed the door against the charging woman, breaking her momentum.

In one continuous motion she kicked her gun hand hard and the pistol went clattering to the floor. Martha grabbed her jacket and flung her across the room toward the kitchen, away from the gun.

Berglund had arrived at the marina by the time he cleared the end of the fuel dock and had a door on her work truck open for him.

"Where's Martha?" MacAuliffe had asked between gasps.

"At Bess's cabin."

"Oh, fuck. How come you're not with her? Jesus, you left her alone to face that mad woman?" Then it occurred to MacAuliffe that he'd never mentioned the woman's name. "You knew about Bess, didn't you?"

The ranger nodded. "It's complicated, okay?"

"It's not fucking complicated. People are dead, Martha may be next. That's not complicated. What's going on, Marlena?"

She navigated a curve going way too fast and hit Highway 61, ignoring a stop sign.

When she didn't answer, MacAuliffe asked again, "Tell me what's going on?"

"Got my hand caught in the cookie jar, and then tried to lie my way out if it," Berglund replied. "People got hurt. No, people died, including my friend, Rose Bumgarten. Rose was my friend." She said it as if she'd been worrying the statement around in her mind for hours. "I'm so, so sorry. I just hope your friend isn't the next one."

She barely had time to give him the briefest of accounts before she screeched the truck to a halt in the middle of Lindskog Road, headlights pointed into the brush. They had passed Martha's rented Subaru a couple of miles back, parked on the side of the road. "Take that path. It brings you to the back of the cabin, by the woodpile. It's a half a mile or so past the hiking trail. You can get there quicker than if I drive all the way around."

"You better fucking hope she comes out of this okay." MacAuliffe flung the door open.

"Oh, I do."

"Call Gould and get him out here *now*."

He began running.

"We meet again," Martha said, coming around to face Bess in the dimness of the camp light. "But this time I won't be so easy to defeat."

Bess came out of her sprawl in a sweeping kick, but Martha hadn't followed her in. She stood back, ready but relaxed.

"Last time, you flailed like a frigging upside-down turtle." Her voice was harsh, raspy, not quite right. The words spewed forth in anger. She crouched, her right side turned toward Martha, her right arm out and flexed, her left close to her body. She was positioned to attack, ready to counter.

"I can assure you I won't this time, Bess. It is Bess, isn't it? Bess and Buzz, sister and brother, hiding out in the woods away from daddy with their pot and poppy farm. Ironic, really, how he wanted someone to follow him into the family business. He just didn't have the right business in mind."

"That bastard can rot in hell," the woman snarled. "You working for him?"

"Far from it. I can help you, but I *am* taking you in. The Bumgartens didn't have to die."

They circled, two opposites now locked in the dance of death, Martha tall and lean, her opponent shorter and full figured. A panther circling a lioness.

"Collateral damage."

Bess kept her right side toward Martha. She wore jeans and a navy blue windbreaker. Combat boots adorned her feet. Her hair was shorn tight to her skull.

"No, Bess, they weren't collateral damage. They were deliberately murdered."

Martha feinted, testing her and her training. She didn't shift left but kept her right side always forward. Good to know.

"I met Lizzie, you know."

The woman lunged with a right-left jab, missed as Martha blocked the first and leaned backwards to avoid the second. Bess followed with a roundhouse kick. Martha took the kick as a glancing blow off her shoulder, but followed with one of her own, a sweeping kick that wiped the legs out from underneath the other woman. Bess tumbled to the floor but immediately rolled away from the following blow.

Only Martha hadn't followed up the kick as she obviously expected. Let her think it's a weakness. She stood back. In the exchange she'd seen why Berglund had called the wounds horrific. The left side of Bess's face was severely scarred, her left eye dull and sightless. She shaved her whole head to match the side that would no longer grow hair. Another war veteran lost not on the battlefield protecting the country but after she returned home, another soldier who couldn't cope with terrible wounds and with the nightmares and the loss of the camaraderie she'd had with buddies who had her back as she faced death many times. Where and when had Bess lost her way?

She flung a cast-iron skillet at Martha's head. Martha leaned away, knowing it was a diversion. The attack came in a series of kicks. But they were high and round, way too wide, leaving her exposed to an inside counterattack. Martha ducked under the first kick and stepped inside the second. She countered with the *Unsu kata*, the cloud hands, and delivered several jabs, one-two to the chest, a third to the nose. A fourth would have ended the fight, but Martha feared she couldn't control the punch and she left it intentionally wide. It let Bess spin away.

Blood now flowed from her nose and down her face. She wiped it away with the jacket, but it kept coming. She ignored it. Her breath came in deep gasps. "That the worst you can do? That's playground shit. You know nothing about real fighting."

Martha ignored her as Bess trash talked to bolster her confidence. By now she knew she was overmatched. Bess was strong. She had skill but her training had never taken her past the usual gun, knife, kick, jab, run. It was military training, cop training; she'd seen it many times. With Palmer in the SPD refresher course. When sparring with some of the young Marines who had come to Jonesy to learn more about fighting. They were bored in Okinawa and thought they could become Bruce Lee with a couple of special sessions with the ex-Marine martial arts trainer. Martha was interested in fighting only if it allowed her to win, to never to be a victim again. She didn't care how or how much damage she inflicted in the process. She was the better motivated and she'd been training vigorously, religiously for over twenty years. Bess was good for one of Jonesy's pupils, but she had never trained with someone the equal of Yamamoto, and Martha had bested him in a no-holds-barred fight. What scared Martha was not knowing how far Bess would push this.

"Bess, we don't have to do this. You won't win."

"Fuck you, bitch."

She charged, head down, intending to wrap Martha in the embrace of a hard tackle. Martha sidestepped the rush and, with a hand on the back of her shirt, sent her crashing into the kitchen table. The kerosene lantern dropped to the floor but didn't break. The lantern's flame fluttered once, twice, but then steadied.

In an instant Bess back was on her feet, in a crouch, now a little more wary if not any less determined. The fall against the table had given her time to retrieve a hidden knife. Arms poised, knife in hand, she started to circle.

Martha stayed ready, her legs flexed, matching each step, her arms curled. She kept her eyes on the knife, only the knife. Bess didn't know how to use it as a feint, she was sure. She was a blunt-force battering ram. The attack came with a body fake to the left, and a lunge with the knife-wielding right hand. Martha grabbed her wrist and twisted it back and sideways until she heard bones snap. The knife clattered on the wooden floor. Martha kicked it over near the gun.

"Next, I will break your legs, Bess. I will break your arms, and then if you force me to, I *will* kill you."

Bess sprang behind the splintered table and fumbled with the drawer. Martha just watched. She came out with a gun in her left hand, pointed, and pulled the trigger. Click click click.

"I found that one earlier," Martha said. "And the wicked machinegun-type thing you keep under the bed and the pistol over the top board in the outhouse. Did I miss any? So many loaded weapons to keep around a young girl like Lizzie. Also saw the bags all packed. Planning a trip somewhere?"

"Fuck you." But it came out with less force, less conviction. She shook her broken wrist but winced with the pain.

"Let's stop this charade now, Bess. I have a solution to your problem."

"The only problem I have is you. When I kill you, Lizzie and I will be out of here before your body's even cold."

"You're not thinking clearly again. Maybe it was the storm. Left you fuzzy and back on the battlefields of Afghanistan. It must be horrible reliving that nightmare with every storm."

"You don't know shit about my nightmares."

"I might know more than you think. Your scars are just more visible."

Bess feinted toward the loaded gun on the floor, but Martha didn't rise to the bait, keeping herself in a crouch between the woman and the weapons scattered across the floor.

"I'm not here to kill you, Bess. But believe me, I will if you force me. I don't care about your little farming activities. I don't even care about trying to frame your father. But I do care about Rose and Amy Bumgarten."

"Fucking ironic, ain't it." Bess gave another horrible laugh. "Uncle Sam turns a blind eye when we smoke a little weed and get high between firefights, but he busts our chops when we bring the shit home. Well, they forgot about me like I was a fucking angel. But I wasn't. I goddamn wasn't. I waited months for them to come get me, and they just forgot about me. Goddamn Ali Baba patched me up and made me a slave in their mountain gardens during the day and their beds at night. Shangri-La shithole. Well, I learned a thing or two before I escaped one night. Took a couple of those towel heads with me."

"Killing the Bumgartens crossed a line, Bess. Even for a war vet with PTSD. I can help you get the help you need, the help you deserve."

"Like hell."

"Then what happens to your daughter, Bess? I guess you haven't noticed—Lizzie isn't here."

She took her one good eye off Martha long enough to dart glances around the cabin. "What'd you do with her, you son of a bitch? I will break every bone in your fucking body until you beg for mercy and tell me where you took her."

"No, you won't. You know you can't beat me. And that leaves you with a problem. What happens to Lizzie when you go off to some psych ward for traumatized war heroes? Because

Buzz is going off to the big boy's jail. Dealing drugs, aiding and abetting two murders—unless he was your active partner in the murders. Then he's facing a life sentence minimum. I didn't check to see if Minnesota has the death penalty. If Mac and I figured it out, you goddamn well know that Gould is just a day or two behind us."

Bess smeared the blood from her nose away from her mouth and across her face. Only half of her mouth moved when she spoke. "And we'll be long gone by then."

"Oh, did I mention I'm also on to Marlena? She thought you and Lizzie might be planning a vacation. Now, she won't be there to care for Lizzie when you and Buzz get put away because she's also an accessory to murder. But she's not strong like you, Bess. How long do you think she'll survive getting locked up with the hardcore felons? So with the three of you locked up, what happens to Lizzie? I may have a solution. If you don't listen to me, Lizzie goes to her closest living relative. That's her grandfather, your father. He can groom her to be the heir that he always desired. It was supposed to be you. Now, it'll be Lizzie. Is that what you want?"

"That bastard's never touching her." Bess offered a lopsided smile and jumped back as the door crashed open.

"Or maybe they'll just disappear into the great north woods." Buzz walked through the shattered door with his gun raised. "Wondered what was taking you so long, sis."

"Do it, Buzz. Now."

"Bess, there's been too much killing already. I never wanted it to go this far." To Martha, he said, "I told you not to get involved, but you wouldn't listen. I'm sorry."

The gun remained steady on Martha, but he hesitated.

"Fucking shoot the bitch," Bess snapped out like a battlefield command.

Bess dove toward the pistol and knife that lay on the floor. Martha jabbed sideways and then reversed course.

The gun boomed, but he missed the now-moving target. A next shot was closer, but still off the intended target. Before he could fire again, an axe handle crashed into the back of his skull, and he crumpled to the floor. MacAuliffe had the handle ready for another blow as he entered the cabin.

Bess tackled Martha on her way to the gun. The ex-soldier had the pistol in her hand when the axe slammed into her shoulder. The gun spun away. The blow didn't hit squarely but it caused her to twist sideways. It was all the leverage Martha required to throw her over her head and roll up in one smooth motion. One foot smashed Bess's other hand as it reached for the gun, breaking fingers and hand bones; the other foot swept the gun and knife away. Martha stomped on her collarbone and heard bones breaking. The woman screamed and struggled to get up.

"Goddamn it, Bess. Stop! Stop now! Or you'll see a wrath that *will* destroy you. You'll never see your daughter again. But your father will."

MacAuliffe stepped up, axe raised again, ready to deliver another blow if Bess didn't cede.

She slumped to the floor, the fight over.

"You okay?" MacAuliffe dared a quick peek at Martha.

"Better now that you're here."

"Sorry I couldn't get here sooner."

"You got here in time."

THIRTY-ONE

Parked on the street, they watched Detective Mark Monahan escort Craig Nettles Senior from his Duluth estate. A woman in a Coast Guard uniform followed a step behind. The big detective pushed him into the back seat of a squad car. The woman removed her hat and slid in beside Nettles. Two pedestrians and one of the neighbors gawked on the sidewalk.

"He had to suspect something," MacAuliffe said. He stood apart from Martha, enjoying his first cigarette in a couple of days. It scared him how good it tasted. "Buzz had stripped the interior cabin. It was too obvious not to notice."

"Suspecting is not knowing," Martha said. She linked her arm in his. "He'll be home by end of day. Or he would be if he were my client."

The squad car pulled away with Nettles in the back seat. Monahan moved across the street with an easy grace. His little black tie hung askew down his white shirt. He joined them on the sidewalk.

"This is all for show, you know," he said, stuffing his hands into his pockets.

The three of them stared across the street at the white-sided estate house bathed in bright sunlight.

"I know," Martha said. "But a good show in front of the world can do wonders for getting people to talk. And for scaring away any investors."

"Gould said we'd get the daughter after they're finished with her in Cook County," Monahan added. "They're still figuring out how much the son was involved."

"Either Bess got lucky finding Amy at Canal Park," Martha said, "or someone was staking out the bus station while she watched the coffee shop. Somebody had to switch out the maps at Rose's place. He's really the only candidate for leaving the toilet seat up. And he certainly came into the cabin with every intention of using that gun on me. Oh, I think there's plenty of incriminating evidence."

MacAuliffe remembered seeing the Coast Guard swarming all over *Executive Suite* when they returned from the woods. They had taken his phone and a statement. "Buzz isn't going anywhere. He's up to the brim of his ratty old baseball cap in the pot- and poppy-growing operation. Gonna cost his daddy one very nice boat."

"Yeah, but growing and distributing drugs, even hard drugs, is a lot less serious than aiding and abetting murder."

Suddenly, they both laughed and turned to Monahan.

"You've still got some work to do, Mark," MacAuliffe said. "And with the drug farm, you're now playing in the feds' sandbox. Good luck with that."

"We'll work it out," Monahan replied. "You guys okay?"

"We'll work it out," Martha said. "Thanks for asking. You're the first one. But, yes, I think so."

The large black man said to MacAuliffe. "Ester Petrowski died yesterday. Her sister had them pull the plug and she passed away in a couple of hours."

"I'm sorry," MacAuliffe said. "I'm really sorry. I liked her."

"So did I," the detective said. "I'll be adding a third murder to the butcher's bill."

"As you should," Martha said.

No one said anything. In time, Monahan slapped MacAuliffe on the shoulder and to Martha, touched his forehead in a two-fingered salute. "Okay, we'll be seeing you soon, I'm sure."

They sat in the sunshine in the cockpit of the *Virginia V.* A cooling breeze blew off the big lake. A halyard on the neighboring boat slapped lightly against the mast. His mother was bringing dinner down to the boat despite MacAuliffe's protests and offer to order take-out. His father should be showing up at any time in *Mac's Place.*

"I can't tell you how nice it is to be sitting on a boat and not being eaten alive by mosquitoes," Martha said. She rubbed lotion on her arms and her ankles and calves where she'd pulled up her jeans. About the time MacAuliffe screwed up the courage to offer to help, her phone beeped in the back pocket of her jeans

She opened a text message from Ray Palmer. "found Olsen, em & kids all at Fish Term on boat. thanks for tip. arrestd O for vilating restrain order. released Em/kids." She thumbed a quick message back.

"Everything okay?" MacAuliffe asked.

"No. It's a client back home. I'll have to refund her money. It's too bad. She'll be back. Not to me, but to another attorney soon enough. It's so hard, so hard. I just hope she'll be okay."

She leaned back against the combing and closed her eyes, basking in the sun and the gentle rocking of the *Ginny.* MacAuliffe stared at this beautiful woman. Tall and slender, she stretched across most of the cockpit. The faint rise of her breasts captured his gaze. Her clear face, the sensual lips were flawless and smooth; the dark eyebrows arching over the large nose hinted at the exotic. All capped with the curled short black hair.

She sat up suddenly. He quickly glanced away, trying to conceal the fact he'd been staring. She smiled to let him know he hadn't been successful. Or that it was okay?

Down the row of slips, he saw a car and panel van pull up against the boardwalk.

"You really believe Berglund?" he said, to cover up the awkwardness of getting caught leering at her. "And you really trust her?"

"I don't have to trust her. We have enough evidence to ensure her cooperation." MacAuliffe let himself be sucked in by those clear, mismatched eyes. "It's her one chance not to go to jail with the Nettleses, and she's devoted to those girls and her grandkid. You should have seen them together. Lizzie will need someone to care for her, and someone to care for. She knows and loves the Berglunds. They've been her family longer than her mother. Craig Junior went to Marlena for help when he learned Bess was pregnant. He didn't know where else to turn. They worked together, he respected her, or at least as much as he respected anyone other than himself. Bess had the baby and rejoined her unit. The whole time Marlena was raising Anna and Lizzie. Bess didn't see her daughter for nearly five years. That's a long time when a kid's young, a very long time. So if she doesn't do right by Lizzie and if she betrays us, we turn over what we know to Gould."

"Three women died in all this, Martha."

"And Bess and Craig Junior will pay for that. Craig Senior will pay in some way. But I'm confident Berglund didn't know about Rose and Amy until afterwards. She wasn't involved in the murders and didn't suspect anything until you found the missing map. Then she knew it had to be Bess. I agree, it's terrible, but by then she was desperate—afraid of what Bess might do, and afraid she had just lost everything she held dear." Martha watched the shimmering water over his shoulder. "I think she deserves a second chance, Mac. Lord knows I've done some terrible things in my life, some of which I'd do again in a heartbeat, some of which I'm ashamed of. I was given a chance to make them right, make myself right. I just think Marlena deserves the same opportunity. And I think Lizzie deserves to be someplace where people will love her."

Neither spoke for a while.

"If you really disagree, Mac," Martha said, finally, "let's call Gould right now. Maybe they'll go lenient on her if she's willing to testify against Bess and Craig Junior. I'll go along with it. Lord knows, I don't have all the answers."

"Bess and Buzz both have to go along with it."

"And they have a powerful motivation to. They hate their father and what he did to their mother, to Bess, what he did to the whole family. They turn on Berglund, and Craig Senior gets custody. Just because he's a jerk won't matter. He's the closest living family."

"But if Bess turns on Berglund and her father?"

"Then Lizzie goes into the foster care system. I don't think Bess will do that. Despite all her psychotic and destructive behavior, she's still a mother who loves that little girl very much. Knowing she's safe with the Berglunds is her best shot of giving Lizzie a chance in life. And right now, that's also the only hope for peace that Bess has."

MacAuliffe felt torn. Berglund had been involved in hiding facts about the murder of two women, two of her friends. For what? Did she receive a kickback from the drug operation? He understood she was scared. There were times during all of this when every one of them was scared. But that didn't excuse her for helping the psychotic war vet and her asshole brother. Why would Martha consider it okay? Maybe that puzzled him most. The shifting sands of morality troubled him more than not turning in Berglund. He wondered what else Martha had experienced that he didn't know about, how that made her more forgiving of Berglund's mistakes when she compared them to her own?

"You want to call Gould?" Martha said. Her face had gone serious. "I won't try to talk you out of it. I understand how it offends your sense of right and wrong, of justice. But it doesn't mine. Marlena's past will always be her present. She'll have the deaths of Rose and Amy on her conscience for the rest of her life."

She offered her phone across the cockpit. It hung there for a time.

He shook his head. "Her secrets will be safe with me." For a while he didn't say anything. "Right and wrong have this troubling habit of changing positions when I'm not paying attention. Funny how I tend to think of myself as being open-minded, able to see nuance and the world as shades of gray. And then life throws it back in my face, and I find I'm none of those things."

Martha took his hand and held it between both of hers. "Mac, you are those things. I know it without a doubt."

He squeezed her hand and withdrew his own. "You're a mystery, Martha Whitaker."

"Not all mysteries are worth solving," she said, glancing away. "Here comes your father."

Mac's Place had turned the corner and was approaching the drawbridge. His father blew the horn—one long, one short. The bridge responded in kind. MacAuliffe stood up. Warning bells that signaled the bridge was about to open began to ring.

"So what's next?" Martha asked.

"Think I'll stay here a little longer before going home. Spend some time with the folks, with Katie and the kids. I imagine there'll be a memorial for Ester Petrowski. She sang in the choir at Saint Andrew's by the Lake. I'd like to be there. The world is too short of decent people." His voice softened. "Besides, I've got a story to write about a young woman. Another tragedy, unfortunately. Maybe I'll go back to Grand Marais and finish building Amelia's kayak. Monahan'll have some ideas on what to do with it. You?"

"That'd be nice. I was thinking I'll drive over to see Dad."

But MacAuliffe wasn't paying attention. Down the dock he saw a camera being set up and a woman with a microphone getting her makeup touched up. What the—?

It didn't matter. They knew Ted MacAuliffe was involved in something worth reporting. The Coast Guard must have said his father was the source for the big drug bust that had been all over the day's news.

Suddenly, the sailboat lurched, and his mother and then Newton joined them in the cockpit. Newton couldn't understand why no one paid any attention to him.

"Oh heaven forbid," Virginia said, putting her bags down on the cabin deck. She wore a floppy sunhat and had her silver-blonde hair pulled back behind her large ears.

Mac's Place eased into the slip; with a touch of reverse, a small hit on the bow thruster, he had her perfectly lined up to come in.

"He's going to be insufferable if he goes on television," Virginia said. "Just insufferable."

"He already is, Mom."

"I mean more so." She pulled the hat down lower to hide her face. "He'll probably nominate himself for First Citizen of the Year."

Both Martha and MacAuliffe laughed.

Out of the corner of his eye, MacAuliffe watched the mysterious Martha. She didn't try to hide as the scene on the dock unfolded in front of them. She sat there confident, almost bemused. She reached out and began scratching the back of the dog's ears. Newton's tail swished back and forth in the cockpit.

Why wasn't her mystery worth solving? In the end, he suspected, it wasn't about trying to hide her past, but about trying to hide her innermost self, her soul. That he'd look inside and find her lacking.

But aren't we all?

All of this flashed through his mind in a few seconds. He smiled and tucked his hair behind his ears. He jumped off the *Ginny* and headed down the dock to help his father tie up.

ACKNOWLEDGEMENTS

There are always so many people to acknowledge in the creation of a book that's it daunting to even start. I'm afraid I'll leave out someone. If I do, please know it is not a lack of appreciation for your contribution to making *Within A Shadowed Forest* a better book.

Let me start by thanking all the Minnesota clan for welcoming me into their hearts and homes, long before *Within A Shadowed Forest* was ever a germ of an idea. They gave me ideas and inspiration, as well as food and hospitality for many years, and allowed me to stay at the family cabin in the Great Mosquito Forest so I would be inspired to finish the novel.

Profound thank yous are in order to the 15th Avenue Group. Your continued inspiration, support and wonderfully creative ideas on marketing helped sustain me through the early days of being a clueless author. Special thanks are in order to the late Waverly Fitzgerald for inviting me into the group; and to Alice K. Boatwright for freely sharing of her friendship, knowledge and experiences, and whose tenacious faith that stories remain important proved infectious when we were all self-isolating during the coronavirus pandemic.

I would also like to thank editors William Boggess for identifying some of the fundamental problems of the book and offering detailed suggestions on how to fix them; and Anne Doe-Overstreet whose attention to detail found and fixed all the lingering problems overlooked by everyone else.

Thank you to the many beta readers—family, friends, acquaintances. Every single one of you made an invaluable contribution to making the book better.

All errors that remain, whether small or large, are entirely mine.

And finally, to Mary Jo, the love of my life, who took me sailing on Lake Superior and introduced me to the northern Minnesota woods—and encouraged me to write about them.

ABOUT THE AUTHOR

Jeffrey D. Briggs, a writer and journalist, has been writing about the Seattle waterfront since he moved onto his sailboat over thirty years ago. He now lives on land with his wife and dog and can often be found on the shores of Puget Sound, wondering what secrets lie hidden beneath those cold waters. His first book in the Waterfront Mystery series featuring Martha Whitaker was *Out of the Cold Dark Sea*.

Made in the USA
Columbia, SC
18 July 2020

14200856R00226